Desta

TO WHOM THE LIONS BOW

Desta flying over northern Ethiopia in his self-built aircraft with Eleni, the Wind Woman from the land of Nogero

Getty Ambau

Book three of the epic adventure series of an Ethiopian shepherd boy in search of his ancestral family's twin sister Coin of Magic and Fortune

Published by Falcon Press International
P. O. Box 8671
San Jose, CA 95155

Cover Art and Illustrations by Philip Howe of Philip Howe Studios
Cover arrangement by Getty Ambau
Flying craft design by Getty Ambau
Coin Illustration by Jin Chenault
Coin Design by Getty Ambau

Library of Congress Cat. No. 2010927259

Desta: To Whom the Lions Bow: a novel/Getty Ambau—1st ed.
Volume 3
310 p. Manufactured in the United States of America

ISBN: 978-1-884459-04-7

1. The settings – actual 2. Finote Selam school scenes–actual. 3. Alem, Konjit, Dagim and all the characters and events related to them—fiction. 4. The story David Hartman and their trip to Desta's parent's home—fiction. 5. Colonel Mulugeta and his family and related events—actual. 6. The Debre Marcos hospital story—actual. 7. Dinknesh and her sister, Hiwot's condition—actual. 8. Governor Asrat's story—partly fiction; 9. Desta and Abraham's trip to Zegay and the meeting of Grazmach Belay—actual, although names have been changed. 10. Desta's brother, Asse'ged's story and death—actual. 11. The flight of Desta and Eleni to Washaa Umera—fiction. 12. The reunion of Dr. Petrova and Desta in Bahir Dar—fiction.

Dedicated to:

my parents, who gave me the opportunity

to go the distances in life.

PREFACE

Although this book is a sequel to volume 2: *Desta and Winds of Washaa Umera* and Volume 1: *Desta and King Solomon's Coin of Magic and Fortune*, every effort has been made to make each volume independent of each other. Still, to get the most out of the story of Desta and the Ethiopian culture, the first two volumes should be read ahead of the third.

This ambitious book series is a narrative about Desta, the character, told in the context of his environment and his adventures, but this series is also intended to serve as a document about the Ethiopian people and their culture. The story explores certain traditional details and historical events. Historical descriptions are provided where practical, and translations from the Amharic are given to lend as rich a cultural experience as possible.

This volume follows Desta from fourth grade through the eighth grade, when he was between the ages of fourteen and sixteen and a half years old. What he has been able to accomplish on his own in this volume, as with the previous two, would be an inspiration to anyone, particularly to students.

A complete list of characters and cultural terms and their definitions are provided at the end of the book for the reader's convenience. Western readers should take particular note of the Ethiopian geography and calendar.

Although Ethiopia is located north of the equator, the seasons are the reverse of the seasons in most Western countries; hence, it is not unusual in Desta's world to find a carpet of wild flowers adorning a mountainside in September and October.

The Ethiopian calendar has twelve months of thirty days each and one mini month of five or six days (depending on whether there's a leap year). The Ethiopian New Year customarily occurs on September 11 and on September 12 during a leap year. The calendar lags behind the Gregorian (Western) calendar by seven years (from September to December) and eight years (from January to August). This difference stems from the perceived date of Jesus's annunciation, about which the Ethiopian Orthodox Church and the Roman Catholic Church cannot agree.

Being near the equator, most of Ethiopia receives nearly equal hours of sunlight and darkness. However, this does not always hold true for the more isolated, mountainous areas, such as where the story of Desta takes place. In such locations, the sun often rises and sets half an hour later or earlier.. .

Although the story is fiction, the setting, natural features, and events, culture, and customs presented are true to life. This tale is probably unlike any you have read before. I hope you have a fun ride to Desta's far-off world! –GTA

"To read is to fly: it is to soar to a point of vantage which gives a view over wide terrains of history, human variety, ideas, shared experience and the fruits of many inquiries." –Alberto Manguel

Maps of Africa and Ethiopia

Desta flying over the Blue Nile gorge

Chapter 1

1963

No school certificate. No kinsfolk in town he could live with. No money of his own sufficient to pay for a room or more than one week's supply of food. No close relatives in the nearby countryside who could give him assistance or pay him a visit—to remind him that he didn't just pop out of the bare earth like a weed or wash onto a riverbank like driftwood.

The soles of his feet felt sore. Pain and stiffness had seized his leg and thigh muscles, all manifestations of his twelve hour journey on foot from Yeedib to Finote Selam the day before. He had come here to pursue his modern education and continue his search for the second Coin of Magic and Fortune.

He was staying with his former school friend named Fenta and his family as a guest. He had shared a room in an external building with Fenta and had just woken during the wee hours of the morning when he started thinking about his past fears and current problems.

He had finished the fourth grade in his hometown two years earlier, but he stayed in school because he didn't have anyone he could live with in the bigger towns where education through the eighth grade was offered. His family in the country didn't understand the value of modern schooling, so they weren't about to give him dependable assistance. They either were against it or took the attitude that Desta, like a church school student, should fend for himself.

For Desta fending for himself meant first having faith and confidence in himself and in the world. Second, it meant learning how to solve his problems and overcome his challenges.

In the two years he spent stuck in the fourth grade, Desta built and flew his own aircraft. This effort and experience gave him the self-assurance he needed to leave town and pursue his dreams. To his credit, Desta had always believed in the kindness and benevolence of strangers. With this in mind, he had decided to go to Finote Selam when the second semester started in January.

Then as if to ratify his belief, a mysterious secondary-school teacher, a *Ferenge*—white man—sent an emissary, a student named Mehiret, to bring him to the town of his dreams toward the end of the first semester. The Ferenge lived in the province's capital a hundred and fifty miles away, but Desta had no idea who he was or why he had sent for him.

No matter, Desta readily accepted the invitation, knowing that going to the bigger world was the only way he could find the kind of people he hoped to meet and live with, and thereby pursue his goals.

But now that he was in Finote Selam, faith and belief seemed very far from reality. He had no idea where or how he would find those benevolent people of his imagination. Then something disturbing occurred to him. He would need support not for one semester or one year but his four years of education—from the fifth through the eighth grade. It all sounded like a pipe dream. Where could he possibly find complete strangers who would be willing to help him for those many years?

He knew, too, that if his previous experiences of living with people were any indication, his future in this new town, where he knew no one other than Fenta, may not bode well. Desta's heart sunk in despair.

He could work part time and try to support himself, but there were no jobs for adults, let alone a fourteen-year-old boy. When Desta realized all these problems were formulas for becoming a homeless beggar, he shivered.

There was the immediate snag that he hadn't brought a transfer certificate from his school. He left in a rush and didn't think about getting one at that moment. Desta understood the added potential obstacle. Suddenly, everything looked as dark and void as the pitch black of the night he was now staring into.

A kind of fear and doubt he had never entertained before seeped into his consciousness. That he was too small to face the big, wide world on his own, without family or even a good adult friend, like Masud of Dangila, took a foothold in his brain. Then there was the possibility that he could get sick or be hurt by people—bigger students at school, fractious boys in town, or adults who might take advantage of his vulnerabilities.

He turned over and lay on his back, gazing into the darkness before him, as his mind devolved into another realm. Trying to bring himself back, he placed his fingers over his forehead and drew a line to the tip of his nose. This act always settled Desta's mind and helped him focus on his problems, specifically his feelings.

He wondered how close the night was to dawn. He wondered whether there were any roosters in the neighborhood. After the first cock's crow, he would more or less know the hours left before daybreak. The cock's crow also would take him back to Yeedib and his home in the country for a moment, something familiar to calm his nerves in this strange place. With his ears cued, he waited for the heraldic calls. But no rooster crowed. He wondered whether people in Finote Selam didn't keep hens and roosters. He wondered whether the night had stopped advancing and the roosters were patiently waiting.

Dawn finally arrived but no rooster had crowed.

A tear welled up in his eye and trailed down the side of his face. It cascaded into his ear and slid down the lobe, trailing along his neck, and finally nestling in the crater between his collarbones. It felt like a thawed ice fragment. Desta saw the tear as a metaphor for his life— representing how far he'd come and the distance he'd yet to go.

A faint and faraway voice came to him, packed with words he didn't understand at first. "Have you already forgotten who your family really is?" It asked imperatively. Desta lifted his head and listened once more. The voice repeated. This time it urgently commanded him to answer.

"The coin," Desta said, finally.

"And its image on your chest," the voice added. "You should know by now that from here on, the world is your family. The coin is your protector and guide. No family, relatives, or friends will travel with you, but the shekel and its image on your chest will."

Desta rose and went to the door and opened it. Thickly grown eucalyptus trees shaded much of the ground beyond the leaf-covered courtyard. He stared at the trees as he thought about the message he just heard. At that moment Desta didn't want a clairvoyant declaring the infallibility of his future. He needed arms that would embrace him and soothing words to console him.

The air was motionless. The eucalyptus trees lent a familiar feel to the place. They were everywhere in Yeedib and in Dangila. They were everywhere here, too. . . .

After both Desta and Fenta had their breakfast, the friend left for school. "I need to get there before the gate closes, at nine sharp," he had said. "My uncle will bring you to register. . . . I'll see you at the mid-morning break."

"I hope so," Desta said, looking away.

"Don't be pessimistic," Fenta said. "I'm sure the director

will accept you even if you came at midterm. He has great
respect for students who come from our little school."

Desta sat on a bench outside the front entrance and waited
for *Ato*—Mr.—Bizuneh, a stern and quiet man whom he had
seen only in passing when the family lived in Yeedib.

"Do you have your notebooks and your transfer document from
your school with you?" Ato Bizuneh asked, coming out of his home.

Desta rose and said he had his notebooks but
not his certificate. He explained why.

Ato Bizuneh's chubby cheeks trembled, his eyes studying
him. "I'm afraid they may not admit you, then." He hesitated. "We
can go and see. . . ." His voice dragged. "I know the director is not
an easy man, but we can at least go and see what he says."

A searing wave went through Desta. He wanted to ask why.
Then he realized what Ato Bizuneh's answer would be. He left
the question hanging on his tongue. Under his breath he let it roll
out. He shook his head and asked, "Why?" just the same.

Ato Bizuneh didn't answer, but he placed his big hand on
Desta's small shoulder. "Cheer up. We've not talked to the director
yet. Let's go quick. I need to get back to my office soon."

Desta followed. Once they emerged from the tree-shaded grounds and
moved onto the main road, going south, they found the day in full bloom.
This was November, one of the dry months when the sun shone blissfully.

The straight road that came into town from somewhere below arrested
Desta's eyes, just as it had the day before. He enjoyed looking at it, tracing
its linear course. Would it be an indication of the life he would lead in this
new town—straight, flawless, and trouble free? This notion was consoling.

Farther down, the road became an arrow that pierced a circle, splitting the
town's center in half. On the left, shops, teahouses, and food places lined the
perimeter. On the right, a mammoth warka tree had claimed much of the half
circle, behind which squat grass-roof homes had sprouted next to corrugated
tin-roof buildings. Eucalyptus trees swayed here and there. Desta loved
seeing the giant warka. It was under the same kind of tree where he met his
grandfather's spirit the first time, and where the mystery of his family's past
and his future began to unravel. The town was slowly growing on Desta.

The school was situated on the south side of the plaza. Bound by a wire fence, the campus seemed the original settler, the town growing around it later.

A dusty sidewalk ran along the fence, parallel with the road. Between the sidewalk and the road, there was a strip of grass along which thorn bushes grew freely, their leaves dry and shriveled from the strong sun. The grass looked as if it had gone without water for many years.

The sidewalk led the visitors to the school's entrance. Closed double iron doors were moored to stout stone pillars. Behind the gate a stern-looking guard in a gray jacket and shorts stood with a long leather whip in his hand.

"Registering a new student?" he asked, partially opening one of the doors.

Bizuneh replied that he was.

"Isn't it a bit late? We're already three-quarters into the semester." The guard looked down at Desta.

"I know. Can we talk with the director just the same?"

"Sure. I know Ato Tedla will say it's too late, but . . ." He lifted the vertical latching rod and fully opened one door.

"You probably don't remember me. My name is Bizuneh," Desta's host said, putting his hand out to the guard.

"My name is Sitotaw," the guard said.

"Follow me," Sitotaw said, leading the visitors along a stone walkway, at the end of which a tall stone building sat like a majestic bird. The lower roofs on either side appeared like spreading wings. Beneath the high-pitched roof at the middle of the building a gray plaque read HAILE SELASSIE THE FIRST ELEMENTARY SCHOOL, both in Amharic and English, the letters arching around the image of a flaming torch. The first such building Desta saw named after the emperor of his country.

On a grassy patch of earth to the left, the green, yellow, and red flag rippled gently in the breeze atop a silver pole. Three identical buildings sat to the right, past a few scattered oak trees.

They continued on the stone walkway, which was now flanked by a series of rose bushes. Some of the roses were in bloom and filled the air with the fresh scent of spring. The visitors climbed a half-dozen shallow steps, following Sitotaw, and landed inside the stone building, on a gleaming tile floor. Bizuneh's hard-soled shoes echoed throughout the hallway they now found themselves in. Desta loved the cool, smooth surface beneath his bare feet.

"Please wait here," the guard said, pushing open a partially closed door. Moments later he came out and invited the visitors in.

Tedla, a tall man with a slightly bulbous nose and neatly trimmed mustache, rose from his desk and, with a familiar air, shook hands with Bizuneh. Tedla wore a smoke-gray suit and crisply ironed white shirt. "Please sit down," he said, motioning to a chair in front of his desk. A blue fountain pen with a brass nib lay squarely in the middle of a white pad of paper.

After Bizuneh sat down and Desta stood next to him, the two men engaged in small talk for a few minutes. Then Tedla quickly changed the subject to the obvious. "I suppose you brought this young man to register," Tedla said, glancing at Desta for a second.

"Yes," Bizuneh murmured guardedly. Something in Tedla's tone of voice hinted what was to come.

"The students will be taking their end-term exams in three weeks. It won't be fair to the boy if we accept him now and expect him to take the exams also. Although the curriculum is the same throughout the country, each school and instructor teaches the lessons differently. . . . So I'm afraid he may have to wait till the beginning of the second semester, in January."

"I realize that, but . . ." Bizuneh trailed off.

"There is just no point to his being in class this late in the term," Tedla said, filling the void left by Bizuneh.

"I mean, if you could let him sit in class, he can still learn something I'm sure. He traveled all day hoping to continue his education at your school."

"Traveling all day—where did he come from?" Tedla asked, his voice rising a notch.

"From the high country—Yeedib, the little town where we used to live before we came here."

A sardonic smile passed Tedla's face. "Where students get one hundred fifty out of one hundred on their exams!"

When he noticed Bizuneh was at a loss, the director said, "There is a running joke here in our school about the Yeedib school director. When some students complain about their grades, the teacher often asks the student, 'You mean, I should give *meto amsa inde Aba Goosa?*'— one hundred fifty out of one hundred, like Aba Goosa?" Tedla chuckled. "I actually have seen one hundred fifty for a grade on some of the report cards that come from that school." Tedla now openly laughed. Then when he realized he was the only one laughing, he stopped.

He leaned slightly forward as if confiding a secret. "The story is, Aba

Yisehak was a former priest. He doesn't have formal training in modern academics and he doesn't know much about percents and fractions. So we often see grades higher than one hundred for some of the good students, the highest being one hundred fifty. Because Aba Yisehak is an older man, somebody nicknamed him Goosa—the term for an old monk who lives in the forest. And so the joke still persists among the teachers here."

"Aha," Bizuneh said awkwardly. A polite smile spread across his face.

"He is a brilliant man otherwise, a strict disciplinarian. All his students are well-mannered and good academically," Tedla said, attempting to make up for disparaging Aba Yisehak, the highly respected teacher of Bizuneh's nephews.

As Tedla rephrased his comments, Desta couldn't agree more. He could see Aba Yisehak clearly in his mind—Aba Yisehak's fierce brown eyes behind his gold-rimmed glasses. He could see him standing by the door of his old school, exacting punishment with his *chenger*—a twig whip—to any student who arrived late, or hitting a boy over the head with a ruler for the crime of idleness or talking in class. This same exacting punishment was applied to any student who had not done his homework.

"Let me show you what I mean," Tedla said, eyeing Desta. "If this boy is a good student, we are likely to find grades above a hundred." Tedla placed an outstretched palm on his desk.

Desta fidgeted on his feet. "I'm sorry, but I didn't get a chance to bring my report card," he mumbled under his breath.

"No certificate then?!" Tedla exclaimed.

"From what I understand, due to circumstances beyond his control, he came here on short notice. The boy used to be a classmate of Fenta, my nephew. I understand he is a good student. He has finished the fourth grade at the top of his class. Regarding the documents you seek, we can easily arrange to have them sent," Bizuneh interjected.

"Students who come from that school generally are very good, but they don't learn much beyond arithmetic, Amharic, and some English. Our students learn science, geography, and history—and all of them in English, starting in the third grade. This boy doesn't even have a rudimentary knowledge of these three subjects.

"Like I mentioned, he should go back, spend his Christmas at home, and come here in January with his certificate and report card. There is no more discussion of this," Tedla said, withdrawing his palm.

He picked up the pen, capped it, and put the instrument in the breast pocket of his jacket, indicating the visitors were now dismissed.

Desta's eyes brimmed.

Bizuneh rose awkwardly. He looked down at Desta. "We need to honor Ato Tedla's wishes. It's only a month, and it will go very quick," his companion said, bending down a little.

Sad and dejected, Desta and Bizuneh left the director's office. Bizuneh walked briskly to the gate, the boy trotting behind him. Outside, Bizuneh stopped and turned to Desta. "I'll find someone from Yeedib who has come here for a court case or business, and you can go back with them. Then you can return in January with all the things Ato Tedla asked for. *Ishee*—okay?"

Desta bent his head down and drew lines in the dust with his big toe as he contemplated Bizuneh's suggestion.

"What do you think?" Bizuneh said, nudging Desta's shoulder.

"Can I give you my answer later?"

"You don't have to answer me now or even later, I'm just repeating what Ato Tedla indicated. Go home. I'll see you when I come for lunch." Bizuneh shuffled off, crunching the gravel on the road with his big feet.

DESTA WAS GLAD TO BE ALONE. He watched for a few moments as Bizuneh walked up the gravel road and then across the eastern portion of the plaza, edging the shadow of the warka tree. He connected to a divergent path and soon vanished into the trees.

The pleasant morning sun had now become cloying. Desta could see the road dust shimmer in the heat. Instead of going to Bizuneh's home, he decided to make his way to the warka tree, sit in its cool shade, and think about his problem.

Once he got there, he sat down on a bench facing east to the shops, restaurants, and teahouses across the road and past the open, bare earth. His eyes intensely probed into nothing in particular as his mind reeled. He was not sure who to blame: himself, the white man who sent for him, his dire circumstances, or the lack of relatives in faraway towns. More likely, it was his family's complete indifference to his efforts that was truly to blame. After all, this caused him to readily accept the suggestion from Mehiret, a strange boy, to come to Finote Selam, at the behest of a man Desta had never even heard of—some American named David Hartman. Changing his earlier plan of coming after Christmas and with very little to go on, Desta had dropped everything to immediately accompany Mehiret to Finote Selam.

He reserved criticism of the white man whose intentions he had no knowledge of. Desta knew only that the man had sent for him and provided him with fifty birrs. But he blamed himself for making the journey without learning more about the man or why he had sent for him. And he was sorry for having a family who never understood him, his needs, or his ambitions.

Desta suddenly realized that as dismal as his current situation seemed, his coming here at the wrong time of the semester was not necessarily a waste of time. He had learned a lesson from his mistake. Now that he was here, he somehow needed to find a solution to his problem. He knew there was no going back—no matter what happened to him. Besides, he had no desire to celebrate Christmas with his host family in Yeedib or on his own in the country.

His mind went to the Ferenge man—for whom he reserved judgment. He needed to meet him somehow. He reached into his breast pocket and pulled out the card Mehiret had left him. He studied the text on the little rectangular white card, trying to pronounce the words.

He whispered "Da-vid Hart-man" under his breath, after studying each letter. He incorrectly used "ən-iversity" for "u-niversity," recalling the *u* sound in "under," "understand," and "unknown." He pronounced "Che-ca-go" for "Chicago" and "p-hone" for the word "phone." And he didn't know what "phone" was or what the number next to it meant. The text was meaningless to him. Just as the names and man were meaningless. He put away the card and reached for the five red bills Mehiret said the man had sent. He fanned them out in his hand and studied them. For a moment he concentrated on the intricate patterns on their surfaces and the ever-peremptory presence of Emperor Haile Selassie in the center of the bills.

Then he thought of their value to him. Regardless of the power the bills contained—their purchasing power, specifically—they were as meaningless as the white man's card. The money didn't come from a father or mother or sister or brother, neither from a dear uncle or aunt. It came from a man he had yet to meet—whose intentions were unclear and who was not from Desta's own town or country. This man seemed to take things for granted.

Hunger gnawed at his belly. Desta pulled the bills together, folded them, and put them away. He passed his right hand over his chest, above his heart. His hunger subsided. He would find people who needed a shop attendant or an errand boy.

He rose and walked toward the shops on the other side of the road. The first shop he came to was a clothing store. A middle-aged woman was standing behind the counter, knitting a sweater. Her hands moved mechanically as she talked, glancing down at the long needles occasionally. She said she had her own children for help around the house and in the shop.

Desta continued to talk to the shopkeepers, offering them his services, but no one had any need for him. The smell of food coming out of the restaurants made his stomach growl. The temptation to spend some of the money he had in his pocket was great, but his resistance to acting on his desire was greater.

He looked down at his shadow. It was a circular gray blob around his feet, indicating midday and the time the students and office workers would come home for lunch. To honor Bizuneh's earlier suggestion, he needed to go report his decision to Bizuneh. And he would share with Fenta the outcome of their meeting with the director.

He crossed diagonally from the first row of shops to the second row, which ran perpendicular to the first. In front of the corner building, near the area where Desta would turn to go to Bizuneh's house, he saw a corpulent young man standing near a flatbed scale, his head down as if laden with thoughts. Adjacent to the wall was a pile of bulging sacks.

Desta stopped. "Excuse me, my name is Desta. Would you by any chance be in need of an errand boy?" he asked, trying to sound casual. Having been turned down by a few merchants already, his hope of finding work was quickly dwindling.

The man looked up with a start. "Right now I don't, but on Saturdays I would," he said hesitantly.

"What would I have to do?"

"I need boys who can pull the farmers' donkeys when they come loaded with grains from the country."

The merchant studied Desta. "But I need someone bigger and stronger—and a good talker. Sometimes the farmers or the donkeys are not cooperative."

"How much do you pay?"

"Twenty-five cents for every donkey you pull."

Desta thought about the offer for a few seconds, computing quickly in his head how many donkeys he would have to pull to get his weekly supply of meals. Ten donkeys would be two and a half birr. Assuming there are restaurants that sell twenty-five-cent meals, he could cover five days of his food expenses. If he pulled four additional donkeys, he would have enough to cover a week's worth of meals.

"When can I start?" he asked, satisfied by his own conclusion.

"Next Saturday . . . if the work appeals to you, but you'll see it's not very easy. And it's competitive. I have boys who do this kind of work for me, and other merchants their own. Come early Saturday morning and we will go to my veranda near the market.

"I'll . . ." Desta started to say, trying hard not to show his excitement.

"Better yet . . . ," the man said as he walked over to Desta. "My name is Amare. Come here tomorrow and I'll take you to my veranda. That way you can see where it is."

"Okay, thank you," Desta said, turning and walking off briskly.

When he arrived at his host's home, neither Ato Bizuneh nor Fenta had returned yet. Senayit was busy in the kitchen preparing lunch. Fenta was the first to arrive. "What happened? I didn't see you at school," he said, the moment he saw Desta.

Fenta shook his head firmly once he found out what had happened to his friend. "So what're you going to do?" he asked anxiously.

"Well, stay put," Desta replied, smiling. "Look, I'd already decided I wouldn't return to Yeedib for the month of December and come back to Finote Selam after Christmas, as the director was suggesting. I don't ever want to look back again. I did that when things didn't work for me in Dangila. I returned home and attended our little school once more.

"That's because I believed in father's advice that it was best to have a relative to live with in order to continue my education. I'm not going to have a relative everywhere I go. I have accepted my fate in life and belief in the existence of good people in this world who'd treat me like their own. I had a taste of it when I lived in Dangila. And I have faith I will find good people here."

Fenta dropped his books on the table and sat down. He stared at Desta, registering the deep emotion that tinged his words. "I've no doubt you'll find people to live with, like I told you last night. I'm just sorry that the director didn't accept you for this semester."

"It's not the end of that yet. I plan to see him by myself tomorrow morning. And I've already found work with a merchant. I'll be pulling the farmers' loaded donkeys for him on Saturdays. He'll be paying me twenty-five cents per animal."

"You're amazing!" Fenta said. He sat back and stared at Desta in awe.

"No, I'm not amazing. This is what can happen to you when you don't count on anybody but yourself," Desta replied sharply. The two years he wasted in Yeedib repeating the fourth grade when he couldn't find relatives to live with had just flashed in his head. "Well, I still have to find someone to live with," he added, his voice starting to flag.

"You've not been here a full day, yet you're halfway there," Fenta said, smiling. "If you found someone to live with by the evening, I won't be surprised."

"Don't be so sure," Desta lobbed back. "I believe I'll find a family, but I'll probably need a week. I want to talk to enough people before I decide. I'd be grateful if you would ask your aunt and uncle whether I might sleep with you in the kitchen house until I find a family to live with. I'll see what I can do for my meals."

"No problem. You can stay with us as long as it takes for you to find someone. I'm sure my aunt and uncle won't mind. Aunt Senayit was happy to see you. Uncle Bizuneh, too. My nephew Sayfu used to be here. Now he is gone. Aunt Senayit knows your situation with your family and the people you lived with in Yeedib. She will be offended if you eat outside."

"Thanks. This arrangement would be of great help to me."

Bizuneh arrived. "Good afternoon, boys," he said, and walked passed them. He seemed preoccupied with something.

After lunch, Bizuneh went to take a nap. Fenta and Desta left to go to their sleeping quarters in the kitchen house. Fenta wanted to study for a test he was having that afternoon. Desta lay on his back and thought about what he must do in the morning to convince the director that he should start school straight away.

After Fenta left for school, Desta got ready to see the director. He went through his pouch and pulled out all his recent exam papers, as well as his unofficial report card and the commendation letters he had received from his teachers. He took out the parchment and recited the legends around the coin, all the while visualizing meeting the director in the morning and gaining admission to the school. In another round of recitation, he saw himself meeting a loving and kind couple who would take him into their home. This done, he folded and returned the parchment and documents to the pouch and left for the center of town. Encouraged by his morning success, he was determined to speak with more people this time.

To his amazement, he found everyone to be extremely friendly. They seemed to be intrigued by the novelty of a boy his age walking around asking for work and looking for a family to live with. Some asked whether he lost all his family through some catastrophe. Others wondered if he had run away from home.

Some of the shopkeepers and restaurant owners wanted to give him money or food; he refused both. He wanted work. He wasn't interested in charity. One tall and handsome man named Aklilu, who at first was taken aback by

Desta's refusal of money, said he knew a single woman in need of someone
to look after her chickens while she visited her ailing mother in the country.
And after her return, there was the possibility that she would need an errand
boy to stay on full time. But Desta would have to check back with Aklilu in a
day or two to make sure the woman had not found another person already.

That night after Desta and Fenta went to the kitchen house to sleep, Fenta
lay on his belly and began to study, the little kerosene lamp next to his pillow. Desta lay on his back, staring at the ceiling. He envied his friend and
hoped to be studying like Fenta very soon. He became even more determined to go back to the school the next morning and plead his case with
the director. Things had already started to look up. He would have work
on Saturdays and possibly would have someone to live with before long.
Desta stayed awake the entire time Fenta was studying. Then the moment
his friend blew out the light, he closed his eyes and went to sleep.

"WHAT BRINGS YOU HERE AGAIN?" Sitotaw asked when he found Desta
standing at the gate.

"I want to speak with the director," Desta replied, eyeing the man nervously.

"What for? He told you to come back in January with all your
documents. Do you have them already?" Sitotaw said, dropping his eyes on the stack of papers Desta had in his hands.

Desta said he didn't, but he had something to show the director.

"Let me see what you got," Sitotaw said, putting out his hand.

After Desta gave him the papers, he watched the guard's face
intently for any hint or reaction. The man bit his lip and slowly flipped through the pages, his eyes completely absorbed by what
was before them. The report card held his attention the most.

"These grades are better than what many of the students get here.
"C'mon in," the man said, smiling. "Let's go to the director and see what
he says." When they got to the director's office in the main building, he
wasn't there. Sitotaw told Desta to sit on the steps and walked away. Shortly
before the flag ceremonies, the director emerged from behind the building, followed by Sitotaw. He had Desta's documents in one hand.

Desta stood and waited nervously, his hands crossed over
his chest, the right pressing the area above his heart.

"You came back so quickly," the director said with a smile.

"*Awwe*—yes."

"This is what we'll do. I'll register you for the fourth grade. You don't need to take the exams if you don't want to, but you can sit in the classes and learn as much as you can for the rest of the month. Follow me."

Desta wished he could kiss the man's knee. Instead, he simply said, "Ishee," and followed the director. As soon as he registered Desta the director took him to the fourth-grade classroom and sat him down at a desk with only two other students. Desta had to fight hard from shedding tears of joy.

Chapter 2

Desta had *driven* many donkeys in the past but had never *pulled* them. The stubborn animals have their own minds. They don't often listen. Now every Saturday he would have to stand by one of the market entrances and convince a farmer to follow him to see Amare, who might purchase the farmer's grains. If the men agreed to a transaction, Desta would go grab the farmer's donkey by its leash or ear and guide the animal to his employer's veranda. He would have to do all of this while competing with a dozen or more boys who worked either for Amare or the other half-dozen merchants.

The day of his registration, after school let out at five o'clock, Desta went to double-check with Amare that he would in fact have the work for him each Saturday as promised. When Desta got there, the man was standing outside, looking as if waiting for someone.

"So you're serious about working for me, eh?" Amare asked.

"Yes," Desta chirped.

"Let's go to my veranda and the warehouse."

As they walked, Amare explained everything Desta had to do, including the end-of-day veranda cleanup all the boys were expected to help with.

A row of flatbed gray scales with columns and bars was arrayed across the dirt floor of the veranda. Other than the scales, it looked deserted. And it smelled like a tanning shop. The air was thick with the odor of animal hide, from the piled goat skins and leather sacks filled with grains.

"That is *teff*—a type of grain," Amare said, pointing to one pile halfway up on the wall. "And the sacks farther down are barley. These are mostly the kinds of grains we buy from the farmers." He turned to the left wall. "Quite often we also buy these goat skins, especially around the holidays when there is a great supply of hides and skins."

All Desta wanted was to get out of that room before he started choking or throwing up. His stomach was already roiling.

Amare seemed to have read his face. "You will get used to
the odor. It's nothing," he said, as he headed to the door.

"No, I'm fine," Desta said, mechanically.

"There is not much for you to do inside the warehouse. I brought you here so
you could see the kinds of things I buy and to show you where my business is
located," Amare said, locking the door. They left the veranda and went back to
the center of town.

ATO BIZUNEH was surprised, and a little hurt, that the director hadn't
accepted Desta at his behest the day before. Desta gained admittance on his
own—what the man of power and influence wasn't able to do on his behalf.

"I told you so," Fenta said, smiling broadly. "The director has a high
regard for students who come from our little school. Because of your
unusual circumstance, he just needed a little more convincing."

"He told me I don't have to take the exams if I don't want,
but I *do* want to take the exams," Desta said. "Do you have your
notes for science, history, and geography from last year?"

"How can you study the full semester's worth of work for three subjects in just three weeks? Plus Amharic, math, and English."

"I'll be okay with these last three subjects. What I need
is the material for the other three. As you know, our school
never taught science, history, or geography."

Fenta padded over to a cardboard box at the foot of his bed and brought
out three dog-eared notebooks. The back cover on one of them was missing. Desta lay on his belly with the notebooks and began leafing through the
pages of one, stopping at places where a word or phrase caught his interest or the handwriting was not clear. Once finished he did the same with
the other two, one subject at a time. All the material was in English.

In the end, he concluded that the history and geography lessons were easy.
One covered mostly dates and events in ancient Egypt and Mesopotamia. The
geography notebook contained names of Ethiopia's fourteen provinces and
what each produced, as well as the names of their capitals—plus the names
and details of other countries in Africa and their capital cities. The material
for the science class was a different matter. There were many terms and English words he had never heard before and diagrams and illustrations he had

never seen. The science class caused him to rethink taking the exams altogether. If he couldn't pass all of them, he would simply rather not take them.

"What's the matter?" Fenta asked when he heard Desta sigh.

"Frankly, I think you're right. It will be a lot of work for me to study all these subjects and pass the exams."

"You have one great advantage many of us don't," Fenta said, turning over from his bed to look at Desta.

"That *is*?" Desta asked.

"Your English. I've no doubt you'll do well on all the exams, but you won't be able to learn the material and remember it all in the little time you have."

"Yes, I'm comfortable with that aspect of the challenge," Desta agreed, closing the last notebook and placing it on top of the others. "Whether I'd have the time to study all the subjects and be ready for the finals is what I'm not sure about."

He crossed his hand over his brow and thought.

"It's something I need to think about for sure," Desta said, finally. He moved his hand from his face and sat up.

"Can I keep these notebooks for a few days?" he asked, glancing at Fenta. "I'll return them if I decide not to take the exams."

"Sure. I've no use for them, for now, anyway," Fenta said. "Go through them again. Think some more whether you really want to take the exams."

Desta said he would give himself one week. In that time he wanted to go through Fenta's notebooks carefully and get a feel for the classroom lessons and the teachers. In that time, he also needed to find someone to live with and get a handle on the job he was supposed to have with Amare.

"It looks like you have planned out everything well," Fenta said.

"These are the kinds of things I must do if I'm going to make it in this town. I have nobody I can depend on. I have come to terms with that aspect of my life. I'll continue to try my best in everything I do. Thanks for being my friend and for allowing me to stay with you and your relatives for this one week." Desta held back his emotion.

"It's nothing. We're all happy you could finally come here. Cheer up! . . . Let's go to bed now." Fenta blew the light out and the night draped the two boys in darkness.

FOR THE REST OF THE WEEK Desta became completely absorbed in the things he had to do—at school with his studies, in town with his search for people to live with. Although he was auditing for the remainder of the term and the teachers didn't expect him to do the homework assignments or participate in the class discussions, Desta was still fully involved.

After interviewing with several families, he decided the single woman with the chickens had the best offer. *The fewer personalities to navigate the better*, thought Desta. And he could study in peace and quiet for a full month while the woman was away visiting her mother.

With this in mind, Desta went to see Aklilu, the handsome man who had suggested the arrangement.

"Where have you been?" Aklilu asked. "I was expecting to see you earlier in the week. Are you still looking for someone to live with?" He was standing behind the counter rolling a spool of fabric.

Desta said he was.

"Wezero Alem had wanted to meet you. . . . Now I'm not sure if she is still in town," Aklilu said. He put away the cloth on the shelf behind him. "Mulat, attend to the window. I'll be back in a while," Aklilu said, turning to a young man who was opening a box of something on the floor.

He came out from behind the counter. "Let's go see."

Desta followed Aklilu through a maze of paths that resembled termite tracks.

Alem lived in an out-of-the-way corrugated tin-roof building that sat like an island in the middle of a nearly circular expanse of land. The property was bound by a dense grove of eucalyptus trees to the south. A tightly built wooden fence separated the inner sanctum of this place from the outer world. A heavy wooden door was the eyelid that opened the gate. It looked onto the backs of two thatched-roof homes that were located across the street.

Aklilu banged on the gate with all the power he had in his fist.

"C'mon in," Alem said, after opening the gate. By her quick response, she appeared as if she had been waiting for them. Her big eyes flashed with pleasure. She took one quick glance at Desta. Then just as quickly, her eyes dimmed and her smile faded. "Is this the boy you told me about?" she inquired, finally.

Aklilu's face tightened. "Yes, his name is Desta."

"I was hoping he was . . ." Alem's voice left her.

"What?" Aklilu asked, knitting his brow.

"I was hoping he was a little bigger."

The ground under Desta's feet felt like quicksand.

"If you're looking for a husband, I can't help you. But he's big enough to run your errands and keep you company whenever you're alone." Aklilu's voice was firm.

Desta winced. "Whenever you're alone?" he murmured under his breath. He looked up at Aklilu to see whether he could discern the meaning of this reference. Aklilu didn't react.

"I was . . ." she looked down on Desta again. "I was hoping he was big enough to carry heavy sacks when I go to the market, to cut firewood, and to help me with bigger things around the house that I cannot handle myself."

"That's called a man! Not a boy, as you told me you wanted," Aklilu growled, his face grievous. "You wasted my time as well as this young man's. Let's go." He motioned to Desta.

"No, no," Alem interceded. Her hand came down swiftly on Aklilu's arm. "I can still use him for the smaller things. I can hire porters for the heavier work." Her eyes went past Aklilu to Desta. "Desta is your name, right?" she asked, flashing her beautiful white teeth.

Desta nodded, still apprehensive and nervous.

"How can I lose with a name like that? Desta, "happiness" is what I need at the moment. As I told you, my mother is severely sick and I have been rather depressed." She looked at Aklilu. Her voice suddenly took on a somber tone. "I plan to spend a month with her, which is one of the reasons I wanted someone who could look after the house, open and close the chicken coop, and collect the eggs the hens lay."

Aklilu's eyes hardened. "If you're going to be gone for a month, who will attend to the needs of this boy?"

"Oh, no problem," she said. "My sister will supply his food and I'll have her son, Dagim, stay with Desta at night. I need someone here at all times for the things I just mentioned.

"It sounds a bit complicated, but it's up to Desta," he said, resting a hand on Desta's shoulder. "What do you think?" Aklilu asked, bending a little.

Desta studied the woman for a bit. Despite her initial air, he liked her easygoing and friendly disposition. He quickly processed in his head her suggestions. Having any place to live, let alone a home to himself for the month he needed to study, was definitely better than his current situation. Regarding food, he could always feed himself with the money he would earn from his Saturday job. Having settled this concern, he said, "Ishee."

"There you have it. You two work out the details. I must go now."
Aklilu said. He patted Desta on the shoulder, indicating they leave.

"Glad to hear it. Then come tomorrow morning and I'll show you the
kinds of things I would want you to do while I'm gone," Alem said.

As they retraced their steps back to the center of town, Desta thought about
Aklilu's suggestion that Desta might keep Alem company when she was
alone. Did this mean he would be with her when she was alone and asked to
leave when she had company? Did Alem have a lot of family in town who
came to visit her? If so, why did she need Desta? He wanted to ask Aklilu
these things, but asking adults too many questions could set him up for
reproach, which, he remembered, had happened when he was little. If things
didn't work out with Alem, he could always try to find someone else. During the month she was gone he would get to know the town and its people.

Chapter 3

Getting the farmers to listen to him or the donkeys to oblige seemed a job made for a different person than Desta. Merchant Amare had made it sound so easy. Despite what Amare had told him, he wanted to see how other boys procured and persuaded the farmers and donkeys to follow them to their employers' verandas. He stood on one side of the market entrance while the others took their positions on either side ahead of him. The moment they saw a farmer and donkey appear at a distance, they moved their mouths, cleared their throats, and smacked their lips, their eyes steely and unwavering from the approaching beast and man.

To Desta the boys' stance reminded him of a cat who was lying in wait and ready to pounce at its victim at what it instinctually felt was a precise and deadly moment. Desta didn't want to mimic a cat. He didn't want to spring at unwitting strangers. He was feeling ambivalent about the work already. But he knew he must force himself to do it. He was counting on the money he would get from the work to live on. He had to learn to be independent. These were the kinds of things he must learn to adapt to, to get used to—as he had gotten used to so many things.

The boy on the left was the first to go. "*Betru waga*—top dollar—betru waga, betru waga!" he began to shout. The boy on the right chimed in as if waiting for a cue from the other boy before he began his own mantra. The moment a man and his donkey neared the market grounds, the first boy stepped forward. He kept repeating the phrase, "Betru waga, betru waga, betru waga," his eyes alighting first on the load and then on the man.

The man ignored him. Instead he whipped his donkey to go past the boy, who now followed the farmer and his animal to the market grounds. Desta followed as well, curious to see the outcome.

The boy kept glancing sideways as he repeated his phrase. He now also appended "*Abaye*—father" to his line. "*Abaye, tru waga, negaday*—merchant—is waiting. *Abaye, tru waga, ishee?*"

Then the boy pointed out the day's rising temperature and how hard it would be for man and beast to stand all day waiting for someone to come buy his sack of grain—worse if he planned to retail it by the basket. The man's feet slackened and then stopped altogether. He turned to the boy. "For how much will he buy my sack of teff?"

The boy stopped abruptly. "Well . . . I don't; I don't know! The merchant has to weigh it first." His voice calmed—and the tight, anxious look on his face faded. "It depends on the weight. . . . Let's go," the boy said, taking a half-dozen long steps to grab the donkey who had now wandered away.

Somewhat uncertain still, the man followed the boy and donkey.

"So that's how it's done," Desta murmured. He returned to the market entrance. He found the second boy clutching a donkey's mane and pleading with a couple to follow him and their donkey to a veranda so that his negaday would purchase their sack of grain betru waga.

The man seemed unable to decide whether to follow the boy. The wife spoke for him. "Either you follow this boy and find out how much the merchant will pay for our sack or drop the idea entirely and we'll go to the teff row." With this input from the wife, the boy's patter picked up speed to the point where he didn't even seem to be listening to what the couple was saying. The intensity in his eyes and on his face was visible.

Desta didn't like the boy. He didn't like the work. *This is what he will have to do with every seller before he finally convinces them to come with him?* It looked degrading. Losing his dignity and self-respect was the last thing he wanted to do, no matter how dire his circumstances.

When the man couldn't make up his mind, the wife yanked the boy's hand from the mane of the donkey and began guiding the animal into the teeming crowd. The boy just stood where he was, looking sad and dejected.

Desta approached him. "Did you need to talk so much to convince these people?" he asked.

"Sometimes it's like this. At other times, it's not," his said somewhat emotionally. With his arms crossed over his chest, he looked down thoughtfully.

Desta felt sorry for the boy. "I've never done this work myself and I can't tell you how well I'd do by the end of the day," he said, waving his hand before the boy to get his attention. "Isn't it still early for that couple's refusal to upset you like this?"

"You don't understand," the boy began to say, until he noticed a man approach who was driving a donkey loaded with neatly folded goatskins and cowhides. "Do you boys work for a skin merchant?" the man asked without hesitating.

"I do!" the boy said, quickly raising his hand. Desta was not fast enough. He was actually surprised there were farmers who came looking for boys in this way. Now he didn't know what to think. Within a short time he observed a wide range of interactions between the boys and the farmers. Standing there alone, his eyes on the surging crowd that was now coming like a tidal wave, Desta wondered which stance he should assume. The first boy worked hard, and he did so with equanimity and self-assurance. The second boy talked too much and appeared nervous, in the end losing a potential customer for his merchant and compensation for himself.

The last situation was probably not the norm, Desta thought. As a rule, farmers are not going to actually come looking for boys to take them to the merchant's veranda. Desta thought he would have to work like the first boy, persistent and self-assured but with a slight modification. Instead of immediately convincing the farmers to come see his merchant, he would ask them questions unrelated to his intentions—like how was their day going? How far had they walked to get to the market? Once he got to know them a little, he would mention his merchant.

In the crowd he noticed another man driving a loaded mule. He certainly wouldn't try grabbing the man's mule by her ear or mane. She was too tall and dangerous for Desta to try anything like that. Instead he spoke to the farmer. "How are you? Are you selling the content of that sack?" he asked, the moment the man and mule came near.

"No," the man said after a quick glance at Desta. "I'm taking this grain as a gift to a friend."

Desta clamped his lips, trying not to show his disappointment.

The two boys returned, their faces bright as the morning sun.

"No luck?" the first boy asked, noticing Desta's forlorn face.

"I'm still trying to figure out this work before I can blame or hail my luck," Desta said.

"You watched us do it. You must learn quickly or you won't have money at the end of the day, and Amare won't ask you to come back next Saturday," the second boy said smugly.

The thought of having no money by the end of the day and not being called back the following Saturday sent shivers throughout Desta's body. "I know. . . . I'm doing my best."

"This is your first day. Amare will probably let you come back even if you don't do well. If the same thing happened next Saturday, it would be a different story. Let's get to work," the first boy said. He strode farther along the market entrance. Now Desta had to wait until each of the boys got a farmer and donkey to take to the veranda.

As if on cue, the second boy followed the first, and they walked down the footpath on the opposite side of the street, their eyes scanning the back of the distant crowd, which tapered like a snake's tail.

From midmorning on, farmers came one after another, allowing the boys to take turns with the grain sellers. Even so, the first boy got the lion's share of the business, pulling a total of fifteen donkeys by closing time. The second boy collected ten donkeys. Desta got only six. This amounted to one and a half bir, covering only six of his meals for the week. He became disheartened. He didn't like the work. He couldn't talk passionately because he didn't believe in what he was doing. At times he talked mechanically like the other boys. He felt hollow inside when he did that.

The farmers with whom he succeeded were those he felt connected to emotionally. There were times when he was compelled to reach for the coin image on his chest, seeking its assistance. But he was discouraged by a fight that broke out between the two boys. One boy accused the other of stealing the farmers he had brought from down the road. The bigger boy punched the other, much smaller boy in the nose, causing him to bleed profusely. If he tapped into the power of the coin and collected a lot more loaded donkeys than the other boys, he would bring unnecessary animosity upon himself from them.

At the end of the day, the three boys went to the merchant to collect their pay.

Desta decided he would rather not come back. The idea of cajoling people and the competitiveness of the work made the job unappealing. It was not in his nature to be aggressive. Desta never fought with kids when he was growing up, not even so much as an argument. He had no kid friends. His only companions were his dog, Kooli; the vervet monkeys; and his immediate older sister, Hibist. Now he would be working with boys who were loud, aggressive, and fractious. His heart tightened. But given his circumstances, he knew he must learn to adapt and grow into the work and get along with his kid friends. Choices were never a part of his world. He had to force himself to like the work, Desta told himself.

Amare gave Desta in coins the equivalent of one and a half birrs for the day's work. He had pulled six donkeys, earning twenty-five cents for each. Despite his ambivalence about the job and the kids he worked with, he loved the feel of the coins in his hand. He earned them. Nobody gave them to him. He was proud of himself. He put the coins in his pocket, enjoying the jangling sound they made.

"See you next weekend," Amare said, raising his hand in farewell.

"Thank you," Desta said, raising his hand in tandem, but he didn't say he would see him the following weekend. He needed to see how things would work out with Alem first.

Chapter 4

On Sunday morning, shortly after eight o'clock, Desta arrived at Alem's house. She had asked him to drop by so she could show him around before leaving to see her sick mother. When he got there, he found a horse hitched to a post by the gate.

"Good morning," Alem said cheerily. "Glad you got here on time. We were waiting for you." She was dressed in a riding habit—cream-colored breeches and a long cotton costume. A turbaned middle-aged man in sandals sat on the high bunk seat.

Alem excused herself. "Let's go outside and show you the chicken coop," she said, stepping toward the door. In the back, attached to the wall of the house, was a small shed. Inside, several parallel wooden bars hung down from the ceiling. On the floor along one wall were patches of grass. This, said Alem, was where the chickens laid their eggs. Desta's job was to collect the eggs, bring them inside the house, and close the shed door every night. She showed him the chickens' feed storage and water trough and told him to remember to refill it regularly.

Then they went to the front gate. Alem showed him how to close and lock it, which he was instructed to do every night. To the right, halfway along the fence, was a wooden box with a door. She opened it and said that it was where the milkman left a bottle every morning, and Desta was welcome to collect the milk and drink it before he went to school. Inside the house, Alem showed him where the kitchen items were—the baskets and pots he could use to make his sauce and tea. And she pointed to the wooden chest where he would store the eggs he collected. He could eat as many eggs as he wished and give the remaining to her nephew, Dagim, when he brought Desta's food. Then Alem showed him his room and where he'd sleep.

Finally, she gave him the keys to the gate and house padlocks. Her sister had a spare set that Dagim would use as Desta's nighttime housemate.

Then both Alem and the man stepped outside. The man unleashed the horse and stood waiting for her by the door. "We need to get going," he said when he noticed Alem linger as if forgetting something.

She tapped Desta on his shoulders. "We'll see you in one month," she said. "That's assuming everything turns out well with my mother."

"Ishee," Desta said reluctantly. He felt a sudden emptiness inside.

As soon as they exited, Desta closed the gate and latched it. He pressed his back against the rough surface of the gate and stared at the house, his daily companion until its owner returned. The two open windows on either side of the entrance stared back at him like hollow eyes, echoing the emptiness he was feeling inside. The enormity of the place, sequestered from the outside world as it was by the tall fence that encircled the compound, had the sense of reducing Desta to a speck of dust.

He pushed away from the gate and started walking to the back of the compound. Nearly two hundred feet deep and as many feet wide, it was strewn with dried corn stalks. The chickens were scratching the earth with their feet, their heads bobbing as they searched and picked morsels of food from the dirt. On the south side, the eucalyptus trees, thick as thieves, hugged the outside of the fence; on the north, leafy thorn bushes overlooked the enclosure from a sloping swath of earth. And back there he sensed something foreboding but he didn't know why or what the cause of it was.

With his eyes still fixed on the tableau, Desta sat on a wooden bench under the eaves and tried to assess his feelings. There was the fear that if a robber broke into the home while he was asleep or a monster lurking in the shadows attacked him when he returned home in the evening. When he remembered Alem's nephew will be there at night, his frights were allayed. It was then that he saw a small figure—thin and frail, like a ghost, walk along the edge of the property and then vanish into the woods below. She looked sad and was pulling something behind her, a box of something. Desta shook his head as if waking from a dream. He stood up and scanned the perimeter of Alem's compound but saw nothing.

"Weird," he said. He sat down and continued to assess his feelings. In his heart he had this uneasy sense of abandonment. The person he came to live with left before he got to know her. This feeling reminded him, in a strange way, of an experience from years ago. He had climbed the mountain above his home and attempted to touch the sky and gather clouds in a sack. Both vanished from him when he got there; the sky was too high to reach, the clouds intangible—impossible to grasp. Alem reminded him of the cloud.

And then there was the underlying anxiety that this living arrangement with his host may be only temporary, until she returns. It seemed unlikely to Desta that such a well-to-do woman wouldn't already have a woman servant who could run her errands. Had her servant gone on vacation, too?

A loud, booming voice burst before him. "This arrangement is for your own benefit. Don't fret over nothing. Take advantage of the month you have to yourself. Study hard and do well on your exams."

Desta lifted his head and looked in the direction of the trees, wondering whether the voice would continue. It fell silent.

Later in the afternoon Desta was sitting on one of the benches in the front when he heard someone knock at the gate. Startled, he went and looked through a gap in the posts. It was Aklilu.

He explained that he came to check in on him and to see whether he needed someone to keep him company at night. When he learned Alem's nephew would be coming to spend the night with him Aklilu said, "Oh, yes. I forgot about that. We don't have to worry about you being alone and afraid to be by yourself in this big place then."

"I grew up in a place much bigger than this and surrounded by a thicker forest, where there lived just about every kind of animal. There are no wild animals here and I am not afraid. . . .

"I wanted to ask you," Desta said, glad he remembered something more important to ask Aklilu about.

"Who exactly is my benefactor? I mean, what does she do? She lives in this big place, yet she has no husband or children to help her with it?"

Aklilu smiled. "This property used to belong to her father—Mersha—who died a year ago. It was one of her inheritances. He also passed down to her a leased farm in the country, where she gets her supply of grains, peas, and beans. And she inherited a few dairy cattle, which graze nearby and make possible the milk she receives each day. She has been married before but has no children. If everything works out, you couldn't have asked for a better arrangement."

Desta processed this information, that a single woman could be a proprietor of all this wealth. "What did her father do for a living?"

"He used to be a businessman, traveling all over the country and abroad. He used to own a couple of cargo trucks and several properties here in town as well as in the country. All of his belongings have been divided between his two children—Alem and her sister, Konjit. Have you been to the main bus stop down by the highway?"

"No," Desta replied, still in awe.

"The largest hotel & bar in town is located there, and it's owned by Konjit."

"So Dagim is her son, the kid Alem said would be staying with me?"

"Yes, he's Konjit's son."

"I really don't need company, but . . ."

"You need a companion in a big house like this. I'm glad Alem thought of it. She is good that way."

"Can I ask you another question?"

Aklilu acknowledged with a toss of his head.

"What did you mean by 'Alem can use my companionship whenever she is alone?' Does she have company a lot of the time? Does it mean I will only stay here whenever she is alone?"

Aklilu smiled benignly. "How shall I explain this . . .?" He looked away for a few seconds, and then turned and gazed at Desta. "I told you that Alem is a single woman, right?"

Desta nodded.

"That means she has a few men friends who come visit her."

"Aha," Desta breathed. "I remember women like that."

"You do?!" Aklilu asked, his brow arched.

"Yes, there were a few in the little town where I used to live. My mother called them *shermuta*—prostitutes."

"Sheee. Don't ever use that word in front of Alem or anybody else. It's not a nice word. A nicer term is *set adaree*—a woman who lives alone."

Desta held his hand over his mouth, embarrassed. He felt as though Alem had just heard the word he called her by.

"Don't be ashamed. You didn't know. Just remember not to use that word again. . . . Got to go." Aklilu rose and prepared to leave.

Desta rose too and followed him to the gate. Returning, he gathered his notebooks and went inside the house.

"How about that?" Desta thought, humored. "When you're free and independent, you get a chance to do what your parents don't approve of." Because his mother wouldn't permit his living with a single woman in their little town, Desta was forced to go to Dangila, where he ended up being starved and physically abused. He didn't have to ask an adult for permission anymore. He was his own person, making his own decisions on all matters concerning his life.

IT WAS NEARLY TWILIGHT when Dagim arrived. He was a tall, acned young man of about fifteen or so, with a wisp of hair on his upper lip and jawline that made him look older than he was.

As soon as Desta opened the gate and their eyes met, the visitor held him with a fixed gaze, as if trying to remember where he had seen or met him before. He was carrying a basket of food in a bag. The spicy aroma caused Desta's stomach to jump. "C'mon in," Desta said, opening the gate wider.

Inside the house, Dagim placed the colorful straw basket on the table. "The aroma is amazing. What do you have in there?" Desta asked with a smile.

"Our dinner," Dagim replied, opening the basket. "Do you want to take a look?"

Desta peered inside. He saw eggs marinating in a thick, succulent red sauce. There was cheese, a range of legume sauces, and cooked carrots, cabbage, and potatoes. "This is high living!" Desta added. He smiled at Dagim.

"This food is not even from our house," Dagim
boasted. "It came from the restaurant."

"It's more than I'm accustomed to seeing. And certainly very inviting."

They sat down to have their dinner, conversing as they ate. Desta learned that Dagim was in the sixth grade. He had started school when he was ten years old because he lived with his grandmother in the country most of the time before that. His parents had divorced when he was five. He didn't like school but loved playing soccer, running, and marble games, which explained the pads of muscles on his legs and shoulders.

Desta shared some of the things he deemed worthy of mention. He touched upon where he came from, his auditing of the fourth-grade class, taking the exams, and wishing he had a life that allowed for soccer.

When the two boys had their fill, they put away the leftovers. Before going to their rooms, Desta washed his feet outside and Dagim took off his tennis shoes. Dagim retired to his aunt's bedroom, Desta to the second, or guest bedroom. Prior to falling asleep, Desta took out the parchment from the folds in his notebook and recited the legends with light from a stubby beeswax candle Alem had left him on a little table by his bed. He said his gratitude to God, blew the light out, and covered his face.

When Desta woke the following morning, Dagim had already gone. Desta went outside to let the chickens into the yard and to make sure their water trough was full. He came back inside to prepare his breakfast of *firfir*—eggs, onions, and garlic, which he sautéed together from the previous night's leftovers. He made his tea with three cubes of white sugar. He ate his firfir and drank his brown, steaming liquid. Afterward he gathered his notebooks from the bedroom and left for school.

As he walked, Desta realized he was in a new world. Not just geographically but also circumstantially. He had found himself in a world in which he alone charted his course. It was he who made both the day-to-day decisions and those with long-term effects, like the choices surrounding his education as well as his finding the second Coin of Magic and Fortune. No parent, sibling, or other relative would offer advice or have a deciding role in his life. He would enter his fifteenth year in about a month, old enough to be considered an adult. He hoped he now had enough experience in his years on earth to make wise decisions in nearly every aspect of his life.

That morning, Desta also made a firm and final decision to take the exams. He had a full month to prepare, a comfortable living arrangement, a quiet place to study. Even if he didn't get top grades, he was confident he would pass the exams. Fenta's notes from the previous year would be helpful to him. Plus he would learn a lot in class until exam time and would be on equal footing with the rest of the students when school opened after Christmas. With these thoughts in mind, Desta ran and skipped his way to school. He arrived at the school's gate about fifteen minutes before nine.

Sitotaw stopped him. "Good morning, Desta. Come here for a second," he said. After Desta walked up, he said, "Having come in the middle of the semester, you're at a disadvantage on many levels. One of them is regarding our rules. One of my many jobs is to ensure that the students respect and uphold our punctuality rule. That means for you to be here by no later than nine sharp each morning.

"When I say nine o'clock, it means just that. Not a minute or two later. The gate will have been locked by then. If I'm here, I'll let you in, but with a price. You get three lashes for the first offense and six for the second. You are sent to the director on the third. He decides the punishment—more whipping or a suspension or even dismissal from school, which is more likely if you have other offenses on your record. Is that clear?" Sitotaw waved the whip in front of Desta.

"It is," Desta whimpered.

When he arrived at his fourth-grade class, the other students were outside and lined up in preparation for the flag ceremony. Next door, the third-graders had readied themselves as well. They marched to the front of the building and stood in single file by class—from the eighth to the first grade—facing the flagpole. Before the flag was raised, the monitors from each class came out and checked to see that there were no mouths moving and the lines were as straight as they could be. Each monitor had a whip in his hand. Once they fixed any infractions they found, they got back in line themselves.

After they sang the national anthem to the rising flag and said the Lord's prayer, the students returned to their classrooms the same way they left them: in a single line and perfectly quiet.

As the fourth-grade students filed into their classroom, the monitor, Dagne, a strong-boned and older student, pulled Desta aside and said, "I know you didn't have the advantage of starting with us in September and you don't know many of the school's rules. As the overseer of the class, I need to make you aware of the rules that govern all the students in the classrooms," Dagne said, fixing Desta with his small sharp eyes. Desta was looking down, and then he looked up, waiting for the rules he must comply with.

The monitor continued. "One, you don't talk, whisper, or do anything that would distract the rest of the students' attention while the instructor is teaching. Two, you don't get up and walk from desk to desk, engaging in any tomfoolery or making jokes that would cause others to burst into laughter or otherwise create a disturbance. Three, every morning you're to arrive before the class is assembled for the flag ceremonies, and after each morning and afternoon break, you are to be at your desk before the teacher starts the lesson. Is this clear?" Dagne asked, with his piercing eyes still on Desta.

Desta said it was.

"There is more. You'll learn the rest as we go along—and the retribution for breaking any of the rules is getting your bottom whipped or your hands slapped with a ruler or your head rapped with my *koorkoom*—knuckles."

Desta flinched. Except for the ruler, Desta had had similar beatings while he lived with his family.

As Desta was about to go sit at his desk, Dagne said, "Wait," and looked around. Turning to Desta, he said, "I'd be remiss if I didn't tell you my own personal rule."

Desta blinked in anticipation. *Dagne's personal rule?*

The classroom's boss went on, "You are not allowed to bring me snacks, money, or any other form of bribery to get favors from me. I know this goes on in other classrooms but *not* in mine!"

"Don't worry," Desta said, feigning a smile. "I've never even heard of students doing that in either of the previous schools I attended. It certainly wouldn't be a habit I'd indulge here."

"Good. I make myself clear on that score with all the students I'm in charge of. Let's go in now," the monitor said, tapping Desta on the shoulder. There was a ring of authority and satisfaction to his voice.

Desta followed all the rules. Nobody complained about him concerning anything—from the guard at the gate to the class monitor or any of his teachers. Nobody told him he didn't arrive on time or had made any noise inside, or even outside, the classroom.

During breaks he went to the wing that housed the fifth- and sixth-graders and stood leaning on the balustrades to watch the students play soccer. He didn't feel comfortable enough to play the game with them yet, nor did he feel privileged. Watching from a distance is something he cultivated when he lived in the country: it was the way he observed the mountains, the clouds, and the sky.

His notebooks, however, were his place of comfort. Whether at home or at school, Desta read. As he studied for his finals during the month of December, he discovered something about himself he hadn't realized before. He could memorize things easily. Often he didn't need to read the notebooks more than once or twice to retain all that he had read. And he was not tapping into the power of the coin image on his chest.

Within two weeks he had memorized all the historical dates, events, and names of history's important personalities and the names of all the countries of Africa, Europe, and the Middle East, along with their capital cities. He accomplished the same for his science, English, and Amharic classes. By exam time he felt confident he could pass all his classes.

The good food at home—Konjit still continued to send along prepared food, through Dagim or the restaurant workers—the quiet and secluded place he lived in, and the willingness of some of his classmates to loan him their notebooks for a night or two, together with Fenta's books from the previous year, made his effort fruitful.

In the morning when he arrived for the flag ceremony with his classmates, he looked across the rows of lines, and he counted. The four lines formed by grades five through eight represented the four years he would be going to the Finote Selam school, before he graduated and went to Bahir Dar to look for the Sweet and Sour woman who held the second Coin of Magic and Fortune.

Desta took his exams along with the rest of the students during the last week in December. The results wouldn't be announced until after the Christmas break, in January. Desta wasn't going home for the holidays. He had not been back home to celebrate them with his family since he fought with his mother exactly three years before. She had insisted Desta be treated with holy water and the cross for associating with Muslims and eating the meat that came from an animal they killed. Desta thought the treatment absurd.

It was that evening as he sat down at the bench in back of the house, waiting for the night to turn color and before he put away the chickens, when he met the spirit he had seen before. He had spied the little girl right after Alem had left for the country, and two more times, like a vision out of the corner of his eye, while he was studying at the same spot. Before, he thought he was imagining the figure or had ruined his eyes from too many hours of reading, compromising his ability to see clearly. But there she stood, looking right at him. She wasn't substantial, like a flesh-and-blood human being, but ethereal, like the Cloud Man, his grandfather's spirit.

"My name is Emnet," she said, fixing her soft eyes on Desta. "I need your help to transition from this world to the next."

Before Desta had time to answer her or find out who she really was, Dagim banged at the door, asking to be let in. "Wait here. Be right back," he said to Emnet, and he went to open the gate. When Desta returned, the apparition was gone.

"Where did you go?" Dagim asked, when Desta returned to the house. Dagim had put their dinner on the table and was waiting for Desta.

"I saw a little ghost in the back just before you came and now she's gone."

Dagim jerked his chin in surprise. "A ghost?"

"Yeah, a little girl."

Both boys went out to the back looking for her. "I don't think she is going to reveal herself again," Desta said.

"My grandpa or aunt never mentioned seeing a ghost here. Do you think you might have seen a small animal or even just the shadow of a moving tree limb?"

"I don't know," Desta said. "The air is quiet and animals don't talk. Let's have our dinner." He was annoyed by Dagim's ridiculous suggestion.

That night when Desta lay in bed, it was not just his physical body that fell into a state of deep relaxation. It was also his mind and spirit. The three weeks of academic rigor had ended. He could sleep late every morning and go to bed at a decent hour every night for the following two weeks of his Christmas break. He no longer had to stay up late or get up early in the morning to study.

Then something hit him. His stay in this beautiful place might end once Alem returned and by the time school started again. Alem never actually mentioned his staying on. And then there was her nebulous comment about needing him only when she was alone. "To be on the safe side," he said to himself, "I should probably look for an alternative arrangement."

The idea of starting over after only a month and a half was daunting to him. Where could he go and who would he ask? Did he really want to deal with another face and set of eyes? This was not just for the next semester. It was for the following four years of his stay in this town! Desta shuddered.

He lay on his belly and held his face in his hands, his elbows propped on the pillow. He thought and thought and thought . . . and then thought no more.

In his dream he heard the familiar voice. Who it was or where it came from he had no idea.

"Again the answers to your questions lie in the coin. You recite the legends from the parchment often without really understanding their meaning or import." The voice faded. Desta lifted his head and listened, puzzled by its sudden disappearance. But it came back, saying, "Tomorrow when you wake up, go to your study bench. On top, pinned to a rock slab, you'll find a new document. Instead of reciting all the twenty-one items—just concentrate on the seven selected for you. The others you will learn as you gain more knowledge."

Desta was surprised, not to mention anxious and excited. "Will I find it if I go there now?"

"No! Tomorrow. It's not ready. You must learn to be patient." The voice ceased.

Desta sighed deeply. Tomorrow seemed a long time to come. *Like the voice said, I have to learn to be patient.* He rearranged himself and lay on his back. He closed his eyes and begged sleep to come and transport him to tomorrow.

IMMEDIATELY AFTER he woke in the morning, Desta went to his study bench. He found a parchment cut exactly fourteen by fourteen inches. In the center was a table of three columns, each containing seven of the legends. Below the table were seven words, evidently chosen for Desta to recite regularly.

King Solomon's Message and Legends
To All My Descendants: With All My Blessings

Benevolence	Equanimity	Courage
Diligence	Guardianship	Honor
Excellence	Justice	Humility
Integrity	Magic	Leadership
Magnanimity	Spirituality	Love
Scholarship	Wealth	Loyalty
Temperance	Wisdom	Prudence

The Coin of Magic and Fortune legends reorganized on the new parchment the mysterious spirit hand left for Desta outside his home.

Recite the following words daily. Morning is always a good time.

Courage—I have within me the ability to face difficulty or pain without fear. I have the courage and fortitude to deal with the known and the unknown challenges I face. I handle my failures, mistakes, and setbacks courageously. Hardships are opportunities for me to grow and succeed in my missions.

Diligence—I persist and persevere in my studies. I continue to work hard to find the person who owns the second Coin of Magic and Fortune. When I'm employed by others, I treat all work with an equal degree of industry and care, as I would do for myself. I thrive on details. I don't waste time, neither do I engage in trivial things.

Equanimity—I keep a constant balance in me. I hold neither positive nor negative experiences in my heart. I let them pass through because I require peace and serenity to stay focused on the things I need to accomplish.

Excellence—Every day I do my best in everything I undertake. I have infinite power within to excel and overcome hardships and obstacles I encounter. I accept my failures as well as my successes with equal reserve and grace.

Magic—My thoughts and beliefs spring from a source most powerful and all-knowing. This source enables me to control the outcome of things. My mind has the ability to connect to the mysteries and sublimities of the universe, to achieve great things and perform spells. With the proper intensity of focus, my mind is a force for change and control.

Prudence—I'm cautious in my dealings with people and things. That way I can protect myself, maintain my equanimity, and stay focused on my mission. I am neither gluttonous nor materialistic. I wish not to enslave myself to either vice. I'm stronger than my sexual urges and too noble for vanity or anger.

Spirituality—Every day I connect to my feelings and emotions. When I am in touch with my spirit, I am connected with the spirit of the universe. My spirituality is the source of my comfort and strength. It's the foundation of excellence, courage, and diligence. I'm small and delicate, but my spirituality lets me know I'm much greater than what I think. I'm strong beyond measure, fully able to finish my education and find the second Coin of Magic and Fortune.

"Wow!" Desta said, when he finished reading the parchment. He closed his eyes and slowly released the air from his lungs. "This is exactly what I need: a mentor. Thank you!"

Now Desta had something new he could recite every morning during his Christmas break. Maybe this would help lessen his fear of losing his comfortable arrangement with Alem. During Christmas break he could also look forward to meeting the Ferenge teacher from Debre Marcos, assuming the Ferenge was coming as he had told Mehiret he would.

Chapter 5

Desta's best friend came to get him for the Christmas Day celebration. Desta had received an invitation from Dagim, too, but he had declined, preferring to spend the holiday with Fenta and his family. They had killed a lamb. A cow was the usual choice at Christmas, which neighbors would kill and share after pooling their money. Fenta and his family were new to the town and didn't know many people.

The celebration was simple and the gathering small, consisting of Fenta, Aunt Senayit and Uncle Bizuneh, a newly hired cook, and Desta. He ate the food without relishing it. It was almost as if the special day had lost its meaning to him. That the day also happened to be his birthday and would usher in his fifteenth year without as much as a single happy birthday wish from anyone, as it had been so the previous fourteen years, didn't make him feel any better. That he had not had a birthday celebration all his life made him feel, in a strange way, as if he didn't exist. Desta remembered, too, that this was the first time he was spending Christmas in his new world—a world where his family would be the people he happened to be staying with at the time, whoever they were and wherever he was.

After dinner he thanked his hosts and left. Fenta wanted him to stay longer so they could visit, saying they had not had much opportunity to do so since Desta came to Finote Selam. Desta said he needed to go check on the house he was tending but promised to get together with his friend soon. In reality Desta just wanted be alone. When he had a choice, he preferred to be alone on holidays, especially on Christmas Day, one of the few times of the year when he connected to his deepest thoughts and feelings. The day when all those things he had stored over the months were released, giving him room for the things that would come in the new year.

He walked along the shadowed path to the graded traffic road. He turned left and headed toward the center of town, to the open plaza. Free of dust and noise, the air was still. It was as if even the atmosphere had taken a pause to celebrate the day. The mirage above the roadway he often saw on a warm day like today was not there. It, too, must have paused to celebrate the day.

The warka tree stood in what seemed an eternal pause, eclipsing the sun and forming a dark disk on the ground, its edges nicked in places, like the ancient Coin of Magic and Fortune. Although the day called for an umbrella, a hat, or a jacket over one's head, as protection against the strong sun, Desta began to feel cold, so cold it was as if the draft had gone past his skin and bones and into his marrow. He crossed his arms over his chest and hugged himself, trying to keep warm. He wanted to go home, but the warka tree was more inviting.

He was not sad or sentimental, although he was wistful, wishing he had someone close he could trust and with whom he could share how he really felt—someone who would accept him without question or judgment, a kindred spirit and true friend, like his dog, Kooli, or the vervets. He wanted to fill the void in his heart with something. He felt slightly light-headed, as if he might faint or hallucinate.

He cut over toward the warka. Meditatively and thoughtfully, he approached the tree's shadow, which was now moving east, far from its perfect circular configuration, when the sun was at its zenith. He stopped at the edge of the shadow, afraid to step inside. There was something peremptory about its presence and preternatural to its being, a holy place, where one cannot trespass without first washing one's feet and paying homage with prayers and prostration. Desta had the advantage of neither.

He simply stood there—his feet positioned at the cusp of the tree's mighty shadow. He rested his right hand over his chest, above his heart. He closed his eyes and said, "You who have set me on this journey, the destination of which is as obscure as this shadow, the responsibility as great as this tree: I have neither the physical strength nor the mental ability to fulfill this grand quest to find and reunite the two coins of Magic and Fortune. I await your guidance.

"You, giant tree—the symbol of the task ahead of me, near whose shadow I stand—please grant me the privilege to take respite under your canopy and give gratitude to my creator, and to all my ancestors of this land and others who guarded the coin we own. I thank the ancient prophecy that chose me as the ultimate shepherd of our family treasure. I want to rest under your massive branches and acknowledge, in the absence of any formal ritual, the passage of my fourteen years; specifically, seven years and seven more—'two seven' years. You who are in charge of this mission, please grant me the privilege of entering the shadow of this honorable tree and giving my prayers and appreciation."

"Wait until the shadow invites you," a voice said. Desta turned around to see whether there was someone behind. There was no one.

"Look down and wait until the shadow inches past your feet."

Desta noticed the dark crescent edge of the tree's silhouette had already reached the arches of his feet. He looked up, still frozen in place where he stood. It was as if his ankles were shackled. When he noticed the border of the shadow had gone past his heels and was now climbing his legs, he moved.

He walked straight to the benches near the trunk of the tree and sat down. There wasn't a soul in the growing heat of the plaza, despite the tree's cool beckoning—its canopy offering a cloak of serenity to anyone in search of shade. Desta clutched the bench with both hands, tipped his head back, and closed his eyes. That's right! This day, two seven years ago, he was born, prematurely. It was on the seventh day and seventh month of his gestation. He was seen by some members of his family as an incomplete human being who would not survive past a few days. His own mother shared this sentiment, rejecting him immediately. And once Desta made it past those critical few days, she would treat him as an outcast and an enigma for much of his childhood, as would many of the adults around him.

Later, when he would leave home to go to school, he would be accused of shedding his native Christian faith and adopting Islam. He would be viewed as a rebellious spirit who willfully pursued a modern education against the norm.

Overcoming anger and abuse—from family and benefactors alike—Desta would still pursue his dual mission. He would pay homage to the many ethereal entities who worked with him unseen. And he would be forever grateful for all the experiences he'd had—good and bad—up to this point. He felt that he was now a better, stronger person, ready and willing for what would come next. He didn't need the birthday celebration. Just being here, under the analogous tree where he first met his grandfather's spirit, where mysteries began to unravel, bringing peace and happiness to his family, including his sister Saba and her husband, Yihoon, was a great privilege and honor.

He felt the presence of something or someone. He raised his head and opened his eyes. His whole body convulsed. He was not sure whether he should scold her or greet her for showing up unannounced. So instead, he stared at the figure.

"Hello! Happy birthday!" Eleni said, with a sweet maternal smile.

"Thank you. You know how to time yourself, don't you?"

"I was on a long journey to somewhere. I thought I'd stop

by and acknowledge this very special day. This is not just
an ordinary birthday and I didn't want to miss it."

"Is that so? Tell me."

"It *is* so. Do you mind if I sit here on that bench and talk to you for a
bit? Before I get to the information I have for you, let me share something you should know about your birthday and about this warka."

"Ooh!" Desta exclaimed.

"This tree is exactly the same age as the warka where you met your grandfather's spirit seven years ago. . . . Your emperor, Haile Selassie The First, spent the
night under this tree when he returned from exile in early 1941. He had the most
peaceful and restful evening here beneath its canopy. Because of it, he christened
the town Finote Selam—'way of peace.' The town used to be called Wojjet. And
in gratitude to his blessed night here, he had the elementary school built, bearing his name. He made sure it was located in close proximity to this tree. You
may not know it, but the school is the most beautiful in the whole province.

"What's more, when the sun is directly above the tree, the outer edge of
the tree's shadow is exactly eighty-four paces from the center of the warka.
You know what that stands for, right?" Eleni asked, glancing at Desta.

"Yes, seven added twelve times."

"Good!" Eleni said cheerily.

"Also they stand for my birthday and the seven channels of the coin
and the twelve-month cycle of a year, round as the coin and the sun."

"Good again! You know what the two stands for, right?

Desta nodded. "For the two coins or the head and tail of one."

"Now you know why the emperor had the most peaceful night under this
warka. It represents the two most blessed numbers—seven and twelve—
signifying harmony and wholeness. Twelve is the symbol of spiritual
perfection and completion. Seven signifies peace and tranquility. These
numbers, which are connected to the coin, also link you to the tree."

Desta placed his hand over his mouth, astounded by the revelation.

"Respect it. Always wait until you receive permission before
you step into its shadow. For you, this will be a good place of comfort. Come here whenever you feel down or sad. Okay?"

"Okay," Desta said. The melancholy that had pervaded his heart earlier was now melting away, like a hailstone on
a warm day. And he was not feeling cold any longer.

"Let me go on," Eleni said, once she noticed Desta felt better. "This is the first year of the twos," she announced. "The two sevens of your age and the two you get when you add the numbers in the year 1964. These twos are significant in that they represent the two coins, or just one, for the head and tail—the universal symbol of balance and harmony.

"Without this fundamental principle, the world would not exist. This birthday of the two sevens is very special and very important. If your family knew what it meant and the whole world knew what it meant, they would celebrate it in a grand way. As it is, you are in this faraway place, under this great tree by yourself, watching the time pass as if you had popped like a weed from the dirt." Eleni turned away as if trying to stop from crying. Then she looked at Desta and smiled instead. "For you, this year of the twos will be the year of balance. You will make up the two academic years you previously lost. . . . But know that I'm privy to something else. . . ." Eleni said, grinning broadly.

Desta peered up at her.

"This should please you. The next time you encounter fourteen or two sevens, your journey ends. I don't know when that will be or anything about the outcome. Just watch for that year and day. You may not even know it until after it has happened."

"Will I have found the second Coin of Magic and Fortune by then?"

"That . . . I don't know," Eleni said, dropping her voice. All of a sudden she went silent. It was as if the very idea scared her or she had spilled a secret she shouldn't have.

"What is the matter?" Desta asked, gazing at the ghost.

"Nothing, nothing," she said, shaking her head. "I need to go."

"Eleni, I wish you would stop revealing such cryptic and meaningless things and then vanish. Can you tell me if I am ever going to find the coin?"

"I made a mistake. Good-bye." Eleni said rising to the air. She looked over her shoulder and added. "I still want to take you to *Washaa*—cave—*Umera*. I'll let you know when, but have your flying craft handy." Seconds later she was gone.

Desta shook his head. He rose and went home.

Chapter 6

Fenta was panting when Desta arrived at the gate. Breathless and sweaty, he shouted, "Desta, Desta!" as he strode through the open gate.

"What's the matter? Are you all right?" Desta asked, looking up from *Ali Baba and the Forty Thieves*.

Fenta restrained himself. "I *am*. Some Ferenge people are looking for you. One of our teachers sent me to bring you to them."

"Did you have to run so fast for this?"

"He gave me this money," Fenta said, unfurling his fingers to reveal a five-birr note. "And he said I should look for you wherever you might be and bring you promptly. I figured if you weren't at home, I might find you at the merchant's veranda."

Desta didn't like surprises like this, but given the fact he had been curious about the mystery Ferenge man, assuming it was the same man who sent for him, he would respond to the urgency appropriately.

He went inside the house and placed the book in his *borsa*—carry on hand bag. From the bedroom, he unlocked the wooden box that contained his personal belongings and brought out his money pouch. He fished the silver coins out of it so that he could leave them behind in the box. He kept the remainder, the birr notes, inside the pouch. He slung its handle over his shoulder and secured it under his arm. He locked the main front door and joined Fenta in the front yard. He closed the gate securely and they left.

Fenta's quick sidelong glances, brisk steps, and puzzled eyes spoke to Desta what his friend had failed to fully articulate in words. Everything about him seemed to say, "How could a poor boy who doesn't even have a relative in town get a visit from a Ferenge who lives far away?"

"Tell me, Desta," Fenta said finally. "Who is this Ferenge?"

"I'm as much in the dark about the man as you are," Desta said calmly. He was surprised by Fenta's excitement, particularly since he rarely showed his emotions.

"You don't know anything about this man?" Fenta looked incredulous.

"Let me back up. I'm guessing it's the same man who sent for me when I lived in Yeedib, but I have no idea who he is or what his intentions are," Desta said. Then he added, "We'll find out who he really is soon. I'm sure."

At the center of town, they crossed the open plaza and walked south on the roadway. Up to now, Desta, as if obeying an urgent call, merely loped along following his friend. He had no time to think things through. But then again, he had no more information about this Ferenge than did the withered thorn bushes along the ditches or the rocks strewn on the ground.

Regardless of who this man was, Desta knew one thing. He should be cautious. A stranger so far removed from him as the sky, or the moon from the earth, cannot be an ordinary person. He must've been sent by someone—someone who knew about Desta's search for the coin. As anxious as he was earlier, he had now become even more apprehensive about this meeting with the man. He slowed down as these ideas took hold in his head.

"What's wrong? . . . Are you tired?" Fenta asked, turning back.

"No, just thinking about things. . . . Can we walk at a regular pace for a bit—what's the hurry?"

"Aren't you excited? No kid in this town gets a visit from a Ferenge. Maybe this man can give you money to buy a new set of clothes."

Desta shook his head. "I'm not seeking alms from this man. I have a greater love for the clothes I have on than a new set of clothes because they were given by someone who means so much to me. Don't bother yourself with my needs," Desta retorted, annoyed by Fenta's impertinence.

"I am hoping to get another tip myself." Fenta smiled.

This time, Desta shot Fenta a sideways glance, saying, "That sweat on your temple is worth more than double the amount you received." He forced a grin through clamped lips. Then he opened his mouth and asked, "Where exactly are we going?" He wanted none of this mindless conversation he and his friend were engaged in.

"To one of the hotels—Emma Tiwab's, to be exact."

Desta had never been to this part of town and he was as curious to see it as he was the man from America.

Desta stopped when they reached the main north-south gravel road that skirted the town. All along the road, on either side, new buildings had sprouted up, their corrugated tin roofs coruscating the light from the midday sun. Some were painted white, a few in hues of pink, red, and yellow. Fenta said the colored ones were mostly hotels, bars, and restaurants. Beyond the buildings to the west, an expansive bare land terminated in a grove of acacia trees and leafy foliage.

"That is where we are heading," Fenta said, pointing to a pink building with a multicolored beaded curtain swaying at the main entrance. "That's Emma Tiwab's hotel."

Desta followed right behind Fenta, who parted the beaded curtain with a swoosh as they entered the hotel. At one corner of the lobby, two Ferenge men sat with their backs against the wall. One of these men was playing the *masinko*—a bunched horsehair string instrument played with a bow— and singing in Amharic. His tune was credible. The other man snapped his fingers and clapped his hands as an accompaniment to the musician.

A group of men and women gathered in a semicircle before them, seemingly mesmerized by the genius of the man who was singing and playing the ancient Ethiopian instrument better than most locals. Desta and Fenta, too, stood at one end of the arching crowd and watched.

Desta's eyes went from the men to the fingers of the masinko player who, with the ease and proficiency of a native musician, was extracting a melodious sound from the pair of bunched horsehair strings.

The crowd began to clap as the men continued to croon, harmonize, and sing to the tune of the instrument.

Suddenly, one of the bystanders stepped into the center of the crowd and began to dance. His shoulders shook and twitched, his head moved from side to side, all in perfect rhythm with the singer's voice and instrument. For a few minutes, both Desta and Fenta had forgotten why they had come, for they, too, found themselves clapping, their eyes now on the dancer, who seemed lost in the heat of the moment.

The musician stopped singing and playing when he noticed sweat was breaking out on the dancer's brow. It was then that Fenta's English teacher, Kidane, spotted the two boys. Kidane leaned over and said something to the second Ferenge, who in turn leaned over and said something to his friend. Then the three men conferred, their heads bent together. Coming back up, Kidane excused the crowd but asked Desta and Fenta to remain.

"Which one of you is Desta?" the masinko player asked in perfect Amharic.

Desta hesitated, caught off guard by the musician's fluency in Amharic as he had been by his fluency in the masinko. Then the man raised his hand to shoulder level, as if in benediction.

"My name is Petros," the musician said, extending a hand for Desta to shake it. Shy and nervous, Desta stuck out a meek hand and held the musician's. After they let go, the second man offered his hand and said, "My name is Dawit." Desta's hand felt tiny inside Dawit's expansive palm and long fingers.

"Where we come from, we are called Peter and David. Here we like to be called by our Ethiopian names,"Petros said with a smile. And then they turned to Fenta and shook hands with him, each repeating his Ethiopian name.

"We don't really need introductions, do we?" Kidane said, grinning.

"*Ayee*—no," both boys said coyly.

Then the three men discussed the fact that Kidane didn't have to translate for the Americans in the talk they were to have with Desta. Peter could handle any necessary translations.

Kidane drained the last of his beer and got up. He shook hands with the two Ferenges, gave a nod of farewell to the boys, and left.

Dawit reached in his pocket, pulled out a wad of bills—a five birr note among them—and handed the money to Fenta, saying, "Thank you for your time." Fenta tapped his friend's shoulder and said, "See you later," and left, his face beaming.

As Dawit pulled up a chair for Desta to sit on, Desta was taking inventory of his feelings. His stomach was knotted, his palms had gone clammy. He turned around and looked to see who else was in the salon.

At the bar was a beautiful woman wearing a red scarf. She was attending two men who were sitting at the other side of the counter with beer bottles in their hands and cigarettes in their mouths.

At the opposite corner, where the Ferenge men and Desta sat, a couple was eating at a table. And there were a few people coming in and going out of the bar.

He had felt at ease to learn that Peter played an Ethiopian musical instrument and doubly comfortable when he heard him speak Amharic. Why Desta felt this way all of a sudden, he couldn't understand.

The two men had sensed the tension that was mounting inside Desta as well. Dawit said something to Petros.

"Would you like a Coca-Cola or Fanta or tea?" Petros asked.

Desta had not wanted to feel obligated in any way, but if one of these drinks could help calm him, he would accept.

When he realized Petros's eyes were still on him, Desta said, "I'll have tea."

Petros signaled to the woman at the bar. When she came, he ordered tea for Desta and two St. George beers for Dawit and himself.

The first fifteen minutes or so of their conversation centered around Desta: his family, his life in the country as a shepherd, his new school, and how far he planned to go with his education. Petros served as a conduit for Dawit's questions as well as his own. Desta was surprised these people knew so much about him.

Although Desta discovered later that these questions were merely intended to relax him and serve as a means of getting to know him, at the time he resented them and gave only short, mechanical answers. When Petros noticed Desta's discomfort—his facial gestures, shifts in his seat, wandering eyes—he stopped.

Petros apologized. He cleared his throat and continued. "To get to the main reason we invited you here, both Dawit and I are Peace Corps teachers. We teach English at the secondary school in Debre Marcos. Dawit is a student himself. He studies things that were made a long time ago, particularly those things that were made in *Gibtse*—ancient Egypt—and Israel and other places like here in your country. It's believed that many things that were made in the countries I mentioned are here. Also, there are things that are made in this country that trace back to events and happenings in Egypt and Israel and other countries in the area."

Dawit, who kept his eyes on Desta, interrupted Petros for a brief moment.

Desta heard and understood some of the words, but he couldn't make sense of the sentences.

Petros continued, saying, "Well, during his spare time, he collects and studies old things from Israel and Egypt, which are believed to be here. When he finishes studying these things, he will become an expert, a doctor, but not a *hakim*—medical doctor." Petros turned and smiled at Dawit.

"Dawit has been aware of the existence of two coins made during King Solomon's time and was excited to learn that one of the coins might be in this country. He knows a coin has come down through your family line and you're supposed to be the bearer of it. That was why he urgently sent Mehiret to bring you here. We wanted the opportunity to meet you and to help you continue your schooling. Dawit very much wants to see this coin to determine whether it's the real one. He is willing to support you through the remainder of the year in exchange for viewing the coin."

The corners of Desta's mouth twitched. A cold sensation ran down his spine from the base of his head to his tailbone. He looked away for a few seconds, trying to determine the appropriate response to this unexpected and unwanted request from these Ferenge people. He needed a safe way out without having to lie.

"Do you know who I am?" Desta asked, trying to buy time for
the proper answer but trying as much to deflect the question.

"Not a lot, why?"

"Well, I'm a former shepherd who was born and raised in a hole.
I don't even have a change of clothes, let alone a precious coin, as
you have indicated. . . . Who is the source of your information?"

"Someone who knows you very well wrote Dawit a letter," Petros said.

Desta winced. "Someone wrote him a letter? . . . Who?"

Dawit took a folded letter out of his breast pocket and opened it. "Here is the
letter." Desta took it and studied both the handwriting and the signature at the
bottom. Neither the hand nor the initials, HMS, at the bottom were familiar to
him. From the firmness and the right tilt of the letters, Desta thought it was probably a man's handwriting. He shook his head and gave the letter back to Dawit.

Dawit glanced at Petros and said something.

"The person who wrote Dawit the letter said he was certain about
the authenticity of the coin. All Dawit wants is to see it for himself. He is willing to pay for your meals and perhaps also for your living arrangements for the remainder of the school year," Petros said.

"Has he ever met this person who has told him all these things?"

Dawit said some things to Petros.

"If you allow him to bring the coin to America with him so that
his university could do further investigation, he will arrange with his
department to pay for your education through high school and possibly arrange to bring you to America so you can go to college."

"I appreciate Mr. Dawit's grand plans, but I
have no coin for him to show or lend."

Petros ostensibly relented. "Okay, let's not even talk about the coin for
now. Dawit is still willing to help you. He has heard good things about
you, and he thinks you'd be worth any money he spends on your behalf."

Dawit tilted to his left and reached for his back pocket. He brought forth a fat
brown wallet and cradled it in the palm of his right hand. He opened it and leafed
through the stack of bills, counting. He pulled out a bunch and handed them to
his mate. Petros held them flat in one hand and tapped their edges thoughtfully
with the other. He said, "Here! These 100 birrs should last you two months."

Desta hesitated, took the money, and set it on the table. He pursed his lips and looked away, thinking how he would decline the offer without offending the man.

"You don't need money?" Petros asked, motioning for Desta to pick it up. The air around them seemed to have sagged.

"I cannot accept money whose purpose or meaning is not clear to me. If Mr. Dawit was hoping, with his support, to 'purchase' the viewing of a coin he presumes I have, I am afraid he is going to be disappointed."

Petros and Dawit looked at each other.

"By the way," Desta added, as if an afterthought, "I've brought the initial fifty birrs Mr. Dawit sent me." He opened his pouch and took out the money. He then put it together with the wad of bills on the table and held them in his hand. "That you sent Mehiret to accompany me to this town so I could continue with my education is more than anyone has done for me. For this I'm grateful. I hope to return the favor in some way. But I cannot take this money because it won't accomplish the purpose you have intended it to." Desta passed the money to Dawit.

When Dawit hesitated, Petros said, "Respect his wishes."

With that, Dawit took the money. Desta sighed silently, feeling relieved. The last thing he wanted was to lead someone into something he couldn't meet or fulfill.

"These are proud people," murmured Petros.

"This is why it is the only country on the continent that has kept its independence," Dawit said.

"In most of the world, for that matter," Petros added.

Desta felt the eyes of both men on him as he closed and tied his pouch.

"I hope this will not be the end of our acquaintance," he said with a half smile. "I would like to stay in touch with you."

"There is your chance," Petros said to Dawit. "This boy is worth getting to know."

Dawit smiled. The dark cloud that seemed to have enveloped him lifted.

"I need to go," Desta said, rising.

"Do you mind if I escort you out?" Dawit asked.

"Not at all," Desta said.

"Be right back," Dawit said to his companion.

Outside, Dawit, with the few Amharic words he knew, and Desta, with his mangled English pronunciations and truncated sentences, communicated enough that they arranged to meet again in a month. Dawit would come on a Friday afternoon and stay at the hotel; Desta would come in the morning and have breakfast with him. They shook hands and parted.

As he walked home, Desta didn't know how to make sense of his encounter with the two Ferenges and their request. No matter, he was glad he returned the money. Just as important, he was happy he didn't accept the additional amount offered. He could now live with a clear conscience. But gnawing at his mind were the other possibilities Dawit offered—supporting Desta through his final four years of elementary school and then through high school, with the possibility of going to the United States for college.

These promises assumed Desta would show Dawit the coin and allow him to bring it to his country to investigate its authenticity. "That would be out of the question!" Desta said aloud.

FOR THE REMAINING FOURTEEN days of his Christmas break, Desta decided to study English and history. He needed to know more English so he could converse with David (Dawit) Hartman when he saw him in a month. He didn't want to rely on an interpreter again. He was frustrated and disappointed with himself that he didn't carry on the conversation in English with the two men. He wouldn't allow that to happen again. So every morning he read his green primer book, the stories of *Ali Baba and the Forty Thieves*, and *Aladdin*, as well as a number of other stories he found in his fourth-grade English book and in Fenta's fifth-grade one. Any new words he didn't know, he wrote down in his notebook and asked his teacher for their translation, writing them down, too. He memorized the words and tried to make sentences with them.

In the afternoons he read the history book, again writing down in his notebook any new words he came across.

It was during one of these afternoons, when the shadows from the eucalyptus trees had become long and spear-like, reaching Desta's bench under the eaves, that the image of Emnet, the little girl, appeared on the side of the chicken coop. He could see only the outline of her human form, like a silhouette or a shadow on a wall.

This time, more than before, he was convinced she was a ghost. The usually warm afternoon air turned suddenly chilly. He scanned the grounds, searching for even a glimpse of the phantom. When he surveyed the area near the chicken coop, the vision was gone, blotted out of existence. Now he didn't know what to think. Did he actually see something or were his eyes playing tricks on him? He shook his head and bent down over his notebooks. He tried hard to return to studying, but he couldn't. He kept raising his head and looking toward the chicken coop and around, wondering whether perhaps the image had relocated itself.

Giving up, he folded his notebooks and went inside, where he would be safe, or so he thought. He lay on his bed thinking about the image. It was then someone knocked on the window. He jumped up and went to look. There was no one. Now he was really scared. He lay back again, his eyes wide open, every fiber of his being cued to the slightest sound outside. Everything was quiet once more. He fell asleep. He was awakened only moments later by the piercing cry of a girl. She seemed to be saying that she needed help to get to her father. The screaming voice, which came from the back of the house, repeated this message again and again.

This time Desta got up and went outside. He had to find out for himself who this little girl was. He moved slowly to the back of the house.

There she was, standing near the fence under the shade of the eucalyptus trees. She looked like a normal child but frail and thin. She was the same girl he had met briefly a week earlier, just as Dagim had arrived with their dinner.

"How can I help you?" Desta asked, when he got close enough to her.

"I need my bones removed and buried," she said. "They are down here in the trees. Come. Let me show you." She took steps toward the fence.

"Who are you?" Desta asked, causing the girl to stop and turn around.

"I'm Alem's half-sister. I was killed by an agent of her mother when I was five. The man left my remains in the shallow grave. The soil cover had been washed away by flood, exposing my bones. They must be buried in a cemetery. Then I can go to my creator. . . . Let me show you. . . ."

Stunned but focused, Desta followed her through the gap where a few fence planks had fallen. They made their way down the leaf-covered ground. "Here they are," Emnet said, pointing with her little hand to the strewn bone fragments. "These remains are the cause of Alem's childlessness, her mother's health problems, and our father's—Mersha's—sickness and death. Once these bones are removed from here and buried, we all will be free—my sister and I, anyway."

"Who did this to you?" Desta asked, shaking his head. His grandfather's remains loomed before his eyes. And he was thinking of the men who murdered him because they wanted back the family's magical coin that one of them had stolen.

"Let's return to the compound and I'll tell you."

Once they had returned and were standing by the chicken coop, Emnet resumed her story. "Alem's mother, Melke, hired a man to murder me. I was the bastard child of her husband, Mersha." Beginning to lose control, Emnet stopped for a moment. She quickly regained her composure and continued on.

"At the time, my mother was married and working part time as a servant for the family when she conceived me from an affair she had with Mersha, just about the same time Melke conceived Alem. We were born just a few days apart."

Noticing Emnet was getting overwrought, Desta suggested she might sit down, but she refused. "Anyway," she said, continuing with her story, "when my mother's husband found out I was not his daughter, he became furious. He divorced my mother shortly after I was born. He didn't want a child he had not fathered." Emnet stopped and looked down for a long time.

Then she lifted her face and resumed her story. "When Mersha, my father, heard about my mother's divorce, he began reaching out to us; he was very concerned for our well-being. This made Alem's mother, Melke, furious. She soon divorced him. My father continued to support my mother and me and came to visit us more often, but he was not spending much time with Alem, partly because he didn't want to deal with Melke.

"Then Melke had a clever idea. To simplify things, she hired a man to kidnap and kill me. Afterward, this man brought my remains and threw them into the shallow grave I showed you. The result of this deed is that I became a curse—to the property, to my father, to Melke, and to my sister. My father died of cancer, Melke is chronically ill, and Alem is childless . . . ." Emnet paused and looked away. She turned her face and glanced at Desta. "The conclusion to this sad story is a request. I want you to tell Alem what I told you. Have her remove my remains and bury them at the church cemetery so we can have closure to this woeful affair that's ruined our lives." Her voice dropped almost to a whisper.

Desta released a great breath, letting out the air he had forgotten filled his chest, mesmerized as he was by Emnet's account. "I'm very saddened to hear this. I thank you for sharing it with me and will do the best I can to bring some sort of healing to you all."

"Thank you, but I need to go now," The ghost said, and she instantly vanished. Desta remained standing, for a moment feeling spooked by the girl's sudden disappearance, and then thinking about what she had shared.

When he finally came to his senses, he went back inside the house.

Chapter 7

By the time the vacation was over, Desta felt far advanced both in his knowledge of English and history. He couldn't wait to see David Hartman so he could test his proficiency in the language.

Alem finally returned from the month-long trip with the same man. She looked pale, tired, and sad.

"I don't want anybody to know I'm back," she said to Desta. "I need to rest for a few days. . . . Keep the gate locked."

"Ishee," Desta said.

"You will be my hands and feet—going to the store and market for some of the things we need for the next three days. Hopefully, my *injera*—soft spongy bread—baker is back from her trip, too. That way we won't have to buy it, and I won't have to make it."

When Desta told Fenta about Alem's request, his friend said, "So long as you return by the third day of the start of school, you will be fine. No guard or teacher would punish you."

Desta was relieved with this news. He would be of help to his host and, just as important, would get to know her during her time of critical need. He had hoped this opportunity would allow them to bond.

WHEN THE SECOND semester began, Desta was still a fourth-grader—but a fourth-grader with a future. Assuming he did well, and he would make sure this was the case, in six months he would be promoted to the fifth grade; in one year to the sixth; and in one more year to the seventh. By the time he finished his fourth year in Finote Selam, he would be ready to go to high school, to Bahir Dar, the place of his dreams, where he believed he might find the lady who held the second Coin of Magic and Fortune.

These thoughts buoyed Desta as he walked to school that morning. A few times he even skipped and hopped when he realized what his new-found freedom meant to him. He no longer had to count on family or relatives for support. Humanity was his family. Human beings were his relatives.

When he arrived at school, the flag ceremony was done and all the students were already in their classrooms.

Sitotaw waved his whip at Desta. "This is the last day you're allowed to come in late and not receive punishment."

"I know," Desta said loping toward his classroom.

The homeroom teacher had just put out his things in preparation for the lesson when Desta entered. "Good morning, Desta," he said cheerfully.

This salutation made Desta feel good. Since he had come to the school, no one called him by name, not even his classmates. At break they hung out with their own friends. Desta simply stood leaning against the wall or the balustrade and watched the boys playing ball and the girls standing in clusters and chatting. These things never bothered him. He was just as happy to be left alone so he could be with his own thoughts. There was an advantage to observing things from a distance, the way he used to when he lived in the country. When he stared at the distant mountains and looked up at the sky, he always felt more in touch with himself and his thoughts. His eyes certainly looked out, but they were looking inward, too.

That morning, there was the teacher's unexpected greeting, but the class greeted him too—not with words but with their eyes. Their eyes locked on him the moment he entered and followed him as he walked to his seat in the back. Nervous, wondering what was going on, he managed to drop his notebooks on the floor. The room was now eerily quiet, and Desta was on pins and needles.

The only other time he had an experience like this was in the Dangila school, when his seatmates had abandoned him, believing his malnutrition to be caused by some sort of disease. They had feared they would catch whatever he had contracted.

But the eyes in his fourth-grade classroom were not disdainful. They were curious, awed. No matter, Desta was still nervous. It would not be prudent to ask why they were looking at him.

He felt the cool morning air flow into his nose and fill his lungs. Then he let out a deep sigh.

The teacher began the roll call. When he finished, he had not called Desta's name. Another mystery. Desta raised his hand to say his name hadn't been called. It didn't seem to be on the list.

"Wait for a few minutes. Sitotaw will come for you," the teacher said.

"Sitotaw will come for me?" Desta hissed under his breath. Now he was breaking out into a sweat. This meant punishment. What had he done wrong? To make matters worse, some of the students were turning around and looking at him.

It was as if the teacher was not going to start the morning lesson until the guard arrived. The teacher was drumming his fingers on the desk, occasionally looking at the door.

Desta closed his eyes and again sighed deeply. "Take it easy. It's nothing bad," the boy next to him whispered. Desta wanted to ask him what the problem might be, but the monitor was sitting one row down. Being quiet during class was one of Dagne's cardinal rules. So he gulped down his question.

Sitotaw finally arrived. Desta immediately checked for a whip. Sitotaw didn't have one. Desta sighed yet again.

"Desta, gather up your notebooks and come out," the teacher said.

Shaking like a leaf, he stuffed his notebooks into his borsa and clambered out of his seat and onto the floor. He tentatively inched toward the door. The teacher got up and put his hand out. Still unsure of the unfolding drama, Desta extended his own to shake the teacher's. "Great job!" the teacher said. "Keep doing well," he added, patting Desta's shoulder.

"Why are you sweaty and nervous?" Sitotaw asked. "I have nothing but good news for you," he said, smiling. "For being first in your class, you have gotten a double promotion. I have come to take you to the sixth grade. It was all announced yesterday afternoon at the school-wide meeting in the auditorium. Your name was called, but you weren't there. All those who were first got promoted either one grade or two grades. All those who achieved your status were recognized by the director and received awards. Yours is a science book; your teacher recommended it. He said you were the best he's ever had."

"If by the end of the sixth grade you rank first again, you could end up in the eighth grade come September."

Desta was not thinking of what could happen at the end of the year. What happened for him in his short time at the new school had not fully sunk in yet. He said nothing.

All the anxiety and nervousness that was building in him up to this point needed an outlet. His throat prickled with emotion, he heaved as if he might vomit or cry. He needed to control what was surging through him. He reached under his jacket and pressed the area above his heart. He calmed down.

The sixth-grade classroom was open. Class had already started. Sitotaw knocked on the door with the knuckles of his left hand, his eyes on the back of the teacher.

The teacher placed the chalk on the blackboard ledge and walked to the door.

"This is Desta, the boy who earned a double promotion for being first in his fourth grade."

"Oh, yes," the teacher said, smiling. "C'mon in."

All the eyes of the class were on Desta, but he had no fear or concern now. He just needed to hold himself together until the morning break.

The teacher placed two fingers on his lips as his eyes scanned the room. "There, I will sit you with Girma and Yodit," he said, pointing to a desk occupied by two students.

The teacher turned to the guard and said, "Thank you." Sitotaw immediately left.

Sitting on the edge of his seat, Desta listened to the lecture. He was not mentally ready to take notes yet. He would rather be out running around like a maniac, expressing his joy, celebrating it with the world. The time till he would go to Bahir Dar was now shortened by a whole year. Instead of waiting four years, it would now be three. The prospect of shortening his schooling by another year, if he became first again in the sixth grade, was equally thrilling.

During the morning break, he walked to the farthest oak tree he could see on campus and sat under it. He had yet to deal with his bottled up emotions. He should either laugh like there was something wrong with him or cry. Desta decided to cry. He placed his head between his folded knees, and let his tears be his moment's companion of joy.

Once done, he felt calm, happy, and grateful. But to whom should he give thanks? David Hartman or the president of America? The president had been killed, and because of this, the Peace Corps teachers were given the day off. This permitted Mehiret, David Hartman's messenger, to come get Desta. Desta was grateful to everyone, for all of it.

Desta thought it was everything working together that had enabled him to be here the previous semester.

Chapter 8

Having recuperated enough, Alem was ready to receive visitors. She decided she would entertain guests from noon to dusk on the coming Saturday. She sent a message to one of her friends to inform their mutual friends of the event.

On the day of the occasion, both Alem and Desta rose early. First, the house needed to be immaculately cleaned. This was Desta's task. So he swept the living room and cleaned the tables, chairs, and bunk seats arranged them neatly. Afterward, following Alem's instructions, he put down plush skin mats and pieces of colorful handmade rugs on the floor and on the high earthen seats. Then he was to wash the columnar drinking glasses, array them on the long plastic serving tray, and place the tray on the dining table.

This done, Alem warmed bathwater in a large aluminum pot. When the water was heated to a comfortable temperature, Alem and Desta held the pot by the handle, took it to the shed, and set it on the floor near a wooden bench. She told Desta to step out for a while. She dowsed her body with ladles of the water and lathered her arms, shoulders, and hair with Lux brand soap, which filled the room with a floral fragrance.

Outside Desta could hear splashing water.

This activity was followed with Alem scooping and pouring several ladles of the warm water over her head while she worked her hair with the fingers of her free hand. After a few more ladles, she had rinsed the last traces of soap, leaving her hair and upper body squeaky clean.

Once done, Alem came out, her hair damp and limp, droplets of water clinging to her face. She scuttled to the house and disappeared through the open door.

From the time she finished bathing until half an hour before the guests arrived, she lined her big beautiful eyes with black antimony powder and her brows with fine soot dust. She chewed the end of an aromatic stick into fibrous bristles and brushed her teeth white with it. She clipped all her twenty nails and oiled and massaged her hands and feet. She applied pats of cream to her forehead, cheeks, and nose, rubbing them in until nothing remained on her fingers or skin. She combed her hair out into a black halo, but covered it with a red scarf, whose reflection made her fine skin glow with the crimson hue of the setting sun.

While Alem was doing all these things, Desta swept the front patio, leaving no trace of the twigs and leaves scattered there. Inside the house, he polished Alem's leather shoes and set them just inside the front door, near the threshold.

Just before noon, Alem put on her calf-length white silk dress and pinched her slender waist with a colorful fabric belt. For the finishing touch, she graced her shoulders with a white *netela*—single ply cotton shawl. Then Alem perched herself on the center bunk seat and waited. To Desta, Alem appeared more like a bride who was anticipating her groom than someone about to receive friends.

By all measures of expectation, Alem should have been married. She had a long, graceful neck and prominent cheekbones that tapered into a delicate square chin. Her big eyes flashed like beams of light and her smile like a ray of hope. Her svelte figure was made to fit the half-circle of an adoring man's arm. Although it was too early for Desta to tell, she also appeared an easygoing, kind person. Despite all these qualities Alem was single.

At noon, no groom came. Instead, women began to arrive, some carrying kettles of *tella*—home-made beer or bottles of *areqey*—home-made whiskey, others the round rye *dabo*—loaf. Staggered throughout the afternoon, single men and couples came. They all entered the house after a salutation and a bow to Alem and to the guests who were already there. They all kissed Alem.

Desta filled the glasses with tella and passed them out to the visitors. The women sliced their loaves into small wedges and piled them on a colorful platter. When he returned after passing out the drinks, Desta circulated the platter of dabo among the guests.

As Alem's friends ate and drank, they talked. At the forefront of everyone's mind since Alem left was the well-being of her mother. This steered the conversation for a time. They asked after the welfare of the rest of her family, their animals, and their harvest. Once these niceties were exchanged, the women talked about their own affairs and any juicy local gossip. Then each at different times rose, gathered their things, gave a bow of farewell to Alem and to everyone else, and left.

After all the visitors had departed, Desta suggested that he should close the gate, but Alem indicated she wanted it open for a while longer. The last traces of the sun's light had faded and darkness was offering its evening cloak. As if out of nowhere, a tall, well-dressed man arrived carrying a sealed bottle. He was neither followed by best men nor dressed like a groom. But from the scent he was leaving in his wake, Desta presumed this guest of the night must have taken a bath before setting out for Alem's.

"Alem home?" he asked. "My name is Aberra. You must be a relative of hers."

"Yes, she is," Desta replied. "No, I'm just her errand boy . . . living with her and going to school."

"Aha," the man said, walking past Desta. Desta followed Aberra, his head abuzz with questions. Why had this man arrived past dusk and after all the other visitors had left?

Aberra rapped his knuckles on the open door. When nobody answered, he knocked again and with greater force.

Desta was just about to go past him and see what was keeping Alem, when a muffled voice said, "C'mon in."

As Aberra stepped in the middle of the living room, Alem came out of her bedroom. "How have you been, stranger?" the visitor asked, smiling with his eyes as much as his teeth.

Alem grinned broadly. "I'm well, thank you. How have you been?" Her voice was happy and teasing.

"Can't complain," Aberra said. He turned and bent down, depositing the bottle on the dining table. When he stood straight up again, he found Alem standing before him. He embraced and kissed her—with a knowing and lingering intimacy—three times on alternating cheeks.

When he let her go, Alem fought to maintain her composure, but Desta could see in the glare of the kerosene light that her eyes were glittering with joy. She tugged on Aberra's hand. "Come, sit down," she said, pulling one of the chairs out from underneath the table. Then almost as an afterthought, she said, "Did you meet my young friend?" She cast a furtive glance toward her attendant. "His name is Desta."

Aberra told her he did. "How did you two meet?" he asked.

As if avoiding Aberra's question, Alem said to Desta, "Could you go and close the gate and latch it?" And then added, "Make sure the chicken coop is closed and locked and . . ." Alem's voice trailed off. Desta could see she might need a private moment with Aberra.

"Ishee," he said chirpily and headed for the door.

He went to the chicken coop merely to honor the request of his host.

He had closed the door and locked it earlier. He grabbed the padlock and jiggled it just the same, making sure the chickens were indeed safe and secure. He sat on the bench under the eaves and stared into the absolute void. He could hear the tall eucalyptus trees—their rustling leaves—at the south side of the compound and the cicadas singing their songs in the bushes behind the tall fence.

Alem called his name. Desta walked briskly. When he entered the house, he found his benefactor and Aberra sitting side by side, both looking quite content. The brown bottle was open, a portion of its contents filling two long-stemmed glasses to their brims. The smell of alcohol filled the air.

"Desta, could you bring water for Aberra's hands?"Alem asked, getting up to serve dinner.

"Ishee," Desta said and brought the hand water to the guest.

Alem placed the tray of food on the table and sat down next to Aberra. After they ate, Alem picked up the bottle and poured another half-glass for Aberra. Raising the bottle higher, she studied its remains, saying, "The rest is for next time." She smiled at her guest.

"Please take it away," he said, lowering his glass. "I've had more than I should. All because I'm happy to see you." He smiled back.

She stowed the bottle and set about preparing Desta's dinner. She placed a platter of food on the other side of the same table where she and Aberra had eaten. "Come, have your dinner," she said, waving a hand. She pulled one of the chairs out from under the table for him.

Shortly, Alem and Aberra went to the bedroom. "Take care of the platters, Desta," Alem said, looking over her shoulder.

He finished his meal, cleaned up the kitchen, and went to bed.

Chapter 9

The next morning, Desta was up just before dawn broke. He put on his clothes and went to the door, which, curiously, was unlocked. After meeting the demands of his body in the shed, he came indoors, gathered his parchment and notebooks, and went outside. He sat on one of the benches by the gate, opened his parchment, and began to recite the legends on the facing side of the coin image first, and then those found on the back.

By the time the sun's long rays had penetrated the tall eucalyptus trees, creating a dappled pattern of light on the ground, Alem had awakened. She was standing before Desta in deep thought, for what must've been a long time, her veiled head leaning lazily against the doorjamb. When Desta looked up, she said, "Why did you have to get up so early? It's Sunday!"

"I always get up early," Desta replied, his eyes still on her. "These are my best hours to study."

"Would you like to go to church with me, then?" she asked.

Desta shifted in his seat. His Sunday ordeals with Zewday's family in Dangila suddenly appeared before his eyes. The long journeys, his struggle with hunger during the lengthy services—these were etched deep within him. Then, back in the present, realizing he was well-nourished and could travel anywhere without feeling famished and tired, he said, "Sure."

"Good!" Alem said, and went to the back of the house.

In the intervening moments, Desta couldn't help but wonder what had happened with Aberra that Alem wanted Desta's company instead. From the unlocked door Desta found in the morning when he rose, it looked like the man had left under cover of darkness, much as he had come. Why the clandestine departure?

Desta didn't have the answers, but he gathered his things and went inside. He put them away in his bedroom, and then walked over and sat by the front door. The sun appeared the warmest at that spot.

"Ready to go?" Alem asked when she found Desta waiting.

"When you are," Desta replied.

Alem studied Desta's clothes. "We must at least change your shorts," she said. "You can't go to the house of God dressed in those."

Desta looked at Alem, puzzled. "These are all I have."

"I suspected that was the case," she said. She pursed her lips grimly. "Let me see what I have."

She dashed to her bedroom and returned with clothes draped over her left arm. "Try these," she said, lifting a pair of brown shorts. "I bought them for Dagim a year ago, but they were too small."

Desta took the shorts, stood up, and held them against him to assess the fit.

"Go try them on," Alem suggested.

When he returned in the shorts, Alem could immediately see they were long and wide in the waist. She dashed to the bedroom again and returned just as quickly. She had a safety pin and a belt in her hands.

To Desta it was as if his host kept a merchandise store in her bedroom. She said both items came from her father's old trousers.

"When father continued to lose weight from the cancer that finally killed him, we kept buying smaller clothes, as well as belts and safety pins. We didn't want him to look like he was wearing borrowed clothes."

With the safety pin, Alem tightened the waist of the shorts. The cinching of the belt served to adjust the length.

"Now drape yourself with this," she said, handing him a netela. "It'll hide all those holes in your jacket. Do you not have family that cared for you?"

"That is a long story," Desta said, as he draped the netela around his shoulders and very nearly his entire upper body. "If you really want to know, I'll tell you someday."

She went back to her bedroom for the third time. When she returned, she was putting on a long cotton dress and a netela with pink edging. She then exchanged her slippers for her polished leather shoes.

"Let's go," she said, heading for the door. She locked the house first and then secured the gate. Desta was not carrying a bible, or cane, or trotting to catch up with Alem, as he used to do with his host in Dangila. And he didn't always follow behind her, like an *ashker*—houseboy. When the streets were wide, they walked side by side, as equals.

After ambling through long paths, groves of eucalyptus trees, and seared thorn bushes, they finally reached the church. It was a circular structure capped with the familiar corrugated tin roof and somewhat obscured by a nearly seamless wooden fence.

"You go inside the compound and stand with the men, and I will go and stand under that tree by myself," Alem said, pointing to a lone tree far from the church grounds.

"Why?" Desta asked, turning and looking Alem straight in the eye.

"Because I don't deserve to be there with you."

Ordinarily, a reply like this would cause Desta to seek an explanation, but he understood. He first saw women standing at the outer limits of his parents' church when he went with his mother to receive communion for the dog disease the family thought he might have contracted. Then his mother had told him the situations in which women were relegated to the outskirts of the church—when they had just given birth, they were having their periods, or had engaged in sex with their husbands the night before.

Later he had heard adults say that it was sinful for women to even come to the church property if one of these situations was true for them. Although only she and God knew what sinful act Alem had committed, it was not hard for Desta to guess. He certainly wasn't going to ask her.

As Desta walked Alem over to her position outside the church, he simply said, "I think I'll be perfectly happy here. And God will hear our prayers as well as he would if we were inside."

"You're a wise young man. You're right," she said. "Let's just stay together and pray, then."

Alem crossed herself three times and dropped to the ground and kissed it. Desta did the same. Then they rose, and standing side by side, they faced the church. Mass had already begun by the time they arrived, but for the remainder of the service, they listened to chants and the singing of the priests inside the church, the words inaudible from where they stood.

They listened to the drums and the priests' hypnotic salutations to God. Their noses took in the sweet fragrance of incense carried to them by the languid morning breeze. Then they heard the tinkling of bells during the communion. Desta could imagine mothers with swaddled babies in their arms, older women with their heads covered—all lined up to take the blood and flesh of Christ. Finally, the benediction was delivered by a priest standing at the entrance to the church.

"Let's go home," Alem said right after the conclusion of the services.

They were not going to break their Sunday morning fast with the blessed *Makfalt*—bread—in the chapel, as was the custom. If Alem couldn't come near the fence, there was no way she could cross the gate's threshold and join the crowd in this ritual. Desta was glad that he was not famished as he certainly would've been at church in Dangila.

The two left. As they walked back, Desta screwed up his courage and decided to ask Alem about her having to stay outside the church today.

"Do you mind if I ask you a question, Alem?" he said haltingly.

Alem turned around and looked at him for a few seconds. "What is it?"

"Why weren't you permitted inside the church and why did you feel undeserving of my company today? You made it sound like it was some sort of punishment you were willing to take."

She stopped, turned around, and fixed her big eyes on Desta. "The answer to your question is kind of personal and complicated to explain, but since you're staying with me, I need to share with you the nature of my living arrangements. Let me think for a little bit, and I will tell you about it when we get home."

From that point till they got home, which was about twenty minutes, Desta and Alem didn't talk.

When they got home, Alem quickly made tea and sliced and warmed the dabo her friends had brought the day before. From her white tea set in the kitchen cabinet, she brought two cups, sugar in a bowl, two spoons, and a serving kettle, placing them on a colorful wide-rimmed tray. She poured the tea into the serving kettle and placed it on the tray as well. She asked Desta to bring everything to the picnic table outside. She put the sliced dabo into a basket, covered it with a cloth, and followed behind Desta with it.

When they were several minutes into their dabo and tea, and after swallowing a morsel, Alem said, "To answer your earlier question, the church prohibits us from entering the compound when we're having our periods, have had an affair with a man the night before, or have given birth recently. The church says it's unclean to come to the house of God while experiencing any one of these situations. So we keep away from the holy grounds but stand within viewing distance of the church. We still can pray and ask God for forgiveness wherever we are.

"Why aren't there men who are standing outside of the church grounds? Do you think they all are pure and free of sin?"

"Men make the laws. They can break them, too. They think themselves blameless. They try to make us pay for our ancestral mother's sin," she said bitterly.

When she noticed Desta seemed lost at the last suggestion, she added, "They say Eve, our mother, is the downfall of Adam. We, her progeny, have been doomed to pay for her transgressions."

Desta remembered about Adam and Eve from his Morals and Ethics classes. "It's very unfair. My brother lost his priesthood because he didn't want to obey the church's celibacy laws."

"Did he?—there you are," she said, pleased to find someone who shared her plight. "If they had their way, they would make us all celibate."

Desta followed Alem's eyes. They were now on the gate. She turned around and said, "While we're on the same subject . . . let me tell you about me and my situation. I don't want you to be confused or surprised later on." Alem looked at him and tried to gauge Desta's thoughts.

Then she hurried through her story. "I live a single life, but I have a few male friends who come to visit me. Some stay over, like Aberra did last night. Others may come for just an afternoon visit. They are all nice, respectful, well-to-do men. They will treat you kindly and I am sure you will do the same. When you come from school or from playing with your friends in the afternoon, you may find the door closed. Don't panic. More than likely, I am inside with one of my friends. Don't knock or try to come in. Attend to the chickens or study until the door is open." Alem sighed deeply. It seemed this had been heavy on her heart and she was pleased to let it out, finally.

Desta for his part didn't know what to make of this report. He wondered how much of this daily influx of men would affect his study time. He needed to be first in his class again by the end of the year so he could get another double promotion. That way he could shorten his stay with Alem by two years. He certainly didn't want to inconvenience her by being a mole in her private world. "How many are there?" he asked, for lack of a better question.

"There are five regulars and two who come to see me every other week. Some of them smoke and will probably ask you to go to the store for cigarettes—one of the reasons I needed an errand boy."

Desta shifted in his seat. While he was in Yeedib, smoking cigarettes was considered one of the dirtiest vices one could engage in. People who smoke were ostracized. As a result, no one smoked. Here not only would he be exposed to the dirty smell, but he'd be perpetuating bad behavior. Desta thought he should start looking for new living arrangements—and soon!

Alem appeared to read his mind. "Look," she said, pressing her hand on his. "Although I have this home and land and get food supplies from my father's leased properties, I have no source of cash to buy all the things we need in the house. You will see. They are very nice men. I know you will like them and vice versa."

"I'm sure I will," Desta said mechanically.

"Cheer up! Let's bring the things inside." She rose and put the dishes on the platter and handed them to Desta. She brought in the empty bread basket. Alem seemed to regret having said so much to Desta.

After putting the dirty dishes inside on the table, Desta gathered his notebooks and went to the back of the house to sit on the bench. Thinking about leaving Alem because of his repugnance of cigarettes and the people who smoke them had caused his mouth to go dry.

No matter, he had never had it this good, even when he lived at home. Here he was drinking milk every day and eating meat dishes three to four times a week. He wouldn't go hungry as before. What's more, after only a month at Alem's, he'd had the peace and quiet to study hard, become first in his class, and skip a grade. He shuddered. He needed to think about the source of this sudden turbulence in his head.

The men Alem said were smokers were not standing in front of him and blowing smoke in his face. He had not even met these people. He had never actually known a cigarette smoker. He had seen some Muslim merchants smoke those hook-shaped things but not cigarettes.

What he was doing was judging them based on what other people had said about cigarette smoking and those who smoke, and not based on his own observations. This is exactly how his mother reacted toward Muslims when she suspected he had become a Muslim. He was ashamed of himself and was doubly sorry for his mother. He told himself never to do this again.

No, he would stay put. He wouldn't judge Alem or what she did with her men. As far as he was concerned, he would embrace any and all friends who came to visit her, including the smokers. With this affirmation, he felt good . . . and free.

IT HAD BEEN several weeks since Desta and Alem had shared their deeply personal conversation. Since then, Desta had met a few of her friends, including the ghost of her half-sister, who had been the cause of Alem's worst troubles, which included, in part, to her clandestinely receiving men in here private residence.

There was the patient, resourceful, and kind Aberra, who always came a little past seven o'clock on Saturday and left a little before dawn on Sunday. Like his temperament, the night was quiet when he was around, and Alem seemed at peace, too. What Aberra did for work Desta didn't know, but he always came well dressed, in a suit or khaki pants, with a light blue jacket and polished shoes.

Then there was Tessema, the tense smoker. He always came on a weekday in the early evening, with a wad of money in his pocket and a request for cigarettes. Invariably, he reached into his pocket, brought out the folded stack, opened it, and peeled off a bill, handing it to Desta to go buy him a packet of cigarettes. It was as if he didn't want Desta around the house.

And often, by the time Desta returned, he found Tessema sitting on the bench by the front of the house blissfully smoking a cigarette. The tension around his eyes would be gone as he smiled beneficently, appearing content with himself and the world.

After collecting his cigarettes, if he had extra change, Tessema would give Desta a twenty-cent tip or more, and then he would leave. If Alem was outside, Tessema would say, "See you next week." If she was not within earshot, Desta received the salutation. As it happened, Alem chose never to be outside when Tessema was smoking. She said the smoke caused her to sneeze and gag. Yet she always seemed ecstatic whenever he came. "He is always generous with me," she told Desta.

Girum was Alem's third male friend. He came only once every two weeks, and the intervals between his visits could not go fast enough for her. A day or two before he came to see her, Alem's nerves seem to smolder with excitement, and she took extra time adorning herself. When Girum was visiting, she always found an excuse to send Desta to the store or to return something she had borrowed from a friend. Then one day she forgot to send Desta away, and so he gathered his notebooks and went to the back of the house, perching on the bench to study.

Not long after he sat down, a sharp, pained cry breached the walls of the house and filled the air. Desta rose with a start and listened. This unfamiliar noise devolved into a grunt, then into a steady squeal. The sound of gibberish soon followed. The cacophony seemed to go on forever and Desta was not sure whether Alem was in heaven or hell. There was one more sharp cry, followed by a groan and then her nervous, self-deprecating laughter.

It was then that he knew all was well with Alem.

Desta never met the remaining four friends of Alem's. He only knew their names and wasn't sure whether they came to visit her when he was in school or out playing with his friends.

Chapter 10

With Desta's double school promotion, he would no longer have to share text-books with up to three students, as the others did. He could borrow texts that he alone used. Early in the second week of the start of school, the guard came and took him to the storeroom. There, on top of a long table, thick hardcover text-books were piled two to three feet high. "Choose one book from each of those two stacks," Sitotaw said, pointing to the piles on the left. "And one of each from those, on the right."

"Thank you. . . . Do you know which book is which subject?"

"I don't know what they are, but I'm sure you do," Sitotaw said. "I don't know English."

Desta reached up and pulled a volume from one of the stacks. He looked at one side and then the other, studying the condition of the book. Threads from the corners grew out like moss. The spine was well worn.

His eyes rested on the face of the book. *The March of Time*, it read, in bold letters. These words didn't give him any clue what subject the book covered. He knew the meaning of the individual words, but they didn't connect in his mind to anything he would be studying.

Sitotaw read Desta's face. "Hurry up. You'll have all day to find out what these books are about. When in doubt, ask your teacher."

He set aside the first volume and pulled down another hefty book from the second pile. *Thorndike Dictionary*, it announced. These words meant nothing to him, either. He placed it on top of *The March of Time*.

He would need the thin "Green Primer" Fenta had, except unlike his friend's book, this primer was red. The fourth book was as thin as the primer and said, *Sewasew*—Grammar—in Amharic.

Desta cradled the four books in his arms like puppies and lumbered under the load to his classroom.

"You got your books, Desta?" his homeroom teacher

Girma asked when they ran into each other at the door.

Desta said he did but didn't know what each book was for.

"Follow me. Let's see which ones you got."

Desta trotted behind Girma to his desk in front of the class.

After he sat down at his desk, Girma picked up the first book and said, "This book is for your world history class." The teacher put it down to his left and picked up the second cumbersome volume. "We'll come to this book later," he said, and put it down to his right.

He grabbed the third volume. He leafed through it, and said, "This one is for your English lessons." He set it on top of the first book. "You can read the *Sewasew* text and find out for yourself," he added. "It's all in Amharic."

"This," Desta's teacher continued, picking up the tome he had placed on the right, "is the mother of all books. You look up any word you find in any of your other textbooks in this one. It's called a dictionary. Do you know how to use one?"

Desta shook his head, indicating no.

"Let me show you," Girma said. He split it open and laid it on his desk.

"Let's, for example, look up the meaning of the word . . . ummm . . . " Girma trailed off. "*Shepherd!*"

Desta looked up at the teacher, startled.

Girma turned over several pages and stopped once he got to the word he was looking for. "Here," he said, planting his index finger on the page. He read out the definition. Then he came back and read slowly the hyphenated letters in parentheses. "*She-pərd* is how you pronounce it. Is that clear?" Girma asked, an air of finality infusing his voice.

Desta said it was, and he began gathering his books. He looked up at Girma.

"Why did you choose that word—do you know I used to be a shepherd?"

Girma smiled. "Yes." That's one of the few things I know about you. . . . I was once a shepherd, too."

This declaration by the teacher made Desta feel good. There were important people like teachers who were once like he used to be.

"You heard what the director said at the school assembly last Tuesday about students who rank first at the end of the year, right?"

Desta said he was not there.

"Well, if you are at the top of the class again, you have a chance to be in the eighth grade in September."

Desta's heart leaped at the possibility. "I'll work as hard as I can to become first again."

"Bravo! Now go to your seat." Girma turned to the class. "Of course, you all have an equal chance. This boy used to be a shepherd. He had been in this school just for one month, yet he became first in the fourth grade and was awarded the double promotion. We like to encourage students who have these kinds of backgrounds. We want them to do well. They can be a good example to others. We want them to continue to do well. . . . They had to overcome so much to be here."

Desta studied the faces of his new classmates. They appeared to be equally awed by the fact that Desta became first after just one month of study in the new school and by his background as a shepherd. He wished Girma had said nothing about him or what he did at home. He had hoped to keep his promotion a secret. When he sat down, Yodit, his seatmate, asked, "These books are just for you?" her voice hardening.

"Yes, why? Is there a problem?"

"Because we share the same books with two or three of our classmates. Considering the kind of favors the school is showering you with, you should be ashamed of yourself if you didn't meet their expectations."

Desta didn't answer her. He placed his books under the desk and kept one hand on top of them.

The other seatmate chimed in: "You were just a farm boy until you came to this school only a month ago?!"

A third from across the aisle leaned over and whispered, "How did you do it?"

Desta didn't answer any of these questions.

"You over there—mind your own business," the teacher said.

The class went hushed for a while.

During the break, Desta stayed behind. He was afraid of losing his books.

More students, only a few with friendly intentions, came over, wanting to talk to him. He maintained his silence under the cross-examination.

When he went home for lunch, his books under his arm, Alem capped her brow with her hand and asked, "What kinds of boxes are those you're carrying?"

Desta smiled. "I didn't tell you, I'm in the sixth grade now. I was double-promoted early this month for being first in my fourth-grade class. These are the kinds of books we study in my new grade."

Alem dropped her hand, a look of confusion spreading across her face. "Didn't you say you started in our school early last month?"

"Yes. Thanks to you, I took advantage of the quiet home you left me. I studied hard and did well enough in my exams to skip a grade."

"You're an amazing young man."

"No, I just worked harder and Providence played his part."

"Do you want to take a look?" Desta put all the books down on the table.

He opened the history book and began leafing through it. He stopped at the pictures. "Did you ever study books like these when you were in school?"

"I never went past the fourth grade. And I've forgotten most of what I learned up to that point," she said wistfully. "But I am just thrilled you have advanced so much in a breath of time."

"Thank you," Desta said. "You know what else? The director said those who are at the top again this coming June will have a chance to skip grades. This means if I'm first again, I could get promoted to the eighth grade." Just thinking about it made Desta want to jump again.

Alem shook her head as if she had a bug in her ear. "This is almost like a joke. How can you possibly learn all there is in these books between now and June to become first again?"

Desta had to contain himself. What Alem said was true.

She thought for a second and said, "If you think you can, all the power to you. I'll get you a separate kerosene lamp so that you can study at night, and I'll tell my friends not to bother you with their errands," she said, holding Desta's eyes. "What you do for me will be enough."

"That's very thoughtful. Thank you so much."

"*Minim aydel*—don't mention it," she said, tapping Desta's shoulder. "Come inside. I have your lunch for you."

Desta had eaten a skimpy breakfast four long hours earlier. Still, he was not hungry. What he was craving was the knowledge stored in the books he brought home. He knew that to properly get into the books, he needed to be alone and undistracted. That usually meant at night, early in the morning, or during the day, when no one was around. In the next four days he would be in school and the daytime hours would be dedicated to his classwork. The weekend was far away.

He brought the books to his bedroom and placed them on the little table next to his headboard. Then he went to see Alem in the kitchen. She was squatting on the floor mincing onions, her face mirroring the excited feelings that seemed to have pervaded her whole being.

"I'm going to follow-up with your offer," Desta said, smiling.

When Alem seemed at a loss, Desta blurted, "The kerosene lamp. I was hoping to get one today. I'll be happy to return the money when I get some for pulling donkeys on Saturday."

"Pulling donkeys?" Alem asked, arching her brow.

"Yes, so that I can buy things like a kerosene lamp."

"Don't do it. It's not worth it. Just ask me. I'll give you money for the small things. In fact, I'd love to buy you a new set of clothes. I just have enough cash at the moment. . . . Be right back." She went to her bedroom.

She returned with a birr note. "Buy your kerosene lamp with this and bring me the change."

He said thank you and was about to run out when Alem continued.

"I've a new friend coming to see us this evening," Alem said, grinning." His name is Yimer."

Desta lingered a bit, thinking. That was the second new man he would be meeting in two days.

That afternoon while he was at school, he thought about the kerosene lamp he was going to buy and the book—specifically, *The March of Time*—it would illuminate. He couldn't wait to learn about all those animals and things he saw on the ancient coin box at home; a lot of them were in the book.

Finding the right kerosene lamp was harder than he might've thought. He wanted one that had a handle on the side. This way, his fingers were less likely to get wet with kerosene and stain the pages of his books. The small, cylindrical tin lamp had a flute for the wick in the center of its circular top, which could carry kerosene residue from accidental spills. The guard at school had told him that he must keep the books clean and return them in the same condition as they were given to him.

He went to several stores but most were out of them. The last shopkeeper sent him to an old man who sold kerosene and the lamps out of his home and at the outdoor market. Desta found the lamp he was looking for there.

By the time he got home with the lamp, the sun had already set and Alem's new friend was about to leave. "You must be Desta," Yimer said, looking down from his six-foot height.

Desta acknowledged that he was.

Yimer shook hands with Desta and left after saying, "See you next time."

Desta felt as though a complete stranger—as Yimer basically

was—had just shown him the kind of familiarity that comes with the
regularity of a sunrise or the cycle of the seasons. He wondered who he
was going to meet next. Alem had said she had five to seven friends.

Before dinner he brought out the kerosene bottle and filled the new lamp
with the flammable liquid. Then he went inside and placed the bottle to one side
of the catchall table by the entrance. He lit the regular lamp and placed it on its
pedestal at one corner of the dining table. Later, before Alem went to her room
with the regular house lamp, Desta lit his from hers and took it to his bedroom.

The little kerosene lamp was a welcome change from the dingy
beeswax candle he had been using since his host returned from the
country. It puffed out the darkness in the room, revealing all the
imperfections of the whitewashed walls and bringing out the more
sharply defined shadows the objects cast around the room. Desta knew
that this lamp was also going to illuminate the world within him.

The knowledge contained in the books piled on the little table next to
his bed was as alien to Desta as the moon or the distant stars in the sky.

He put the lamp down next to the books on the table. He picked out
the history book and placed it adjacent to his pillow. Anxious to get to his
reading, he quickly undressed and got under the covers. He lay on his belly,
opened the book, propped his chin on one hand, and began reading.

His main objective that night was to read about the people, animals,
and objects he had seen early in the section of the book that described
ancient Egypt. These seemed very similar to the images on the coin box
at home. Desta didn't make it that far. He got lost in the early part of
the book, which covered Mesopotamia, Hammurabi, and Babylonia. He
didn't so much read the text as study the images, the captions that went
with them, and the places that dotted a map along with the squiggly rivers,
whose names he couldn't quite pronounce. The carved faces and strange
characters on walls and smoothed stones, a particular stock of block
building called Ziggurat and structures covered in leafy vines that cascaded
from balconies and window ledges were intriguing and absorbing.

By the time he got to the Egyptian history section, Desta was overwhelmed.
While he scanned the early part of the book, he saw many words and names that
were hard to pronounce and even more challenging to remember. Some of them
he tried to look up in the Mother of All Books. The import of Alem's comment
came crashing down on him.

How could he possibly study all there was in these books
in the little time he had and pass the exams, let alone rank
first in his class and get another double promotion?

While contemplating these thoughts, he fell asleep. Several hours
later he awoke to find the lamp still on and burning through the precious
kerosene. He quickly blew out the light and went back to sleep.

Shortly after the first cock's crow, Desta stirred again. He was
sorry to have fallen asleep without getting to the Egyptian section of
the book. Before the day broke and he got ready for school, he wanted
to read up on the animals and people that reminded him of the coin
box. Otherwise, he was going to be wondering about them all day.

So he lit the lamp once again and dragged the book toward
him from the bedside table where he'd left it. He opened and
leafed through it until he got to the Egyptian section.

To his amazement the images of the animals and people were depicted
on walls. Many of the people wore loin cloths that hugged their waists and
thighs. Stiff yet somehow animated, they appeared to communicate something
to one another and to anyone looking at them. To Desta, who grew up looking
at distant mountains and clouds in the sky in which he saw animals, people,
and strange creatures that morphed into one shape or another, seeing these odd
beings on these pages brought him happily back to his childhood. In some ways
these images reminded him of the murals on the walls of his parents' church.

For the time being he was not interested in reading the text. From
observing the posture and attitudes of these people, the angle of their faces
and eyes, and the way they held their hands, he wanted to know what they
were saying and doing. Strangely, some of these figures were half human, half
animal. Who exactly they were he would have to read the book to find out.

The most important things to Desta, however, were the animals and
people that appeared on the ancient coin box he had at home. He couldn't
remember if the animals he was seeing in the book were the same ones on the
coin box. Unlike his father, Desta had spent little time studying the creatures
on the chest. No matter, he needed to learn about the animals. Why? Because
they were on the box that contained the ancient treasure. Desta very much
wanted to know the connection between the animal symbols and the coin.

To increase his understanding and retention of the information about
these animals, Desta decided he needed to be a little more organized. First,

he went back to the pertinent captions for each of the images in order
to make his list. Then using the Mother of All Books, which Desta now
called MOAB, he looked up the meaning and attributes of the creatures.
Then he studied them, memorizing as many of them as he could. This
was followed by reading the chapters that talked about the animals.

To his surprise many of the creatures in ancient Egypt were not
ordinary earthly ones, like trees and humans, but many had perceived
power over the lives of deities, people, and things. Yes, the people had
animals such as cattle, horses, goats, donkeys, dogs, and cats, like his
family in the country had, but these same animals and many others
represented the gods and goddesses and pharaohs who ruled Egypt.

Desta remembered his grandfather's spirit had told him that many of the
animals on the box were valued for their protective power as well as for their
ability to make people fertile so that they could reproduce and populate the land.

Desta learned that while the cat, cobra, falcon, lion, scorpion,
and vulture were protectors, the bull, cow, frog, and ram represented
the gods and enabled people and other creatures to reproduce and
multiply. Other animals, such as the heron, monkey, and scarab beetle
symbolized the rebirth of people, animals, plants, and the sun.

From these readings Desta concluded that all the creatures that
appeared on the coin box were meant not only to protect the coin
itself but also enable Solomon's descendants to reproduce and grow.
Interestingly, some of these animals also represented royalty, justice,
respect, responsibility, and strength, to mention but a few attributes.

These characteristics, in one form or another, were also found in the coins'
legends. Desta shook his head, fascinated by this continuity of themes.

He closed the book and put it away. His head was heavy with information
and fuzzy with sleep. He blew out the lamp and pulled the blanket over his
face. He hoped slumber would come soon and relieve him of his burden.

Chapter 11

When Kidane, the English teacher, saw Desta outside during the morning break, he told him that David Hartman was expected to come the following Saturday. "Put on your best clothes and go meet him at Emma Tiwab's hotel. He wants to see you for breakfast at nine o'clock," said Kidane.

Desta thought about his "best clothes." He had none. And he was not going to borrow Dagim's shorts, which was what Alem had him wear when he accompanied her that one Sunday. This swirling around in his mind, Desta simply said, "Thank you. I look forward to seeing him again." He tried to sound upbeat.

But before the appointed day, Desta would wash his only jacket, shorts, and shirt. In Alem's large aluminum pot, he heated slices of the orange Martello soap in water, until the mixture boiled in wild protestation. Then he gathered his clothes and dropped them into a large wash basin.

With two folded rags, he held the ears of the pot and poured the now-milky water-soap solution into the basin, feeling triumphant over the lice that always embedded themselves in the seams of his clothing. Doing this every so often rid him of the parasites, at least for a time.

He bunched his clothes in his hands and beat them against the bottom of the basin. To the more soiled areas, like the front of his jacket and shorts, he applied a liberal amount of soap, clasping the fabric between his fingers and rubbing it vigorously. He rinsed them several times, both to reduce the strong waxy smell of the soap and loosen any remaining dirt. Then he squeezed out much of the water by twisting the fabric between his hands. This done, he shook and hung them on the benches to dry in the sun.

The next project in preparation for his breakfast with David Hartman was to have the holes in the elbows and shoulders of his jacket patched and his shorts hemmed.

Aklilu got this done for him through a tailor he knew.

Desta was ambivalent at the time about the patches but grew to see them as respectable looking. Taking a bath was the next order of business. His newly washed clothes demanded a clean body. Friday afternoon he warmed water and scrubbed and washed himself thoroughly in Alem's bathing chamber.

On Saturday morning he got up early and cleaned his face and wet down and brushed his hair. After putting on his newly washed and mended jacket and shorts, he draped his gabi around his shoulders. He figured his gabi would shield his patched-up clothes from the amused eyes of pedestrians.

As he walked down the roadway, Desta ran into Fenta. "You look so dressed up—where are you going?" his friend asked.

Desta told him.

"Era! Wrapped in your gabi, like a shepherd?!"

Desta fixed his eyes on Fenta, surprised. "What's wrong with that? After all, I used to be a shepherd. You think I should shed the cloak of my past, like a snake, just because I now live in town? See you later." Desta trundled down the dusty footpath along the roadway. Although Fenta never talked about it, he used to be a shepherd, too, which made Desta especially bothered by his remark. Desta was proud of his beginnings. They made him what he was today. He couldn't be more grateful!

As Desta got nearer to the hotel, butterflies invaded his stomach. His mouth twitched as if succumbing to a palsy attack. He was not afraid of seeing the guy. Desta had anticipated their meeting by reading and studying his English. Still he worried that words might fail him, that all of a sudden he might have nothing to say or he might misunderstand the Ferenge man. And David Hartman didn't say whether his translator was going to be there. He let out a big sigh, trying to calm himself, when he reached the hotel gate.

While Desta was crossing the courtyard, he saw the white man through the window. His arms were crossed over his chest. His eyes were tense and his mouth clamped. He seemed to be grinning at his own thoughts.

Is he nervous too? Desta wondered. This possibility made him feel more at ease.

Then a surprise of a completely different sort presented itself. A man came out and asked, "What brought you here?" in a voice that went beyond what the simple question conveyed.

"I'm meeting a Ferenge. His name is David Hartman. He's the one standing in the lobby." Desta explained himself quickly to prevent the man from kicking him out of the compound, like a dog.

The man peered into the window. "That one there?"

"Yes."

"How do you know him—who are you?"

These questions annoyed Desta. "I don't think my answers would give you any reason to bar me from entering your hotel. I ask that you let me pass." By this time David Hartman had his face on the window. Realizing what was going on, he came to the door and began to step out, saying, "Can you let him go? He is a friend of mine."

The man turned around. "He is?!" he exclaimed. To Desta, this sounded more like an expression of surprise than a question. "Go," the man said. He followed them inside the lobby and trotted past Desta to the white man, who was now walking toward the entrance of the restaurant. "My apologies," he said to Desta's host. "There are street boys who come here and bother the guests. I thought he was one of them."

"I understand," the Ferenge said, without breaking stride or turning back.

Inside the restaurant he went to a table where two walls met, adjacent to a large window. There were no people here, and it seemed the quietest and most private spot.

"Good morning!" he said in English, extending his open hand across the table for a shake.

"Good morning," Desta said, putting out his own and clasping the white man's hand.

"It's not easy being a kid around here, is it?" he asked with a smile.

Desta considered the question. If he disagreed, it would be untrue. If he said yes, it would sound cynical. He chose the middle of the road and said, "It can be." But he didn't smile.

The waitress came. David Hartman ordered tea with dabo and scrambled eggs. Desta ordered tea, dabo, and firfir.

"How do you like this town?"

"I like it."

"And school?"

"I like it."

"You're in fourth grade, right?"

"Sixth."

"I'm sorry. I thought Mehiret said you were in fourth grade."

"I was. I was double-promoted to the sixth grade."

David Hartman scratched his head, trying to make sense of this information.

The waitress arrived with their tea in tall glasses, which she put down in front of them, and left.

David Hartman sipped his tea. "I love Ethiopian tea. All those wonderful spices. So flavorful." He glanced to his left at no one in particular. He planted his elbows on the edge of the table and propped his chin on the tips of his long fingers.

"So tell me," he said to Desta, "in one month you went from the fourth grade to the sixth?"

"That is because I had the highest average in my class. When students are first in their class, they skip one or two grades, depending on whether the promotion occurs at the completion of the first or second semester."

"Very good! Congratulations!"

He extended a hand to shake Desta's, but at that moment the waitress arrived with their breakfast.

As they ate, they talked. David Hartman asked Desta about his family. What they did. Where they lived. Whether he had brothers and sisters. Simple questions, all requiring simple answers. Desta was relieved. He grew more confident as the conversation progressed. He didn't ask David Hartman about himself.

Instead the Ferenge himself volunteered information about his family— that his mother had died in a bad way when he was very young so that he was raised by his paternal grandparents. He never met his grandparents on his mother's side because they had disowned his mother. And that he had one brother, who was studying to become a doctor of physics.

Not only was Desta sorry that David Hartman had lost his mother, but learning about him in this way made him seem like a regular person. Desta was still cautious.

David Hartman reminded Desta of his father, with his long, prominent nose, high forehead, and perfectly square chin. If not for the skin and hair color, the two men could be related. And Abraham didn't wear glasses as this white man did. David Hartman also had the habit of pushing his glasses up the bridge of his nose every few minutes, always with his left index finger, blinking his eyes and twitching his nose in the process. It was not so much annoying as it was distracting.

Shortly after they finished eating, a group of people came in and sat at the table next to them.

David Hartman ordered some more tea for both of them. As they drank, they talked, with Desta again talking more than his companion, in answer to questions about school. Science, math and English were his favorites, but his current love was ancient Egyptian history.

The man smiled broadly. "What's it you found so fascinating about ancient Egypt?" he asked, delighted that their conversation had shifted to his own passion and area of expertise.

Desta told him about the pyramids, the pharaohs, the mummies, the wall writings and drawings. Desta said he was particularly keen to learn about the animals and symbols that he saw in the drawings on the walls and on various objects because some of them are exactly those that appear on his family's coin box.

"Is that so?" David Hartman asked, now smiling even more broadly.

Just then Desta realized what he had done. He wanted to cover his mouth, but it was too late and it would be futile. He couldn't take back what already had spilled out. He had not planned to talk about the existence of the coin or the coin box. A film of perspiration veiled his brow. He wanted to wipe it, but that would be too obvious as well.

He had to regroup. He passed his hand over his chest and pressed on the area above his heart. He felt calm immediately.

The Ferenge took over. "Those are the kinds of things I study," he said. He rested his arms on the table and leaned forward.

Desta tilted back in his chair and studied the man's face. He felt a little more comfortable with his host because of their shared interests. "So you know all that stuff?" Desta asked, fascinated.

"I know a lot about Egypt, but I also want to learn more," he said, smiling again. "Let's go for a walk, and we'll continue our talk about Egypt."

Desta liked the idea. Walking in the company of someone had always been one of his favorite pastimes. The man scored another point with Desta.

Though it's a matter of honor with Desta not to accept charity, he let his host pay the bill with the hope of reciprocating in kind sometime in the future. They left the restaurant. The man who nearly barred Desta from coming into the hotel was standing outside talking with someone. He eyed them furtively.

Once they were a few paces away from other people, David Hartman said, "The reason I'm interested in the coin, and now the box you mention, is because I'm studying to be an expert in ancient artifacts, particularly those from Egypt and Israel. I have come to your country because there are artifacts here that trace their roots to both ancient Israel and Egypt. One of them is the Ark of the Covenant. You probably have never heard of it by this name, but it's an object that was made during Solomon's time. It carries the original messages from God. When I learned there might be another object of antiquity, a coin, just as old and with its origins in the same two places, I was very excited. At the moment I can think of nothing else but seeing the coin."

He stopped and looked at Desta.

Desta looked down. He kept rolling a rock on the ground with his toes while contemplating the request.

David Hartman continued. "You said the coin box has images of animals and people on it, right? If I get to see the coin and the box, I can tell you more about the purpose of the animals and writings because those are the kinds of things I study."

Desta looked up. "I know what the writings on the coin say. It's those on the box I don't understand a lot."

"That's why you need to show it to me. I can tell you what they stand for."

When Desta didn't answer, the man said, "Look, you don't have to give me an answer now. Think about it and let me know. If you decide to show them to me, I would like to see them before I leave at the end of July."

"Ohh," Desta said, "you're not coming back?"

"After I finish my studies, I might come back in two years, or earlier, if I need more material in Egypt or here for my dissertation."

Desta was sorry to hear this. It meant they might never see each other again. He would have liked to get to know him a little better.

David Hartman seemed to sense Desta's wistfulness. He said, "In the meantime we can keep in touch by mail."

"Okay. Let me tell you about the coin and the box. One, they are not with me. My father keeps them. Two, I'm not sure if it would be right to show them to you. I need to ask my grandfather's spirit first."

"Your grandfather's spirit?" The man bent down a little. He couldn't believe his ears.

"Yes. Please don't ask me to explain this. It's a bit complicated.

I will tell you the full story sometime, if you want to know."

Now doubt was creeping into the Ferenge's mind. Was he wasting his time? Was this just African superstition?

"I will let you know after I see my father in three weeks. And if I get permission from grandpa, then you must be prepared to travel to my parents' place," Desta said, looking up at David Hartman. "It's a long and difficult journey."

"Let me know. I will send a note through your English teacher. His uncle works at the school I teach."

With that, David Hartman and Desta shook hands and parted.

Chapter 12

Desta's new life in Finote Selam couldn't have been better. He lived with a woman who fed him well. He had never had it this good, even at home. He drank milk every day and ate three square meals, many of which were augmented with meat and eggs. In just two months, he filled out nicely, pads of muscles on his shoulders and chest, thighs and legs. He appeared to have grown taller, too. People who had seen him when he arrived wondered what Alem was feeding him. Some of Alem's gentlemen friends joked about marrying him off to one of their beautiful daughters when he fully matured. Desta simply smiled with all these exaltations, grateful for his good fortune.

Academically, he was doing well. He was absorbing everything he read and all he was taught with great ease and speed. Mostly, he needed to read a book only once and he retained most of it. In the classroom he was the one the teachers called on to solve a math problem or lead the class in the discussion of science, math, or English in their absence. When a teacher in the lower grades was sick or gone to a funeral service, the director chose Desta to fill in. All of Desta's problems appeared behind him, and he felt on top of the world.

But lately there appeared to be something brewing inside his body that had become increasingly worrisome. Not only was he growing and filling out, but he was also starting to feel wound up, in a sense. In the mornings he woke to find his male organ uncomfortably rigid, which made it difficult to pass urine. A dowsing with cold water often did the trick, but the fix was often temporary.

During the day while sitting in class or standing outside chatting with other students, the same bodily part came to life, stretching and expanding outside his control. Each occurrence was a discrete event. There seemed to be no specific cause. The feelings that came with these occurrences, however, struck him as pure, felicitous, and natural.

His voice cracked and screeched like an out-of-tune string instrument, making Desta wonder whether his vocal cords might be giving out. And seemingly overnight, mossy hairs sprang up under his arms and around his groin. Desta wondered whether these hairs might eventually transform into the same thick, furry patches he saw on his father and older brothers' bodies. The idea that someday he would have this same abundant growth crept into his mind like an unwelcome friend. Without really meaning to, he checked to see whether the hair between his thighs had grown any thicker since last he checked.

In the mornings after he washed his face, he found himself in front of Alem's wall mirror, examining his body and the details of his facial features. He was happy he didn't have acne like Dagim and some of his classmates.

Then one morning Desta woke up wet and sticky, at a loss as to the source or its nature. He had had a passionate dream the night before. He had remembered it briefly, and although the dream had vanished once he opened his eyes, it left him with a wonderful out-of-this-world sensation. Yet he couldn't make any connection between the forgotten dream and the stickiness in the morning. Nothing like this had ever happened before.

What was troubling to Desta about these physical changes was he had no will or control over them. If they got much worse, they could easily affect his young life, his education, and his effort to find the second Coin of Magic and Fortune.

Desta shuddered at these thoughts. He had no solution to what was happening. And he couldn't tell a soul; there was no one he trusted with this information. He assumed he was the only boy having this problem, and others, like his friend Fenta, if they knew what was happening, would laugh at him. He bottled up his feelings.

He prayed. He placed his hand over the coin image above his heart when things got especially tough. This helped to calm him but didn't relieve what was going on physically.

As if in answer to Desta's prayers, at the beginning of February, Abraham came. He was visiting for two reasons. In addition to seeing Desta, he wanted to file an appeal for a case he had lost at court in Yeedib. Desta didn't take offense to being secondary on Abraham's list of importance. He had long accepted his insignificance to his family and not to expect much from them.

"You're looking so well," Abraham said, his eyes going wide. "Who is responsible for your radiant health?"

"Not a relative," Desta replied, happy to be able to disprove his father's belief—that only relatives had the heart to extend assistance and good will. He was genuinely pleased to see his father. He kissed his knees, and Abraham grabbed Desta's chin and planted three of his own, alternately, on Desta's cheeks.

"I'm so happy to find you in this wonderful state of well-being." He examined the figure before him with both his eyes and hands. "You have filled out well and grown taller, too."

"Providence has been kind to me."

"Let's go to that teahouse and talk," Abraham said, pointing with the tip of his walking stick to the least crowded of the beverage vendors. "I have some important details I want to share with you. Something you are going to like," Abraham said, flashing his chipped tooth.

"That makes two of us," Desta said. "You couldn't have come at a better time."

"Ohh!" puffed Abraham. "We can talk about anything on your mind. I have all afternoon free."

They sat near the front window of the teahouse. Abraham ordered two teas with two rolls of bread. Soon after they finished eating their rolls, Desta asked, "Who should go first?"

"Let's hear yours first. Mine can wait," Abraham said.

This was Desta's opportunity to share the things that had been going on with his body. If there was one person with whom he could share these things without fear of judgment, it was his father.

Starting with the first physical signs he noticed, Desta told Abraham. Some things, like finding the wet sticky stuff in his bedding and the stiffness to his male organ were awkward to talk about. Abraham for his part listened attentively. He didn't interrupt nor did his big eyes veer from Desta.

When Desta stopped talking, his father smiled. He rested a big hand on Desta's shoulder and said, "These are signs you're now becoming a man, my son. There is nothing wrong with you. All the boys go through them. The girls have their own challenges as well. This phase of a young person's life is the most difficult—and the most dangerous."

Desta turned and looked at his father. "Most dangerous?"

"Yes. If you give in to these feelings, you could end up losing yourself, your dreams, and your aspirations, as well as destroying the dreams and aspirations of someone else. Do you remember my telling you once how you test the purity of gold?"

Desta nodded and said, "With fire."

"That's right. Just as you test the purity of gold with fire, you test the strength and character of a young man with hardship. What you're facing now is probably the ultimate test of your strength and willpower. . . . So do you think you're gold, or not?"

Desta had never thought of himself in these terms before. He considered the suggestion for a few seconds and said, "If I survived all the bad things that happened to me in Dangila, I suppose I could survive this, too."

"If you don't, let me explain what you could be facing. Suppose you acted on your desire to have a physical relationship with a girl. Two things could happen. You might find out you enjoy being physical so much that you would spend all your time at it. Then she could end up pregnant. Her father might insist you marry her, and you would be forced to quit school, in which case you might fail to fulfill your other dream, which of course involves finding the second Coin of Magic and Fortune. Would you want that?"

The very idea sent shivers through Desta's body. "No!" he exclaimed.

"Then be strong. Don't give in to your thoughts and feelings. I've witnessed many a man who forsook his planned life path because of a woman. We don't have to go far. Think of your brother Tamirat. He abandoned his twelve years of education and gave up becoming a priest because he wanted to remarry. Becoming celibate, as the church required him to be after his divorce, was something he couldn't bear. He was not strong enough to resist his physical urges. Should I say more?"

Desta shook his head to say no. He knew the story of his brother very well. He had witnessed his father's grief when he found out that Tamirat had abandoned the priesthood and remarried.

"What your body is calling you to do now, you have plenty of time for, and you'll be able to do it the rest of your life. But this is the time of learning and achieving things. Once it passes, you will never have this chance again. All right?"

Desta nodded. Finishing his education and finding the second Coin of Magic and Fortune were more important to him than anything in the world. He resolved not to give in. *I'm the gold that's being tested. I will fight my body with all the power I have in me,* Desta thought.

Desta left the teahouse with Abraham shortly after more people came in. They were heading to the home where his father was staying when Desta asked Abraham to tell him the story he had said he would share with him.

"I've not forgotten," Abraham said, smiling. "I just didn't want to tell you what I had in mind while we were within earshot of all those strangers."

Desta's ears perked up. He looked around. "Is this open space here private enough for us to talk?" Desta's lips parted into a smile.

"Yes," Abraham said, gesturing with his hand. "I think we'll be better served by the added cover of that beautiful warka tree. We can sit on one of the benches there and talk."

Desta followed his father, wondering what was so important that Abraham needed the cover of the great tree to share the news with him. As they walked toward the warka Desta pondered if they would need the spirits permission before they could enter the tree's shadow. When they approached it, Desta was about to tell Abraham to stop when his father walked right in. Then realizing it was probably safe to trespass, Desta followed suit. They sat side by side near the trunk of the tree.

"I think you will be happy to know that I have a contact who is acquainted with the owner of the second coin," Abraham said in a hushed voice.

Desta's eyes bloomed. "You do?!"

"I cannot be one hundred percent certain, of course, but the person who told me said that he had seen an illustration of an ancient coin with the image of a man, and it was supposed to have come down from King Solomon."

Desta couldn't believe his ears. "How did you find this out?"

"He is an old, trusted friend of mine who asked what you were doing, and I told him you were in school in Finote Selam, and at the same time on a mission trying to find a long-lost ancient coin. I gave him the details of the coin, and that was when he said he knew someone who had the coin."

"Where does this man live?"

"In Zegay, not far from Bahir Dar."

Spasms of excitement went through Desta. "Did he tell you what the owner's name was or whether it was a man or woman?"

"What difference does it make?" Abraham asked, shooting a side glance at Desta.

"The person who owns the coin is supposed to be called Sweet and Sour and they were supposed to be . . ."

Desta went blank for a second, trying to remember what Eleni, the Wind Woman, had told him the owner was called. Then it came to him. After a few whispered stabs at trying to pronounce it correctly, he said it. "They were supposed to be hermaphrodite—*Finafint*."

"What?!" Abraham cried.

"I'm just repeating what someone told me," Desta said, dropping his voice.

"I didn't get much detail," Abraham admitted. "But if you want to find out, we can go there during your Easter break. I told him you would be available to travel then."

"Yes, of course. I would go to Bahir Dar anytime with anyone who would take me there," Desta said, excited by the very idea. He had been somewhat down at the thought of having to stay in Finote Selam all four years of his schooling. Now there was the possibility of getting a bit of a break, and in Bahir Dar, no less.

"Yes, I can come home for my Easter break and we can go to Zegay then," Desta said.

"Good," Abraham said. "Let's do it."

The father rose. Desta followed. "Come, let me introduce you to the woman your brother and I stay with whenever we come to town.

"Here is Desta, Wezero Dinknesh," Abraham said. "I have told you so much about him. I want him to meet you, finally."

"What a handsome boy," Dinknesh said.

"Thank you," Abraham said. "He is at that age when all children bloom."

Desta liked Abraham's friend. Dinknesh was a round-faced, fair-skinned woman who smiled genuinely and readily. She seemed to wear her heart on her sleeve.

As the father looked on, Abraham's host asked Desta how he liked his new town, school and his living situation.

Desta told her that he was content with everything and couldn't have asked for more.

Dinknesh wanted Abraham and Desta to come inside so she could make coffee.

But Desta needed to go. He had an errand to run for Alem. "Nice to meet you," Desta said, waving at Dinknesh.

"Come and see me tomorrow afternoon. We can visit some more," Abraham said. He kissed Desta on the brow before he left.

Desta walked home, his mind whirring with Abraham's news.

Chapter 13

Abraham and Desta were planning a visit to Zegay, near Bahir Dar, following an inconclusive lead. For a quest of this magnitude, they didn't want to leave any stone unturned. Desta yearned for this trip. For Desta's sake, Abraham was anxious that the trip succeed. Desta had been spending way too much time thinking about the second coin, sometimes at the expense of his education. For Desta, it had become an obsession that had no end. The only one in the family who could really relate to his dream of finding the second ancient treasure was his father.

Even Desta didn't quite understand the ultimate importance of seeing the two coins united at long last. He couldn't fathom what their eventual union would look like, partly because his grandfather's spirit was not specific. All that his grandfather said was that when the two coins came together, something grand would happen, and it would affect all of humanity. For Desta, though, the challenge the Cloud Man gave him was just as important.

He would use every fiber of his body and brain to find the second coin and unite it with the one he already had. Sometimes he thought about what it would be like for identical twins who had been separated for three thousand years to unite. What stories would they have to tell each other? Just thinking about this, alone, made him shiver.

This was the first holiday Desta was spending with his family in two years. But his primary purpose for coming was so he could go to Zegay with his father and determine the identity of the person who supposedly owned the second Coin of Magic and Fortune.

To his absolute surprise, Desta's mother, Ayenat, had dropped her demand that he be blessed by a priest's cross before entering her home. It was a mandate she put forth believing he had converted to Islam when he lived in Dangila a few years back.

This time, though, it was as if she had been baptized with holy water and blessed with a priest's cross herself. He found her transformed from the cold, exacting mother he knew to a warm and welcoming person. She greeted him with a smile, and hugged and kissed him. Desta was almost beside himself. He had a hard time believing what he was witnessing.

To her credit, Ayenat was never a temperamental, changeable woman. She was actually quite an even-keeled person. So there was hope. Does absence indeed make the heart grow fonder? Does time by itself change people?

Although he had forgiven Ayenat, as he had all members of his family, Desta hoped this would lead to a meaningful relationship with his mother. For Desta, time, distance and life experiences have taught him to have a more sober outlook toward his mother.

"Maybe now she felt powerless" he said to himself. He had been totally independent, asking very little of his family in the past few years. Whatever led to Ayenat's transformation, he hailed the change in her. Although he was no longer drawn to his family, he would continue to visit his place of birth, and it would be nice to feel welcomed when he did.

Three days after Easter, Abraham harnessed Dama and hung from either pommel at the horse's flanks, the *dabo kolo*—the apricot-sized rye snack rolls—and the aluminum water canteen.

Zegay was a two-day journey. They were going east. This meant traveling through mountains that grew like trees—some whose tips were sharp and pointy like needles, others whose facades were wavy, and ridges razor sharp. The first time he saw these mountains was when he climbed the peak above his home with his half-sister, Saba. At that time he had only a bird's-eye view of them. Now he was going to have an up-close encounter with these imposing giants.

After the trio climbed the peak facing their home and stood and looked at what was awaiting them that day, Desta turned to his father and said, "Isn't there another way to go to Zegay?"

"There is, but this is the shortest distance," Abraham said, studying Desta's face. "Why, are you afraid to go through these mountains?"

"I just wondered how we will be able to climb up and down all those peaks and still remain in one piece at the end," Desta said. He smiled apprehensively.

"You're trying to find the second coin, right?"

Desta nodded.

"We don't know where it is for sure, so you need to be prepared to travel through mountains and valleys like these, across vast deserts, and around vast bodies of water. If you are to achieve the prophecy you were meant to fulfill, these are the kinds of challenges you will have to face. Right?"

Abraham couldn't have said it better. Desta pursed his lips and slowly moved his head up and down.

"In fact, think of it as the start of your journey. If we're lucky enough and find the coin with Belay, whom we're going to see, then you would be blessed. This journey would be your first and last."

Desta corrected his father. "Actually, it would be the last of three. I traveled to Lake Gudera in my search and Bahir Dar once before."

"No matter. You just have to be prepared for such challenges," Abraham said. "Let's move on."

Move on they did. Around the time the sun was looking down on the western edge of the sky, they had cleared the last mountain and emerged onto a summit. They stopped and gazed at the vast land that spread like a fan in front of them, giving their eyes freedom to travel as far and wide as they could. They welcomed and enjoyed the change of scenery. Then they pressed on.

It was here they encountered a small, wiry woman who looked a thousand years old. She had a pair of teeth that jutted out from her lip, like a single fang, and dark, sinister-looking eyes. At that moment Desta was reminded of the story his sister Hibist used to tell him about *budas*—a class of evil-eyed people whose spirit possessed persons and made them do all kinds of crazy things, until they finally died. When a person was dead and buried, a buda would come riding a hyena at night, dig out the corpse, load it on the hyena, and bring the body to share among the buda's family and beasts of burden.

As they walked along, Desta eyed the sun, anticipating the splendid colors he was sure he and his father would witness when it finally met the horizon. But he was also thinking about the old woman, wondering whether she might indeed be a buda. The more he thought about her, the more convinced he became. When he asked Abraham if he thought the same, his father said he didn't pay attention to the details in her face. At that moment his father was more concerned about getting to their destination before darkness fell.

Strange thoughts entered Desta's head. What if he happened to get sick that night? They might have to return home. In the dark, and through those mountains? And it would mean another failed attempt trying to get where he'd been wanting to go for so long. If so, he would never find out whether this man, Belay, had the coin.

With these thoughts, Desta was getting sicker by the minute, until he finally collapsed. Shocked, Abraham turned and tried to pick him up, but Desta slipped from his grasp like a wet rag. Holding the horse's leash in one hand, he secured Desta in the saddle with the other and trudged toward a set of houses several hundred yards down the hill. Desta was alert, but he just didn't have energy anymore; it was as if all vitality was sucked out of him.

A woman was watching, her hand cupping her face, as Abraham struggled toward the houses. She stepped a few paces in their direction. Abraham kept moving.

"Stop, stop, stop!" the woman shouted. "What is the matter with him?" She asked, at the top of her lungs.

"I have a sick boy. Can you help? I need garlic," Abraham said.

"Stay there, please. Stay there!" the woman echoed. She walked back and disappeared into her house, but moments later came back out. She took a few steps toward them and said, "Here," throwing the head of garlic with as much power as she had in her.

"I hope that helps. Now please go," she said, waving them away with her hand.

Abraham didn't go. He put Desta down on the ground and went looking for two flat stones, with Dama still in tow. Finding a pair, he returned and dropped them near Desta. Then leaving the leash on the ground, he removed two cloves from the garlic and smashed them between the slabs.

Desta had kept his eyes split between Abraham's hands and the morphing sun over the western sky. He also watched the group; people were gathering outside the woman's home, all cupping their faces with their hands, spying on the strangers up on their hill.

"Here, smell this," Abraham said, placing his palm with the smashed garlic under Desta's nose. "This is one of the cures for buda."

Desta didn't know that the cure for a buda's spell could be that simple and instantaneous. Hibist had told him the effect of a buda's evil eye but not the remedy. Grateful, Desta inhaled long and deep several times. When he looked up after drawing his last deep breath, the sky above the now-vanishing sun was painted in hues of red, pink, purple, and many shades of gold. Desta took a long, hard look at the scene.

Abraham, who was pulling out the rolls of bread and placing them on a section of his gabi, asked, "Do you feel better now?"

Desta said he did.

They munched on their rolls and shared the canteen of water
between them. They watched the people, Desta and Abraham
themselves intrigued by the crowd's intense curiosity, as if the two
of them were aliens that had dropped out of the blue sky.

When Desta asked why, Abraham said, "They probably
feared you might be carrying some disease."

Once they finished their rolls, Abraham closed the sack and hung it and the
canteen on the horse's pommels. "We need to save the remaining garlic just in
case," he said, stuffing Desta's lifesaver into the big lower pocket of his jacket.

They turned and looked at the benevolent woman and her
company. The people had dropped their hands from their faces,
relieved, Desta figured, that the intruders were taking their leave.

"We still have a long way to go before we reach our
destination," Abraham said, glancing at the eastern sky. "I hope
we at least have the company of the moon tonight."

Once the sun set, night fell rapidly. Abraham had been eyeing the
eastern horizon for any sign of the moon. Now Desta was doing the same.
The longer they walked, the harder it became to see ahead of them.

To their right loomed a giant spherical shape.

"We better take shelter under that tree until the moon rises,"
Abraham said, pointing to the form with his walking stick. "At the rate
the night is falling, I'm afraid we might not find the home where I was
hoping to stay over. I've not been to this area for a long time."

Desta's stomach knotted. "Do you think the moon will be out tonight?"

"Why—do you think she will have reason not to?" Abraham said,
chuckling a little.

"I think, under the circumstances, it's better if we take shelter
under that tree. There are no homes around here where we can
present ourselves as *yegzi abhere engdawech*—guests of God."

Abraham, with Dama's lead wrapped around his hand, got off the
road and began walking in the direction of the tree. Desta, ambivalent
and uneasy about the whole idea, followed. Abraham tied the horse to
one of the branches and removed the load from his back. He took off the
layers of fabric from the saddle and spread them on the ground near the
trunk of the tree. Then he said, "We'll rest here for a while, sleep if we

have to, and then if the moon comes, we'll get up and go in the moonlight all the way to Zegay. That way we can arrive early tomorrow."

"And if there is no moon?" Desta asked, looking at the blurred figure in front of him.

"We'll sleep here until we see any hint of light in the morning and then go."

Abraham seemed incredibly adapted to nighttime activity. He opened the bag of snacks and poured a handful for Desta and another for himself. He closed and tied the bag. They ate listening to the grinding and masticating of each other's food. Once done, they wrapped themselves in their gabis and lay on their backs. The tree branches that seemed so close earlier now looked far away.

Abraham muttered, saying if they had left early and Desta hadn't gotten sick, they would have been in the warmth of his friends' home.

Desta didn't say anything because he was listening to the hyena's howl, which was coming from somewhere up in the hills.

"Are you awake, Desta?" Abraham asked, sounding like he wanted to talk about something.

"Did you hear that hyena?" Desta asked.

"What about it? Hyenas roam the countryside in the evening. They are the kings of the night."

"Just wondered. That's all," Desta said, trying to make light of the disquiet that was mounting inside of him.

"I'm going to tell you a story. Are you listening?" his father asked him.

After Desta told him he was, Abraham continued. "There once was a rich man. He had two sons. He sent them on a long journey, with an assignment. Wherever they spend the night, they needed to build a home. At the end of their journey, they were to come back and report to the father the number of homes they had built."

There were now three hyenas howling, the second to the east, the third to the north. "Did you hear that?"

"What?"

"The hyenas?"

"Are you listening to my story or the hyenas?" Abraham snapped.

"I'm listening to your story. So what happened after the children returned?"

"Good! You heard. The man asked each son how many houses he had built while they were traveling to faraway places. Each son gave his accounting. One son stood up and described the places he visited, the people he met, and the houses he built wherever he spent the night. He said some of his houses were built from sturdy materials and would last a long time. Others were merely shacks and would last no more than a few months to a year. He sat down.

The next son rose. He described the different places he saw and the people he met. He then talked about the different families he befriended and formed relationships with. He detailed the things he did for them and in turn what they did for him. When he left, he gave them his name and address and invited them to come and see him if they ever visited the area where he lived. He wrote down the name of every place he visited and the people he met, but he didn't build a single home.

There were a lot more hyenas howling now. They didn't seem very far away.

"Baba, in all your travels have you had any close encounters with hyenas?"

"It sounds like you are really scared of these hyenas. You grew up hearing them at home. It's no different here. They are just roaming the countryside. Did you hear the rest of my story?"

"Yes. What happened to the children in the end?"

"Good. Well, their father got up, placed his hand on the shoulder of the son who built relationships wherever he went, and said, 'You are my true son. You have a great future ahead of you.'"

Desta was no longer listening to the howling hyenas. He was thinking of the story. "And what did the father say to the son who just built houses?" he asked.

"He sent him back to try to build relationships with the people he would meet. . . . Do you know why I am telling you all this?"

"Why?"

"Because if you really want to find the second coin, you have to build relationships with every person you meet. People can be the bridges that help you reach your goal. That's why I'm pleased that you met that Ferenge from Amarika."

Just then the horse snorted and Abraham raised his head. He whispered, "You know what . . . those disgraceful creatures are here." He sat up and reached for his walking stick. Desta sat up but froze.

"I knew they would eventually come near us," Desta said. "There was something ominous about the way they were howling."

They listened. The hyenas seemed to be all around them, now circling the outer perimeter of the tree.

The moon had gone to another world. The night was as dark as a night could be.

Abraham rose and stumbled forward past the horse. He whipped his stick through the air, prepared to strike any hyena that would come near his horse. Then suddenly, all was quiet. He came back and sat on his heels, waiting. The beasts cackled and laughed from farther away, as if to mock the old warrior.

"Desta," Abraham whispered. "Go to sleep. We have another full day's journey tomorrow."

"Are you sure you'll be all right?"

"What—do you think you can save Dama and me if we're attacked by these beasts?" Abraham retorted sharply. "They will give up and go away soon."

Desta placed his hand over his chest above his heart and tried to doze off, but his mind and ears were on the hyenas. They were milling around them. Then all of a sudden everything was quiet again.

A short time later, Abraham said, "Like I thought." He had believed the whipping of his stick through the air had done the trick. He lay down next to Desta. Desta knew it was the coin image on his chest that had chased them away, but he didn't say anything.

In the morning they awoke when the scene before them was barely illuminated. After placing back the saddle seat covers and hanging the snacks and the canteen, they hit the road. Although the night was relatively warm, the morning was a different story. A cold wind was coming from somewhere in the east and the dusty road felt like ice under their feet.

After the sun rose and fully shone over the entire land, they began to walk comfortably. Late in the afternoon they reached a V-shaped pass covered with lush trees and bushes.

"We are just about to arrive in Zegay," Abraham said.

Desta shook with excitement. "Baba, will we be able to see the man who has the coin tonight?" he asked.

"No. Probably tomorrow. We have to go across the *Abayi*— the Blue Nile—river for that," Abraham said. "Besides, my friend said he saw drawings of a coin, not the actual object."

"Wouldn't it be safe to assume the man has the coin, too?" Desta said. "Both the coin and image of the coin are on the goat skin parchment."

"It's true. But at this point let's not assume anything." Abraham warned. "It's always better to be surprised."

Desta tightened his lips.

Embraced by the mountains that curled around it, Zegay looked and felt like a charming place. The evening shadows of the peaks draped over the scattered village, reminding Desta of his own valley.

They arrived at the home owned by Abraham's friend named Tekle. Inside the residence, everything—the food, furnishings, and bedding—was spare.

Abraham noticed Desta glancing around with a puzzled look on his face. "These people are *zelans*—nomads. They stay in their homes only half the year."

Then the father explained that nomads are people who travel great distances, following their cattle wherever the good pastures are. They always have somebody staying behind to farm the land and take care of their homes in their absence. They leave during fall and return in spring.

Desta now was more pleased to have met the zelans. He hadn't heard about or met them before. Something he would cherish remembering in the future, he thought.

After dinner Tekle said, "I've sent a messenger to *Grazmach*—commander—Belay, alerting him to expect us in the morning."

"The man who holds the coin?"

"Yes, but don't quote me on that part. All I know is, he has interesting drawings of a coin."

Desta's heart leaped but fell back as quickly with what Tekle said next.

"We need to go to bed early and get up early. Grazmach Belay is a district governor. Although tomorrow is Saturday, he still has visitors from mid-morning on."

With this reminder from the host, all went to bed.

Chapter 14

That night, sleep was merely a concept for Desta. His thoughts of the coin were like electric currents running through him. His mind flitted from worry over the shekel's authenticity to what he would say or do if Grazmach Belay refused to let Desta take the coin with him. Then when he considered all the clues his grandfather's spirit had provided, doubt crept into his head.

For one, the coin's owner was to have a name that meant sweet and sour. That was not true of 'Grazmach Belay.' And then according to Eleni, the owner of the second coin was supposed to be a hermaphrodite. "Was the governor one of those people?" Desta shook his head, baffled by this notion. Finally, after the first cock's crow, he fell asleep. He was awakened a few hours later.

Once he was alert, Desta quickly dressed and joined Abraham and the host, who were ready to go see Grazmach Belay. They took a path that went across an expansive flatland. Farther up on the left, steam rose from the sibilant falls of the Blue Nile and spread languidly through the trees like fog. Up ahead the same powerful liquid roared as it came tumbling down into what sounded like the deep crevices of the earth.

The ground trembled as they neared the river. The path ended at the foot of two carved planks, connecting the narrowest points across a deep chasm. Higher up in the air, a pair of ropes spanned the same distance, linking two stout posts. One of these was supposed to be the pedestrians' lifeline. Desta felt one of the ropes between his fingers. They were hopelessly old and frayed, looking as if they might snap under the slightest pressure. To Desta, the bridge was more like a death trap than a lifeline.

Abraham and Desta stared at each other. Tekle looked at the father, then the son, and said, "Don't be afraid. Lots of people cross this bridge every day, and there has never been an accident, that I know of."

"Watch me," he said, stepping onto the planks.

To Abraham and Desta's amazement Tekle strode across the wobbly bridge as if walking on solid earth. The planks sighed heavily under the pressure

of his steps but responded in synchronized rhythm and all without Tekle
touching the hand ropes.

Abraham turned to Desta. "There you have it," he said, speaking more to
their guide. "I'll go first," his father declared, and stepped onto the planks.

Desta's eyes rested on Abraham's back. His heart was in his
throat. His father was so much taller and bigger than the small, wiry
Tekle. Were the aging boards strong enough to support him?

Desta placed his hand over his chest and prayed. As he watched
his father totter across, he thought about the challenges Abraham
said he should expect to face—vast deserts and oceans, hunger and
hardship—in his quest for the second coin. His father had forgotten
to include crossing deep gorges on flimsy plank bridges.

Abraham made it across, although still his
hand grazed the left rope as he swayed.

With the bridge's safety record intact, Desta took his turn. Looking
straight ahead, with his right hand still on his chest above his heart,
he marched swiftly across the span as if there was nothing to it.

"See, I told you so," Tekle said triumphantly.
"I must admit, you're a brave boy."

Abraham winked at Desta and said, "He *is* courageous, isn't he?"

"I should say so. The young ones are generally skittish
when crossing this bridge for the first time."

GRAZMACH BELAY WAS a tall, handsome man. The chiseled outlines of his
face were accented by a noble nose. He was outside, perched on a chair. There
was a book on the table next to him. Desta thought this probably was his Bible.
He rose and took steps toward them when he saw the visitors at his gate. Then
he lingered a bit and locked eyes with Abraham, as if trying to remember where
they met before. After shaking hands with his guests, Grazmach Belay invited
them to come and sit at his table, which overlooked his expansive courtyard.

The first several minutes were spent getting to know one another. A
woman—Desta couldn't tell whether she was a servant or a relative of Grazmach
Belay—came out of the house and asked what they wanted for food and drink,
suggesting they could more comfortably eat inside. Grazmach Belay ordered
coffee and some snacks, announcing, "Let's have it here. It's a lovely morning."

After they finished the third round of coffee, Tekle said, " Grazmach

Belay, Abraham and Desta are who I told you were interested in seeing the drawings of the coin. They also wanted to find out if you or somebody else had the actual coin. They walked here for two days just for this purpose."

"I see," Belay said, again fixing his eyes on Abraham. "Are you so interested in the coin?"

Abraham explained the purpose—that they had an old coin themselves and they knew of an identical companion coin that was important they find.

Desta kept his eyes on Belay, as he played with his fingers under the table. He searched the man's face for any hopeful signs that he had the actual coin.

"I don't have the coin, nor do I know anybody who does. But it's true we have a goat parchment with drawings of what look like the head and tail illustrations of a coin. We found it among my father's important documents."

He signaled to the woman. When she came near, he said, "Bring that wooden box from our bedroom." The woman came cradling a box measuring roughly twelve by eighteen inches and set it before Belay.

He opened the box and brought out two items: a rolled fuzzy parchment and large, rectangular object wrapped in black satin. He placed both on the table. He picked up the covered object. "Ato Abraham," Belay said, glancing at his visitor. "Forgive me for staring. But the resemblance is uncanny."

He brought out from under the black satin a framed portrait of a regal-looking man and held it up for all to see. "Do you know who this is?" Belay asked, fixing his eyes first on Abraham, and then on Tekle and Desta.

They all shook their heads, but their eyes didn't waver from the portrait.

"Belay wrapped one arm around the frame and said, pointing with an index finger, "This man is His Imperial Majesty Emperor Lebna Dengle of Ethiopia, who was also known as Dawit the II."

Hushed, the audience of three stared at the picture. Belay could discern their struggle to derive meaning from his passionate announcement. He laid the picture face up on the table.

Belay continued, speaking directly to Abraham. "You're the spitting image of this man who ruled our beloved country four hundred years ago, and I want to know if you might be related to him."

Abraham, stunned by this sudden and unexpected revelation, looked away for a few seconds. Then he turned his gaze on Belay, saying, "I've no knowledge of my background. I've lived in an isolated valley nearly all my life, having gone there with my mother after my baba vanished."

"I've no doubt you're related to this man," Belay said, and began an accounting of the facial features that linked Abraham to the man in the painting: the long, prominent nose; brilliant big eyes; high sloping cheekbones that terminated in a perfectly square chin; beautifully curved lips; ears shaped like conches, all indicating a blood tie between the two men that no one could question. He added, "My family descends from him too but no one resembles him."

Tekle picked up the picture and held it closer so all three could examine it. As he studied it, Tekle kept glancing at Abraham's face. "You're absolutely right," he said, turning to Belay. "It's an amazing resemblance. You don't find this kind of likeness among siblings, let alone two people who are separated by four hundred years, as you say."

"That is like thirteen generations apart," Belay concurred, after crunching the numbers in his head.

Abraham had no reaction whatsoever. When the picture was before him, he studied it like someone who was looking at a piece of art.

Desta thought it was a very interesting resemblance but had no other feelings.

"Well, let's get to what you came for," Belay said finally.

Both Desta and Abraham pointed to the rolled parchment. "We would like to see what this is."

"This," Belay said, unrolling the parchment, "purportedly was in the emperor's possession. The actual coin should've been with his belongings; we don't know what happened to it." He handed the curled skin to Abraham.

Abraham opened it and anchored one edge with his arm. He handed one corner to Desta and held the bottom right side with his free hand.

Both father and son tingled with goose bumps. Despite their being old and somewhat faded, the drawings of both sides of the coin were identical to those the grandfather's spirit had drawn for Desta. Even the handwritten legends seemed identical to the ones on the drawings they had at home. They kept shaking their heads as they stared at the images for a long time.

"You find it interesting?" Belay asked. "The unfortunate thing is, we have no idea what happened to the object from which those images were drawn. It was rumored to have great powers."

Father and Desta looked at each other for a few seconds, debating whether they should tell Belay they actually had the coin. "Later," Abraham whispered.

Then he turned to Belay and said, "It's very interesting, indeed. We were hoping you had the coin we were looking for, but this finding is also very helpful to us."

Desta was assessing the dimensions of the parchment while Abraham was talking. He elbowed his father. "Baba, look here, I think these measurements are fourteen inches by fourteen inches, the same measurements grandpa's spirit had me cut out from the goatskin for Hibist's wedding return."

Abraham looked down. "The shape looks identical," Abraham said, after fixing his eyes for a few seconds.

Belay excused himself for the moment. Abraham tapped Desta and said, "Let's talk for a second." After excusing themselves from Tekle, they walked a few yards away to discuss whether they should reveal their ownership of the coin. Abraham suggested they shouldn't. It would do Belay no good to know. Anyway, it would be a violation of the vow to keep it secret.

Desta suggested they should tell the man because "it would make him happy knowing the coin existed and was in good hands. Besides," he said, "it will no longer belong to us or anyone else, once it reaches its final destination—its fate yet to be determined. I'd rather walk away from this man, who was obviously pleased to meet us, knowing we kept nothing from him."

Abraham agreed. Having come to terms, they walked back to the table and sat down. Tekle rose in respect to the father and sat down once Abraham settled in his seat.

Then Belay returned with a leather-clad sword. All rose in respect to him. They sat down only after Belay reclaimed his chair.

Abraham cleared his throat and said, "God has a way of arranging things that can be mystifying to us humans. We came hoping you held the Coin of Magic and Fortune. Instead we found that we might be related to you *and* you hold pieces of our ancestors' history. I know you're not going to believe this, but we have the coin."

Shock and disbelief spread across Belay's great face. His big eyes got bigger. His great nose flared and then narrowed, and his ample lips trembled. "Tell me more," he said.

"Without going into too much detail," Abraham said, "we've this identical illustration at home. It's supposed to be with the coin that came down through our family. Do you know where it comes from?"

"Yes, I do. It was supposed to have come from King Solomon. It's because of its antiquity my father and others who knew about it had been

saddened by its disappearance. That illustration there has remained the
only reminder of its existence in our fold, and later the coin's loss."

"It's lost no longer," Abraham said, cracking a smile.
"It's still in the family—for now, anyway."

"Very pleased to hear it," Belay said.

Then Belay offered: "Let me give you its background. During the Muslim
Jihad invasion of our Christian kingdom, from 1531 to 1543, many valuable
ancient properties were lost. Our Muslim neighbors from the East, aided by the
Ottoman Empire and led by a powerful ruler named Ahmad Gragn and his army,
ransacked hundreds of ancient monasteries and burned down churches. They
destroyed thousands of ancient books, works of art, and other precious objects."

Belay stopped and looked away for a few seconds,
saddened by the story he just recited.

Desta placed his hand over his mouth and shook his head, saddened,
too. Abraham just listened, his eyes fixed on Belay, but looking through
him, not at him. He knew what battles were like, having fought one
himself when the Italians invaded Ethiopia during World War II.

Belay turned back and continued. "During these dark years of our history,
this man you see before you was the emperor of Ethiopia—for most of those
years, at any rate. After many years of battle with the emperor and attempts
to capture his palace atop Amba Geshen in northern Ethiopia, the Muslims
finally succeeded in entering the palace proper in 1540, after getting help from
the Turks. They slaughtered the prisoners along with their guards and looted
the royal treasury. This sword," Belay said, picking it up and pulling it from
its leather sheath, "was one of the few items later found in the compound.
And the emperor himself was killed in a battle afterward the same year."

Sad and thoughtful, Desta just shook his head. After seeing the
painting of Emperor Lebna Dengel and noting the uncanny likeness
to his father, he felt as though it was his father who was killed.

Belay continued on: "You know, the only other Christian country that
might've given aid, like Ahmad Gragn got from the Ottoman Empire, was
Portugal. Their great explorer, Vasco da Gama's, having discovered the sea
route to India at the conclusion of the previous century, used to dock his ships
along the East African ports, including our own, at Massawa on the Red Sea.

"Is Portugal in *Europa*—Europe?" Abraham asked.

"Yes, in western Europe. . . . Anyway, the Muslims in the East were a constant threat and Lebna Dengel's army had engaged in battles with them, winning decisively. Later, when Gragn came to power, Lebna Dengel's army, outnumbered and ill-equipped as it was, still fought and defeated Gragn in one of the battles. They had had contact with the Portuguese from early on, but Lebna Dengel was too proud to ask for assistance."

Desta nodded, remembering his own refusal to take money from David Hartman.

Belay noted, "Near the very end of his fight with the Muslims, Lebna Dengel dispatched an emissary to Portugal. In the letter he supposedly had said, 'Not only do we have our Christian faith to defend but also a treasure much older than Christianity itself to protect.' In 1541 the Portuguese sent four hundred soldiers under the command of Cristóvão da Gama, the son of the celebrated seafarer.

"Our army together with the Portuguese soldiers was defeated. Cristóvão da Gama was captured and eventually beheaded by Ahmad Gragn. The Muslims, with their massive assistance in money, firepower, and troops from the Arabs across the Red Sea, were a superior force.

Desta shook his head, feeling sorry for Cristóvão.

"This would be the Muslim leader's last battle. It happened across from here, near Lake Tana. The Ethiopians, along with the remaining Portuguese soldiers, under the command of Lebna Dengel's son, the Emperor Galawdewos, fought in this battle, defeating the Muslims and killing Ahmad Gragn."

As if coming to the end of his story, Belay lowered his voice an octave, saying, "That was the end of the Ottoman Empire's attempt at erasing the only Christian Kingdom in Africa, a people whose faith in their Christian God goes back to the fourth century."

"Did Lebna Dengel have any other children?" Desta asked Belay.

"A great number of them—three more boys and at least three girls," Belay said with an air of melancholy that didn't fit the content of his reply. He was still trying to shake off the dark chapter of his country and the woeful end of his ancestral father.

Then, "Oh, yes," he said suddenly, collecting his thoughts. "To get back to the story of the coin, one of Lebna Dengel's greatest fears was losing the ancient treasure to the invaders, as he had indicated in the letter he wrote to the king of Portugal. Not to risk this, he passed it on, along with the parchment, to his youngest son—Yakob."

Belay drew a deep breath and continued: "Yakob was instructed to hide in Shawa, not far from our current capital, Addis Ababa. That was how the coin and parchment were saved. Otherwise they too might have been lost like everything else from the royal treasure. Yakob was supposed to have passed the coin to his grandson, Suseyenos, who became the emperor of our country in the early 1600s. From then on nobody knew what happened to the coin itself. However the parchment found its way to us."

Waking up from Belay's mesmerizing account, Abraham said, "We don't know who the owners were prior to my father; he had been killed before I was barely seven years old."

"I think you should have a copy of our family tree and see if you can trace the lineage," Belay said and got up. He went inside the house once again and returned with a big tome, bound by a rough-hewn leather cover. "Do you have a couple of hours?"

Abraham looked at Tekle.

"Don't worry, Tekle can go if he wants to. I'll have one of my helpers escort you across the Blue Nile River or to Tekle's home if you think you might get lost," the governor interceded.

Abraham looked at Tekle again.

"It's for a very important purpose. Stay," the host said.

With that Tekle left.

Belay opened the tome from the middle, flipped through several pages, scanning the text as he went, and then stopped. "After lunch your son can copy a few of these pages—starting here," he said, pointing to the middle of the page. He pushed the book closer so Abraham and Desta could see. "You only need it from Emperor Lebna Dengel on down."

Desta copied the pages with pen, ink, and paper the host provided. He was done within an hour, but he spent another hour reading about the ancestors beyond Lebna Dengel. The writing was very clear. The information appeared to have been copied into the new book fairly recently.

Before they left the table outside, Desta wanted to know about the wording he saw at the bottom of Emperor Lebna Dengel's picture. Can I ask you a question?" he said, looking up at Belay.

After he got permission to ask, he said, "What does *Wanag Seged* mean?"

Belay chuckled. "It means 'to whom the lions bow.' Somebody had given the king that title after his first defeat of the Muslims. 'Wanag' is a Muslim term for lion. 'Seged' is a Geez word, and it means 'bow.' In short it's a metaphor to say that Muslims had submitted to the king."

"What a clever line!" Abraham said with a smile.

"It's clever all right," Belay said, "Given what ended up happening to him, it was an unnecessary affront. I'm sure he would have liked to take it back."

"True," Abraham said. "Sometimes when one is inflated with pride or success, one's humility is tossed aside."

Desta was the only one who thought it was a great line. He kept repeating it in his head.

Desta and Abraham didn't cross the Blue Nile that night. Belay invited them to sleep over. Abraham and the host talked until well past midnight. Of what they discussed, Desta had no knowledge. He had gone to bed shortly after dinner, with 'to whom the lions bow' running on an endless loop through his head.

The next morning Desta and Abraham got up early, ate breakfast, and prepared to leave. Belay sent for one of his assistants, who lived in the next compound. The governor followed them out the gate and waited for a few minutes until the assistant arrived. In those intervening moments, Belay mustered the courage to say what this unexpected visit from Abraham and Desta meant to him.

He shook hands with Abraham. "I thank you for your visit," he said, looking his guest straight in the face. "I thank you especially for the two things you have done for me, and I'm sure for the rest of our relatives as well. One, to know that the coin is still in our fold. Two, to have met a relative who is the very image of our great emperor. Anytime I looked at that picture I showed you yesterday, I wondered if there was any one in his *zere*—bloodline—that might resemble him. I compared his image to all our relatives, but none came close. It pleases me to know he was not lost forever, just as the coin was not lost."

With this they shook hands, exchanging the customary three kisses on the cheeks. When Belay's assistant arrived, they left. At the edge of the gorge, Abraham told the man to stay behind until Desta and he crossed the bridge. After they cleared the wood planks, they waved their hands and vanished into the woods, following the path to Tekle's home. Once there, they harnessed Dama and left after thanking Tekle for his kind hospitality.

"We'll repay you in kind when you come to visit us next," Abraham said, shaking Tekle's hand firmly.

The three got on the road and headed home. For quite a while neither Abraham nor Desta seemed predisposed to talk. The sun was beating down on them. Abraham threw the end of his gabi across his head as protection. Desta did the same. Dama shook his head to chase away the flies, and clambered along, braving the sun.

The conversation they had with the governor had caused Desta to think through things he had never considered before. If the coin had not been stolen and his grandfather had not been killed as he tried to get it back, his father's life and his own life would have been very different. It would have been different if his grandma had stayed put on their old property in Kuakura, too.

Leading the horse, Desta slowed a little so his father could catch up to him. "Are you tired already?" Abraham asked when he came nearer.

"No, I'm not. I just have a question."

"Yes?"

"The governor's story got me thinking. Do you know that if grandpa had not gotten killed and grandma had not left the old homestead, you could have had a different life?"

"Yes. That wasn't lost on me. But there's nothing to be done. Our lives are what they are."

"I was just thinking . . . you know, if things had been different, you could have been king of Ethiopia."

"Maybe. And you'd have not been a shepherd," Abraham said with a grin.

"What's wrong with being a shepherd?"

"Nothing. I was answering your question." Abraham grinned again.

"Don't belittle it. I know what you were thinking. You know I'm proud of being a shepherd, as I would be happy to be a prince."

"Good for you. On a serious note, though, it's good to be proud of your roots. Your heritage is the bedrock on which you stand. From here on you should never wonder where you came from or who your ancestors were.

"From various encounters I knew we had important personalities in our family. I just didn't know it the way the governor told it. At the same time don't be overly proud of yourself. It's not a good trait to have. I know you're doing well in school. Remember this: the higher you rise in what you do, the lower you sink in the eyes of others. People will find any excuse to bring you down."

Desta fell silent as he processed what his father had just said.

"Did you hear what I said?"

When Desta said he had, Abraham said, "Enough of this heavy discussion. Let's keep going."

WHEN THEY GOT home the next day, Desta opened the only notebook he had brought with him and wrote atop the first page:

DESTA

To Whom the Lions Bow

Then when he returned to school three days later, he wrote the same lines in all his notebooks. . . .

Now that Desta was back in Alem's world, he tried to figure out the best way he could tell her about the remains of her half-sister that lie strewn in the grove behind her backyard.

Chapter 15

In reality Desta didn't really want to be the bearer of another bombshell. He realized now that his arrangement to live with Alem was not just for his own and his host's benefit. He was needed for a much bigger purpose. To help free a trapped soul, solve a long-forgotten murder mystery, and hopefully bring closure, peace, and a better future to everybody involved in this macabre tale of long ago that nobody knew had happened.

He knew his involvement in this sensitive family affair would impact his relationship with Alem's family and her circle of friends. He also knew the events that would unfold afterward might affect the quiet he enjoyed for studying, and consequently, his chances of getting another double promotion. Nevertheless, he had to move forward with his decision to tell Alem his secret.

On Saturday morning May first, Desta invited Alem to go on walk. Her response to this was, "I'm not a leisurely walker. I walk for purpose—to go to the market or church."

Reluctant at first, she became willing company when Desta told her it was to talk about something important. She dashed to her bedroom and came back after throwing a netela over her shoulders. "Do you have to go on a journey to tell me what's on your mind?" she said edgily. "We have plenty of space here."

"I've always enjoyed leisurely walks, especially with someone that means a lot to me," Desta said, smiling.

"You know how to put someone at ease, don't you?" she said, herself cracking a nervous grin. "Such delicate affairs don't often bode well, but I will come."

Desta waited outside while Alem put on her shoes and dabbed her face and hands with cream. She closed and locked the door and followed Desta to the gate. At Alem's suggestion he pulled shut the gate behind them.

They turned left on the path in front of Alem's compound and went north, following it through the brush-covered hill. Somehow the conversation through this leg of the walk, which was arduous, centered around Desta, his family, his days as a shepherd, and his life, both in Dangila and Yeedib. Desta spared Alem much of his harrowing experiences. He had never before shared this much of himself with his benefactor, and it felt good. As they chatted, Desta felt closer to her, which would make it easier for him to ask Alem about her own life.

Where the street split at the top, Desta suggested they go left. The caravan road crossed this path, and it was at this intersection where Mehiret and he had stopped when they arrived in the town. Desta remembered being elated by the sight of the tree-covered land, his eyes tracing the long, straight road that came into town from somewhere down below. They hadn't rested on the benches and rock seats available to them at the time because they needed to get into town before dark. Today he would do just that with Alem and ask her to return the favor—to share a little bit of her life story.

They sat side by side overlooking the town. Desta decided to begin with a disclaimer, saying, "I hope you'll forgive me for being so personal as to ask you some of your life story. I'm confident you will forgive me when you find out the reason for my transgression," he smiled. "Actually, having shared a bit of my own story, I don't feel so bad." He emitted a nervous chuckle.

"You want to know about me?!" Alem asked, touching her chest with her index finger, her big eyes grazing Desta.

"Not that I'd do anything with the information, but if I know a little bit about your past, I'll share with you something very important that can be of future benefit to you."

"My goodness, this is getting more mysterious by the minute. You are making me terribly anxious and nervous, now." Alem passed her hand over her face as if shooing away a fly.

"I think that in the end it will be good for everybody."

"The end?" She stared at Desta. She shook her head. "So you want to know where I have been so you can tell me where I should be going, right?" She chuckled, as if she found the mere suggestion ironic.

Desta nodded.

"Might as well get to it, then," she said, and proceeded to open up to Desta.

"I was married and divorced three times, not because I had difficulty making my relationships work, but because I couldn't conceive a child. Each one of the men I married wanted children, and not one of them wanted to stay in the relationship if we couldn't have children together." Her voice cracked. "Then hoping to find that one person who would accept me for who I am, I rented a place in the business section in town and became set'adaree. I lived on my own for a year, trying it out, and I still couldn't find someone. Most of the men were either married or didn't want to commit themselves to someone like me." Alem batted her eyes as if to chase away her emotions.

"What do you mean 'someone like you'? You're one of the most beautiful women I have ever known. Generous and kind as well."

"Oh, you're so sweet to pin those kind words on me, Desta." A small, sad smile appeared on her face.

"Those things don't seem to matter. And I do take care of myself, just in case. After a while I may just give up and go join a *gedam*—monastery." She rested her mouth on the back of her hand and stared down at nothing in particular.

"What about the men you have now?"

"Some of them are taken. The others want children or don't want to obligate themselves long term."

"If you could have a child, would one of them be interested in marrying you, and vice versa?"

"A couple perhaps," she said, still struggling with her feelings. "You know, I've not thought about the idea of getting married lately. The reason I continue to see my gentlemen friends is, I have no source of cash. They help pay for a lot of the little things we need in the house, like I mentioned before. Luckily, I now have my own home. My father left it to me for as long as I live. After I die it goes to my sister's children, because I don't have my own. It was stipulated in the will." Alem shook her head. She gathered her knees together and wrapped her arms around them, lowering her chin to her knee caps, her eyes probing the earth near her toes.

"If you have your own children?"

"Then it would go to them."

"Did you ever have any other siblings besides your sister?"

"No—not that I know of, anyway." She smiled benignly.

"You don't ever remember seeing a little girl around the house when you were a kid?"

Alem had to think. "You mean like a sister? It's kind of a silly question, but . . ."

"No, just a girl about your age at the time—five or so."

"We had a young servant, not that I remember very well, but my mother told me about her, and she had a girl. But then they left, and we never saw them again."

"Well, let's go back home."

"Don't leave me hanging. What about the girl?"

"I think your difficulty having children, your father's cancer and death, and your mother's issues with her health may have something to do with that girl."

"What?!"

"Let's go home and I'll show you something. I think if we can solve this mystery, your problems can be solved."

Alem lifted her face and looked at him incredulously.

"Trust me. I've been through this once and I know what I'm talking about," Desta said, thinking of his sister Saba's problem with her miscarriages and how he helped solve that problem.

"Whatever you say," Alem said, now feeling like she was under some sort of spell.

"Let's go."

"Why don't you tell me what you have in mind right here and now?"

"It's not something I can tell you. It's something I need to show you. I may be entirely wrong. I want to show you and see what you think. That's all."

"You really know how to put a person through hoops, don't you? Do you enjoy this?"

"Of course not. I just think you will believe your eyes more than your ears. It might not be what I imagine it is. Let's see what your perspective is. If it is, I know you will be happy in the end."

"You have me under an *asmat*—spell. I'll just have to follow you like a sheep for now," she said, her voice tinged with resentment. "I need to tell myself I am going to be happy in the end. I'm going to be happy in the end. I'm going to be happy in the end."

"Hold on to those thoughts," Desta said, pleased to see the change in Alem's attitude.

As they walked, both were quiet for long stretches. Alem with her head down and her face forlorn looked like she was in another place. Every time Desta tried to nudge her away from her thoughts by asking her questions or making a comment about one thing or another, Alem appeared as if she had not heard or gave just one- or two-word answers.

Then all of a sudden she stopped. "You know, there once was a rumor about this crazy man, a friend of my mother's, who supposedly killed someone and buried the body on our property. Apparently, my father knew something about the incident, but nothing came of it. It's not about some skeleton you found, is it? Alem asked, challenging Desta with her eyes as much as her voice and words.

"We're almost there, so let me show you the object of your curiosity, and you can see what you think."

"Desta, you're dragging this out way too long. I'm not looking for drama, please!"

Desta walked on without answering Alem.

Inside, he turned around and said, "Follow me," and continued walking to the back of the house, Alem on his heels.

Down the sloping grade into the eucalyptus grove on Alem's property they went. Desta lost his footing in the pile of dead and slippery leaves, and fell, nearly breaking his leg.

Alem picked up one of the dead branches and used it to balance and support herself. They finally reached their destination.

The skull of the child leaned against the base of a tree, her hollow eyes staring up at them. Part of the rest of the skeleton was crushed and buried in the undergrowth.

Desta stared back at the hollow eyes, almost at a loss for words and struggling to hold back his tears. Alem, now grim faced, gazed at the remains and then at Desta, as if waiting for him to say something. Just then Desta raised his hand and said, "These bones once resided inside the skin and flesh of your half-sister, Emnet—the one who used to play with you— the jewel of her mother, your father's favorite child but, unfortunately, an eyesore to your mother." Desta said, his voice laced with anger.

The horrible crime his grandmother's cousin had committed against his grandfather out of greed and jealousy had suddenly hit Desta. He shook his head and sighed deeply, trying to calm himself. He wiped his tears—the tears he couldn't shed when his grandfather's spirit took him to the ravine where his remains were buried because he was too young and too confused to feel and react.

He had been carrying years of hurt with him, and his feelings were not far below the surface. Every time he saw someone wronged or mistreated, his tears came faster than his anger. At that moment he reached for one of the lean trees near him and wrapped his hands around it. He rested his head on his arms and let the emotions flow that had been building since he first saw these bones. He cried until his eyes turned strawberry red.

Alem had her hands on his shoulder. Forgetting her own thoughts and feelings, she tried to comfort and soothe Desta. She kept saying, "Why so many tears? You don't even know this child." She caressed his hair and patted his back. Desta didn't reply to Alem's croons or questions.

Finally, he wiped his tears, dried his eyes with the back of his hand, and said, "Let's go. I want to tell you what we should do next." Having cleansed himself, Desta was now all business.

Returning to Alem's compound, they sat on one of the benches at the front of the house, facing each other.

"Here is what we need to do," Desta said. He noticed Alem had not yet pulled herself together. Her face pale and bloodless, she looked confused and sad and not disposed to receive further information or instruction. Desta held back on what he was about to suggest.

Alem shook her head and asked, "How do you know all this—I mean, how do you know what we saw is my half-sister?"

Desta told her how he knew. "You met her spirit here on this property?"

"Yes, I did. It's she who told me the details I've shared with you and other specifics I've yet to share."

Alem looked around, evidently disturbed by the report.

"There's nothing to be afraid of. She is just a stranded little girl who needs help. Her spirit has been trapped here for so many years, and now she needs to go home—to her creator."

"I'm just astonished by this finding. Are you a *tenquay*—wizard—that you have such ability to connect with creatures of the woods, as I suspected?"

"No, I'm not a wizard. Nor do I come from a family of wizards, but I do have the ability to connect with spirits because of what I've been given. I've been able to unscramble the mysteries of my vanished grandfather and an ancient family treasure. Similar to what might be the case here, I also solved my oldest sister's childbearing problems."

"Did you find out who killed her and why?"

"It was pure jealousy and fear. For a few years nobody knew Emnet was fathered by your dad. Emnet's mother was married at the time, so there was no reason to suspect there was another man in the picture. When your father began to dote on Emnet, your mother became suspicious. What's more, the girl resembled you a great deal as she got older.

Finally, your mother confronted your father, and he told her the truth—that he'd had an affair with their servant woman. Your mother immediately fired her. To make matters worse, months later the poor woman's husband divorced her. Now your father was morally obligated to support Emnet and her mother. In the long run it also meant that Emnet would share your family's inheritance. To your mother, this was intolerable. So she hired someone to kill the little girl. To prove he had completed his task, the assassin brought the body here and placed it in a shallow grave, where I just showed you."

Alem pressed her hand over her mouth, her eyes glistening with tears.

"Guess who the beneficiary of this horrific deed became?"

Desta answered his own question: "All of you, minus Dagim's mother. You, and your mother and father. Your father died, your mother is chronically sick, and you aren't able to have children—or keep a husband."

The last part of Desta's report had hit Alem the hardest. Now tears began to flow. "It's because of my mother's deed that I became a *mehan*—childless. The mother I have spent the full month and a half caring for," she cried. The tears she had forced back earlier now found sufficient reason to flow freely.

Desta rose and put his arms around Alem. "Go ahead. This is your chance to let go of what has been accumulating in your heart and soul for so long. Get rid of it. When you're done, you will feel better. And your life will begin anew."

As he was saying these things, Alem was crying, but not with the kind of intensity Desta would've expected. With his last comment, she turned and looked at him.

He said, "Yes, after the bones are collected and buried and the girl's spirit leaves this compound, you will have a new life with unlimited possibilities."

"Unlimited possibilities, eh? I like that." She wiped her eyes with the long side of her index finger. "This is like a dream. The idea is thrilling. I just have to hang on to that, even if it doesn't come true in the end."

"Believe it. My sister's situation was worse. Her problem was losing her unborn babies only after carrying them for several months."

"You're amazing. Thank you!"

"Here is what we need to do. Find Emnet's mother, even if you have to pay someone to search for her. She needs to have closure, too. I'm sure she has suffered a great deal."

"Of course."

"Then collect the remains and bury them. Keep this strictly a family affair. Nobody has to know." Desta remembered the long discussion with his family members and whether they should let outsiders know and have a formal funeral. It was done by vote, more of them favoring the idea of announcing it and having a formal funeral. Emnet's case was simple, and Desta felt it should be handled as such.

"We should end this catharsis now. We both have had a gratifying emotional release. I'm sure Emnet is happy. We'll soon free her from her captivity. I cannot get involved, but you should try to take care of this within a week."

"My thanks to you has no end, Desta. I've a feeling this may be the start of my freedom, too. I'll not get you involved in any way. This is my family's problem, not yours. But I hope you don't mind my consulting you a little. You're the expert, after all."

"Of course! I'll respond to any questions if I know the answers. Like I mentioned, find Emnet's mother first. Bring her here and show her the remains and see if she could verify their identity and corroborate the story. Then arrange the funeral, same day if possible."

"I'll," Alem replied, cheerily.

With this they both rose and went inside the house.

Chapter 16

It was the day of Emnet's funeral. Desta was walking toward the house from school when he came upon Alem. She was sitting alone on one of the benches in the front courtyard. Encircling her bent knees with her long, graceful arms, she seemed faraway. She perked up a bit when she saw Desta. They greeted each other.

"How are you doing?" he asked, piling his schoolbooks next to him as he took a seat across from Alem.

"Oh, I am fine," she said, with some effort. Her voice sounded small. "I'm just sitting here and reflecting on the funeral. . . . My family and the other visitors just left."

To Desta she didn't look fine. Her eyes were lusterless, her lips cracked and dry, her face pale. All in all she appeared as if utterly parched by the grief she bore since Desta showed her the remains of her half sister—the sad spirit that had unwittingly plagued her life.

Desta looked at the horizon; the sun had begun its descent. The trees cast their shadows all around them, as if to mirror Alem's somber inner world. Thin rays of light from the setting sun penetrated the tall eucalyptuses and flickered on the metal strips of the wooden gate.

"Cheer up," Desta said. "From here on your life can only get better."

Alem smiled. "Mr. Positive!"

"I have to be. It's always better to be optimistic than the other way around," Desta said, smiling.

"So tell me, how did Emnet's mother react when she saw her daughter's bones?" he asked. "I've been anxious to hear all about it."

"Oh, my! You should have been here," Alem said, shaking her head a little. "Trufat collapsed directly on the threshold. It was one of the most heart-wrenching scenes I have ever seen."

"Really! What happened?"

"Aberra went to the poor woman, picked her up, and led her to one of these benches here. Thin and frail, she looked a lot older than she was. She glanced around and asked, 'Where is my baby?'

"There were five of us. Aberra; me; my sister, Konjit; my Aunt Kibret; and Emnet's Aunt Asmarech. We looked at one another, wondering whether Trufat was hallucinating. Aberra, who was still standing next to her, leaned in a little and asked, 'Baby?'

"She replied, 'Yes, my Emnet.'

"We four women huddled together, discussing how to break the news to her—that this wasn't a living child but her dead daughter."

"Heartbreaking," Desta said, shaking his head. "She must have been terribly distraught."

"Very much so," Alem said, her face tense and forlorn. She released her legs from her arms' embrace, shifted her body a little, and planted one of her hands on the edge of the bench.

"It was a harrowing situation, to say the least," Alem said, squinting her pale eyes, "the little casket Aberra built was only a couple yards away. He brought it over and set it before Trufat, saying, 'We invited you here to see if you could identify these remains. Not really by these bones but by what we found along with them.' Trufat couldn't even wait until he pulled the necklace from his pocket. She scooted closer to the box and peered inside. Aberra handed it to her. She sat back and asked, 'You found this with the bones?'

"Aberra told her that they did. With this response, Trufat clutched and held the necklace against her mouth and began to wail. Then we all sat down around her and wept. We were moved by the mother's intense grief as much as we were by the sadness we felt for the little girl whose life was cut so very short. It was the second sister I would never have."

Alem tossed her head a little, straightened her back, and folded her arms across her chest. She stared into space for several seconds. Then she turned to Desta and carried on with her story. "Trufat found the courage to speak: 'I had picked up clues that something horrific had happened in our household, but nobody came out and said and I couldn't confront anyone. Your revelation and the finding of these bones were the answers I was looking for. For this I thank you.'

"Then Emnet's mother dropped to the ground and held the casket and cried into the remains. It was as if she had never formally grieved because she had never known what really happened to her little girl. I sat on my heels next to her and put my arm around her spare frame and tried to comfort her. Shortly afterward, she stopped, and I nudged her to get up and sit on one of the benches."

"I guess her years of hurt finally found reason and an outlet," Desta said.

"Indeed," Alem concurred. "To come back to Trufat, after she came to her senses, she started to ask me questions. How had we found her remains? Who had I thought killed her? Had their father known the killer? I told her that you, Desta, met Emnet's spirit here in the compound and it was the spirit that led you to her remains. She has stayed here almost thirty years, waiting until somebody buried her remains.

"With this Trufat got up and began to pace the grounds, just looking around. Then she inched close to the fence, near the wooded part of the grove where the bones were found. She began to call her daughter's name. 'Emnet!!! . . . Emnet!!! . . . Emnet!!!' she hollered into the woods. I followed her at a distance. When she didn't get a response, she turned around and headed toward the front of the house. She was startled when she found me standing alone, looking in her direction."

"Poor Trufat," Desta said, wiping a lone tear from the corner of his eye. "This is heart-wrenching. She must have been disoriented by the intensity of her emotions."

"No doubt," Alem said, undoing her arms. "Anyway," to go on with the rest of the story, "I walked up closer to Trufat and said, 'Spirits are not revealed to everybody. I am sure she heard you. She just chose to remain invisible.' Trufat replied, 'I know. I just want Emnet to know that I came to see her this last time.'

"With this testament she broke down and wept uncontrollably. I patted her shoulders, but I couldn't come up with meaningful words to comfort her. Emnet didn't die of disease or by accident. It was a vile, senseless killing.

"Anyhow, once Trufat calmed down, Aberra picked up the casket and all of us went to the church. A couple of priests and deacons held a short mass for the little girl. Aberra dug a grave in the church's burial ground while we women stood outside the church, with Trufat between us, and prayed.

"At the end of the church service, one of the priests came out with incense. He stood by the graveside and said a few prayers. He made the sign of the cross with the burning incense in its holder at the end of three swaying chains. After that Aberra gently set the little bones into the grave, covering the casket fast and furiously with shovelfuls of dark soil. He packed the dirt with his feet and topped it with a few planks of wood.

"Trufat shed a few more tears. We did, too. Then we came home to a meal prepared for us by my cook. After lunch we hugged and kissed and parted. I encouraged Trufat to come visit anytime she could. Later on, as I mentioned, some more friends came to offer their condolences.

"That in a nutshell is how we closed the dark and sad chapter of my family's life."

Alem's face had taken on a more serene quality. Desta couldn't tell whether this new sense of calm was a result of fatigue or from the dawning realization of a fresh start, like the flicker of light that shone on the gate at sunset.

"How do you feel now that it's all over?" Desta asked, trying to understand what Alem must be thinking.

"My sorrow for Emnet will linger for a while, I am sure. But knowing that the simple removal and burial of her remains could be the solution to my childlessness gives me peace and comfort. . . . I know you're the major contributor to this, Desta, and I'm enormously grateful."

"Oh, don't mention it. My part was incidental. I am just glad the spell that has plagued your life has finally been removed," Desta said.

He looked around. "Do you get a sense of tranquility in the compound?" he asked, offering a warm smile.

"Yes, I do. I am not sure if it's in my head or truly in the air."

"I think it's in the atmosphere. The earth and air surrounding us here are happy to be free of their burden," Desta assured Alem.

"I think you're right. It's going to be a new and good beginning for me and for this land," Alem said. She looked away with a hopeful face. "And as part of this new start," she said, smiling broadly at Desta, "Aberra and I are going to get married."

"You are!" Desta said with surprise. . . . "I'm happy for you."

"We are, too."

"Isn't it a bit fast? I mean if you're planning to have children, shouldn't you wait to see whether your problem is fixed first? . . . Although, I hope you don't take what I told you as God's word."

"We're not going to hold you responsible if that is what you're worried about."

"I know your previous three marriages failed because you couldn't have a baby. If Aberra wants one, are you prepared to live with another divorce?

"One, I have been a happier person for the past several months. Two, I hope things will look up now the remains of Emnet are properly buried. I have been happier ever since.

Three, Aberra told me that although he would love to have a child with me, he is okay if I can't have one because he has two children already from his previous marriage. Four, I am not getting any younger. All the guys I am currently dating will leave me when they begin to see even the vaguest lines around my eyes. And I don't want to be a spinster the rest of my life," Alem said, smiling a little. "We're getting married next month."

"You are?!!!" Desta was stunned.

"We're both ready. There is no reason to wait."

Desta was not sure how to handle this report. So he kept quiet for a few seconds. But he could see the writing on the wall regarding his living arrangement with Alem.

"Of course, you're welcome to continue to live with us. Aberra likes you a lot."

"How old are his children?"

"Fifteen and twelve."

"And you're marrying when?"

"May 21st."

"A good number," Desta said. Then he propped his chin with the heel of his hand and thought. Despite the disruption their marriage would cause to his quiet and peaceful existence, Desta was genuinely happy for Alem. She was a good person. She deserved to have somebody in her life who was there for her all the time instead of different men who came and went.

He put his hand on her shoulder and said, "I've the sense that this is going to work out for you just fine. You're a kind and generous person and you deserve to be happy. I pray that you have your own baby to give you meaning and purpose in your life."

"Oh, thank you," Alem said suddenly. "For a boy of your age to convey such wisdom is humbling."

"I know I'm only fifteen, but sometimes I feel like I'm thirty-five—because I have seen so much in my short years."

"Admirable" was all what Alem could manage as she got up to go inside.

Chapter 17

A few days after the wedding announcement, both Desta and Alem were peaceful-ly coexisting in the backyard, he sitting on his bench with his notebooks and she feeding grain to her chickens. Alem had come out with a small bag of barley. She would reach into the bag, take out a pinch, and toss the grain to her chickens. The animals greedily picked up the barley as if deprived of food for days. Their heads bobbed, their beaks stabbing the air, the earth, and each other, as they fought over the precious kernels.

Alem seemed to derive pleasure from watching these creatures rush excitedly toward the grain she pitched and then battle it out with each other. She smiled often and even openly laughed when she saw a chicken snap up a kernel before it hit the ground. To Desta this activity seemed Alem's only source of entertainment when she was alone, but he could see it also gave her time to reflect and connect with her feelings and thoughts.

The corners of her mouth twitched and her eyes squinted, as her hand mechanically scooped up the barley and tossed it to the winged creatures. Thoughts formed, were considered, and dissolved; Desta could read all of this on her face.

Having finished feeding her chickens, she came and sat next to Desta.

"Are you ready for our wedding?" she asked, teasingly, as if her wedding was all she was thinking about as she fed her chickens.

Caught off guard, not by the subject matter, but the specific question, Desta contemplated his answer. "I've next to nothing to do to prepare, but you have a lot. Are you ready?" he said, glancing at his host. He grinned.

"Our wedding will be simple this time," Alem replied casually. "I had three big, extravagant weddings before and Aberra had one of his own. We wanted to save our money for something more practical and we wanted to spare others—close relatives—from having to spend money and energy on our behalf. Nevertheless, we may still have fifty to sixty people, not the three to four hundred we had in our previous weddings."

"I remember my parents' preparation for my sister's and brothers' weddings. They were long and involved affairs," Desta commented.

"Yes, it can be backbreaking. . . . This time we also want to have a church wedding. Our previous marriages were civil."

"What's the difference?"

"Church weddings are more binding than civil weddings. God willing, we both want to be married to each other until death takes one or both of us away."

"The ghost of Emnet is gone. I think everything should work out fine for you and Aberra," Desta said cheerfully.

"Thanks. Do you know what else?"

Desta turned and looked at Alem.

"We'll be wearing crowns."

Desta was just about to ask her what the crowns were for when someone banged at the gate.

"I'll tell you about them and their significance after the wedding," Alem said, rising to go to the gate. "I think that's Aberra."

ON THE WEDDING DAY, Alem wore a long white dress that flowed gracefully behind her. It was marked by intricate and colorful needlework, which circled the neck of the gown and continued down the front, culminating in an elaborately stitched cross. She wore low-heeled leather shoes and around her shoulders a black wool cape, which was also colorfully embroidered.

There were half a dozen bridesmaids helping Alem look perfect for her groom, who was expected to arrive at any moment. While the bride was sitting on one of the chairs, one bridesmaid fixed her hair, combing it out into a perfect sphere. Then she wreathed it with a *shash*—a strip of white fabric. The second bridesmaid manicured and polished Alem's nails and massaged her hands with olive oil cream. Alem applied moisturizer to her nose, cheeks, and chin and rubbed it in. With this treatment, her fine skin shone and her eyes beamed with happiness.

When Alem stepped outside, she looked magnificent in the morning light. Just then a green car that said OPEL on its trunk rolled to the gate and stopped.

Aberra was also dressed in gleaming white—jacket, shirt and trousers. He got out of the car and held the door open for his bride. When Alem reached him, he flashed her a bright smile and planted a kiss on her lips. Once both were inside the car, Aberra closed the door and whisked them away to the church. The rest of the wedding party, Desta included, followed behind in separate vehicles.

The church courtyard was packed. Mass had not yet begun. The priests would be conducting the wedding ceremony prior to starting the service. They stood by the entrance behind a table, upon which lay two crowns, a heavy book, and a silver cross.

When the bride and groom arrived in the compound, the crowd parted to let them pass. They were lead to the table and stood next to the priests.

Then the head priest placed a crown on the groom's head, while saying, "The servant of God, Aberra is crowned unto the handmaiden of God, Alem." He said this three times. Then he placed a crown on Alem's head, reciting, "The handmaiden of God, Alem, is crowned unto the servant of God, Aberra." He said this three times, also.

Next the priest chanted, "Oh Lord, our God, crown them with glory and honor," while lifting the crowns from off their heads and switching them between bride and groom three times. Then the priest hallowed the proceedings with the cross, passing it over their heads and faces. This crown-blessing ceremony was followed by a formal mass and the receiving of the bread and wine of communion. With this final act Aberra and Alem were formally deemed husband and wife—until death do them part.

At the conclusion of the church services, Alem and Aberra strolled out, followed by their best men and bridesmaids. The congregation applauded as they passed. The wedding party got in their cars and headed to Alem's house, where a lunch awaited them. The customary elaborate dinner party would be held a week later.

THE NEXT DAY AFTER returning from school, Desta had a few questions about the wedding ceremony, the crown, and why the dinner was delayed by a week. Alem explained it all for him.

"First, we cut the traditional church wedding by half. We just wanted the services, *not* the elaborate romantic events that take place afterward, as if we were first-timers. Second, the dinner was delayed by a week because you cannot go eat and drink and be merry after you have taken the Holy Communion."

Desta knew about this. He had taken the Communion a few times and knew the importance of respecting the rite.

"Third, why the crown?—I can't give a clear answer. A priest once told me it's to remind us what would be waiting for us when we go to heaven if we're good Christians. Maybe just simply to say that we have become queen and king of our newly created family." Alem laughed.

"To produce princes and princesses," Desta joked.

"You got it!" Alem agreed. She smiled, her eyes flashing. Somehow the idea of having "royal" children had given her happy thoughts.

Chapter 18

When school closed at the end of June, Desta found himself at the top of his class yet again. He had earned his second double promotion in less than a year, making big news across campus and the community. During the summer break, he would be keeping close to his heart the thrill of skipping two more grades, which meant he'd be starting eighth grade in September. Then he'd have only one more year before setting off for high school in Bahir Dar, where he could begin in earnest his search for the second Coin of Magic and Fortune.

Way before that though, he was poised to fulfill a promise he made to David Hartman—that Desta would take him to his parents' home before David left for America in July, so that the student of ancient Egyptian and Middle Eastern artifacts could see for himself King Solomon's Coin of Magic and Fortune and the sandalwood box it was kept in.

Two days after school let out, David Hartman and Desta were on a bus from Finote Selam headed to Tilili, a small town off the main highway, where they would be renting horses to make the day-and-a-half trek to Desta's home in the highlands.

They arrived in Tilili a couple of hours after the sun rose. They quickly arranged their rental and were ready to hit the road, when the man who owned the horses took a quick glance at David Hartman and, directing his question to Desta in Amharic, asked, "Do you think he can make it?" The tone of voice conveyed more than the words.

"I don't know. He said he could. I'd given him all the particulars about this trip," Desta said.

"From here to Yeedib he could probably handle it. What concerns me is the rugged terrain to your parents' home."

"I know," Desta said, now himself uncertain. He glanced at David Hartman, sizing him up.

"Look at him," Desta said, turning to the horseman. "What's your name?"

"Hailu."

"Hailu, this man is the size of you and me combined."

"It has nothing to do with size," Hailu said. "It has everything to do with endurance—stamina."

"Isn't that true with everything we do in life?" Desta retorted. Having his will and stamina tested since he was little, he could talk like a grown-up.

David Hartman sensed that they were talking about him. "What's he saying?" he asked Desta.

"He thinks you might not make it."

David Hartman laughed. "I grew up playing all kinds of sports—basketball, football, baseball—so no problem."

Of all the sports David Hartman mentioned, football was the only one that sounded familiar to Desta—you kick the ball with your feet. Kids at school played it. The others he had never heard of. He was about to ask David Hartman how he played the other two sports, when a thought occurred to him. He turned to Hailu and said, "That's why we are renting your horses, to rest on them when we get tired."

"Even then. . . ." Hailu thought for a moment. "But I'm only going to Yeedib. I'm not taking you to your parents'."

"You're not?"

"No. Once we get to Yeedib, you're on your own."

Desta explained to David Hartman what the horse renter had said. "If we cannot find a horse to rent in Yeedib, we may have to walk for a half day," Desta said.

"No problem. I can handle it," David Hartman said.

Desta glanced at Hailu and said, "Can you tell me why you won't take us to my parents'?"

"Because I love my knees, my back, and my horses. I've been there twice, and each time was an ordeal climbing and descending those mountains," Hailu said.

The horse renter was going on foot.

"In that case, we'll take just one horse," Desta said. "My feet will serve me just as well, especially since you will be walking, also."

June was the month when the rainy season officially arrived. There were rains starting as early as April, but these were light warning showers, coming sometimes as sporadic sprinkles, other times as sudden downpours. It was a warning of what was yet to come, a nudging to wakefulness the life that had lain dormant under the earth during the dry season. By June, clouds piled high like mountains in the sky—black, white, and dark gray—and rains were almost an everyday occurrence.

To Desta, the day looked as promising as any nice day in June could be: he knew he must enjoy it while it lasted, and be prepared for anything. The sun glowed over the entire countryside as it climbed into the cerulean-blue air, leaving a smattering of fleecy clouds below.

The land was flat and green in places but the color of burnt sienna in freshly tilled lots. Groves of eucalyptus trees hugged villages like a hen gathering its chicks under her wings.

The three travelers pressed on, their conversation pared down to a single word or phrase, exchanged mostly between Desta and David Hartman. Desta and Hailu talked more at length.

Other travelers passed them from the opposite direction, but almost nobody stopped or lingered to look at the man who looked so different from them. They exchanged greetings with bows or words as they passed one another.

David Hartman refused to ride the horse because Desta and Hailu were walking. If they were on foot, he felt he should be, too. He saw himself as a strong, fit man.

Around noon, David Hartman turned to Desta. His feet were still moving him forward. "How long before we reach Yeedib?" he asked, his forehead now beaded with sweat.

Desta turned to Hailu and asked the same question. "We'll get there before sunset if we go at our current pace," he replied. Desta translated for David Hartman, who grunted and said, "That long?"

"We could get there sooner if we travel faster," Desta said.

"We should, then," David Hartman said. "But let's rest first and have something to drink."

With that suggestion, they sat on rocks they found along the embankment of a river. David Hartman and Desta each drank a bottle of Fanta. Hailu walked up along the shore and scooped the river water into a plastic cup and came back. His horse helped himself to the running water as well as to the tufts of lush grass along the river's edge.

After they quenched their thirst and rested, David Hartman rose with the spirit and vitality of a runner who's just gotten his second wind. "Let's press on, then," he said, striding purposefully along. Both Desta and Hailu had to double their speeds, sometimes breaking into a trot, just to keep pace with the Ferenge.

Soon after they were back on the road, a gauzelike shadow fell over them. Desta looked up. The sun had been overtaken by a voluminous white cloud that had come surging from the east. He looked down at the horizon ahead of them and noticed it had begun to ink. His stomach tightened.

He glanced at Hailu. "You think it will take us all day to get to Yeedib?"

"If we keep up this pace, we may get there a lot sooner."

Desta communicated this news to David Hartman. "Good!" the Peace Corps teacher said, and he began to take even faster and longer strides.

Overhead, the cloud's inky darkness intensified, building from a steely gray to coal black. The three travelers watched as the drama unfolded before them. Without warning, the sky had become a roiling mass of dirty clouds.

They needed to get to Yeedib before the rain caught up to them. David Hartman couldn't maintain the pace he set earlier. He was walking slower now. At the urging of both Desta and Hailu, he got on the horse. The animal grunted at first.

As Desta had feared, sheets of rain came bearing down on them well before they reached Yeedib. They managed to find shelter under a tree, but only after they were soaked to the skin.

The rain passed on. When they returned to the road, their clothes were clinging to them like glue. They finally reached their destination but only after the sun had been lost to another world. The notorious Yeedib wind was tossing and battering every moveable object, including people and animals.

"Where are we staying?" David Hartman asked.

"I know there are no hotels here, but let me think where we might spend the night," Desta said, buying time. His father-of-the-breast had been transferred to Dangila. He really didn't have any other close acquaintances he could impose upon. He had met the governor a few times. Maybe he would offer them accommodation, especially since they had an out-of-country visitor with them.

When Hailu saw Desta vacillating, he became increasingly anxious. "I need to find a place to stay before it gets too dark. Can you let me have my horse back?" he said.

"Take us to Governor Alula's house," Desta said.

When they arrived, the governor was not at home. There were two women and three boys. He had never met any of them. After they learned that Governor Alula was in town and would return soon, they took down David Hartman's knapsack and returned the horse to Hailu.

"Let me know the next time you need a horse,"
Hailu said, as they shook hands.

"Will do. Thank you," Desta said, waving his hand.

David Hartman waved good-bye, too.

Wet, cold, and shivering, they sat on a log outside and waited. The governor finally arrived. After handshakes and exchanges of niceties, Governor Alula invited them in. Everything was spare, including the meal and the accommodations. Considering that they had dropped out of the sky, both Desta and David Hartman were grateful for whatever they could get.

The next morning after a breakfast of tea and bread, they left. Nobody rented horses in Yeedib. And Abraham didn't know when exactly they were coming, so he couldn't send one of his sons with his horse Dama to meet them.

They took the caravan road out of town and stood at the edge of the plateau. "David Hartman," Desta said. "Do you see those mountains at the other end of the valley before us?"

David Hartman nodded.

"That's where we're going. First, though, we need to descend this mountain in one piece. If we make it down without twisting an ankle or breaking a leg, then we can say "Thank you" to God. The walk from the bottom of this plateau to the foothills of the mountains across the valley is pretty easy, fun even. Part of the terrain is padded with soft, springy turf. Climbing the other mountain and descending the far side will test all the athletic endurance you have in you."

David Hartman smiled. "Rest assured. I'll not disappoint you. Shall we go?"

Go they did. Desta wheeled down the familiar slope, sliding along the trail with great control. He moved from one ledge to the next, avoiding rocks and flood-washed potholes. David Hartman, staring down at his own feet, watched his every step. Even so, with his smooth-soled shoes and no traction to speak of, he looked as if he might come crashing down at any moment, the loose rocks and soil unsteady conveyors. He stood so high up in the air that gravity kept tugging at him more than it did Desta.

Desta looked around for a stick. Finding one, he handed it to his unsteady hiking partner. "That is what I needed, a third leg," the Ferenge said, grateful to have something to catch him, should his own feet miscalculate their steps.

They reached the bottom of the mountain unscathed. The flat terrain was easy to traverse by comparison. Then there was the next challenge—climbing the next mountain, which stood before them like a wall.

When they reached halfway up, David Hartman glanced at Desta and said, "You know what? I think each of our bodies uses different sets of muscles when we climb and descend. Climbing was easier for me."

Desta turned and looked at him. He was astounded. There was not a hint of perspiration on David Hartman, whereas Desta was soaked in it. "I wish it was the other way round," Desta said. "Our ultimate challenge is yet to come."

The next hour of climbing was easier. The trail skirted the mountainside for several miles and split in two—one path going east, the other north. They took the northward branch. It meandered along a wavelike peak for quite a distance. Then it split again, one trail going east, the other continuing north. They took the eastern leg, Desta leading the way to the edge of the mountain. "That is where we're going," Desta said, pointing to a cluster of domes far below.

"Down there?" David Hartman asked, springing his index finger into the air.

"Yes, down there. Those are circular thatch-roofed homes, where we will share one of the homes with horses and goats." Desta said this with a straight face. He fixed his eyes on his companion, waiting for a reaction.

David Hartman sensed the intended alarm. "I'm not worried about that. The question . . ." He didn't want to admit what had come to mind.

"Just to reassure you, we'll have our quarters and the animals have theirs. We'll cross paths by the entrance though," Desta said, smiling.

"I'm not so concerned about the horses and goats but getting down there is going to be tricky," David said, finishing his earlier thoughts.

"I know," Desta said, "playing football—what did you say the other sports were called?"

"Baseball and basketball."

"Yeah, playing football, basketball, and baseball is different from scaling down a cliff, requiring as you say, a different set of muscles. But I'm sure you can handle it. Let's go."

If they had gone farther along the previous trail, they would've found a path that traversed the gradient of the mountain before it dipped down the hill. Going that way was easier on the back and knees. But almost all young people preferred to go the route David Hartman and Desta were taking. There was a particular challenge in coming this way because there was no marked or beaten trail. People walk all over the land, finding their path of least resistance.

Desta glanced at David Hartman. "You can follow me if you like, but you can also create your own route," he said.

"Thank you. I'll see how I can manage," he said, appraising the slope analytically.

Desta started walking straight down, as if fitted with wheels. David Hartman charted his own course, seemingly guided by the movement of graceful music. He walked left and right, left and right, cutting at an angle whenever he turned.

"You see, it's not all that bad if you know what you're doing," Desta said when they stopped for a break. He smiled.

"Not bad at all," David Hartman said, almost reflexively. His mind seemed elsewhere. He looked to one side of the valley and then to the other, finally stopping at a mountain, whose craggy face reflected in the waters of the Davola River. "Tell me," he said, glancing at Desta. "So you were born and raised down there?"

"Until I was eight years old," Desta said wistfully. "I didn't even know there was land beyond these mountains. I grew up believing the sky was joined with the earth at the horizon. Imagine my reaction the first time I climbed this mountain we are on. . . . It was a life-changing experience for me."

"I must say," David Hartman said. "I think you should one day come to America. *That* would be a truly life-changing experience for you."

"I hope I can go someday, but I need to find the second coin before I do. Then I will be free to go anywhere."

"You never know, it could even be in America," David Hartman said. He glanced at Desta. "I'll keep my eyes open for you as I visit the various museums in London, Paris, and New York."

"That I'd appreciate to no end."

Then they got up and started walking. David Hartman explained what museums were. Desta doubted the second coin would be in those kinds of places, if it were owned by the person with the confusing name. But he didn't say anything to the Ferenge about this. It was not necessary.

When they arrived at his parents' home, they found Abraham all decked out. He was outside pacing the grounds as if waiting for someone. "Era," he cried, the moment he saw Desta and his companion. "This is a nicer surprise," he said, after kissing Desta on the cheeks.

Desta looked at his father. "*Nicer*? Who were you expecting?"

"The children came rushing to say that some government officials might be coming to see me."

"Let me introduce you to my friend. His name is David Hartman—it means 'Dawit.'"

Abraham extended a hand. "A pleasure to meet you, Dawit. Come on inside. Ayénat should be preparing something."

Abraham had spread out plush cowhides on the living room floor and had a big fire going in the hearth.

"Sit down, please," Abraham said, gesturing to the floor. At this moment Ayénat came from the kitchen. She kissed Desta and greeted Dawit, bowing her head. Then she went back to the kitchen.

As they sat down Desta realized he was just about to confront what he dreaded when he thought of taking David Hartman to his parents. What could he ask his parents to give the visitor from America to drink and eat? Ayénat quickly brought two tumblers of tella. She handed one to Desta, the other to their guest. Desta stole a glance at David Hartman, who barely took a sip before putting down his glass. Desta guzzled his as if overcome by thirst.

"Do we have any more of the Fanta left?" Desta asked, turning to his companion.

When David Hartman replied there were two left, Desta said, "Let's save them for the return trip. We may have something close to Fanta for you."

"Baba," Desta called out. Abraham was in the kitchen with Ayénat.

Abraham came. "Do you have any honey wine?" Desta asked him.

He looked over the parapet and asked Ayénat. They didn't.

"Can you make *birz*—honey diluted in water—then?"

"That we can," Abraham said, relieved to find a solution to the unexpected dilemma.

David Hartman liked birz. He drank all of it.

The next concern was what he might like to eat.

Knowing eggs were enjoyed by city people, Desta asked his father if they could cook a few of them.

"How about porridge?" was Abraham's swift and unexpected reply.

When Desta seemed at a loss, Abraham said he thought all white people ate porridge.

Desta turned to David Hartman. "Is it true all you eat is porridge in your country?"

David Hartman laughed.

"I guess not, huh?" Abraham said, immediately realizing his mistake. Desta asked his father where he'd gotten this idea. Abraham explained that his cousin, who worked with the British for a short period after the Italians left in the 1940s, had seen them eat the gruel every morning.

After Desta translated the story, David Hartman chuckled some more, saying, "I'll be fine with injera and shiro wat."

"That we have plenty of," Abraham said happily.

So they had freshly made injera with shiro wat and boiled eggs for dinner.

After dinner they chatted for a while and then went off to bed. Both David Hartman and Desta were utterly exhausted.

Chapter 19

The next day, after breakfast, Abraham brought out a few goatskins and spread them on the grass. Desta approached Abraham and said, "As I told you before, the reason David Hartman came here is to see the coin and coin box. Can you bring them out?"

"I'll not bring the coin. You don't know what this fellow is up to. Nobody is supposed to know it even exists, other than close family members. But I'll bring the box," he said, and left.

David Hartman and Desta made themselves comfortable on the skins.

Abraham brought out the preciously wrapped object, cradling it in his arms like a baby. He removed the cloth wrapping and placed it down gently in front of David Hartman. He took his place on the skins.

"Thank you," David Hartman said, looking up at Abraham. For a few seconds he just stared at the box, almost afraid to touch it. "Is it okay if I pick up the box and inspect it?" he asked, glancing at Desta.

Desta asked his father's permission.

"If he wants to, sure," Abraham said.

He lifted the box with both hands and placed it on his lap. Desta could see David Hartman's mind churning. He rotated the box one way and then the other, turning it completely over, his eyes lingering on each side for a long time. Then he lifted the lid and studied the carved figures, noting with amazement the array of color.

Both Desta and Abraham were watching their guest with the kind of anxiety reserved for a courtroom verdict.

"What do you think?" Desta asked.

"It looks very old, but I can't say how old," David Hartman replied.

"What both Baba and I want to know is what all those illustrations and drawings are doing on the box," Desta said.

"The ancient Egyptians didn't have the alphabets we have today. They used symbols to express their ideas, thoughts, and wishes. So all these animals and illustrations you see have purpose and meaning. They are not just for decoration." Desta translated David Hartman's words for his father.

"I suspected something like that because some of them are not exactly good-looking images," Abraham said.

Desta had to suppress a laugh.

David Hartman continued on. "The lion, here, for example," he said, pointing to one of the images on the side of the box, "is a protective symbol. You see it appearing in all kinds of places where protection is required. It's also a symbol of the pharaoh, or king, of ancient Egypt. . . . The same thing is true of the cobra. Someone wearing a mask with the image of a cobra about to strike is trying to say, 'Don't come near me—I will kill you with my venom.' This is the literal meaning; it can also have a figurative meaning when used in a different context."

"But why on this box?"

"It's to warn others that the content of this box, the coin, is not to be touched."

Then he pointed to the large carved image of a cross and a circle on top. "This is called *ankh*. It's a symbol of life and eternity. Why here? Whoever had the box made, they wanted the coin to always be a part of the family."

He went on and talked about the baboon, cat, crocodile, falcon, frog, hippopotamus, jackal, vulture, and others.

He also talked about the different gods and why they were always masked with the heads of animals. He discussed colors and their meaning for ancient Egyptians. Black was the color of night and death. It also stood for life and fertility. Blue, the representative of heaven and the sea, also denoted life and rebirth. Green stood for growth and life. Red signified blood and fire. White was associated with cleanliness, sacredness, and ritual purity. . . ."

"My grandpa's spirit said the box and coin were made by Shoshenq, the Egyptian Pharaoh."

David Hartman perked up. "Is that what he said?"

"Yes," Desta said.

"If that's the case it wouldn't be hard to trace the origin of the box and coin. There are many artifacts from Shoshenq, the most famous being his ring."

Desta leaned down and asked Abraham to please bring out the coin.

His father resisted at first, but Desta convinced him. However, before showing the ancient coin to the eager David Hartman, Desta decided to take him to some landmarks in the area.

THE FIRST PLACE David Hartman wanted to go was to the site where the grandfather's remains and the coin were buried for forty years. They went straight down the field and then across the creek to the property of Desta's older brother, Damtew. The land appeared as a freshly tilled lot. Along the edge of the farm, they went to the only place where Abraham's eucalyptus trees were swaying in the wind. He had planted these trees—seven in number—so that future generations could locate where his father's remains and the Coin of Magic and Fortune had been buried for so long.

Once they reached it, Desta led David Hartman through the trees and stood at the edge of the ravine. "There," he said, pointing to the bowl-shaped depression before them. It was thickly covered with thorny vines and bushes.

"There?" David Hartman asked, incredulous.

"Yes. It looks like a jungle now. That was where my grandpa's remains and the coin were buried for many years, while his soul roamed the land, waiting for someone to come along and set it free. That person was me."

David Hartman shook his head. "Nobody in America would believe this story. Having met you and your family and hearing your stories, I feel honored and privileged to have seen this. Can I take a picture?"

"Yes, of course."

David Hartman took a couple of close-up and long-range shots, and one more with Desta standing in front of the trees.

Afterward they went across a creek and the Davola River to visit the warka tree where Desta first met his grandfather's spirit, under the invocation of Deb'tera Tayé, the shaman.

Then they headed to the grave of Desta's dog, Kooli. They passed by the spot where Damtew's goat had been killed by an animal, now memorialized by the eucalyptus tree Damtew had planted.

"This place holds my saddest of memories. It cradles the remains of my beloved friend and companion, Kooli," Desta said, staring down at the mound of rocks.

"Sorry to hear it," David Hartman said, after Desta conveyed the circumstances of his dog's death. The Ferenge continued, "Our pets can sometimes be the closest and best friends we ever have."

"Yes, Kooli was everything to me," Desta concurred. He wiped away a few tears.

Next they came to the place where, together, Desta and his sister Hibist sought comfort. "Here," Desta said, once they reached a clearing in the bushes back toward his parents' home. "This is where Hibist and I plotted, counseled each other, shared our secrets, laughed as well as cried. It was our retreat and hide out, away from the adults and our problems. This is one of my favorite places here."

"What a grand view," David Hartman said, as he pointed his camera and took several shots.

"Now let me take you to the happiest of my memories," Desta said, heading down to the field where he used to look after the animals.

"We'll be going to that shola tree," Desta said, pointing. After reaching it, he exclaimed, "This tree saved me from rain, hail, and strong sun when I was tending to the animals."

They walked around the gentle leafy tree. "This is also the place where our family's past and my future were unraveled. I spent a good number of hours with my grandfather's spirit, learning the details of the coin by making drawings of it on a goatskin he made bring, and having the image of the coin tattooed on my chest, by my grandpa's own hand. All the things I know about King Solomon and Shoshenq and the coin and box were also told to me under the tree. Much of this, including my travels in search of the coin, was predicted since ancient times. . . ."

David Hartman was awed. He walked around the mighty shola. He took pictures of the tree, a few including Desta.

When they returned, Abraham was sitting outside on the goatskins. Next to him were two cloth-wrapped objects and the scroll containing the coin images. After Desta and David Hartman sat down, Abraham turned to Desta and said, "I don't think it's a good idea to show the coin to anyone we don't really know. But it's your coin and your idea; I am not going to refuse. You're old enough to make these kinds of decisions yourself."

"Don't worry about it, Baba. It'll be okay."

With this, Abraham picked up the package nearest him. He unwrapped it and handed it to their guest.

For a few seconds David Hartman said nothing, his eyes and the silent

concentration of his face spoke the words he couldn't articulate. He seemed both enthralled and overcome. "So this is it, huh?" he said, finally.
He continued his inspection, examining one side and then the other, occasionally running his fingers over the channel reliefs.

"What do you think?" Desta asked.

"The letters are definitely paleo-Hebrew, and the coin looks very old, but without doing an in-depth examination, I can't determine how old. That's why I was hoping to take a picture of it."

"No, it's not necessary. We know how old it is," Desta said.

Abraham glanced at Desta. "Please tell him that we made the exception of showing it to him because he troubled himself in coming the long distance in this wet season."

"Can I copy down some of the information?" David Hartman asked.

After consulting with his father, Desta said it would be okay. With that he went inside and returned with David Hartman's knapsack for his writing things. David Hartman sat down with his notebook on his lap and sketched the coin—heads then tails. Next he transferred the cryptic letters individually, like they themselves were works of art.

Then the student of ancient artifacts copied and transferred the legends from the scroll. This done, he closed his notebook and thanked the father once again.

Abraham picked up the next package. Although his face was thoughtful and he seemed far away, he carefully unrolled the cloth. The object fell into his palm. Glints of light reflected brilliantly from its surface in the early afternoon sun. He shifted to Desta. "Could you ask him to take this watch and give it to the owner's relatives?"

Desta studied his father's face. "I don't think so. He is American. The watch supposedly belongs to an Italian, but I'll ask him."

Desta explained to their guest that the pocket watch came from an Italian soldier who was fatally killed during the Italo-Ethiopian war. Abraham had been in possession of it. But he had no use for it now and wanted it returned to the soldier's family.

David Hartman smiled. "I live so far from Italy and even if I came from there, I wouldn't know where to find the dead soldier's family. . . . Can I see it?"

After Abraham handed the watch to him, the Ferenge tried to read the inscription on the case, but with the afternoon glare, he could make out only a few letters. He flipped it open and studied the dial and the crystal.

"This is a beautiful watch," his said. He closed it and tried to decipher the fine printing on the back. He couldn't make sense of this, either. He tossed it in his palm as if to determine its weight. "This watch is gold."

Desta translated for his father. "I don't care what it's made of," Abraham said. "I just want it back with the soldier's family. I bet it's a special family treasure to them as the coin has been to us. And I bet they would be very happy to have it back."

After Desta bridged Abraham's thoughts and intention to David Hartman, their guest said, "This is what he should do. Bring it to the Italian embassy in Addis Ababa and let them trace the owners. That will be the easiest."

Abraham thanked David Hartman for his suggestion as he returned the watch to its cloth wrapping. "I think *you* should do that," Abraham said to Desta. "I've never been to Addis Ababa and I wouldn't know where to go."

"When the time comes for me to go there, I'd be happy to do it, Baba," Desta said.

With this Abraham wrapped the coin in its cloth, placing it in the box. He took the box and the scroll inside.

Since he met David Hartman, Desta's sense of travel and adventure had been heightened. During his upcoming two and half months of vacation, besides reading the books for the seventh grade, he'd hoped to fly to Washaa Umera, the famed cave of the spirits known as Zarrhs and Winds. Back in January Eleni had indicated she would take him there and he must be ready when she did.

With this idea in mind Desta told his father to bring his flying craft with him the next time he came to Finote Selam. Abraham said either he or one of Desta's brothers would bring it to him.

Desta had built the flying craft when he lived in Yeedib more than a year and a half ago, hoping it would be a source of freedom and adventure. He had plans to travel to the distant towns in the hope of finding a place to stay while he went to school. He also intended to use the flying equipment to fulfill his dream of following the setting sun to discover where it really went after leaving the world each day.

The next day, they rose early and got ready to leave. Ayénat had prepared three loaves for them to take as snacks, which Desta carried in a cloth pouch. David Hartman secured his writing things and the two bottles of Fanta in his knapsack.

Right before they left, the visitor from America asked to take a

couple of photos with Abraham. The host gladly complied and went inside
to change into his more formal clothes. He returned wearing a jacket
over his long shirt, his nice breeches, and a newer gabi over the rest.

In terms of height David Hartman found his match in Abraham.
When they stood side by side, they seemed nearly identical, at six
foot three inches, although Abraham would fall short of that mark if
measured from foot to skullcap. Abraham kept his salt-and-pepper hair
as a *gofferay*—combed-out halo—giving him an extra one to two inches.
David Hartman's was a brown pile, with several rioting arcs and curlicues,
which a comb and pat of the hand would lessen by an inch or so.

The architecture of their faces and profiles was nearly identical,
and as with their hair, differed in the texture and tone of their skin.
Abraham's was a smooth cinnamon, while David Hartman's had
turned rubicund bronze from the long day's journey in the sun.

David Hartman handed Desta the camera. The two men stood
side by side, the Ferenge resting his arm across Abraham's shoulders.
With the quilted green and brown landscape in the background,
Desta knew this was going to be a photograph for posterity.

First a test run. Desta aimed the camera at his subjects and
looked through the lens. Two sets of eyes—one pair deep brown,
the other two thunder blue—stared back at the camera.

"Ready?" Desta asked, raising his right hand as in benediction.

The pair rearranged their shoulders and shook
their heads a little before striking a final pose.

 Click!

"Now turn sideways," the cameraman commanded. With their curving
noses lined up against the eastern mountains, Desta engaged the shutter.

Click!

How about *facing* the eastern mountains? With David Hartman's arm
over Abraham's shoulders still, the pair looked like the best of pals.

Click!

"Thank you," David Hartman said, after they turned around. He smiled.

Ayénat stood by watching everything, intrigued.

"Ma, would you also like to have your picture taken with David Hartman?"

"Nooo!" she said vehemently.

When Desta asked why, she replied, "My soul was made for God,
not for that thing."

Desta jerked his chin, surprised.

"You're not taking a picture of just my body but also my soul," she said, clarifying her assertion.

Desta knew his mother was superstitious but this was something. He was almost certain Ayénat had never seen anyone take pictures, let alone a camera. How she came up with this idea was beyond him. Instead of asking her to elaborate, he simply said, "That is a new one, Ma!" He chuckled a little.

Now they were ready to leave. David Hartman shook hands with Abraham and thanked him profusely for showing him the coin and box and allowing him to copy the legends from the parchment.

Desta kissed his father first and then his mother. He picked up the pouch with the loaves in it and flung it over his shoulder. David Hartman did the same with his knapsack. The pair waved their hands and headed up the mountain.

Once they were halfway up the mountain, they turned and looked all around them. The sun was out. The wet season was festooned with clouds configured like small islands in the sea. The valley, a patchwork of freshly overturned earth on a field of emerald green, was stunning. "Let's sit and enjoy this beautiful place once more before we leave," David Hartman said. Then he took several shots with his camera. They also took a few photos of each other, with the valley as backdrop.

"You know what I regret?" David Hartman asked.

Desta's stomach tightened. "What?"

"Not being able to talk with your father. I wish I knew Amharic or he English. He just seemed like an incredible man—regal, courtly, and discerning. The whole time we were with him yesterday, I felt like he was talking to me with those sharp and intelligent eyes."

"Thanks for your kind comments about my father," Desta said, relieved that it was not about something they had forgotten. "You're not the first one to talk about my father that way. I see it all the time when we're out in public together, people treating him with so much deference.

"What's unusual about him is, he grew up fatherless. He had no uncles or similar father figures around to pick up those qualities from. He is just naturally like that."

"Yes. He looks as if he is from another place and time," David Hartman added.

"As we found out recently, his ancestors were once kings of Ethiopia,"

Desta chipped in proudly. "And the coin you saw used to belong to them."

"That explains it. He has ancient blood that makes him act and behave the way he does," David Hartman said. "It was an honor to meet him."

"Thanks. Although I didn't get a chance to ask him, I'm sure he was delighted to meet you. Like you say, he is very discerning. . . . We better get going. We have a long way to travel."

They got up and pressed on.

As they walked side by side, Desta said, "The pictures will be nice mementos of your trip here."

"I know. I can't wait to get them developed."

"I'd love to have a copy of each."

"I'll mail them to you."

Desta scratched the side of his face. "To where?"

"Doesn't your school have a post office box?"

Desta hated these moments, especially now, when he thought he knew so much more about the world. It troubled him when boys or adults cast sharp, sidelong glances and said things like "Have you not seen a *biyee*—marble— before?" "You've not eaten *timatim*—tomatoes—before?" So Desta became a bit guarded when he saw things he had not heard about or seen before. His unfamiliarity with David Hartman's question made him feel laughable.

He was thinking how to answer the question without giving himself away, when he heard himself say, "Post office box. . . ." It was not a question but an intoning of the words to himself. He held his breath.

"You know, an assigned box in an office where people receive letters and whatever someone sends them," David Hartman elaborated.

"Ohh! Our town doesn't have one," Desta replied quickly. He let out the air from his chest.

David Hartman stopped. So did Desta, as if his legs were tied to his companion. "How do people from far away send and receive letters and things?"

"I'll show you how my father sends and receives letters when we take a rest later. For now let's keep walking."

David Hartman shook his head a little and followed Desta. For a long while they didn't talk.

Desta occupied his head with *post office* and *post office box*, thinking of a simple way he would explain to David Hartman how his father sent and received letters.

David Hartman's mind buzzed with the new world he had visited and
the lives of the people he had been a part of. . . . He also thought of the
ways he could incorporate the information he gathered on the coin, box, and
parchment into his dissertation. He was both excited and daunted. He would
have to conduct research to confirm that the items he saw were authentic.

After they had walked for a long time, David Hartman glanced
at his watch. "It's one o'clock. Shall we take a break?"

"A good idea," Desta said, happy with the
suggestion. "I'm a little bit thirsty and hungry."

When they found a spot on the side of the road where there
were rocks, they sat. Each had one loaf and a Fanta.

"In the interest of time, I'll wait until we are on the bus to show you
how mail is sent and received here," Desta said, after glancing at the sun.

When they finished their Fanta and dabo, they rose and continued
walking. They arrived in Tilili as the sun was about to set. Luckily,
they found a bus with its engine running, ready to leave for Finote
Selam. They boarded at a quick pace and, squeezing in with other
passengers, were forced to sit separately. In Burie several passengers
got off, giving Desta and David Hartman a chance to sit together.

"Now we can breathe," Desta said, joining his companion in the adjacent
seat. "I can also show you the mail delivery system while we still have light."

David Hartman brought out his notebook, opened to a page
where there was no writing, and handed it to Desta with a pencil.

Desta quickly sketched a man wearing country garb. He created
a long and thin bamboo stick on the man's shoulder, the end tipping
down into one hand. He drew a sealed envelope on the split top of
the stick and penciled in a string, for holding the letter in place.

"This man is the carrier of the letter," Desta said, pointing with his index
finger. "He is not to touch or disturb it in any way while in transit. Only the
recipient can undo the knot and open the envelope. This, David Hartman, is
how our postal system works." He looked at the American for a reaction.

David Hartman shook his head. "What if he
were delivering more than one letter?"

"If two or three, I suppose he still could carry them on top of the stick,
but this almost never happens because the senders and recipients are often
individuals and don't exchange more than one letter at a time. The carrier can be

a family member or a hired person. And he can travel on horseback or on foot."

Then the Peace Corps teacher explained how the modern Western postal system works.

Desta thought it was great, particularly if it meant he could receive letters from faraway places, including America.

"Even though you have no post office in Finote Selam, we can still correspond," the Ferenge explained. "I'll mail a letter to my friends in Debre Marcos and they will forward it to you, and vice versa."

The idea of receiving a letter, addressed to him and from America, sounded like something he would look forward to.

"And then when you go to Bahir Dar, we can correspond directly because they have a post office there," David Hartman said.

"Really?"

"Really! I know Peace Corps teachers there I regularly correspond with."

Now Desta had one more reason to go to the town by the famous lake. "A year from this coming September, I'll be in Bahir Dar," Desta said chirpily.

"Good! They also have a telephone there, so we can talk occasionally."

"Telephone?"

David Hartman explained to Desta what that was.

Desta's eyes went wide. "You mean we can actually hear each other through a wire like that from so far?" He shook his head. He couldn't imagine or believe this report. What was disappointing was that he still knew very little about the modern world he lived in. He just couldn't wait now to go to the place where there was a post office and telephone.

"A year from September I'll be starting my second year in graduate school. Two years later, I will be returning here to do more research so that I can have all the material I need to complete the dissertation for my doctorate."

This was good news for Desta. It meant he would see his friend again.

When they reached Finote Selam, darkness had enveloped much of the town. Only the section of the road taken over by hotels was illuminated. There were bright, far-reaching lights from the hanging porch lamps.

"Since it's late to go home, why don't you come stay at the hotel?" David Hartman suggested. "I'll rent a room with a double bed." Desta liked the idea.

They ate their dinner at the hotel restaurant and went straight to their room. Exhausted and sleepy, Desta passed out the moment he hit the pillow, his clothes still on.

The following morning they rose early and ate their breakfast. Then they returned to the hotel room, gathered their things, and headed to the bus station. David Hartman needed to catch a bus for Debre Marcos.

Just before David Hartman got on the bus, they embraced warmly. He handed Desta his card. "Don't lose it," the teacher from America said. "It has all the information you need to get in touch with me."

"I still have the first card," Desta said, smiling.
"But it doesn't hurt to have another."

David Hartman waved his hand right before he stepped on the bus and waved it again as the bus swayed and roared off, leaving in its wake a trail of exhaust—one more physical evidence left of a friendship with a man from so far away, who taught Desta how the telephone and modern postal system worked.

Chapter 20

When Desta returned from visiting his parents with David Hartman, he found Alem and Aberra had combined their household. Because Alem's home was much bigger and secluded, they had decided to keep her house and rent Aberra's for a while.

Aberra's children were going to spend much of the rainy season with their mother, who lived in Debre Marco, but they were still in their new home when Desta arrived. The compound was now bustling with activity, and every one was ready to laugh or smile at the slightest provocation. Desta, too, felt eager to laugh and smile, but his joy was skin deep.

He quickly reminded himself that his arrangement with Alem was not to be forever. He would be staying with Alem and Aberra only one year, now that he would be skipping the seventh grade. The question was, with two kids in the house, would they still want Desta, a third? They had no obligation to him in any way. The obvious answer scared him.

He needed to make backup arrangements in case things didn't work out. For now he would stay put. Aberra's children, Mesfin and Adane, would go to Debre Marcos to be with their mother for the next two months. He would be the only one living with Alem and Aberra. His services as an errand boy would still be needed.

During the coming months he wanted to read the material for the seventh grade and he needed a quiet place to study. He also hoped to go to Washaa Umera, Eleni's abode, to meet her spirit friends and see the place. She had promised to take him there.

Aberra's children left. As luck would have it, his flying craft arrived a day later, brought not by his father but by Asse'ged, his second oldest brother.

It was great to see Asse'ged, despite Desta's mixed feelings about him. This brother, like most of his older siblings, had never spent any time with Desta. They saw each other only at family gatherings and sometimes when they crossed paths in their travels.

Upon reflection, of all his older brothers, Desta would have liked a closer relationship with Asse'ged. He always had a warm smile and kind heart. He certainly was Abraham's favorite son. Asse'ged didn't know the meaning of the word *no*. He was willing to do anything in his power for anyone.

Desta was pleased to see his brother's handsome, smiling face. Along with the flying craft, Asse'ged had brought on a donkey a sack of teff and a few kilos of butter for Alem to have during the rainy season, when the supply of food at the market was at a minimum. The grain and butter they took inside, the craft to the back shed.

The arrival of the unexpected largesse surprised Alem. She seemed pleased and appreciative, quickly inviting Asse'ged in and offering food and drink. He contentedly ate a dabo snack and sipped tella. Alem kept stealing glances at the guest, but he avoided locking eyes with her for any length of time. With his good looks and regal presence, Asse'ged was used to women's attention and advances. However, he was very much married and loyal to his wife.

Afterward, the two brothers went to town, leaving the donkey to graze in Alem's compound.

As they walked, Desta told Asse'ged all about his plans—that he would complete his education and find the second Coin of Magic and Fortune.

The brother was silent for a few seconds. Then he turned to Desta. "You know, you're like that one single bean that comes out whole and perfect in a pot full of cracked and overcooked beans. Of all our family members and the entire valley, you're the only one who is driven to do these things. Why?"

"If you had accepted a responsibility, you would, too. It's a promise I made to our grandfather's spirit. I am privileged to be entrusted to fulfill the ancient prophecy."

Asse'ged shook his head. "It just worries me that you're doing this all by yourself and so far from home."

"My life has been great here," Desta said. "It's the future that concerns me, like when I go to Bahir Dar in a year."

Asse'ged's eyes flared. "You're going that far to study?"

"Yes, I am. I'm not worried about the distance," Desta said. "But never seeing anyone familiar might bother me some."

It was true. When Desta lived in Dangila, Aunt Zere's children came on market day and he used to go looking for them whenever he had something important to send his father.

Here in Finote Selam Abraham came every so often to attend
court and there were people from Yeedib who were often in Dangila
on business. Nobody visited Bahir Dar. It was too far.

"I'll come visit you," Asse'ged said.

Desta knew he would. That was a comfort to him.

"You know what I wish, though?" Desta asked.

Asse'ged threw a keen glance at Desta.

"I wish you had the opportunity I did. Father always
talks about how you and Tamirat finished your church school
lessons in half the time it took other students."

"The timing was not right for me. Father had gone to fight
in the Italo-Ethiopian war. We had no one to farm for mother,
and there were no modern schools then. I'm no longer a farmer,
though," Asse'ged said, his fair skin brightening.

When he saw the surprise on Desta's face, he said, "I've become
a tailor. I saved up my money and bought a brand-new sewing
machine. I took lessons from Teferra and am doing well already."

"Since when?"

"Since about six month ago."

Desta thought for a few seconds. "At the rate the forest and soil have been
depleting, I think it's a good idea to start doing something else," he said.

"That's part of the reason. And the other . . ." Asse'ged trailed off.

In response to these dwindling words, Desta turned to his brother.

"Now that you're serious about your schooling, I'd like to support you.
Probably not a lot, but I could maybe give you a little money for your pens and
pencils and notebooks and clothes." He surveyed what Desta was wearing.

"I know your success will make Baba happy, and me and Tamirat
in particular, because you will make up for our failures. I know how
hurt Baba was when Tamirat abandoned his priesthood, probably
not so much with me because I had not gone far before I quit."

"I appreciate that," Desta said warmly. "What's always the hardest for
me is having enough cash to pay for my things. I can always get food from
the people I live with, but I cannot ask them to pay for clothing and school-
related expenses. As you know father doesn't have income unless he sells a
cow or goat. Even if he covers my expenses once, he cannot do it all the time.
So I cannot thank you enough if you are willing to help me in some way."

"I'll do my best. Having seen how much money Teferra makes, if I can make half that, I should be able to help with your spending money."

They had reached the center of town. They had walked leisurely. It was Asse'ged who invited Desta along with him. Desta didn't know what his brother's plans were, so he lingered a bit, waiting to see where Asse'ged intended to go.

"Let's head to one of those stores," Asse'ged said, pointing to the south side of the quadrangle. "I want to buy you a jacket and shorts."

Desta was a little overwhelmed. All this generosity from a brother he had never been close to and even at one point disliked! It was almost too much to handle.

The first store they stopped in didn't have clothes in his size. Neither did the second or the third. The attendant in the last shop suggested that they simply buy fabric and have the clothes custom made. "Most stores no longer carry premade children's clothes because they don't fit well," he said.

So that's what Asse'ged and Desta did—they bought charcoal-gray fabric, chosen mostly because it tended not to show dirt or stains. A tailor next door took the measurements and promised to have the order ready the next day. Having finally agreed on the price for the man's labor, they left.

A few doors down from the tailor's shop was a teahouse. Asse'ged suggested that they could go there and talk some more. They ordered two teas and two loaves, after sitting down on a section of bench along the wall. Desta learned that Asse'ged was getting divorced from his wife of twelve years and would be moving to Talia to live with a woman he planned to marry; it was a half-day's journey south from his current home, which was near their parents.

Sad to hear the news and disappointed that his brother would be moving away, Desta shook his head and stared into space for a few seconds.

"Don't worry, I still plan to help you and come visit you here in the next school year and when you go to Bahir Dar," his brother said when he noticed Desta was crestfallen, his head hanging.

"It's not that," Desta said, turning to look at his brother. "I'm just sorry for your children."

"Me, too. It was a marriage that was not destined to work from the start. I never knew anything about my wife. Our parents arranged the marriage, of course. But now I've found somebody I love and with whom I know I'll enjoy spending the rest of my life. Her name is Lulit." Asse'ged's face glowed as he was saying these things.

Then Desta learned that Asse'ged's oldest child, a boy, would be staying with their parents until after Asse'ged and Lulit got married. Asse'ged's daughter would remain with his ex-wife, who was soon to move back with her parents, a half-day's journey west.

"I can see that you are a lot happier now. I look forward to meeting Lulit sometime," Desta said.

"You will," Asse'ged said. "I'm thinking of coming to see you and possibly bringing Lulit before school opens in September. . . . Let's go back to the house for now. I'd like to visit with Alem and Aberra."

They left. On their way back to Alem's house, Desta started to feel uneasy. He was not sure how to handle this gesture of goodwill from his brother. Was he expecting something from him?

"Asse'ged," Desta said, "You've taken me by complete surprise and I'm very appreciative of the trip you made to see me and buy me clothes. Are you expecting me to pay you back for this favor any time soon?"

Asse'ged laughed. "The clothes I purchased for you today and the assistance I hope to offer you in the future are not and will not be a loan. As I mentioned earlier, I just want the one bean that came out of the pot whole to succeed," he said, cracking a grin.

"You're the only one of our extended family and from all the people of the valley who is pursuing a modern education. After Tamirat abandoned the priesthood, Baba was never the same. Since we both failed him, I wanted to make sure he has at least one son who will make him proud. If I support you and you finish your education and find the coin, I know Baba would be very thrilled. This is enough for me. I won't expect you to pay me a dime."

"You know what they say about a mother's womb, don't you?"

Asse'ged looked at Desta expectantly.

"They say that a mother's womb is like a leopard's skin. Children who came out of the same place can be so unlike each other. The difference between you and Teferra is an example. He wouldn't buy me tea when I used to see him in Yeedib. But you came all the way from our valley with my food supplies and bought me clothes." Desta had to fight the sudden rush of emotion. "All I can say at the moment is thanks so much, Asse'ged!"

"Don't ever mention to anyone the little things I've done for you. This way others may come forward and contribute something, too. You deserve to be supported."

Desta needed to hold on to his feelings and preserve the inner security and freedom he had found for himself. He had long given up on his family for support, relying now on his own efforts and the kindness of complete strangers who accepted him for who he was and what he could do for them in exchange for room and board.

Now his brother offered assistance out of the blue. Should he count on him, or even believe him? His reasons seemed noble and credible enough. Asse'ged's love for their father was boundless. Asse'ged often said he would rather his father bury him than vice versa. For him life without Abraham would be unbearable.

He quickly reasoned that Asse'ged's intentions were pure and gallant. Refusing to accept the gesture would hurt his brother. Desta would see what developed from this unexpected benevolence from his second-oldest brother.

"Teferra is like father," Asse'ged said. "They are both tight with their money. Me, I put people ahead of money."

"It's not just the tightfistedness that bothers me," Desta said. "It's his lack of feelings—that morose but otherwise handsome face.

"He grew up with grandma because she was alone," Asse'ged said. "I think he must've felt abandoned and unloved by mother. He cannot give what he doesn't have."

The next day, as Desta escorted Asse'ged out of the gate, his brother rested his hefty hand on Desta's shoulder and said, "*Ayzoh*— be strong—I know you'll accomplish your dreams. I'll do my part to be with you all the way." He gave him three kisses and left.

Desta struggled with his feelings again. He wiped a single tear from each corner of his eye and said, "This is what the desert must feel like when it receives a sudden shower from out of the blue sky." Asse'ged's hand, his words, and the gentleness of his voice were nourishing Desta to his marrow.

Desta had to treat this moment as it was—a passing desert shower. He would later linger on tender moments like this, but now he was forced to squirrel them away deep in the protective armor of his heart. Clinging to something that would pull at his heartstrings and interfere with his mission was the last thing he wanted.

When he returned to the house, he retrieved the parchment and headed outside. Sitting on the back bench he recited the legends around the coin images. As always, this exercise helped calm Desta's nerves.

IN THE AFTERNOON, Desta set out to collect his new clothes. To his disappointment he found the store locked. Then as he was about to turn around and
head home, he ran into the tailor. "Coming for your new clothes?" Bekalu asked.
"I figured you would be here by now, so I came without finishing my lunch."
Bekalu smelled of food. It seemed he had not even wiped his mouth.

"I appreciate that," Desta said, following Bekalu back to his store. Soon after
they stepped inside, the tailor brought out the custom-made shorts and jacket.

"I've tailored them a little bit longer and wider in the waist because
if you plan to keep these as long as the ones you're wearing, you want
room to grow into them." Surprised by the presumptuous tailor, Desta
asked for privacy to try the clothes on before he left with them.

Yes, they were slightly longer and wider, as Bekalu had indicated, but not so
much as to be noticeable. He paid the man, collected his old clothes, and left.

"What a nice-looking set!" Alem said, the moment
she saw Desta. "Did your brother bring them?"

"No, we had them made here in town," Desta said,
happy that Alem liked his new clothes.

"That is very nice," she said. "You look handsome in them."

Desta smiled and said, "Thank you."

Then he went out and dashed directly to the shed. He brought out his
flying craft, removed the cloth wrapping, and inspected it. It looked as new
as when he had left it. He knew Abraham would take care of it, and he was
pleased. Now all he had to do was wait for Eleni to show up one of these
days so they could fly to Washaa Umera. He had been looking forward
to this since she first mentioned it to him while he lived in Yeedib.

At night right before he went to bed, he neatly folded his old clothes,
remembering his Muslim friend in Dangila who help buy them. He said,
"Masud, I want to thank you for these clothes. They kept me warm and
protected, and brought to me a semblance of dignity. I'll keep them
with me for as long as I live. They will be reminders of your friendship
and kindness and generosity. May the world be kind and giving to you
as you have been to me." With these testaments of gratitude, Desta
wrapped the clothes and placed them in a carton near his bed.

Before he got under the covers, he thanked Asse'ged for his kindness
and generosity and for his efforts to reconnect with him. He thanked
God for his current living arrangements. Then he fell asleep.

Chapter 21

Desta needed the comfort and council of the warka tree to think about what his brother Asse'ged had decided to do on his behalf. The last thing he wanted at this point in his mission to find the second Coin of Magic and Fortune was an emotional attachment to a family member or someone else. He needed to protect his heart and his feelings.

He knew his vulnerability and weakness. His living arrangements now and in the future would never be secure.

Desta felt as if he were on a cross-road with Asse'ged. Having made up his mind to be self-reliant, he found the idea of being dependent on his brother for support disconcerting. But he also had to be realistic about the benevolence of complete strangers. If he had some critical financial problem, having someone like a family member to fall back on would provide the safety net he needed. Furthermore, Desta had never had a male relative he was close to. *It would be nice to get to know Asse'ged and experience brotherly love*, he told himself.

It was then when out of the corner of his eye, Desta noticed a huge bird descending from the sky. The astounding creature landed in the center of the quadrangle. When he turned and looked, he saw it wasn't a bird at all but Eleni. "I wonder what news she has this time," Desta said under his breath.

"Your aircraft arrived?" she asked, the moment she walked up to him. There was urgency in her voice, as if this was all she came to ask about.

"Yes, the other day."

"Can you meet here this coming Saturday before dawn?" she asked, eyeing Desta sternly. "I'd like to take you to Washaa Umera. We have found important information on the cave walls about the second Coin of Magic and Fortune."

Desta perked up. "Is this for real?"

"It's for real."

He wanted to go. Desta figured he had better make up his mind, quick. "Next Saturday, you say?"

*Desta flying over one of the rock-hewn
Lalibela churches, northern Ethiopia*

"Yes, next Saturday—before dawn. See you then," she said, looking over her shoulder. She flapped her wings and in an instant rose to the sky and vanished.

This is just the distraction he needed, Desta thought. He could get away for a day or two. For the time being he didn't have to think about his brother's proposal or the two children he would be living with when school opened in September. He was eager to go, even though he didn't know where he would be traveling or how far they would have to fly.

On Friday night, Desta told Alem and Aberra that he would be going away for a couple of days. He preferred they didn't ask questions or push him for an explanation.

Both said that would be okay and wished him a good time.

On Saturday morning after having his breakfast, Desta collected his flying craft from the shed and left. When he arrived with his aircraft at the warka tree, he found Eleni waiting for him.

"You're a little tardy this morning, Desta," she scolded, fixing him with her sharp eyes.

Desta mumbled an apology.

"We need to go to the top of the plateau. You will get a better lift there."

Once they climbed the hill, they stopped at exactly the place where Alem and he had perched looking down on the town a few months before. At the moment everything was quiet and gray, with just enough morning air coasting up the hill for a buoyant draft.

Desta was having butterflies. After he unfolded the craft and stood in front of it to harness the belts to his waist, his hands became clammy and he couldn't quite grab the hanging strips.

Eleni was busy with things she was unloading from a narrow blue bag. "Wait, wait, wait!" she shouted. She pulled a long pleated fabric from the bag and shook it. Then she opened it with both hands and fanned it on the ground. Very thin metal spurs ran vertically from the bottom to the top of the fabric, all in all presenting what looked like the wingspan of a bat or a giant bird.

"You're going to put this on first because the material is very durable," Eleni said, pointing to the limp fabric on the ground. "It's a reinforcement lining for your craft to keep it from flipping in a strong current."

While Desta stood in front of her, Eleni picked up the lining and harnessed Desta's body and shoulders in the hanging belts. Then she retrieved Desta's craft. After aligning the two spines, of both craft and the reinforcement material, she inserted the leather strips through the precut holes in the secondary material.

Then she tied the ends of the two materials all around. In the back, the lining had bunched behind Desta. Eleni said that this was fine because when the wind hits it, it would balloon and peg against the ridged pockets of the top wings.

"Are you nervous?" Eleni asked, noticing the film of perspiration on Desta's temples.

"A little."

He was more than nervous. He was actually scared.

"It's normal," Eleni said, "I'd be surprised if you weren't. Nothing will happen to you. Once we're airborne, you are going to enjoy it so much that you may not want to come down."

Next she covered his head with a soft wool hat, leaving room only for his nose and eyes. She gave him velvety leather gloves to wear.

Desta sighed deeply.

"No worries. Just stay focused and be positive."

"If I'm going to find that second coin, this is the kind of risk I have to take, right?" Desta said, trying as much to seed courage in his spirit as stating a fact.

"That is right!" Eleni echoed.

He took a few steps and leaned forward, trying to catch air and fill the balloon pockets with it. He reached across his chest and rubbed his fingers over the area near his heart. He took another deep breath and was about to kick off the ground, when Eleni shouted, "Wait, wait, wait!"

"Once we are in the air, stay right behind me at all times. That way you won't get tired and you will hopefully have minimal problems with turbulence."

Desta let her go first. Then he realized that there wasn't enough pressure built up. He was not ready for a lift. Eleni circled above him, bellowing, "Lean forward, lean forward more!"

As soon as he did, more pockets popped. The whole assembly wobbled for a bit and finally rose to the air.

"Follow me!" Eleni said.

Desta, still on pins and needles, kept his eyes on Eleni's feet and voluminous tunic. This was July and deep into the rainy season. The land below was cloaked in green, the peaks and ridges mere points and lines—and high above, mountains of a different kind rose to the sky like impenetrable barriers. Desta was concerned that if these clouds turned into rain, his balloon might become waterlogged and collapse.

He wanted to ask Eleni this question, but with the noise of the wind and her flapping fabric, he knew she wouldn't hear him.

"There is the Blue Nile gorge!" Eleni exclaimed, her eyes gazing down like an eagle's. Desta tipped his head. Brown water coursed along a timeless, serpentine path, edged on either side by rambling escarpments.

An hour later, Eleni stuck her left hand out and said, "That way over there is Addis Ababa. We're now in the province of Shawa."

Eucalyptus trees hugged the hills, whitewashed buildings, both tall and small, packed much of the sloping terrain and the flatlands below.

Cattle fields, clusters of villages, and freshly tilled farms adjoining level emerald green earth kept their eyes engaged for much of their way north. The air was now less turbulent, making their flight easy and enjoyable.

Farther ahead it was the earth that seemed to have its own turbulence. The land became craggy, shrubs and stunted trees mantling it. Hills popped up here and there, as if urgent swellings of the earth.

"There is Lalibela!" Eleni shouted out, pointing with her right hand.

Desta couldn't believe his ears. They were already in Wollo province and he was actually going to fly over the holiest of places in Ethiopia, the place where his grandfather was once supposed to be living, and the same place where his mother yearned to come and pay homage to God. As he was thinking, he glanced up and saw Eleni cutting right. "This is marvelous. I want you to take a look at this first!" she hollered.

But there was something wrong about the place. He looked around, trying to find the familiar tree-covered mounds, the country churches usually enveloped with a copse of trees, but there were none here.

"How long before we get to Lalibela!" Desta shouted at the top of his lungs.

"Look down," Eleni shouted back.

Below them were a number of huge crosses, seemingly resting on a pedestal and bound by open rectangular earthen boxes.

Desta shook his head. "I don't see any churches— only strange crosses!" he hollered.

"Those are the famed ancient churches carved out of the living rock in the shapes of crosses. Each one of those crosses is hewed from rocks whose insides have been bored into chambers for the priests to hold their masses."

Desta wanted to land and investigate these amazing sights, but Eleni turned around and shouted, "Let's move on! We still have a long way to go before we get to Washaa Umera!"

Now he was just as anxious to see the famed cave.
He whipped around and chased Eleni.

The terrain below them changed again. Rock supplanted
the verdure, shrubs the lush trees of Wollo province.

"We're now in Tigray province," Eleni announced. "A part of your country
rich with history since antiquity."

Desta looked down. His eyes saw rocks, sparse vegetation, low-lying
plateaus, and outcroppings that shot into the air like monuments, but his
mind was in his history book. *This is one of the early crucibles in which
the Sabean people, who crossed the Red Sea from western Arabia and
Yemen, merged with the natives to create a distinct race of people, who
became the Ethiopians. It is here where civilization that paralleled the
cultures of Mesopotamia, Egypt, and China flourished*, he thought.

As arid and desolate as it looked, there was a quiet, serene dignity
about the place, something akin to a wise old person who had seen and
been through a lot. Desta could feel what time had not preserved—
the dead men and women, children and animals that roamed the land
through the millennia. The life that used to be here: the marriages,
births, and deaths—people who had passed into eternity.

"We are just about to fly over the battlefield of Adwa,
where your countrymen fought and defeated the Italians in
1896," Eleni said. She had slowed so Desta could catch up to
her, and they talked side by side now without shouting.

Desta went back to his history lesson. *Yes, it was in this province
where the Italians, in their attempt to grab a piece of Africa like many
other Europeans had done, fought and suffered a disastrous loss,
making Ethiopia the only independent country on the continent.*

"Here in this province is the site of the famed monolithic
obelisks, the biblical Queen Sheba's palace, and Tsion—the Zion
church that houses the Ark of the Covenant," Eleni said.

He knew about these historical things, too. *I bet David
Hartman would be interested in them*, Desta thought.

Next they headed toward Eritrea, the fourteenth
province which sits above the other thirteen.

Rocky and wrinkled terrain spanned the greater part of their flight
path. As they went farther north, the land became more rugged, marked

by valleys and patchy green mountains. Cattle grazed in the lower plains, but as Desta and Eleni pushed onward, camels became prevalent.

Near the apex of the map, where Eritrea, the Sudan, and the Red Sea converged, there appeared a concentration of highlands, as well as deep valleys. The vegetation was meager in places, rocky in others.

"We'll be arriving shortly. Prepare to land!" Eleni shouted.

"Do you see that mountain?" Eleni asked, pointing to what looked like a big head atop a stretching spine. Desta couldn't see where it ended from their vantage point.

"Yes . . . where there seems to be a closed eye?"

"Indeed. That is the entrance to Washaa Umera."

"An eye for an entrance?" Desta quipped.

He began to pull the strings to his balloon one at a time.

He kept his eyes on Eleni. When she started to descend gently like a bird, Desta pulled more of the strings. He slowly tipped the bottom of the craft up with his feet to let air out of the pockets. This helped quicken his descent. He landed with a hop and forward motion on a dusty patch of earth. He was exhausted. His muscles ached, his face and eyes felt raw and sore.

With the efficient hands of Eleni, they removed his harness and neatly folded the craft.

He looked around, noticing two men driving a herd of camels near the south side of the mountain. On a path nearby a woman was perched atop a harnessed camel, cradling a toddler in her arms. Surrounded by household items—plastic containers, aluminum cooking pots, and various baskets—that drooped from the animal's sides, mother and child looked as comfortable as if sitting on a mountain.

A man, evidently the husband and father, was on a horse. There were a few household items dangling from his animal's flanks as well. They stopped and stared in the fliers' direction.

"Poor thing," Eleni said, throwing a quick glance at mother and child. "I wonder how long they have been traveling with that child over terrain and in a climate like this."

Desta shrugged. His mind and eyes were on the bulging mass before them.

*Washaa (cave) Umera, northern Eritrea:
home of spirits and ghosts known as Zarrhs
and Winds, and of the famed Hall of Records.*

Chapter 22

The gate of Washaa Umera indeed resembled a giant eye. It swelled from the front of the mountain. Loose rocks and light shrubs veiled most of the peak, but the lid of the eye was shielded with a membranous material, over which a thin layer of grass had grown. When Desta and Eleni neared the gate, the lid opened a crack and then closed just as quickly.

"Follow behind me," Eleni said. "I think the eye saw you first. That is why it opened and then closed. This southern entrance is reserved for us, the Winds. There is an eastern entrance to the cave adjacent to ours, also an eye, but that belongs to the Zarrhs."

"Why did the eye opened and then closed?"

"When someone approaches, they partially open the entrance to verify the individual. Once the identity is confirmed, they open it fully."

"I see," Desta said, looking up at the great sphere before them. With his folded and wrapped aircraft over his shoulders, Desta followed Eleni. When they reached a marked line about twenty feet from the bottom of the eye, the lid opened again. This time it slid upward, revealing a huge white orb, with brown and black concentric circles, marking the middle of its surface.

"Now we're good," Eleni said, stepping past the line with Desta in tow. When they stood within ten feet, the eye split open vertically from the center, and Desta could see a large anteroom.

"C'mon in," Eleni whispered, stepping past the threshold.

Desta, nervous and tentative, complied.

"Stay still—stay still—and don't be afraid," Eleni advised. "It's going to get dark in a moment before we get some light."

Both watched the two halves of the eye draw together and shut tight. A sliver of light seeping through the joining half-moons of the eye was the only source of illumination in this anteroom of the cave. When the lid slid down and completely covered the exterior of the oversized concave structure before them, the room turned pitch black.

Desta could hear the thumping of his heart. "Now what?" he asked, turning to Eleni. It was so quiet he was convinced she had left.

"We'll have light soon," she said finally.

The source was not apparent, but light did shine in the room, putting Desta a bit more at ease.

This room was shaped like a rotunda, three closed doors marking the back wall.

"Come, let's store your craft in that room," Eleni said, walking to the door on the far right. "I need to change my clothes, too."

Eleni took Desta's craft and closed the door. Nervous still, Desta paced the floor while waiting for her. It occurred to him that if the Winds decided to keep him, he had no way to escape. The gate was shut and he couldn't tell how to open it, although it appeared someone was controlling it.

Desta recoiled when he turned around and saw Eleni. "What happened to you?"

"This is what we all wear when we're in Washaa Umera. I'll tell you about our clothes in a minute. Are you okay?" she asked, holding Desta's eyes.

Desta hesitated. "I thought I was coming to a normal cave where the entrance is open and people can come and go. With gates and rooms, this place looks like a building."

"Yes and no—yes, because this place was once home to a great many ancient Nubians and Egyptians. No, because it's still a cave, with stone walls and firmaments, now inhabited by us, the Winds and the Zarrhs.

This news gave Desta the chills. That he was in this historic place where some of his ancestors once lived was both thrilling and frightening. *Were these Winds and Zarrhs his ancestors, too?*

"We'll be passing through that door in the middle," Eleni said, pointing to the now-closed portal. "Before we go, I need to explain something. First, as you can see I have assumed my natural ghostly state. Just about everybody you will meet here looks like me. Second, based on our longevity and terms of service, we take on any one of seven colors.

"Those who left their organic bodies in the not-too-distant past are red, the ghosts following them are orange, the ones after that are yellow, and so on—all the way to the seventh, or violet, color—representing the different shades of the rainbow. Third, there are thousands of Winds with those different shades of color. The representatives of each of the seven color groups are waiting for us in the room behind that door," Eleni said, pointing.

"Fourth, so you won't stand out like a sore thumb, I brought this for you to wear." Eleni handed him a gauzy red garment. "You can change into this in the room in the far left corner. It's our guest dressing chamber."

In the mirror on the wall, Desta was shocked by his transformation. Draped from head to toe in the red fabric, he now resembled the masculine version of Eleni.

"It looks good on you," Desta's host said, the moment Desta stepped out of the door. She smiled.

"I feel strange."

"You look fine," Eleni said, inspecting Desta's new costume. "No one would think you're not one of us. . . . Follow me."

She turned the door handle and opened the door. Seven ghosts, representing the different colors of sunlight, stood in a row. "Good afternoon!" they said in unison.

"Good afternoon, fellow residents," Eleni said.

Desta just bowed.

"Welcome to our world," the seven ghosts of the rainbow said, again in unison, addressing Desta directly.

"Thank you," Desta said, bowing again.

"My name is Rasmus," the violet Wind said, putting out his hand for a shake with the guest.

"My name is Desta,". He extended his hand.

Then Eleni introduced the rest of the ghosts in order: Ahmos, Wesret, Senbi, Setsobeck, Seth, and Kamoon.

Rasmus signaled to Eleni to step closer. The two chatted for a bit. "I think that's a good idea," Eleni said when she finished their conversation.

His companion turned to Desa and said, "One of the reasons we all wanted you to come visit was so you could view the Hall of Records, where information on thousands of historical events is kept, including that about the two coins.

"Like my comrade Ramsus suggested, we'll go there first. If we have time, we can visit our recreational facilities.

"We'll rest for a couple of hours first and then get up and go."

"That's a good idea," Desta said.

"Let's leave," Eleni said, tapping Desta's shoulder.

"Have a good time," all seven said in unison.

Eleni acknowledged them with a wave of her hand and a thank-you.

On the left edge of the reception room were two alcoves. Eleni led Desta to one of these nooks and said, "This is one of the thousands of dens the ancient Egyptians and Nubians used as their sleeping quarters. This alcove, which can sleep two to three people comfortably, has a feather-padded straw mat.

"I'll wake you in a couple of hours," Eleni said, and left.

Desta lay down with his ghostly clothing on and fell asleep instantly.

When he awoke, he didn't remember how long he had slept or what time of day it was. Eleni was at the entrance. "Slept well?" she asked.

"I feel well-rested," Desta replied, his voice rough and groggy. "Do you know what time of day it is?"

"I don't know . . . and it doesn't matter," Eleni said, smiling a little. "Here in our world, day and night do not exist."

Desta jerked his chin. "Why is that?"

"Because it's night all the time. . . . Let's head to the Hall of Records," Eleni said, motioning her companion to get up.

An orange-colored Wind opened the reception room's back door and Eleni and Desta stepped out. The Wind closed it immediately behind them.

"Omigod!" Desta gasped. "How are we going to find our way there?" He groped with his foot to feel the floor. It was rough and rocky.

"From here and until we get to the Hall of Records, it's going to be dark like this," Eleni said. "I know the way. Just follow me."

Desta had a queasy, twisted feeling in his stomach. He put his hand out in front of him. The only way he knew it was there was by drawing it back toward his face and touching his nose.

He inhaled hard, trying to screw up some courage. All he could feel was the dank, stale air passing through his nose and into his lungs. He coughed, hoping to expel the odor. It was no use. He drew in more of the fetid smell instead.

Feeling trapped, he decided to be obedient and follow Eleni's commands.

"I have a flashlight we can use. But so as not to disturb the animals and resting spirits, we'll be walking without it for most of the way," she said.

"Are there hyenas in here?" Desta asked, knowing that these nocturnal marauders sleep in caves during the day.

"Not in the deepest parts of the cave," Eleni explained.

Desta's heart eased a little.

"The path is straight. All you need to do is follow right behind me."

"How far before we get to the Hall of Records?"

"I don't know. We'll get there when we get there."

Desta could feel the uneven floor beneath the soles of his feet. It was deathly quiet. *Did this mean no other animals lived in caves—not even cicadas?*

The temptation to shout so he could hear his echo was great, but he didn't want to upset Eleni or, worse still, wake any sleeping monsters and be devoured by them.

They had only gone a few yards when Desta stumbled and fell.

"What happened—are you that afraid or is it that difficult for you to walk on this path?"

"I'm not used to walking in the dark. And I'd be lying if I said I wasn't nervous."

"Here, grab the end of this rope," Eleni said, extending a length of rope, the other end of which wound around her waist. "Now you should have no problem walking along with me."

Desta thanked her. He felt a little more secure. Whatever animal might come to attack him would also get Eleni. But do monsters eat ghosts?

He didn't know and he didn't bother asking his companion.

They had inched along for a while, taking slow and careful steps, when Desta heard the sound of water hitting a hard surface. Thin and remote at first, it grew louder as they moved farther into the black void.

"You're going to like what's coming up," Eleni whispered, lingering for a bit and turning her head back toward Desta.

"What is it?"

"You'll see."

"Yeah, right. I'll be stunned by what I see in this 'broad daylight' we're walking in," Desta replied sarcastically.

Eleni didn't reply.

Now the sound gave the effect of rain falling on a smooth, hard surface. When they got near it, Eleni took the flashlight and gunned it upward. Sharp, needlelike projections were arrayed along the curving roof like the jaws of a devouring beast. Some of the 'teeth' were white, others yellow to nearly transparent. Water dripped down along each of the projections and splattered on the granite slabs below. "Those are called stalactites. They are formed by acidic water that dissolves the minerals in the rocks above. It takes over one hundred thousand years for them to form."

Desta was trying to imagine how long one hundred thousand years was when Eleni shifted the light downward, pointing to mushroom-like clusters on the floor a few feet away. "Those are called stalagmites. They are created by the same process as stalactites, except the dissolved minerals collect on the cave floor."

Desta yearned to sit on a boulder nearby, stare at the formations, and contemplate what it meant to be one hundred thousand years old. The beam from the flashlight lent a mystical quality to the scene before them, the crystalline projections appearing as if lit from within.

They had not traveled far when they stumbled upon a number of other features—columns, twisted shapes, drapery-like forms, and structures reminiscent of straw—adorning the walls, ceiling, and floor of the cave along the footpath. Reflections from the flashlight dazzled Desta's eyes and fired up his imagination.

By now Desta had forgotten his fears. His mind was fully occupied by what he was seeing and hearing. From somewhere on their left came a thrashing sound. He felt a stinging sensation in his leg; it was unlike any he had experienced. Desta winced and let out a sharp, pained cry.

"What happened?" Eleni asked, throwing light on Desta .

"Something stung me."

"Oh my! You've been pierced with a porcupine needle."

Eleni moved the light around them. There she was, the beast herself, with her babies—a few feet away—angry and puffed up, ready to unload more of her ammunition into whoever dared draw near. The protective mother locked her eyes on the light for several seconds and then turned and scuttled away, her babies in tow.

Eleni bent down, grabbed the needle gently, and yanked it in one swift motion. Blood oozed forth. Desta sat down and pressed his finger on the punctured skin to stem the flow.

Several minutes later, they got up and continued moving. Eleni kept the light on.

They stumbled as they went. Desta heard the flapping of wings and high-pitched squeaks over their heads. Eleni shot the light upward to find a huge colony of bats clinging to the cave ceiling. Dozens of the bats were airborne and fluttering, clearly alarmed by the light and the sudden appearance of these nocturnal intruders.

The air here was thick with the pungent odor of bat guano. Desta knew it well. He used to smell it every time he went upstairs to the school's auditorium. It came from the dark corner beyond the stairs' upper landing.

Eleni quickly killed the light and they stumbled forward. Desta opened and closed his eyes, trying to adjust to the new darkness. It was then that his foot caught a rock and he came crashing down.

He shrieked. Eleni turned around with a start and cast the light on Desta. "Are you that blind?" she scolded, flustered by Desta's continued calamities.

"My eyes were not made for cave walking," Desta snapped.

Eleni helped him up. His knees were scraped and the heels of his hands burned from landing on them in the rough rocks. He rose and limped along, now fixing all his concentration on walking.

"The Hall of Records is only a short distance from here," Eleni advised.

"Is the hall pitch black like here?"

"Unless they did something special for you, the lighting generally is minimal, one of the reasons I brought this flashlight."

"Frankly, I had expected many more exciting things than we've seen," Desta complained.

"I'm sorry," Eleni said, "there has been a change of plans. I decided to skip what I had earlier thought would be a fun adventure for you. Considering the nature of your missions, I thought you would find the Hall of Records more valuable."

"What's in there?"

"You'll have to wait and see."

Desta fell silent.

"Here we are," Eleni announced, as the path began to narrow. She switched on the flashlight. Shallow stone steps reached up to meet a smooth granite landing, on the opposite of which stood a massive wooden door.

Eleni rapped her knuckles on the door. It immediately swung open. The same seven brightly colored Winds they saw the first time were standing by the entrance. Past them in the open hall there were hundreds of the same rainbow of ghosts—a surreal scene.

"Had trouble negotiating the passages?" they all asked in unison.

"Yeah, plus my friend had a few accidents."

Fourteen eyes dropped on Desta. "Sorry to see that he is scraped up a bit," they all said as one. "Glad you made it here nonetheless."

"This particular route is merciless," Eleni said.

"At nighttime it's harder," they said in unison.

The seven Winds sat down at a long table near the door, in the order of the sun's spectral colors. Eleni excused herself and sat down in a chair across from them. Desta remained standing by the door.

The seven Winds talked for several minutes. Desta couldn't make sense of what they were discussing. Afterward, Eleni invited Desta to join them, and he sat down in a chair next to her.

Rasmus spoke. "We invited you here believing that some of the information we have on these walls would help narrow your search for the second Coin of Magic and Fortune. We are equally interested in this coin. Let me tell you why:

"One, we want to know where it is. The last record we have of it is from 1915.

"Two, we want to see if you would be interested in bringing the shekel you own for us to see. We have been tracking the two coins and have heard about them from the Winds who once owned them, but we seven have never seen either coin.

"Three, we want to make sure the two coins are not united. Doing so would violate the basic principle of duality. These coins were not intended as mere carriers of King Solomon's message to his descendants. They are symbols of balance, as the Supreme Being indicated to the king. So trying to unite the coins and make them one goes against God's wishes."

The other six men studied Desta's face, as if looking for any external sign that would reveal his thoughts and feelings. Eleni just glanced at Desta occasionally.

Desta for his part needed to be cautious. He kept his feelings close to his chest. He didn't want to get into a debate with Rasmus, arguing whether uniting the two coins would be a violation of God's laws.

He simply said, "Thank you for your advice and suggestions. I'll certainly keep your wishes in mind. Regarding your desire to see our coin, I'll need to consult my father. I will communicate with Eleni once I have an answer for you. But now I'd like to see what you have in here."

Rasmus glanced at his companions and then at Eleni.

"We think it's a fair answer," they said.

"Eleni will give you a tour of the place and see that what you find here will be helpful to you," the violet Wind said. With this final word, all rose.

"We'll start from the left wall," Eleni said, pointing. She took a few steps forward, stopped, and turned around. "Like I mentioned before, this cave used to be home to many ancient Nubians and Egyptians. It's they who smoothed the walls and leveled the floors you see here. They had planned to use them as slates on which to draw objects and record events and stories. They got as far as covering the walls with their history and art, and then they just stopped. We don't know whether they died or simply left. We suspect it's the former, because toward the end of ancient Egypt's Old Kingdom (2686 B.C. - 2181 B.C.), there was a world-wide drought.

"The Egyptians have depended on your country's annual floodwaters that emptied into the Blue Nile. When the rains stopped, food supplies became scarce, causing people in the caves and elsewhere to perish. It was then that these caves became home for us."

"How long ago was that?" Desta asked, sorry to hear about the catastrophes.

"A little over four thousand years ago," Eleni replied, herself sad and thoughtful.

"To give you some more background about the caverns," Eleni continued, "They have two wings. One goes all the way to Israel under the Red Sea and the other to Egypt, the pyramids of Giza. As you might have read from your history book, the great pyramids at Giza were constructed during the Old Kingdom. The tunnel that connects these pyramids to the second cave passages was built at the same time.

"The spirits of a great many people who died in Africa, the Middle East, Europe, and much of Asia came to these caves to live and work as messengers of God and Lucifer. Many of the documents and illustrations you will see on these walls were created by them. We understand there are other caves elsewhere in the world that serve a similar purpose.

"You should know that we'll have no time to stop and study all the details we see on these walls. Many of them run from floor to ceiling, albeit the information is well-organized; the dates and authors of the work are meticulously recorded. I'll point out certain things as we go along, until we get to the area devoted to the two coins. Any questions?"

Desta had to stop and think for a few seconds. He had been dazzled by the colorful ghosts surrounding them. He really didn't hear all of what Eleni had said.

Instead of asking her to repeat herself, he simply said, "I don't have any questions at the moment, but I'm anxious to see what's written on these walls."

"Let's go then."

Thrilled, Desta trotted behind Eleni. Eleni's index finger stood at attention. "These works were done by the early dwellers—the Nubians and Egyptians."

The writing, illustrations, and sculpture before them were almost overwhelmingly beautiful: carvings of men with sticks in their hands, ostensibly engaged in heated debate; dog-, snake-, and bull-headed humans; scantily clad women sitting with flowers in their hands, facing each other in conversation; hieroglyphics—language represented by lines, birds, fish, bulls, circles, and eyes—similar to that found on the coin box and in the history textbook.

Then came writings and illustrations similar to the first set in some ways but different in other ways. Eleni said they were made by the ghosts who currently reside in the cave. These spirits, many of them dead Egyptians and Nubians, recorded important events in their lives and in the world. After this series, Eleni and Desta came upon works created by the souls of people from the rest of Africa, the Middle East, Europe, and parts of Asia who happened to end up in these caves.

The sheer volume and detail of the works were stunning. The walls on either side were completely covered in writings and art and seemed to go on forever. Desta lingered at every section he found interesting, and then he hurried to catch up with his host, twisting in and out of the vibrant crowd of spirits.

"At the rate we're going, we will never get to the area of the wall dedicated to the coins. We need to skip much of the Mesopotamian and African sections," Eleni suggested.

They scampered along until they got to the part of the wall that said simply Solomon's Coins, in large letters.

On the wall were two large map panels. Each map had hundreds of dots traced by a path and was covered with numbers, words, and the occasional phrase in parentheses. Both Desta and his companion studied the information on the panels for a few minutes.

Eleni glanced at Desta. "These maps illustrate the courses the coins have been traveling. The numbers correspond to the years and the words to the names of the owners," Eleni said, staring at the left panel.

"As you can see, the second coin is the most well-traveled and perhaps also the most elusive, as it has been to so many countries," she said, pointing with a fist the shape of a bird's beak. It has gone from Palestine to Iraq, Persia, Italy, France, many places in Russia, as far as the Mongols' border, back to Russia (but this time the central steppes), and then finally to present-day

Israel," Eleni said. She stopped as if something else had caught her attention.

Desta traced the details of the map with his eyes, following the sea of lines and dots before him. He let out a heavy sigh. Tracking down the second coin suddenly seemed an impossible task.

"See, from 1800 to 1915, it went from Baku on the western edge of the Caspian Sea to Odessa, and then from the west side of the Black Sea to Crimea, on the eastern side of the same sea. From there it went to Israel, the last known place, according to this map."

Desta thought about this revelation for a long time. His heart fluttered with excitement. That it came to its place of origin meant it was drawn to its sister coin—to the one his family holds in Ethiopia. Therefore, the second coin probably had come to Bahir Dar, the largest lake in Ethiopia. It was probably waiting for him there now. He nearly hyperventilated at the thought.

"Are you okay?" Eleni asked, surprised by Desta's behavior.

"I'm . . . I'm. I was just thinking about all this."

"I'm glad you found this information so exciting."

"We gathered the details you find on these maps from different wall drawings by the Winds and Zarrhs, who used to own the coins. That's why we don't know what happened to the second coin after 1915. We believe the person who owns it is still alive."

"I suspect so, and I think I know where they are living," Desta said with a broad smile.

"I know what you're thinking but . . . Let's move to this other panel. As you can see," Eleni continued, pointing again, "it traveled from Israel to Egypt and then to Ethiopia. It has stayed here the whole time—mostly in the northern part of the country—moving next to the center, Showa Province, and then north again to Gonder, the last two series of owners being in Gojjam, the northwestern province.

Desta moved his head, now even more convinced that the first coin ended up in his family's possession because it was preparing to meet the second coin in Bahir Dar.

At this point he felt he had all the information he needed.

Eleni noticed Desta's contented face. "You have it figured out?"

"I think so," Desta said, trying hard to keep his excitement under control.

"You know there is a lot more to see here. Just about every historical event and fact is recorded on the walls by the Winds who lived or observed them."

"I know," Desta said. "I learned that in my history class."

"Do you want to leave the caves then?"

"Yes," Desta said.

"We'll go in a different direction; it'll be much shorter and not as complicated. It's the only way out."

Desta studied the eerie and awe-inspiring sight of the beautifully colored Winds. Some sat on benches, others leaned on rocks, and still others stood and talked quietly.

"It's an amazing number of Winds you have here," Desta observed.

"At night they congregate here because the light we have in the hall mostly come from their bodies.

Noting the amount of light they gave off, Desta didn't doubt Eleni's testament.

They left through a side entrance and entered a new passage. The path was smooth and Eleni's flashlight made the journey easy. When they reached the last room before the main gate, they stumbled upon the same seven Winds, who were sitting at a table.

"What did you think?" The violet Wind asked.

"I think it was great!" Desta exclaimed.

"Eleni worked very hard on your behalf. Your search for the second coin has now been narrowed to Israel and perhaps the surrounding countries. It's not the whole world anymore. For all we have done for you, do you think you can show us your coin? Or can you at least show it to Eleni?"

"Like I said before, I need to consult with my father and then I'll let you know."

"Good! . . . No pressure."

"Thanks."

Eleni took a few steps toward Desta. "Because it's already past midnight, let's sleep until daybreak and then we'll leave," she said.

Desta agreed. She brought him a cot and set it up at one side of the wall. All the Winds left. Desta removed his ghostly clothes and set them aside. Then he fell asleep as soon as he hit the cot.

In the morning before the sun arced over the eastern horizon, they left. They flew into Finote Selam by midafternoon, landing in front of the warka tree.

"We'll do it again," Eleni announced. "On the next visit, we'll spend a lot more time."

"I'd love that!" Desta said, thrilled by the suggestion.

Desta and Eleni hugged and said their good-byes.

Chapter 23

A week before the New Year's celebration, Desta realized his fears. Aberra's children, who spent the rainy season with their mother in Debre Marcos, had returned. Aberra had brought them so that they could celebrate the holiday together and become properly acquainted with their stepmother before school opened later in the month.

Desta became the oddball in this small family unit from the start. Alem and Aberra thought that the brothers could share Desta's bedroom, and Desta could sleep in one corner of the living room, on the floor, "until suitable arrangements could be made," was how Alem put it.

Two days later the hope for "suitable arrangements" came in the form of Konjit, Alem's sister.

Desta was outside sitting on the bench and studying his history book. He was using his break to learn the seventh-grade material to prepare for his eighth-grade promotion. He glanced up and saw Konjit coming toward him. After a greeting and some small talk, she said, "I understand you're a good student, and I came to see if you would like to live with us and help my son with his studies."

Desta stared at her for a few seconds. "If Alem and Aberra permit it," he wanted to say, but this would have been stating the obvious. "Thank you for your offer, but I'll have to think how this would work," he said instead, placing the responsibility of making the decision on his own shoulders.

"Yes, of course. Just know that you wouldn't be asked to do much except small jobs here and there. . . . Dagim is fundamentally a smart boy. He just spends way too much time playing football.

"I'm a single mother running a business, and I just don't have the time to keep after him with his studies.

"Alem and I thought if you lived with us, you could be a good influence on him. And Dagim likes you very much, and I think you two could be happy living together. You could sleep and study in one of the old servant quarters in the back of the hotel. And there is very little noise back there—it's ideal for studying."

Desta looked away for a few seconds, processing Konjit's proposal. He
could feel her eyes on his face, anticipating the response she wanted to hear.

He turned and looked squarely at her. "Can you give me a few
days? I would like to come and see the living arrangements you're
suggesting and find out exactly the things I need to do for you."

"Come later this afternoon or tomorrow. We'll give you
a tour of the place." Konjit said, smiling. It was a sweet,
teasing smile. It made him feel safe and welcome.

Of course Desta was somewhat disappointed with his current host, but
he also understood her predicament. Things probably wouldn't have worked
out, even if Alem and Aberra wanted him to continue living with them. His
moving on was no doubt the best thing for all of them. Besides he would only
be staying in the town for one more year, before going to Bahir Dar. So he
should at least go and see the place and talk to Dagim and some more with
Konjit. And he should go there today before Konjit changed her mind.

"What time do you want me to come?"

"Come around three o'clock this afternoon."

THE SERVANTS' QUARTERS stood about fifty yards behind the hotel. It
amounted to a large, single-room shack, which was tucked away under some
trees. Whitewashed both inside and out, it had a tin roof and cement floor. There
were single beds on opposite sides of the room, and one large table in the middle, with four sturdy chairs. Behind this building was an animal pen where sheep
mostly were kept until they were slaughtered for the hotel restaurant. There were
also a few ewe kept for breeding.

Konjit said she had the little place built when she opened the hotel several
years ago. Having erected bigger quarters for her now-large staff, they used
it only for the occasional guest. Dagim lived at home. The idea was that the
two boys could stay in the shack while Desta tutored Dagim. Food would be
provided to them from the hotel restaurant and sometimes from Konjit's home.

Because Dagim, quiet by nature, didn't say much, Desta couldn't tell
whether he was anywhere as excited as his mother was about the idea.

Something suddenly occurred to Desta. "By the way," he said to Konjit,
"I'll be in the eighth grade when school starts. If it's your intention that I help
with Dagim's seventh-grade lessons, I may not be able to, since I'm skipping
that grade. I've been studying some of the courses on my own, but I might

not know the subjects well enough to help Dagim with the homework."

"No, he should be able to handle his own work. What I need is to have someone like you around to keep him motivated."

It was an arrangement Desta couldn't pass up. That he would have the seventh-grade course material within easy reach was going to be a bonus.

"And what will I have to do for you in the way of work?"

"Nothing much really. I may need you to run errands when my staff is occupied. That's it for the most part."

"In that case," Desta said, glancing at one and then the other, "I'll accept your proposal. When do you want me to move in?"

"Tomorrow if you like," Konjit said.

Upon returning from Konjit's place, Desta told Alem his decision to move.

"I'd love you to stay with us, but it just won't be practical or right with you sleeping on the floor. You're still part of the family, and we'll get a chance to see you. Now I don't feel so bad," his host said.

"No, you shouldn't feel bad. I thank you for the comfortable living situation you provided me for the last eight months. It's because of you this alternative arrangement came to being. So I am more than grateful."

"You're always so gracious, Desta. I'm glad you look at things as you do," Alem said. She rested her hand on his shoulder. When he looked up, she pulled Desta close and gave him a warm hug.

UPON ARRIVING AT his new residence the next day, Desta found the room cleaned, his bed made, and the table and chairs neatly arranged. There was also a kerosene lamp and matchbox on a nightstand near his bed. Desta felt more like a guest than a student who was getting room and board in exchange for work. He liked the isolated setting. Dagim had exactly the same arrangement on the other side of the room.

That night Dagim and Desta ate their dinner together at the table. Afterward, Desta took his English text and notebooks out of his borsa and brought them to the table. "Since part of my job is to help you with your studies, we might as well start tonight." Desta pulled his seat close to Dagim.

The boy glared at him. "Before school starts?"

"If you start now you will be ahead of the class. Plus you will learn it better if you do it at your own pace."

"Not tonight. Let's do it tomorrow when I am better prepared mentally."

"Fair enough," Desta said, putting away his notebooks.

Maybe he will be motivated if he watches me study, Desta thought. He went to his bed, lit his kerosene lamp, and began reading his history book.

Dagim got up and sat on his bed. He undressed and got under the covers. Shortly afterward he began to snore.

Desta closed his book and placed it on his nightstand. He lay down on his back, staring at the flickers of light on the ceiling and thought of ways he might motivate and inspire Dagim.

When he awoke at midnight, the rain was chattering on the tin roof. The sound was as hypnotic and lulling as the flames from the kerosene lamp, which cast graceful shadows on the ceiling. Then with a brisk and vigorous blow, he put out the light and went to sleep again.

Knowing that his living with Konjit was largely dependent on Dagim doing well in school, Desta spent days trying to figure out ways to interest the boy in his studies. Every evening Desta sat down with his books and read or wrote something, hoping Dagim would copy the idea and start doing the same himself. Although his mother had told her son to eat his dinner with Desta and study with him afterward, Dagim began eating at home and coming to the shack only to sleep.

His books collected dust on the nightstand. Even the woman who came to clean the room gave up on the books, allowing them to gather dust.

But there was a glimmer of hope. School would be opening in two weeks. Then Dagim would be forced to buckle down and study, Desta thought. He didn't want to push him now and create an unnecessary rift between them.

Chapter 24

Desta's brother Asse'ged kept his word and came to see him. But Desta couldn't help wondering whether Asse'ged kept his promise for their father's sake or was simply a man of his word—or perhaps he felt brotherly love for Desta and wanted him to succeed in his dual missions. It didn't matter which, but the fact that he came as he said he would made Desta feel important and extremely good. He was someone close who could say to him ayzoh once in a while. Someone Desta could think of when he felt sad or down. Someone who had a genuine interest in him and his pursuits.

"*Dehna neh*—you're well?" Asse'ged kept saying, after he kissed Desta three times on the cheeks.

"Dehna, *enantes*—how about you?"

They were standing outside the little house. The late morning sun was exuberant, smiling at the world, as were the blossoming daisies and forget-me-nots across the neighborhood.

Desta was just about to invite his brother to come inside when Konjit showed up. She bowed a little and greeted the guest.

"Konjit, please meet my brother. His name is Asse'ged."

The two shook hands, smiling warmly at each other.

"Come, I'll ask one of my girls to make coffee." She motioned for them to go to the hotel restaurant. She paused. "On second thought, let's have it here, where there's no distraction," she said. "We'll bring chairs and a table and set them here on the porch. That way we can have our coffee among the flowers." She left.

One of the hotel attendants brought a folding table with a floral plastic cover and set it up in front of the little house. Desta brought the chairs from inside and placed them around the table.

He invited his brother to sit. Shortly after, Konjit returned and took a seat directly across from Asse'ged. The visitor, courtly and dignified like his father, watched the next flurry of activity with interest.

A woman brought out, on a red plastic tray, three white cups, the tops overturned on three white saucers, and placed the tray on the table. A second woman came with a kettle of piping hot coffee in one hand and a basket of dabo in the other. She put these down next to the tray and flipped the cups over.

With all eyes on her, she lifted the kettle and carefully poured the coffee into each cup. Gray steam plumed out as the deep brown liquid cascaded into the cups, filling them to their brims. The rich aroma of the coffee and freshly baked bread had everyone swooning.

Then the woman picked up the basket and passed it around. Konjit, Asse'ged, and Desta contentedly nibbled their bread and sipped their coffee.

Asse'ged and Konjit talked about nothing in particular, and mostly she did the talking—asking questions, expounding upon them, and offering her opinion. She kept her eyes on Asse'ged, forgetting there was a third person at the table. His brother glanced away once in a while and Desta could sense his boredom. For his part Desta cleared his throat occasionally, hoping Konjit would pick up on the hint. The woman was instantly smitten by the visitor and seemed oblivious to all the hints, gestures, and facial expressions thrown at her.

One of the hotel attendants came and told Konjit that someone was waiting for her in the lobby. She excused herself.

"Finally!" Desta said under his breath, relieved.

"How did you end up in this place?" Asse'ged asked quietly.

Desta told him the situation.

"That's it?" Asse'ged said. "That's such a good deal. You shouldn't complain about the minor inconveniences you've experienced with your host."

Desta said he hardly saw her and that she was easy to live with.

"That's good," Asse'ged said. "Just keep to your studies."

At that moment Dagim entered the courtyard. He glanced at the guest indifferently at first. When Desta told him who he was, Dagim bowed a little and extended a hand to Asse'ged. He was wearing his new khaki jacket, cream-colored shirt, long pants, and leather shoes. He looked splendid. These were gifts from his father, who owned a clothing store in Debre Marcos.

Dagim went inside and came out a short while later with clothing rolled up in his hand. "I'm going to give these away to our neighbor's son," he said, flashing the wad of fabric before them. "I'll see you later." He walked off briskly.

Desta saw thoughts churning behind his brother's big eyes.

"Is this the young man you'll be helping?" Asse'ged asked, sounding surprised. He surveyed Desta from head to toe, as if seeing him for the first time.

"Yes," Desta said in a resigned tone of voice.

"But he is so big! Isn't he older than you?"

"So?"

"He should have advanced a lot more than you have. With all that he seems to have, he should be doing better with his studies than you."

"Sometimes things are not what you think. And age or wealth has nothing to do with how much one knows or how well one does in school," Desta said gravely. The problem he had with Dagim loomed before him.

"I just hope this works out for both of you," Asse'ged said, picking up on Desta's tone of voice.

"Don't worry, we'll make it work," Desta said cheerily now. He didn't want to be argumentative with his brother, who had made the trip just to see him.

The hotel people came and collected the dirty dishes. Desta and Asse'ged got up and went into town. They walked all over the place— sometimes holding hands, other times Asse'ged resting his big hand on Desta's shoulder. Asse'ged bought Desta his school supplies—half a dozen pencils, a fountain pen, inkwell, and several notebooks. He also bought him a beautiful blue shirt that Desta could wear under his jacket. Asse'ged suggested shoes but Desta refused, saying he was not ready for a pair.

By the time they returned to Desta and Dagim's little house, their feet ached, but they were both thoroughly happy. This was only the second occasion in which Desta and Asse'ged had spent an extended period together, and they were getting along like old pals.

In the evening Konjit sent one of her employees to invite Asse'ged to join her and a few other people for dinner at the restaurant. Desta spoke for his brother. "Please tell Konjit that Asse'ged appreciates the invitation but he needs to lie down for a while. He's exhausted from walking all day."

They had their food sent to them instead. Dagim had an added excuse not to come to the little house and study because he had lent his bed to Asse'ged.

After Desta put out the light, Asse'ged decided to share some family news.

"Desta?" Asse'ged said, with a bit of urgency in his voice.

"Yeees?" Desta replied, lifting his head.

"We're planning to get a dog."

"You are?!"

"Yes, we wondered whether you'd mind if we called him Kooli."

This news was a great surprise. Asse'ged never wanted a dog before.

182   Desta

In fact he never liked them even coming close to him. Desta remembered how he used to push Kooli away when the dog came to lick his feet.

Knowing this about his brother, Desta asked, "What changed your mind about dogs?"

"Since the last time I came to see you, I asked myself how I could remember you when you go far away on your search for the coin. We thought that having a dog called Kooli, like Baba used to, was one way of keeping you in our thoughts."

"Asse'ged, you're breaking my heart. That is very kind and sweet. But I'm not dead. It's not like you have to keep the memory of me alive. Nevertheless, by all means, call your new dog Kooli. I don't own the name."

"I know," Asse'ged said. "But we're aware how much your Kooli meant to you and how you refused to allow Baba to get another dog called Kooli."

"I'm honored and touched. Please go ahead and use the name for your new dog. I look forward to meeting him."

With that they said goodnight and fell asleep.

The following morning, shortly after they had washed up and come inside, one of the women from the restaurant came to invite Asse'ged and Desta to breakfast. She relayed that Konjit was waiting for them and would appreciate their coming as soon as they were ready.

"We're ready, aren't we?" Asse'ged asked, after listening to the urgent invitation.

Desta acknowledged he was and they could head over to the main building for breakfast with the hotel's proprietor.

"I was thinking of taking you to town to have tea and a loaf of bread, but this might be a sumptuous affair," Asse'ged said, humored by Konjit's overzealous entreaty.

Indeed it was. There was steaming bread piled high in a basket, injera firfir in a deep dish and scrambled eggs in another, as well as bananas, peaches, and oranges in a large bowl. They had the choice of coffee or spice tea in kettles ready to be served.

The presentation was equally impressive, suggestive of a romantic meal. White plates, red napkins, colorful coffee cups, and tall, curvaceous tea glasses, all arrayed on a tray at one side of the big table. And there was a woman ready to serve at the owner's slightest eye movement, hand gesture, or firm word of command.

Konjit rose and shook hands with Asse'ged, quickly asking

whether he had slept comfortably enough in a crude student's bed. The guest said all was well, that he slept rather soundly.

Konjit had arranged the sitting, putting Asse'ged on the right and at arm's length from her side of the table. Desta sat opposite his brother. The chair across from Konjit was empty.

The conversation was entirely between Konjit and Asse'ged. Desta was just as happy in the role of audience. Asse'ged was polite and respectful, yet at the same time controlled and circumspect. He kept his answers concise and avoided anything personal.

When breakfast was over, each told Konjit they enjoyed her food and thanked her for her gracious hospitality. Asse'ged offered to pay, but the host refused. It was her treat. The two adults shook hands. Desta and Asse'ged left after thanking Konjit one more time.

"How long did you say you will be with them?" Asse'ged asked after they left Konjit's compound.

"God willing only until the end of June," Desta said, happy that he would be finished with the eighth grade much sooner than he thought a year ago.

"She is very nice, but she is a bit too much," Asse'ged said.

"She is in love with you," Desta said, breaking into a laugh.

"I've run into women like her before. Please tell her that I've a girlfriend whom I love dearly.

"I almost forgot," Asse'ged said when they reached the bus stop. He reached into his pocket. "Here, I have twenty-five birrs you can use to buy small things. I probably won't see you for Christmas, but I'll be at our parents' for a few days before Easter. I hope to see you then." He handed the bills to Desta.

"Asse'ged!" Desta cried, taking the money. "This is more than even father has done for me. All the things you have bought me are certainly enough, but I appreciate this enormously. As you say, I can always use cash for little things." Desta pocketed the money and wrapped his arms around his brother's waist.

"I want you to continue to do well. In the eyes of our father you're making up for us older boys, and this means a lot to me," Asse'ged said. "I don't want him to die heartbroken." He tightened his lips, trying to hold in his emotions.

"Don't you worry about that," Desta said. "I'm bound by a greater purpose—carrying out my promises to Grandpa and fulfilling the ancient prophecy of uniting the two coins."

"Whatever your reasons—I can't wait to tell father that you have gone from fourth grade to the eighth in just one year."

"I have my work cut out for me. . . . Thanks for your visit and your support," Desta said.

Someone cleared his throat and Desta turned around. It was Colonel Mulugeta, the head of the police. Desta had seen him at Konjit's bar and in the street a few times. A tall, handsome man with glasses, Colonel Mulugeta said, "Excuse me," glancing at Asse'ged. "I need to speak with Desta for a second."

Desta winced.

"Something wrong, sir?" asked Asse'ged.

"Nothing's wrong. I just want to speak with the young man for a moment."

Desta walked off with the colonel, feeling nervous and uptight.

"If I can clear it with Konjit, would you like to come on weekends and spend an hour or two with my son? He needs help with his English. I hear you know the language pretty well."

Relieved, Desta said, "Of course."

"Good. I'll let you know when then," Colonel Mulugeta said, and walked off.

When Desta returned and told Asse'ged what the colonel wanted, his brother replied, "You're that in demand. I'm so proud of you." Asse'ged patted him on the shoulders.

The bus came, blaring its horn. Asse'ged and Desta strolled closer to the unmarked bus stop. They kissed, both brothers wiping away lone tears. The bus came to a halt and people spilled out. After the last passenger exited, Asse'ged stepped up into the vehicle. Suddenly glancing back, he waved at his little brother, who returned the gesture.

Desta turned around and headed to his dorm with a warm feeling in his heart.

Chapter 25

School opened during the last week of September. Desta's dream of starting the eighth grade was finally a reality. On registration day the guard met Desta at the gate. "The director wanted me to watch out for you," Sitotaw said.

Desta's stomach knotted. When a message like this came from a figure of authority, it wasn't a good sign. "What about?" Desta asked nervously.

"I don't know, but I don't think it's anything bad," Sitotaw said. "Follow me."

"Good morning, Desta!" Tedla bellowed affably. The director's enthusiastic greeting put Desta at ease. "Have a seat," he said, indicating the chair across his desk.

Tedla asked him a few questions about his rainy season break. Then he commented about Desta's remarkable academic achievements in one year—going from the fourth to eighth grade. He was the first to accomplish this feat and he and all the teachers were proud of him. "However," he said, "to ensure you have continued success, we thought we would put you in the seventh grade for the first semester. You will need to know the seventh-grade courses to do well in the eighth grade and beyond. If you are first or second in your class at the end of the term, you can move on to the eighth grade. This is for your own benefit and nobody else's."

The knot in his stomach eased some. Desta looked away, thinking of this news. All that Tedla said made sense, and he didn't want to be rushing through his elementary and middle school education. So as long as he finished the eighth grade by the end of the year, he was happy to start in the seventh grade now.

"Okay?" Tedla asked, after letting Desta finish his thoughts.

"I understand what you said. I definitely would like to know the courses for the seventh grade, at least those given in the first semester. So I am fine with your decision."

"Just make sure you rank first or second to prove to the teachers that you deserve the second double promotion in one year and that you can handle all the course work for the eighth grade."

"I'll do my best," Desta said, rising to go.

"You're way ahead of most students. You should be proud of yourself," Tedla said, patting Desta on the back as he escorted him out.

Desta saw the added advantage of starting in the seventh grade. Because Dagim would also be in the same class, he could be of better help to him, fulfilling his commitment to the boy's mother.

He went and registered with the seventh-grade homeroom teacher. Now he was as anxious about getting through the first semester and going on to the eighth grade as he was about making it to Bahir Dar a year later.

Classes started and Desta was immediately immersed in his studies. His focus was not only the courses for the first semester but also those covered in the second. That way it would be easier for him to handle all the course work for the eighth grade.

Dagim on the other hand was forever apathetic about school. He often didn't bother to study at night with Desta. He either never showed up at all or arrived late and went directly to sleep. He came to study with Desta only when he wanted the answers for their homework or tips about what to study a day or two before a test. Desta became increasingly frustrated and worried. His arrangement with Konjit would fall apart if she no longer saw the value of Desta to her son.

One evening he sat Dagim down and asked him why he was so disinterested in school. Dagim's answer shocked and disappointed Desta.

"There is no reason to put myself through the rigors of learning," Dagim said, "because when I'm older, I'll be managing my mother's hotel. And it's in the will of my grandfather that when Alem becomes old and dies, all the property and the country estates she owns will come to me and my brother." Then he thought for a second and added, "She may die sooner, in which case I'll move into her house, get married, and raise my children in that beautiful place." His face beamed at the very thought of this eventuality.

Desta rubbed his brow, trying to think of what profound statement he could come up with to shake Dagim out of this fantasy. Finding none, he simply said, "Don't you think you would still benefit from knowing things rather than not knowing?"

"What for? I don't plan to become a teacher or a judge or anything else. I'll be a businessman. I don't need history, geography, English—none of that." Dagim spoke with such conviction in his voice that Desta saw no need to continue the discussion. But he suggested one last thing.

"Look, for your mother's sake, why don't you at least finish the eighth grade. I'll help you as much as I can while I am still here. Okay?"

"That I would appreciate," he said. He rose and left.

Several days after Desta's last conversation with Dagim, Konjit came to ask how her son was doing. She was standing by the door.

Desta was lying on his bed, studying. He rolled over and stood up. "Please come and let's have a talk," he said. He pulled a chair out from under the table for Konjit. Then he moved to the opposite side and pulled one out for himself. He sat down and faced Dagim's mother.

"Your son is fundamentally an intelligent person," he said, fixing his eyes on Konjit. "I have helped him with his homework and prepared him before a test. However, at times it has been difficult to get him to be studious. He doesn't come here often except to sleep sometimes."

Konjit's brow furrowed and her eyes hardened. "He doesn't come here at night?"

"Not often, I am afraid."

"Where does he sleep then?"

"I don't know. I had the impression he was sleeping at home," Desta said. Realizing the potential feud that might ensue between Konjit and her son and eventually between Desta and the boy, he ventured, "You know Dagim has a lot of friends. It's possible he spends the night studying with them."

"I hope that is the case," she said, her brow relaxing a little. "That is why I want you here. So he has someone to study with."

Desta's lips tightened. He proceeded cautiously. "Konjit, I'll tell you something you're not going to like. I may even be risking the arrangement we have. But when you see the honesty in it and realize my intention is to help both you and Dagim, I believe you will think better of it," Desta said.

Konjit's brows sprang like a pair of crescent moons.

"I think Dagim has long been indulged. You and his father have been too lenient for too long. He has no concept of work or what it means to work hard for something. He has no dreams. He is not trying to achieve anything that would give him fulfillment or happiness. Unless you do something drastic, assume that you have a son who will be lost forever."

Konjit shifted in her seat. Her lips trembled. Desta's incisive remarks had cut though her conscience. She was surprised by this unexpected verbal affront from a young man to whom she had served as benefactor.

"Like I say, you can kick me out of your home tomorrow for speaking the truth and for something you'll come to see for yourself down the road. I say these things from personal experience and from what my father has taught me.

"My family in most respects is not poor. They have large properties and a great many cattle. My father long ago told me that I have to experience hardship to appreciate and value life. I think you should give Dagim less or let him work for what he takes. Then he can learn to have dreams and it will be easier for me to motivate and inspire him."

Desta might as well have entranced Konjit. "Well," she said finally. She held her lips firmly and stared down at the floor, but her eyes had gone inward, deep into her mind. She raised her face and turned to Desta, rocking her head up and down, saying, "I think you're right. His father has spoiled him more than I have, but let me see what I can do." She got up and headed to the door. Just before she reached the threshold, she turned around and said, "I thank you for your advice."

"You're welcome!" Desta said, surprised by Konjit's sudden departure.

DAGIM CAME EARLY to the little house that night. He was pensive and tense but not unfriendly. He lit his kerosene lamp, took his books out of his borsa, and began to read. He stayed up as late as Desta, until eleven o'clock. He said good night, blew out his lamp, and went to sleep. Desta echoed Dagim's salutation and actions.

After Desta's talk with Konjit, Dagim came to the little house to study every evening and he slept there afterward. He was neither friendly nor communicative. It was as if something was brewing in his head but he wouldn't say what. Desta had an idea what was wrong, but he was not going to confront Dagim. He decided to leave him alone until the boy was ready to open up.

Then it happened. One Saturday evening while Desta was lying in bed studying, Dagim came in. His brows furrowed and lips tight, he stood like a pillar in the middle of the room, as if debating something with himself. Suddenly, a look of decision swept his face and he walked toward Desta's bed.

"Tell me," he growled.

Desta had been watching him out of the corner of his eye. He turned around and asked, "Something wrong?"

"Why did you tell my mother I don't come often to study with you?"

"You mean to say I should have lied, Dagim? The truth is, until recently, you've rarely come to sleep here, let alone study. When you *have* come, you've refused to open even one book. Your mother offered me the accommodations here so you could have me as a study companion. She loves and cares about you, and has employed me to help out. I have to honor my agreement with her."

"Because of all the things you said to her, we don't have a good relationship anymore. You've brought nothing but misery to my mother and me."

"Misery?" Desta stared at Dagim.

"Yes!" he said vehemently. "Now she has hotel workers spy on me. Every day she wants to know what I've done and where I've been if I'm not here or at the house. And this nosing around in my life is really creepy and upsetting, and it makes me not want to study at all. She says she doesn't enjoy doing it either, but it's for my own good."

"Shouldn't you be grateful you have somebody who is concerned about your future?"

"Grateful?! For being pestered? . . . I know she wants me to do well in school, but I don't see the point. She says that when I get older, I'll be managing the hotel. Later, when Alem gets old and passes away, I'll have my grandfather's inheritance."

"It's a shame you feel this way, Dagim," Desta said, sitting up now. "No matter what you end up doing with your life, a good education would still be valuable to you. It could also be your path to freedom—from your mother, father, and your own fantasy about your future inheritance."

"Look," Dagim glared. "If you're concerned about your accommodations, you'll be safe so long as you cooperate and don't say anything to my mother about me. If you continue to be a problem to us, I could get you kicked out of here—or worse. Do you hear me?"

"Dagim, you started this conversation, and I'll let you finish it. I've nothing more to say. Perhaps tomorrow or the next day you can think about what I said and try to make some sense of it. If not, may you find meaning and fulfillment in what you hope to do with your life." With that, Desta returned to his history book and continued studying.

Dagim simply walked to his side of the room, got undressed, and went to bed.

Desta thought about the problem he was having with Dagim for a long time before he finally fell asleep.

Chapter 26

Several days later Alem showed up with a big smile on her face. "Guess what?" she blurted, the moment she saw Desta outside. He was still trying to figure out what might be the source of her mirth, when she continued.

"I'm pregnant!"

"Congratulations!"

"Thanks to you!"

"I had nothing to do with it."

"But you did," she said, "I was just telling Konjit and Dagim that if not for you, I would have remained a mehan."

"I don't really have that kind of power, and if you don't mind, I'd prefer you not mention to anyone else my incidental involvement in your good fortune. Please don't mention my name in relation to this again."

"Sorry," Alem said. I didn't mean to. I was just sharing the source of my miracle. I'll not mention you again."

"Thank you," Desta said and went into the little house. The last thing he wanted was to get involved in his host family's problems.

Later that evening Dagim showed up in an angry mood, his face cold and foreboding, like winter clouds. Desta was sitting at the table writing a letter to David Hartman. This was his first letter to his American friend, and he was excited to tell him what had been happening since they last saw each other. Desta had planned to send it through the Debre Marcos post office.

Dagim swayed a bit as he walked; it seemed he had been drinking. He stood in the middle of the room and stared at Desta. Darts of rage shot from his eyes.

"Something wrong?" Desta asked, trying to break Dagim's icy stare.

"I understand that you are the reason Aunt Alem can now have a baby."

Desta glared back at the boy, wondering where he was going with this. "Dagim, I'm neither Alem's husband nor have I the power to create life. . . . Even then, I'm not sure what the real issue is here."

Dagim paced the floor. He stopped and turned to Desta and hissed.

"You think you're clever to talk to me like that. . . . The issue is you! You have been the cause of the problems between my mother and me. And now you've ruined everything."

Then it occurred to Desta. Dagim and his brother were to inherit all the property Alem owned, assuming she remained childless. Now that she would have an heir, the two brothers were unlikely to get anything from Alem's estate. *This must be the cause of his fury*, Desta thought.

"You know, Dagim," Desta said. "This is exactly what I told you before. Never count on anybody or anything but yourself. Education can give you that freedom." Dagim was so wound up in his own rage that Desta could see he wasn't listening.

Dagim blurted out, "This is all your fault! Thanks to you, my brother and I will lose the properties that were supposed to come to us from Alem."

Realizing that nothing of what he was saying was going to penetrate, Desta rose from the table, picked up his writing things, and headed to his bed. He needed to lie down and think about what he should do about the boy and his living situation with him.

It was then that Dagim hurled a mighty punch at Desta, hitting him with all his power squarely in the back of the head, causing Desta to fall unconscious to the floor. Then he kicked and continued punching him, shouting and screaming at the same time. And Desta didn't have the wits about him to access the coin image on his chest to protect himself or make Dagim stop. But his tormentor finally wore himself out and quit of his own accord. He sat in a chair and gazed down at his victim, satisfied and relieved of his rage.

"I should've killed you for screwing up my future. But just let this be a lesson not to meddle with people's lives," Dagim spat out, gazing down at Desta disdainfully.

Desta lay curled on the floor for a long time. Then once he was fully aware of his surroundings, he dragged himself to his bed. The pain was excruciating. He hurt all over.

Dagim was now on his bed, too, staring at the ceiling.

Lying on his back, Desta stared at the air above him. He knew what he must do after daybreak tomorrow. The first thing was he must not let Dagim know how miserable he felt inside and out. He resolved to bear his pain as if nothing had happened to him. The second and immediate thing to do was to leave this place.

The night give way to dawn. Desta hoisted himself up with one arm and sat down, leaning against the wall. It was then that he realized the extent of his injuries. With the incoming sunlight, he saw blood on his legs and thighs, where Dagim kicked him. The back of his head, where the first punch had landed, was swollen.

He swallowed the emotion that had bubbled up in his throat. He had to control it. He had to be strong, even as his body was cut up and bloodied like this. Only by being strong could he go on with his mission. His past hardships were his bedrocks. Those experiences would give him the strength to get through this.

Dagim brought warm water with soap and said, "Here, go outside and clean yourself up."

Desta shot him a dead stare. "Why? So the world can't see what you've done to me?"

"You brought this upon yourself. . . . If you mention this to anybody, know that I *will* kill you."

Desta bit his lip and gazed at Dagim, believing that the cruel boy could carry out his threat.

"Mark my words," Dagim warned. "You go wash yourself before the water gets cold. If you don't, you'll have a hard time explaining to anybody who sees you. Like I said, if you start telling people what happened, you're a dead boy."

Desta thought for a few seconds. He would wash himself not for fear of Dagim's threat but to avoid the scrutiny of others.

Outside he washed all the parts of his body that had visible blood stains from the attack. Since he was terribly thirsty, he drank some of the water.

Desta returned inside after cleaning himself.

Dagim brought Desta a breakfast of scrambled eggs, firfir, tea, and a large chunk of dabo and set them on the table. It was the first time he'd brought Desta anything since they'd started living in the little house. "Mother is probably waiting for me to have breakfast with her, so I'll go. This is all for you," he said, pointing to the large amount of food on the platter.

Desta didn't say a word. He just studied Dagim, revealing no emotion.

"I want you to know that what happened last night won't happen again. I had to get out what was building in my system."

Desta ignored him.

"Go sit and have your breakfast. I'll see you later. I promise to bring something very special to make up for the anger you seem to be feeling." Dagim's acne-covered face beamed.

"I'll see you soon," Dagim said, and he left.

Food was the last thing on Desta's mind. He headed for the door.
He wanted to make sure the animal had fled the scene. He returned
inside and gathered his notebooks and writing things, putting them
in his borsa. He shoved a few items of clothing in a bag.

He had no idea where he was going. He just needed to be out of that little
house and away from the son of the hotel owner. It took him a long time to get
to the center of town because he was limping and had to rest several times. Once
he got there, Desta went directly to the warka tree, unloaded his bundle, and sat
on one of the benches. He needed to feel safe. Open spaces were his refuge.

His brain felt raw and dull. His battered body didn't take well to
sitting. So he slid onto the ground and sat at an angle, leaning against
the bench. He wanted more than anything to be overtaken by emotion.
He knew he would feel much better afterward. But Desta felt nothing.
His inability to feel had clouded his capacity to think clearly. What
should be his next step? Where was he going to spend the night?

He knew Alem's would be out of the question. She would want
to know what had happened and he'd be forced to tell the truth. Desta
didn't like to lie, but he wasn't ready to tell on Dagim either.

His other possibilities were his friend Fenta or Abraham's friend
Dinknesh. He didn't want to be dependent on Fenta and his family
again and he didn't want to reveal what happened to anyone.

He decided Dinknesh's home would be the
better place. There'd be fewer questions.

It was then that he saw Colonel Mulugeta out of the corner of his
eye. He lowered his head, hoping the colonel wouldn't recognize him.

"What're you doing there, Desta?" the Colonel said in a pitched voice.
He was walking up to Desta with another person, who shook hands with
the colonel and left, as if giving the colonial space to talk to Desta.

Desta wished the earth would crack wide open and swallow him.
Knowing Dagim and his mother were good friends of the colonel's, the
last person he wanted to see was this man, the head of the police.

"When are you going to come and help my son with his
studies—you have been promising me for some time now?"

Desta pushed up and sat on the bench.

"What were you doing down there?"

"Just resting."

"Is Konjit making work hard or is it Dagim?

"Neither," Desta replied, glancing up briefly.

"What are all those things?

"My books and clothes."

"Where are you going with them?"

"Nowhere."

"You're not living with Dagim anymore?"

"No."

"What happened?"

"We didn't get along."

"Where do you plan to live?"

"I don't know yet, really."

"You don't look so well, are you sick?"

"No. Not really."

"This doesn't make any sense. Have you eaten breakfast?"

"No."

"Let's go have some tea and something to eat. I meant to talk with you about coming to help my son on weekends, but I didn't want Konjit to think I was taking you away from her. That's why I hadn't asked you."

Desta felt trapped. He hesitated, not because he didn't want to go have tea with the colonel but to avoid having to explain the reasons for his departure from Konjit's house. He was finally getting his appetite back and could use some breakfast. Colonel Mulugeta was one of the few people he'd gotten to know when he ran small errands for Konjit and liked a lot. The colonel often smiled at Desta and said hello when they saw each other in the street or when the colonel came to the hotel bar.

"Get up. Let's go."

Colonel Mulugeta picked up Desta's Borsa and Desta his clothes.

They walked across the roadway to get to one of the teahouses. The colonel kept glancing at Desta as they walked.

"Is something the matter with your legs?"

"No."

"With your feet?"

"No."

Colonel Mulugeta grunted. The police chief dropped his eyes as Desta limped across the threshold of the teahouse and was disturbed by the sight of a streak of dried blood on the back of Desta's leg.

The Colonel ordered tea and firfir with eggs and dabo for Desta and just tea and dabo for himself. After they finished eating, Mulugeta said, "My job as a policeman is to correct as many wrongs as I can, and to make sure that the wrongs don't get repeated. If we as a society don't do this, people will continue to get hurt, robbed, or killed—which is not good. This means people who have been hurt must come forward and tell us what happened so that, hopefully, others won't get hurt in the future."

Desta had never heard anyone talk like this before. At home when his brother or father beat him up for some minor infraction, he didn't tell anybody. No one would do anything about it. And certainly nobody corrected Damtew the time he severely whipped Desta, not even Abraham or Ayénat.

It was reassuring to learn that there were people like the colonel who protected others from getting hurt. This meant that he had to tell the colonel what really happened to him. Dagim had assaulted him and threatened to kill him. To Desta the most important thing was to keep Dagim from hurting anyone else. The cruel beast's threats of retribution were nothing compared to this.

Desta proceeded to tell the colonel everything Dagim had done to him. Mulugeta recorded the details of Desta's testimony in a small notebook. Except for the occasional tightening of his lips and shifting of his head, the colonel gave nothing away as he wrote down the information.

After they left the teahouse, the colonel suggested that Desta could stay with him and his wife.

"I'd accept your kind offer but not today," Desta said. "I know of someone who could probably give me shelter for a week or so."

In the condition he was in, Desta didn't feel like going to the home of complete strangers. He had never met the colonel's family before and he didn't know how his wife might react to a boy who'd been through hell the previous night.

So the colonel escorted Desta to Dinknesh's small grass-roof house. Dinknesh winced when she saw Desta and Colonel Mulugeta outside. "Something wrong?" she asked, looking at Desta first and then the colonel.

"Nothing that would implicate you," Mulugeta said, smiling a little. "I'm Colonel Mulugeta, in case you don't know me. Desta thought you might let him stay here until he finds an alternative arrangement."

Dinknesh looked at Desta again.

The colonel continued. "It turns out that his previous living arrangements weren't suitable for him and he needed to move out. We believe the people he lived with have transgressed the law and I am doing my best to help him with that. As you probably know, his family is far away and there's no other place in town where he can go."

"Yes, I know his brother and father very well. They stay with me whenever they come to town. Yes, I'm happy to share our spare residence."

"Thank you, kindly," Colonel Mulugeta said. He handed Desta's borsa to her, patted Desta on the shoulder, and left, saying, "I'll see you tomorrow."

DINKNESH'S HOME had an unfinished earthen floor. High bunk seats arched around one wall and Dinknesh offered Desta one end of this platform as his bed.

The next day, before Desta had a chance to begin making sense of what had happened to him, Konjit, Alem, and Aberra arrived at Dinknesh's.

Konjit moaned. Alem shed a few tears, but Aberra just looked down with a stern and somber face. They asked a lot of questions, and many of them were whys. Why had Desta gone to the head of the police instead of seeking out Konjit or Alem, whom he knew better? And nobody seemed to believe that it was the colonel who came to Desta and encouraged him to tell the colonel everything. They all left blaming Desta. Konjit also blamed Aberra and Alem for bringing Desta to her home.

MORE THAN THE physical injury, it was the mental and psychological damage that was devastating to Desta. He missed a full week of school. He stayed awake many nights, fearful that Dagim would come after him. Sleepless at night, Desta slept through the day. He lacked the energy to do much of anything. Colonel Mulugeta came and took him to the clinic, hoping to find a cure for Desta's depression. They gave him prescription medicine to take. By the following week, he felt well enough to go back to school

The next weekend, Colonel Mulugeta brought Desta to meet his family. His wife, Fanawork—a fair, moon-faced woman with a generous mouth and almond eyes—peered down at Desta from a window as Colonel Mulugeta and Desta approached the house. When they entered through the front door, they seemed to surprise Muneet, a bay-colored middle-aged woman, who stopped in her tracks and shot her puffy eyes toward Desta. A frog-eyed, brown-skinned girl named Enatnesh was lingering by a tall table, putting away dishes.

The frog-eyed girl stood on a pair of long and spindly legs. She had reddish hair that shot out from her head like porcupine needles. As Desta later found out, these two women were the servants. Then there was a sleepy-eyed teenager called Menkir, who was standing against the wall, watching the women. A boy of about five, named Zelalem, sat on the threshold, fidgeting with what looked like little wooden cars.

Fanawork came out and offered Desta her slight if haughty smile. The others soon congregated around the new arrival, as if inspecting a new puppy before letting it loose in the compound.

Fanawork and Desta engaged in chitchat, talking particularly about his own scholastic achievements and how he might be useful to their son, who was in the fifth grade.

"Our son is doing okay, but with a little motivation, we know he could do a lot better. My husband has been telling me about how you might inspire him, and he definitely needs help with his English."

Desta said he could tutor him as needed and encourage him to study. "That is probably what Menkir needs—a companion to study with," Desta said, trying to lighten the mother's concern.

Colonel Mulugeta took Fanawork aside. After what seemed like a long time, the colonel signaled Desta to follow him to the side of the house, away from the family. "Fanawork and I feel that you would be a nice addition to our family and would like to have you live with us. If the idea appeals to you, you could bring your things as early as tomorrow. You and Menkir can share a room and study together."

Desta wasn't sure. He didn't feel drawn to any of the people, particularly Fanawork. That first brief eye contact through the window—and talking with her about Menkir. She left a metallic taste in his mouth. Of course, for someone who is nearly homeless, any accommodation is welcome, let alone the home of Colonel Mulugeta—the administrator of the country's laws. So Desta said, "Thank you. I appreciate your interest in my welfare and your continued effort in trying to help. I'm very grateful. I can come with my books and personal belongings tomorrow afternoon."

"Good!" Mulugeta said, genuinely pleased. "I have heard many good things about you from many different sources, and I want you to succeed in all your dreams."

Desta tipped his head and swallowed up his emotion.

"Come, let's announce your coming tomorrow to the rest of the household."

Once they got back inside the house, Colonel Mulugeta clapped his hands. He got everybody's attention and said, "Starting tomorrow afternoon, Desta will be our newest family member. You all treat him like he was your own blood brother. Ishee?"

"Ishee!" everyone exclaimed. The redheaded girl seemed less enthusiastic than the others.

Colonel Mulugeta escorted Desta to the gate. He patted him on the shoulder and said, "See you tomorrow."

Desta experienced relief and comfort as he headed to Dinknesh's home. He felt as if someone had picked him up from the dirt.

The following week Dagim was brought to the judge and given a three-month jail sentence.

Desta was relieved. He didn't have to worry about Dagim killing him as he had threatened he would. A year from now Desta would be in Bahir Dar and actively looking for the second Coin of Magic and Fortune. He'd make sure that nobody knew where he'd be attending high school.

As Desta prepared for his finals, he noticed something that disturbed him. He found it hard to concentrate on his studies, and his keen ability to retain information was nearly gone. He often had to read the material two to three times before he could remember it.

He took the final exams but wasn't sure how well he performed. To keep the double promotion he had been granted, he had to rank first or second in his class. If he didn't rank highly enough, his dream of going to Bahir Dar would be deferred for a year. This was something he didn't want to think about. Grade results and class rankings wouldn't be announced until after the Christmas break.

For the first time in many years, Desta longed to spend the holidays with his family. He was hungry for genuine affection. And he'd be able to see the two people who could give that to him: Saba and Asse'ged.

Chapter 27

At long last Desta would have shoes. Not that he needed them, or suddenly felt the desire to fit into the greater population of students that wore shoes made of a variety of materials—from canvas to leather to synthetic—but to honor and celebrate this utterly new gesture his mother, Ayénat, had extended to him at Christmastime.

At the end of his two-week stay, Desta was preparing to return to school when Ayénat asked if he might remain three more days. She wanted him to be part of the annual church festivities. Desta knew he would be punished if he didn't return to school on time. He told her no.

Having said good-bye to most of his family, Desta left. He was half a mile up the mountain when he heard a woman's desperate voice. He turned around. Scurrying up the hill was his mother. He stopped and fixed his eyes on her, thinking she might be carrying something he had forgotten. Desta walked back, "What is it, Ma?" Desta asked, when he was near enough to Ayénat.

She opened her fist and said, "If I give you these two silver dollars, would you stay and celebrate the church holiday with us?"

Desta's heart melted. He didn't care about the money. It was his mother's manner that was changing his mind—the sweet, tender way in which she spoke, her small eyes twinkling at him.

It was as if Desta had been lost in a vast desert with nothing to drink and suddenly stumbled upon a cool freshwater lake. It had taken sixteen years, but he had finally found a quenching oasis of love in his mother. This alone was cause for celebration. "Oh, my! Of course, mother," he said, without the slightest hesitancy.

"Many of my relatives will be coming," Ayénat said, unnecessarily. "I'm sure they would like to see you."

"At this moment, Ma," Desta said, now noticing the glaze of perspiration on her brow, "knowing it'll make you happy that I'm staying on is good enough for me—even without that gift in your hand."

Desta followed his mother back to the house. He was actually
looking forward to the Saint Mary's annual celebration. The people,
the activities around the house, the dances at the church, and the field
hockey games he would join in would take his mind away from himself.
After what Dagim had done to him, Desta had the feeling that some
vital force had been taken away from him. His concept of himself had
been dealt a severe blow. So far, sleep had been his only escape.

Desta went from rising at four or five in the morning to sleeping until noon
or one in the afternoon. "If your body wants to rest, let it," Ayénat advised.

He didn't tell anyone what had happened to him. There was no
reason for such a disclosure. No one could undo what had been done.
He wanted to spare his father and mother any unnecessary grief.

As he walked back with Ayénat, Desta thought about the two Maria Theresa
silver dollars, the precious underground currency nearly all country folks used
to transact business. He knew that for these people, cash was hard to come by.
To get it, they had to sell a sack of grain or an animal, like a sheep or goat.

The grain comes from six months of labor and the animals from one to two
years of extra feeding and nurturing. And Desta was sure Ayénat had saved that
money to buy something important. Therefore, her willingness to hand it over
to Desta was no frivolous matter. The money was an extension of her maternal
feelings—love she had kept close to her breast for so long. That day her love
found an outlet; it found Desta. And he finally decided he was going to take her
love, in the form of those two coins, and run with it. At the end of the three extra
days, Desta left for Finote Selam with Ayénat's two precious symbols of love

For Desta, the silver dollars he would use to buy his first pair of shoes
were significant for another reason. The silver coins evoked the two ancient
gold Coins of Magic and Fortune he was trying to unite. So *purchasing his
first pair of shoes with coins that had such resonance would be a good omen*,
he thought. Just as important was gaining back his self-respect. A new pair
of shoes would improve his image of himself, helping him to feel he was
as good as anybody else. Two days after he got back to Finote Selam, he
went to town with the silver dollars in his pocket. Getting there, he went
from store to store, checking the prices and the quality of the shoes.

The silver coins were exchanged for eight birrs. He finally found a nice pair
of canvas shoes, which were an affordable five birrs. And beautiful sky-blue
socks for one birr. He spent a total of six birrs and still had two left over.

He raced out of the store, half not believing what he just did and half terribly eager to get home so he could put the shoes on and walk in them.

"What have you got in there?" Enatnesh asked when she saw Desta go into the back entrance, his arm cradling his box of shoes.

He told her.

Her eyes widened and followed him inside the house.

Desta set the box down on the edge of his bed and opened it.

"You're going to put them on without first washing your feet?" Enatnesh asked. She was standing by the door looking in.

"Oh, yeah, right."

Enatnesh left. Desta went outside and came in after washing and drying his feet. He put on his sky-blue socks and canvas shoes, tottering across the doorstep to his bedroom and then into the living room, feeling for the first few minutes as if he had two left feet.

Then he went toward the kitchen house, where he could show off his new shoes to Enatnesh and Muneet. The two females came out and stood side by side as Desta romped in the backyard as if he were in a marching band. Left right left; he moved his hands in tandem with his feet. He felt important and special and as good as anybody who ever wore shoes; it was just what he needed now.

DESTA RETURNED SIX days after the second semester had begun. Therefore, he had missed the three-day cutoff for getting back to class and was prepared to receive his punishment. The penalty was usually administered by the homeroom teacher.

The seventh-grade homeroom teacher was not in the classroom yet, so Desta went looking for him in the hallway. He wasn't there either. But he saw Tedla, the director.

"What happened?" Tedla inquired, the moment he saw Desta.

"I am sorry I got back late," Desta began to say, when the director interrupted him. "You're—I was not referring to that. You finished third in your finals this time. That was what I meant."

Desta's heart skipped a beat.

"And it was only by a few decimal points that you missed being second and by one point you missed ranking at the top of the class," Tedla added, as if this unaware would help lessen the queasiness in his stomach. "We know that you had a personal problem last semester and it may have contributed to your lowered performance in the finals."

Desta felt numb. He didn't know what to say.
"What happens now?" he asked finally.

"You will have to stay in the seventh grade for all of the second semester."

Desta looked down, searching for a miracle in the gleaming tile floor. He raised his face and reasoned, "But you said the differences were small."

"Yes, but our rule was that you had to rank first or second in your class after your first semester in order to advance to the eighth grade. We don't make rules only to break them." Tedla was decidedly firm.

Desta realized there was no point in arguing with the director. As he turned to go, Tedla grabbed him by the arm.

"Wait, I'll make a different kind of exception—just for you," Tedla said. "I'll tell the teacher not to punish you for arriving late. As for your grades, what's done is done. Count your blessings. You're already way ahead of where you were a year ago."

That last line hit Desta hard. He simply said thank you and left. For most of the morning he kept shaking his head, as if something was in his ears, whenever he thought of his grades. But he didn't blame anyone, not even Dagim or himself, for the outcome. He accepted it as just another life experience, one of many he was destined to have.

Chapter 28

Sometime in early February, Colonel Mulugeta approached Desta and said, "I heard rumors that Konjit is making threats against you. So I had an idea. We could adopt you as our son. That way she'd likely back off and leave you alone."

The idea thrilled Desta. Colonel Mulugeta was like a father to him already, much to the chagrin of his wife, Fanawork. The colonel bragged about Desta to just about everybody and treated him like his own son.

"I'd be honored," Desta said.

"We could do it legally, through the court, but that takes too long and is too involved," Mulugeta said.

Having gone through the process once already, Desta suggested the Parents-of-the-Breast route, which would make Desta, for all practical purposes, his adoptive son. The colonel thought it was a brilliant idea.

Desta broached the suggestion with Abraham when he came for one of his court cases and his father thought it was a great idea. "Colonel Mulugeta has always impressed me as a very intelligent man and he has my highest regards," Abraham said. A person had to be smart first for Desta's father to treat him or her with respect. Having Abraham's blessing, Desta and Mulugeta went on with their plans for the Parents-of-the-Breast ceremony. Since a killing of lamb accompanies this event, Abraham supplied the animal and the ceremony was held in early March.

A priest conducted the ritual, Desta suckling Mulugeta's thumb three times each after he dipped it in honey and milk. Fanawork refused to be part of the ceremony. Desta was not hurt by or disappointed with Fanawork. He had felt her distance all along.

After the ceremony was over, Mulugeta came up to him and said, "Now I can tell Konjit that you've officially become my son." Shortly after, he added, "And she will get the message." He smiled.

"Thank you. Now I will tell all my friends in school that I have a new father. . . He is called Colonel Mulugeta. . . . and they will get the message," Desta said, grinning from ear to ear.

"I'm very proud of you. . . . I've not forgotten about
finding you someone to live with when you go to Bahir Dar
next year. I know finding that coin is important to you."

"My education and finding that coin are my eternal dreams.
So any effort you expend on my behalf with respect to these
two is something for which I'll be grateful forever."

"We still have a year, right?" Mulugeta asked.

"A year and a half," Desta replied sadly, his
missed opportunity suddenly hitting him.

"We have plenty of time. I will be making multiple trips
to Bahir Dar between now and then. I'm sure I'll find you
someone to live with so you can pursue your dreams."

"Thank you!" Desta said, his heart filling with excitement.

"May I ask you for a favor?" Desta said.

"Sure—"

"I ask that you don't mention it to anyone here in town
where I'll be going to high school next year."

"No worries—"

"For now, though," Mulugeta whispered. "You and I need to work
hard to bring Fanawork into our fold. Do your best to help Menkir.
Once the boy starts to get good grades, she will appreciate you."
Desta's new father patted him on the back and walked away.

The problem with Fanawork was she never stayed at home. She
had a Muslim friend named Medina, and they spent most of their time
together. In the morning the two had coffee together and they were mostly
off to the small Muslim community on the west side of town. What they
did there nobody knew exactly. It's rumored however that Fanawork
was consulting with Muslim *tenquais*—shamans—to stop Mulugeta
from staying out at night. Particularly upsetting to Fanawork was the
allegation that Konjit and her husband were often seen together.

To Desta the woman of the house was little more than a perfect
stranger. However, he continued to motivate and inspire Menkir,
Mulugeta's stepson, and the boy was showing marked improvement
with his grades. When this report reached Fanawork's ears, she smiled
at Desta more frequently, although she was still haughty and distant.

Chapter 29

Desta wanted to think it was the sweet love with which Ayénat graced him when he was home at Christmas that explained his desire to return again at Easter. But this wouldn't be entirely true. This time he was hoping to see his brother Asse'ged—another relative who had shown him unconditional love and devotion—one of few family members who'd rooted for his success. And he was the one relative promising to come visit him in Bahir Dar when Desta finally goes there.

Of course he was looking forward to seeing the rest of his family. This time he was going home mainly to keep a promise he'd made to Asse'ged. Desta had agreed to come early so as to overlap with his brother, who would be leaving before Easter. Asse'ged had planned to help in the construction of their parents' home, and would be there only a day or so before Easter. Afterward he was going to his home in Talia, a half-day's journey on foot.

Having told Mulugeta and Fanawork his plans, Desta left on Wednesday to arrive the eve of Good Friday. When he reached home, the shadows of the western mountains were climbing slowly but deliberately up the flanks of the eastern peaks.

A smattering of workers was still busy with his parents' new home. A man of his word, Asse'ged was there, too, evidently in charge of the project. He moved from one place to another, checking and assessing the work, making sure the job was done to their father's standards. Asse'ged knew Abraham as well as his father knew himself. Quality, detailed work was Abraham's standard.

Asse'ged's big eyes grew bigger, and his fair face brightened when he saw Desta. He dropped whatever he was holding and walked straight up to his brother. "You kept your word," Asse'ged said, pulling him into the circle of his arms.

"I'm glad you kept yours," Desta said, wrapping his own around his brother's midriff. Before he let go, Asse'ged bent down and gave Desta the customary three kisses on the cheeks.

Then Desta went around and received kisses from the rest on the

job site, even from those he had never met before. Abraham, who'd
just arrived, flashed his chipped tooth when he saw Desta. Desta kissed
his father's knee, and then Abraham kissed his son on the cheeks.

"I'm done for the day, Baba," Asse'ged said. "I want to visit with Desta the
rest of this evening. You all will have a full week with him. I only have tonight."

"Go ahead," Abraham said, with a toss of his hand. After dinner Asse'ged
and Desta brought their bedding to the new house. The walls had been
erected, but the structure was still roofless, allowing them to see the stars
and the moon. They slept side by side and talked until well past midnight.

Desta shared all the good things that had happened to him since
the last time they had seen each other, including Konjit's undying
hope to see Asse'ged the next time he went to Finote Selam.

"I'm sorry, I am the cause of her unfulfilled hankering,"
Asse'ged said, genuinely meaning it. "As I am a happily married
man, there isn't a chance in hell something will happen between
us. I think it's better we never see each other again."

"Don't worry about her . . . Incidentally, how was your wedding?"

"It was a great small, intimate affair," Asse'ged said.
"Involving just immediate family members on both sides."

"Sorry I missed it," Desta said.

"We'd have loved you to be there but we knew your
commitments and the distance you'd have to travel to come.
That's why we didn't even send you an invitation."

"I know," Desta said absent-mindedly. He was thinking about the
difference between Asse'ged and Teferra, the eldest brother. Teferra was
married, too, but he had girlfriends in just about every town he visited.

His love and respect for his second-oldest brother just kept growing.

Then Asse'ged talked about his new puppy, Kooli, after
Desta's beloved dog. "He's so much like your old Kooli used to
be," the brother said. "He follows me wherever I go, and he seems
to know almost about everything that goes on in my head."

Desta smiled broadly. "Yes, just like my Kooli used to," he said, looking
away for a second. "I think dogs know a lot more than people give them
credit for. They just lack language to tell you what they think and feel."

Asse'ged agreed and proceeded to tell him what he referred to as
his "secret plan." His wife, Lulit, and he were seriously considering

relocating to Bahir Dar in six months. "That way, when you go there for high school, you can live with us," Asse'ged said. "I don't ever again want to see you bouncing from one stranger's home to another's. And Bahir Dar is so far away and we have no relatives close to the city."

Desta was quiet, thinking and wondering whether fate had intervened. It could be that his inability to skip the seventh grade and finish junior high a year earlier was by design.

"That certainly would be a great help to me," Desta said finally. "I'll pray for your success."

"Part of all this effort is I want Baba to be finally fulfilled. You've been our saving grace, and I just want to do the best I can to see you succeed. That way we all win."

"May your dreams come true!"

With that they said good night to each other and went to sleep.

The next day Asse'ged left early, as he and Lulit needed to get ready for the holiday.

"I hope to see your Kooli sometime," Desta said, as he was just about to say good-bye.

"You'll be living with him," Asse'ged said, his handsome face brightening a little. "By the way, I have left some money and one more thing for you with father. I was not sure if you would arrive before I left."

Desta surged with emotion. He took two steps forward and wrapped his arms around his brother and said, "Thanks so much, Asse'ged!"

Asse'ged bent over and kissed his brother on the forehead. "See you soon."

Desta watched until his brother disappeared into the woods of the northern creek.

To Desta this dream of Asse'ged's was music to his ears. And he had no doubt about his brother's ability to accomplish whatever he set out to do. He was a brilliant businessman.

THE RITUALS OF EASTER celebration had begun. Each of the remaining four couples—Abraham and Ayénat; Saba and her husband; Tamirat and his wife; and Damtew and his wife—killed a lamb in own home. And each hosted a dinner party.

The morning of the third day after Easter, an unfamiliar young man arrived. Abraham and Desta were outside. Desta was perched on the fence, basking in the pleasing morning sun. Abraham was standing farther away, feeding one of his goats.

Desta didn't hear what the young man had said to Abraham.

All he heard was his father saying, "Era," in surprise. "Let me get dressed and we will go with you," Abraham added shortly after.

Desta didn't like Abraham's disconsolate face.

"What happened, Baba?" Desta asked, dismounting from the fence.

"Asse'ged is sick," Abraham said, and went inside.

Desta turned to the messenger. "Do you know what's wrong with him?"

"No. He is just not feeling well," the man answered with effort. His eyes revealing more.

"Shall I come with you?" Ayénat asked, following Abraham as he came out of the house.

"I don't know if it's anything serious. . . ." Abraham's voice dragged. "Tell Damtew to harness Dama and ride over to Asse'ged's," he added.

Late in the morning Damtew left with Dama. Late in the afternoon, Damtew returned riding Dama. He reported that Asse'ged was really sick, with a dangerously high fever. Damtew suggested that Ayénat go see him. "They said it all started with a tingling sensation in his arm, where Kooli had bitten him a month ago.

Desta was mystified. He was once bitten by his own Kooli, too, but he'd never had a tingling sensation or a fever.

Early the following morning, Ayénat and Desta left. They were later joined by Saba and Yihoon, along with Teferra and Tamirat. Damtew came along on the horse.

When Ayénat's party arrived at Asse'ged's house, they found the grounds swarming with people. The atmosphere was palpably tense, and fear seemed to hang in the air and was reflected in the eyes of the visitors. Desta had a queasy, sinking feeling in his stomach.

They tried to enter the house but people were packed in so tight there was no budging the door. Low, mollifying words were punctuated by muffled shouts and tussling skirmishes. Once the people against the door realized Asse'ged's mother was trying to gain access to her son, they parted like a wave. Ayénat, with Desta behind her, rushed into the living room.

The sight at the center of the room confused, saddened, and scared Desta, all at the same time. Three strong men had pinned Asse'ged on the floor. He kicked his feet free from the grips of one man and struggled to free his hands from two others. He begged for water, but no one would give him any. His eyes, when he looked straight into the crowd, appeared red and scared.

With the noise and commotion throughout the room and Asse'ged's shouting, Desta found it hard to ask the question that had formed and was lingering on his tongue: What had happened to his beloved brother?

He had seen women possessed by spirits act wildly, like what his brother was going through, but nobody pinned them down or ever heard them asking for water. And they would generally calm down after fifteen or twenty minutes. Whatever possessed Asse'ged wasn't abating. Just like everybody else around, Desta stood there helpless, worried, and wondering when and how this was going to end.

Then Asse'ged calmed down some. The men relaxed their hold and sat him up. His body was drenched in sweat. He asked for food. They passed to him what seemed like a soft piece of injera. "It's hopeless. He's incapable of swallowing," someone grumbled.

The moment they tried to feed him, he vehemently pushed the food away. At one point he buried his face in his hands as if in a deep thought. Later he aimlessly flailed his hands before him, and then randomly touched his face and head—confused and agitated.

The next wave of what had possessed Asse'ged surged through him, and he started to shake and hyperventilate. "Water, water, water!" he begged. The moment they brought it to him, he became violent and shouted, "Take it away, take it away!!!" Again he went into another series of spasmodic convulsions in which he screamed and attempted to get up and run out of the room.

The men who had been holding down a two-days sick and starving Asse'ged became overwhelmed by his power. His brothers Teferra, Damtew, and Tamirat stepped in to take over. Strong as they were, they had difficulty holding him down, too. One of the bystanders crouched and pressed down on Asse'ged's abdomen. Even so he wouldn't lay still. His whole body was shaking. He said things nobody could understand or associate with anything in the regular world.

Desta's heart sunk. Silent tears began to flow. He feared for his brother, Abraham, and their dreams.

"We cannot just keep him here," Abraham said, after calling immediate family members together. "We have to take him home. And then we must go from there to Dangila or Debre Marcos, where he can get proper medical help."

Because strong sunlight wasn't good for Asse'ged's illness, they decided to wait until the sun was low on the western sky before moving him.

Transporting Asse'ged home had its own challenges, however. He couldn't walk much on his own nor could he endure riding horseback for any protracted time. Luckily, his condition quickly became episodic. There were quiet moments in between the outbursts, and he could travel on foot during those times, a man supporting him on either side. They rested when the walking became too much.

Crossing a creek would send him into a terror so intense that people thought he might die just from the sight and sound of the water. The sounds of water they passed couldn't be controlled, but they could blindfold him to the sight of it, which they did.

It seemed a miracle, but they eventually reached Ayénat and Abraham's home, followed by a great number of people. Asse'ged continued to ask for food and water, but nobody was even trying to give him something to eat anymore.

The valley folks who had heard about Asse'ged's condition and knew that he was now at the parents' home came in great numbers, some bringing what they thought was a cure for the dog disease. Nothing helped.

The family decided to give modern medicine a chance. They prepared to take him to Debre Marcos Hospital the following morning.

By the wee hours of the night, Asse'ged seemed to have burned all the energy he'd had in him. He finally collapsed into a deep sleep. Nevertheless, he awoke at the crack of dawn. All those who catnapped with their clothes still on rose and got ready to take him to the hospital, hoping against hope for a miracle.

Abraham, Teferra, and Lulit were the ones who took him to the province's capital. A dozen men followed behind as far as the highway, where the four boarded a bus.

Chapter 30

Hope and the unknown have a magical ability to sustain and comfort people. Since Abraham, along with Teferra and Lulit, took Asse'ged to the hospital in Debre Marcos, all those at home waited patiently, trusting modern medicine would prevail and the patient would come home cured of his disease. As there was no known treatment for the disease in the small valley, the bigger world beyond the mountains had to offer a solution, they thought.

All awaited eagerly the outcome. Some slept only three or four hours a night. Others, like Ayénat and Desta, nodded off only now and again. Two days later, people who had taken Asse'ged to the city finally began returning, one by one, in the predawn hours.

Abraham arrived first, as casual and natural as could be. Desta and Ayénat had just gotten up. They searched the father's face for news. This was a safe approach. A question could elicit answers they didn't want to hear.

When Desta finally plucked up the courage to ask about his sick brother, Abraham said Asse'ged was in good hands, but there wouldn't be any details about his condition until Teferra and Lulit came back. The cryptic answer left Desta frustrated and anxious. It was like walking a tightrope. Ayénat seemed more discerning, but Desta didn't like what he was reading on her face. Several minutes later Teferra arrived, alone. Questions had become moot. Her face said it all.

The last to arrive was Lulit. She started crying the moment she stepped indoors. Ayénat rose and began crying, too.

Abraham got up and recited a poem he had composed in his head:

A son is dead
A son is dead
Heavy the woe on a father's head
A man taken in his prime
Robbed of life
By the implacable sands of time.

A young man named Asse'ged
A revered son—good and true
Bitten by his beloved dog
In whom rabies grew.

He sunk his teeth in Asse'ged's arm
And shook it rough and raw
Before the rabid cur
Let loose his rugged jaw.

The dog's deadly mouth did foam
A froth so thick and vile
Poor Asse'ged succumbed to shock
After only a short while.

Who can know a father's grief
A damaged heart with no relief
A father's hell, a father's pain
A wound no potion could ever tame.

His heart beat faintly
Baba sped him on
To the nearest town
To save his son.

On to town they traveled
A hospital's help to seek
Desperate for the healing power
Of modern medical techniques.

But before this could happen
Woe, lack, and alas
The shadow of the darkest Death
Over their path must pass.

For poor Asse'ged was so sickened
His consciousness starting to stray
His breathing sporadic and weakened
The man himself draining away.

He died in his father's arms
Finally able to rest
Free from pain and harm
Secure in his baba's breast.

But Hell would not release Baba
No, Hell wasn't done with him yet
Hell blew on his aching heart
With its icy cold breath.

In a final insult to injury
No money for a private grave
Asse'ged's body in the ground
A stranger alongside he would lay.

Baba received Death's message
Death seemed to be poking fun
Baba couldn't afford a private site
He was stuck with a two-in-one.

A son is dead
A son is dead
Heavy the woe on a father's head
A man taken in his prime
Robbed of life
By the ignoble sands of time.

Soon the twelve or so relatives who had been at the house awaiting
news of Asse'ged's condition began weeping. A few of the closest relatives
gathered in a circle, singing mournful songs, following the leader.

Abraham led the group in the first few songs. Those outside the circle formed a chorus, harmonizing with the lead singers.

Desta wandered away and sat in a dark corner, watching and listening to the mourners. Asse'ged's death meant he would never see his beloved brother again. He would not get the chance to live with Asse'ged in Bahir Dar while attending high school, as they had planned. Desta's life was suddenly turned upside down again. As sad as he was to be without Asse'ged, he was sadder that his brother's life was cut so short and that his three children would no longer have their baba. He felt these things but not deeply enough to be completely overtaken by his emotions.

Tears would have been the true outlet for his grief, but Desta had never been able to consciously shed them over a person's death. So he simply sat there watching Ayénat and Lulit wave their hands, thump their chests, and wail in grief. Although some of the more powerful songs of mourning, about the stinging cruelty of death, got to him, he shed not a tear.

Desta heaved and sighed several times, as if he might break down and let loose a torrent of tears. But he couldn't cry, no matter that the air was thick with grief, as Asse'ged's friends and loved ones honored his passing.

Dawn was breaking, pale as the belly of a donkey. Abraham took his sons Damtew and Tamirat aside. He told them that each must climb the mountain on either side of the valley, horn in hand, and announce the death of their beloved brother, Asse'ged. With this announcement, they must invite the members of the community to attend the funeral service at the parents' church.

The sons did as ordered.

Even before the sunlight came down from the western mountains, people started arriving. Desta knew Asse'ged was popular and well-loved by the community, but he didn't really understand the extent of his brother's fame until he saw the scores of people pouring in from all directions to attend the funeral.

Around midmorning, the procession began. The crowd followed behind the family to the church, some of the women still openly crying. Desta's sister Hibist, who had remarried, lived far away and didn't know of her brother's death. She was the only one missing.

Desta had heard that one way he could honor his brother, if not with tears, was by wearing a rope around his waist. So he found a strong rope and wrapped it around himself again and again, piling circle upon circle.

As was the custom, some of the mourners rubbed their faces until they bled as an expression of love and devotion.

Men rubbed their foreheads and women their cheeks.

Asse'ged's ten-year-old boy, Fikray, like Desta, wore a rope around his waist. They walked behind the family as the crowd headed to church. Once there, Desta and Fikray, their faces dry as sand, watched and listened as the people wailed. Desta occasionally rubbed his forehead with the hem of his gabi.

Some of the close relatives wept uncontrollably. Others sang mournful songs carefully written in advance as well as composed on the spot, going around in a circle, signifying the cycle of life.

Then there were those who judged and gossiped. They whispered to each other about one thing or another, but as Desta found out later, the lion's share of criticism went to Ayénat, who exhibited such exaggerated grief that the onlookers were dumbfounded: she rubbed her cheeks until they were streaked with blood and her wailing, which knew no end, rose above all the rest. "She has so many children," these gossipers had said, "just one child is gone and she descends into madness?"

"What might she do if she lost two or more?" others had said.

"God knows. She might actually kill herself," someone suggested.

Desta was also bothered by his mother's histrionics, but for a different reason. This was a woman who seemed devoid of love in life. How could she show so much of it in death? Where had she hid all this love and devotion for Asse'ged? Why had she not shown even a fraction of it while he was alive?

Yet her love for the God she barely knew was boundless. Desta shook his head, perplexed.

Before the conclusion of the memorial service, a procession of priests came out of the church holding umbrellas over their heads, large crosses, and their books. They stood before the crowd, saying their prayers first and then chanting hymns that asked God to provide Asse'ged a beautiful place of rest and forgive him his sins. Then one of the priests read from a book that a younger man held open before him.

This activity was followed by a solemn chanting, again, asking God to offer Asse'ged a place that was comfortable, where he would not experience pain, sorrow, or suffering but everlasting life and peace.

Then they sung melodious hymns of grief and consolation, petitioning God to grant the deceased peaceful rest and eternal life. There was some more reading and chanting, and once again, a soliciting of the Almighty to let Asse'ged rest in a place of light, renewal, and joy.

This marked the end of the ceremony and the crowd gradually dispersed. But Asse'ged's family continued on.

The family members were all quiet now, their faces pale and smeared with tears. It was time they made themselves available to whomever would come and offer their personal condolences. People paid their respects so that they could count on reciprocal behavior when their time came.

At the end of the day, Desta's forehead was raw where he had been rubbing and rubbing it. But still no tears came, even after soliciting his chest for assistance.

Having spent long hours on his feet and under the strong sun, Desta turned in early, going to the loft where he would not be disturbed.

When he finally awoke in the morning, he was drenched in sweat. His nightshirt was so wet with it that he could literally twist and squeeze it out. He had never experienced anything like this before. Then he realized what was going on. Maybe not his eyes, but his entire body had wept for his brother.

Chapter 31

Desta's world felt fractured in a hundred places. It had been too good to be true. Asse'ged had taken the role of father and had been giving him money for his school supplies. As well, he had eased Desta's worries about where he would live when he attended school in Bahir Dar. He was to live with Asse'ged and his wife as he studied and searched for the coin. It had all vanished like a dream.

Now he would have to find his own way to support himself and pursue his dual missions. The greater world will be his saver. One thing he could not allow: self-pity or blame, although he deserved self-judgment. He should have known better than to become attached to anyone. He had long discovered this when he lived in Dangila and he should have kept *that* faith and belief. This clearly was just another lesson. He would take it as such.

School would be starting in three days. Desta needed to leave. When he told this to Abraham and Ayénat, both said he should wait and get at least a couple of days' rest. He also should take time to mourn Asse'ged's death with the family. Then he could go back to his studies.

The last thing Desta wanted to do was stay and mourn a brother he had no power to reclaim. "No. I must go today," Desta insisted. "That's by far the best thing for me now."

Abraham relented. Desta gathered his things and got ready to go.

"Wait here a little then," Abraham said, and left. Minutes later he returned with a package.

"This is for you," Abraham offered, handing Desta the package. "Asse'ged had brought this with him when he came to help with the building of our house a week ago." Desta unrolled the fabric wrapping to find a beautiful new set of clothes—a blue shirt, a jacket, and a pair of trousers. He was speechless. He put them down and then picked up each piece, one at a time, holding each up against him, imagining how he would look.

"Asse'ged said he had them made so that you could dress like that boy you're teaching," Abraham said.

Desta stopped and gazed at Abraham, not seeing him but suddenly finding himself taken back to that awful night and to what Dagim had done to him.

Abraham was busy unwrapping another piece of cloth, saying, "And this money," counting seven Maria Theresa silver dollars, "is to buy leather shoes like that boy's, and with the rest you can get your school supplies."

Desta shook his head and dropped his gaze to the ground. Suddenly, his eyes brimmed with tears. How he missed his brother just then. More tears surged through him, pushing the first wave over, giving way to those that followed. As teardrops streaked and stained his face, he couldn't help but focus on another irony in his life. While he couldn't shed one salty drop in memory of Asse'ged's death, Desta was weeping untold rivers of tears for his brother's kind deeds.

"Thank you, Baba," Desta said, glancing up at his father. "Asse'ged has had a way of reaching deep into our hearts."

"That's why everybody loved him," Abraham said, his eyes moistening. "Me, I didn't just lose a child, but also a friend, a confidant, and a reliable messenger. Asse'ged never knew the word *no*. It was always *ishee*."

A steady stream of emotion in the form of wet tears flowed down his cheeks.

"Look, Baba," Desta said, "you have wept enough in the past two days. And I think I have done my share in the only way my body knows how in this situation. The best we can do right now is to go on—and I need to go on."

"I know," Abraham said. "It's just a shame to lose so beautiful an individual at such a young age."

Desta began gathering his brother's gifts.

"If you insist on going, at least come inside and get something to eat first."

"Yes, I need to go, Baba, because I will spend the night in Yeedib, and tomorrow I'll need to get up early and head to Finote Selam. I only have one day to prepare before school starts."

Ayénat was too exhausted to do anything. She had slept through much of the morning. She prepared Desta's breakfast from the basket of food the people across the Davola River had brought.

After he ate, he said good-bye to everyone there, gathered up his things, and left.

As soon as he set foot on the road, he told himself, *I've two choices. I can either be happy and strong or be sad and cry, thinking about my lost brother. I choose to be happy and strong. These are the attitudes I must maintain to reach where I am going in life.*

This decision set the tone for that day and the next, as Desta arrived in Finote Selam.

Chapter 32

When he reached Colonel Mulugeta and Fanawork's home, he found the gate
locked. Desta was taken aback. He had never seen it locked before because there
was always somebody in the house.

Each house in the row along the main road was nearly identical. Desta
thought that he might be at the wrong one. He stepped back and scanned
the houses on the right and then on the left. Although the houses were
painted different colors, they were each framed by the same wooden fence.
Colonel Mulugeta and Fanawork's home had a slightly greenish cast. Desta
stood right outside the residence. Thinking the whole family had gone
to town, including the two servants, Desta sat on a log by the entrance
and waited. The sun was now rapidly setting, but still no one came.

He walked up to the gate of the house on the right and knocked. There
was no answer. He rapped his knuckles several times and heard only a dog.
It managed a couple of unenthusiastic barks and fell silent. Then Desta
went to the house on the left and knocked. An old man with brilliant silver
hair came out. He said he didn't know of the family's whereabouts.

All was eerily quiet. Desta had to do something or he would not have a
place to sleep come nightfall. Fanawork's best friend, Medina, lived several
houses down. Desta walked to Medina's home praying that she was not gone
as well. Medina's home had no fence. The front door was ajar. Desta was
relieved. If anybody would know where his adopted family was, it was Medina.

Anxious and nervous, Desta knocked on the woman's door. Medina came
to see who it was, furrowing her brow when she saw the visitor. His knees
buckled a little. *This is weird*, Desta thought. "Good afternoon, Medina. Do
you by any chance know when Colonel Mulugeta's family will be back?"

Medina scratched her neck and stepped out. "They have moved," she said.
With so many thoughts in his head, Desta wasn't sure if he heard her right.

"What did you say?"

"They are gone to Bichena—transferred."

Desta recoiled. He stood motionless, not knowing what to say. He hoped Medina was joking.

She wasn't. She was as serious as anyone who breaks such news can be. "They are gone," she repeated. She seemed to enjoy saying it.

"Did they say anything to you about me? I had gone home for the Easter break."

"I know," Medina said, in a cold voice. "To answer your question, no, they didn't say much. They left your things with me."

"But . . ." his mind went blank. He covered his face with one hand, trying to gather his thoughts. "But they were my new family."

"They are no longer, I guess," the little woman said callously. "Do you want to take your things now?"

"At the moment, I don't even have a place to sleep, so can you keep them for a few days?"

"Only for three more days," Medina said firmly.

It was not his things that were a concern to Desta. He had a much bigger problem. He wanted to ask Medina more, but he didn't really want to find out more. He'd had enough. The way his adoptive family departed, without so much as a simple note, begged no more questions.

He simply said, "Thank you. I hope to see you in three days."

He turned around and walked back in the direction of the former home of his new Parents-of-the-Breast. Head down, mind whirling—he kept going. At first he thought this had to be some big joke orchestrated by an elf who derived fun from the misery of others. Occasionally, he looked around to see whether the creature was there and laughing.

If not an elf, maybe it was God, who was having a grand old time. He lifted his head to the sky to see whether the Good Man up there was laughing. He didn't see God. His world was now completely empty. The brother who had just begun showing him so much love and care had been taken away. The family who had adopted him as their own was now vanished from his world. Where could he go? Who could he possibly live with?

School would start the next day. Of all the people he knew in town, the only person he could comfortably ask for shelter for the night was Dinknesh. He could stay with her for a day or two, paying for his own meals. After that he had no idea.

A permanent place he didn't have. His only option was to follow the family.

He was hurt that they hadn't left a note for him—apologizing or telling him
to come—but he came up with a million excuses for them, wanting to think
the best of Colonel Mulugeta and his family.

They were probably in a hurry. They didn't have writing material
at their disposal. They forgot. They thought it would be too far for
him to come. They didn't know whether he would be interested in
going that far away from his blood relatives. . . . Convinced that it
was probably one of these reasons, Desta talked himself into going to
Bichena. They were the closest family he had in Finote Selam, having
adopted him as one of their members. He would follow them like an
abandoned dog who goes looking for his master, following his scent.

When school opened, instead of going to his classroom, Desta
went to the director's office and got his transfer certificate. He knew
he was going in the middle of the semester and there was the chance
the new school in Bichena might refuse him admittance. He would
have to convince them somehow. If they could make room for the
family's other boy, he was sure they could make room for Desta.

He borrowed a bag from Dinknesh and put all his clothes in it. He put only
his essential notebooks and books into his borsa. The rest he left with Dinknesh.

He learned from the bus driver that it would take two to three days to reach
Bichena. There was no direct bus service to the town, and he might have to spend
two nights on the road. So he took a shuttle bus from Finote Selam to Debre
Marcos, where he spent the night with students he knew. To make traveling
easier, he bought a bag for his clothes. Early in the morning, he took another
shuttle, from Debre Marcos to Dejen, a town near the famed Blue Nile gorge.

"From here on," the shuttle driver told him, "you're on your own. You
either walk, which means it will take you all day, or you can hitch a ride
on one of the *chinet mekinas*—trucks. In Dejen, Desta asked the driver of
every truck that stopped about getting a ride to Bichena. Most coming from
Addis Ababa or going the other way were passing straight through.

The next day, around noon, he finally found a truck going to Bichena. It was
packed with goods and Desta would have to sit atop the bulging load and hold
on with his bare hands. The load was covered with canvas and crisscrossed with
rope. He scampered up the side of the truck with a sturdy rope and perched right
in the middle of the load like a bird. The driver tossed him his bag and borsa,
which Desta tightened and secured with the loose end of the harnessing rope.

"Hold on to the ropes," the driver advised. "It can be rough and windy up there."

Desta actually felt he was on top of the world—the way he always felt when perched near the peak of a mountain. It was just that this mountain was moving, and he had to rein in his worries that it wouldn't fling him like unwanted goods.

The driver cranked the ignition and the truck roared to life. It growled, emitting a harsh metal on metal sound, and then lurched forward. Desta was tossed back and then forward, scrambling to hang on to the rope. For a couple of miles they drove on the main highway, and then they cut east onto a road that was little more than a footpath, created from the wear and tear of the many trucks traveling along it. On this ungraded road the truck jerked and rattled badly, causing Desta to cling to the ropes for dear life. The cold highland wind bore into his face and the battering and jostling of the truck was taking its toll on his body. But whenever the road smoothed out, Desta enjoyed the view of the rolling hills and green fields—an unusual sight in the dry season.

After three hours of this punishing ride, Desta reached Bichena, a tranquil town with patches of eucalyptus trees and a lot of open space. Desta immediately fell in love with the place.

As soon as the truck was parked, porters surrounded it, making Desta feel uneasy. One hefty man put out his arms, indicating he could simply catch Desta. Instead, Desta rappelled down from the load, using one of the loose rope ends as his anchor. But the rope came undone, causing Desta to fall off the truck, ending up in the man's arms anyway. Another porter quickly climbed up on the load and started untying the rope before removing the canvas. Then he began tossing down some of the lighter objects.

After collecting his bag and borsa, Desta took several tentative steps, making his way over to one of the benches. He sat down. All the hopeful thoughts he'd had as he walked from Medina's home two days earlier were gone. Instead, a paralyzing anxiety set in. What if Colonel Mulugeta and his family had intentionally abandoned him? What if they refused to take him in? What if they hadn't actually moved here after all? The only report he'd had was what he'd heard from Fanawork's friend.

He knew any of these possibilities might mean he wouldn't finish school this year. Whether he decided to stay here or go to Finote Selam without a secure place to live, he couldn't possibly pursue his education. His face felt hot and there were dragonflies in his stomach. He looked around to see who he could ask, who might verify the existence of Colonel Mulugeta's family in Bichena. A woman had just come out of a store and was about to pass him.

"Excuse me," he said, "do you, by any chance, know who the new chief of police is here?"

She looked at Desta for a few seconds. "No, I don't," she said, and walked off briskly. Next a middle-aged man passed by him. Desta asked him the same question. "Colonel Abinet," the man replied unequivocally.

"Are you sure?" Desta asked. He was feeling queasy inside.

The man retraced his steps. "The last time I checked," he said, smiling a little. He walked on.

What looked like a businessman was the next person to come along. He was carrying something heavy in a bag. He, too, said the police chief's name was Colonel Abinet.

Now thoroughly convinced, Desta got up, intent on finding a place where he could spend the night and get up early the next day to find a truck back to Dejen.

At that moment everything again felt like a dream. Asking any more people about the colonel seemed almost pointless. Now he just wanted to find a place where he could sleep for the night. He rose, gathered his things, and started trudging along the road. It was then that he saw a policeman. As a last resort, he walked up to him and said, "Excuse me, do you know, by any chance, who the new chief of police is here?"

"Who are you?"

"I am looking for him, if he is the right man."

"Would Colonel Mulugeta be that man?" the policeman asked, smiling a little.

Desta sighed. "Yes, that's him. Do you know where he lives?"

"Yes, I do. I'll take you there."

Desta wished he could hug the man. The question now was, would the colonel and family accept him with open arms?

"You must have just arrived from Finote Selam?"

The query made his heart jump. "Why, did they tell you to look out for a boy like me who might be coming from there?"

"No. The colonel came ahead of his family. The rest arrived last week. With all that you're carrying, I figured you must be the last to arrive."

Desta's heart retrenched.

"Who's Colonel Abinet?" Desta asked.

"The former head of police," the man said.

After they walked for a quarter of a mile, the policeman pointed and said, "That's where they live."

Where Colonel Mulugeta's family lived was in a pitched tin-roof building, bordered in back by a grove of eucalyptus trees and in front by a large open field.

"Thank you," Desta said, turning to the policeman. "I appreciate this."

All of a sudden he was having cold feet. Instead of walking toward his adoptive family's home, he stood and watched the policeman go—until he disappeared into the distant neighborhood. Pride, disappointment, and shame got in the way.

He sat down and thought about his circumstances for a long time.

It was out of desperation, the loss of Asse'ged, and any hope of finding someone loving to support him that he came following after a family who, it turned out, cared little for him, *obviously*, he thought. Why hadn't he thought of these things before leaving Finote Selam? Why had he accepted without question the challenges his grandfather's spirit put before him— going off in the world to find the second Coin of Magic and Fortune, for example. Why had he not remained a farmer like the rest of his relatives?

The string of unanswered questions elicited emotion from deep within Desta. He began to cry. After allowing himself to weep for a few minutes, he found relief and clarity. A voice—a single answer—came to him, as if from a clairvoyant. He was destined to have a whole range of experiences, both good and bad, before he would finally reach the place of his dreams. "So banish shame and pride from your mind, immediately," the voice added. He wiped his tears, took a deep breath, and readied himself to face any upcoming challenges, as if preparing to scale the jagged and slippery face of a mountain.

Chapter 33

The plate of food Enatnesh was carrying nearly fell from her hand the moment she saw Desta approach. He was careful to read her face. She gazed at him in cold disbelief. He felt it was no coincidence that the family had chosen this town so far off the beaten track, a place a shepherd boy might have neither the courage nor means to find.

Enatnesh took a few stiff steps and stopped. Desta braced himself, having read her body language. In response to any question the thin, frizzy-haired girl might pose, he had to be decidedly strong, positive, and confident. She was the main conduit of communication to Fanawork. He dare not show any weakness, shame, or fear.

"You came all the way here by yourself—why? Couldn't you find someone to live with in Finote Selam?"

"No, you all are my family; I'm your adoptive brother, as Colonel Mulugeta is my Father-of-the-Breast. Don't you think this qualifies me as one of you?"

"You're right," she said, softening a little. "We'd just wondered if you could make it here by yourself, especially a boy like you, who had not been to many places."

"You're mistaken . . . this talk is irrelevant," he said, making a motion to go past her. "Can you give me something to drink? I am thirsty."

"Sure. Come on in." She led the way to what appeared to be the back of the house. A large room projected, like an appendage, from the side of the main house. This was the *madd-bet*—kitchen. Enatnesh went into the room and returned with a glass of water.

"Let's go inside the house so you can see Fanawork," Enatnesh said.

The back entrance opened onto a hallway and an alcove on the right. Near where the interior partitioning wall and external wall of the house met was a door, which led to a large living room. Enatnesh explained that this was now being used as a bedroom for Colonel Mulugeta and

Fanawork and the two boys, because they couldn't find a bigger house.

The little girl made Desta wait in the hallway as she went to fetch the woman of the house.

"A surprise, indeed!" Fanawork said, evidently repeating what Enatnesh must have reported. She presented a hardened face and supercilious smile.

He moved forward so as to receive the customary three kisses. Instead, she extended a hand to Desta. He steeled himself, realizing what she was trying to do—make him feel bad, unwelcome; she was trying to undermine his strength and fortitude.

He quickly offered his hand and grasped Fanawork's.

Bete sebocheh Dehina nachew—your family is well?" she asked, indifferently, for a lack of anything else to say.

"Very well, thank you," Desta replied. He was in no mood for this.

"Who told you where we had gone?"

"Medina."

"Is she well?"

"As well as when you last saw her, I'm sure."

"Enatnesh!" Fanawork called. "Give Desta something to eat. He is probably hungry."

There was nothing meaningful to talk about. They had nothing in common between them. He was happy their reunion had ended.

Colonel Mulugeta arrived in the early evening. He flashed a genuine smile when he saw Desta. "Glad to see you made it here," he said, after he kissed him on both cheeks three times.

"Thank you," Desta said, truly happy to see the colonel.

"Did you bring your school certificate?"

Desta said he had.

"Good. I'll take you to register at the school in the morning."

"Thank you."

"When I learned you were not coming to Bichena," he said, resting a hand on Desta's shoulder, "I was going to wait until we got established here before going to check on you and our house—that you came here is even better."

Knowing he had at least one solid ally made Desta very happy.

Menkir, Mulugeta's stepson, and Muneet, the cook, were a bit distant and indifferent. Among them was the same undercurrent of disdain and suspicion Desta had gotten from Enatnesh. It was an attitude he hadn't seen in these two when they lived in Finote Selam.

The following day Colonel Mulugeta took Desta to school to register. Desta was accepted without any resistance from the director, and despite feeling unsettled in his new home, he was poised to finish out the last two months of his seventh-grade education here in Bichena.

Although the curriculum was supposed to be the same in all the schools, certain teachers emphasized certain areas more than others and some even taught entirely different subjects. So Desta sought out the top student in the class and became friends with him. His name was Merid.

Instead of copying the lessons for the entire year from his classmates, he borrowed Merid's class notes and read them through once, just to see the variance from what he had learned in his Finote Selam school. He found many differences as well as similarities.

Within a week of Desta's living in his new home, the unfriendly demeanor of some members of the household was becoming apparent. At one point, when Desta was putting away his new clothes, Enatnesh snidely asked, "Did you buy those things with the money you stole from Fanawork?"

Stunned, Desta looked up and asked, "Who told you I stole money from her?"

"We all know you did. That was one of the reasons why Fanawork didn't want you to come with us."

Desta shook his head, disappointed by Fanawork. She had resorted to this petty, common excuse families sometimes used to create rifts among members. "I didn't steal any money from her or anyone," he said firmly. "These things were bought with the money my brother left me. Whoever told that story is lying. Please tell the others what I just told you."

"I think you're lying," Enatnesh challenged.

"I'm not going to argue with you. . . . What was the other reason Fanawork didn't want me to come?"

"Because you were getting all the attention from Colonel Mulugeta, and there was none for Menkir or any of us."

"Ohhh," Desta exclaimed. "This answer explains the fabricated accusation. To convince Colonel Mulugeta of my unworthiness to be part of the household, my integrity had to be tarnished. Please don't repeat this lie to anyone else."

"You better be careful or you will have a problem with all of us," Fanawork's agent warned and walked off.

Desta was certain that this warning from Enatnesh
represented what the lady of the household felt about him.

He was careful never to be deferential or servile to her. The last
thing he wanted was to lose himself or his pride to buy the favor or
kindness of a woman who was already set in her attitude toward him.

Not having a private place in the house to study became his saving
grace. A short distance from the house was a patch of regrowth from
cut eucalyptus trees. Some of the trees were waist high, others taller.
Among these newly-sprouted young trees he made his lair.

In the daylight hours, when he was not at school, he came here to
study and do his homework. On weekends staying at home became too
oppressive, so he came here to find peace and solace. When the pain
inside was too great, he lost himself among the eucalyptuses, breathing
in their scent and the cool highland air, feeling healed and comforted by
his surroundings. This outdoor refuge served as a shield from his misery.
Whenever a pedestrian walked by, he'd lay low and remain quiet.

To abide by his responsibility and appease Fanawork, Desta spent a great
deal of time with her son, helping him with his homework, preparing him for
his final exams. They'd study even after everybody had gone to sleep. At other
times he took Menkir to the grove to study with him. When the exam results
came, both did well. Desta finished second, Menkir in the top ten percent.

Most students looked forward to the two and a half months of vacation,
but Desta saw them as months of purgatory. It rained just about every
day, and he had no choice but to stay at home or go out for a couple of
hours after the rain stopped and gave control of the world to the sun.

When the day brightened, he went out of town and gazed into
the distant, hazy lands. The country in the south was the most
enchanting. Not far from the edge of town, the earth fell deep like a
trench and then rose and ran in a flat, seemingly endless, massif.

He wished he'd had his aircraft so he could fly there and
discover who and what lived in these distant, misty lands. He had
sent it home with his father after his life became unstable.

When he looked north, in the direction of Bahir Dar, where he'd be going
a year from now, his heart leaped with excitement. But it sobered just as
quickly when he remembered he had nobody he could live with there. From the
way things are with his adopted family, now he was not even sure if Colonel

Mulugeta would help find someone he could live with when he finally goes to the place of his dreams. Desta's real hope and promise was gone with Asse'ged, in the nondescript grave his brother was sharing with a complete stranger.

It was then that he got up and walked. He didn't even want to think and worry about his future while he had problems to think and worry about in his current living situation.

He enjoyed looking at the charcoal-gray soil that turned into a claylike paste when wet and cracked like a poorly cured brick when dry. It was in this soil where chickpeas, peas, and beans grew abundantly, a farmer once told him. They grew wheat, barley, and rye, too, but not much teff. The open fields teemed with cattle, sheep, and horses. The whole countryside was beautiful, peaceful, and soothing to look at. Therefore, during the rainy season, Desta came as often as there was a break from the rain, to drink in the stunning surroundings and to daydream.

The people, be they farmers or town dwellers, were pleasant and gentle. This was the sort of place where Desta would like to live after he was done with his dual missions.

Sometime at the beginning of August, Fanawork told Desta and Menkir she wanted them to replace the stuffing in her and the colonel's mattress. The cotton balls that gave the mattress its shape had become lumpy and uncomfortable. The two boys, along with the cook, took the mattress and laid it out in the sun, away from any overhanging trees.

The job of opening the covering of the mattress at its seams and sorting the good cotton balls from the bad was left to Desta. Once he had cut the threads along the seam, he separated the fabric and pulled out the musty balls of cotton, creating a mound of dusty fluff on the ground next to the mattress.

One by one he began sorting the good balls from the bad ones. While doing this, he discovered folded pieces of paper, each about two inches square, wrapped in fabric. The fabric had frayed at the edges, exposing the paper. When Desta held and pressed them between his fingers, the wrapping came apart. He unfolded and began to read them. The ones in Amharic were spells for Colonel Mulugeta, that he should stop seeing other women, particularly Konjit, the hotel owner, show more love to Fanawork and her son, Menkir, and stay at home with the family more often. The second was in Arabic. Desta figured it was probably written by the Muslim sorcerers Medina had introduced to Fanawork.

As he was folding and putting away the papers, Fanawork appeared.

Her fair skin went red when she realized what he was doing. She snatched the pieces of paper from his hand. "You have no right to be opening and reading these private notes!" Her eyes flamed with rage. Her lips trembled. She looked around as if searching for something to hit him with. Finding nothing, she demanded he immediately get up and go away.

Go away he did. He realized his days were now numbered. He would probably have to leave forever, but he didn't know where he would go or when.

Strangely, when he returned in the evening, she was sweet and apologetic. There were no hard feelings. But Desta was skeptical. This seemed more dangerous to him than when she was showing her truer cold self.

His sixth sense was right. About a week after the discovery of the secret pieces of paper, Enatnesh told Desta that he should put their youngest boy in the back sling and go for a walk. Ghion was about four years old. He was a rather sweet, chubby little boy. He liked Desta and Desta liked him.

Just about every time he carried Ghion, the boy urinated on Desta. Both Enatnesh and Menkir laughed and said the boy was in the habit of doing that when they carried him, too.

Ironically, during this time, all the members of the household, including Fanawork, were kind and sweet to Desta. These niceties made up for the unpleasant issue with Ghion.

But then Ghion did more than just urinate on Desta. Now Desta knew the family was united in getting him to go away. The smell came first. This was followed by the feel of a very warm and heavy wad of something. He was tempted to release the strap of the sling and drop the boy like a rock. He didn't. The consequences of such an action would be dire. He had to maintain his equanimity. He lowered himself and Ghion to the ground and untied the sling.

Enatnesh and Menkir came first and burst into laughter at the sight of Desta and Ghion. Next came Fanawork. She didn't laugh but her arrogant face brightened. She appeared as if triumphant, indicating a satisfaction equal to that of someone vanquishing a hated enemy.

That night Desta decided to leave. He gathered up all his things and put them in his bag. He sat down and wrote a letter to Colonel Mulugeta.

In the morning he went to the school director's home. Desta begged him for a certificate of transfer. It was an urgent matter, he told the man. Because Desta was the adoptive son of Colonel Mulugeta, the director said he was happy to oblige.

When he returned, he went to Colonel Mulugeta's office
and gave him the letter. The colonel read it. He was extremely
disturbed and unhappy to learn what had been going on under his
own roof. He asked why Desta hadn't come to him earlier.

"It would have been a vicious cycle and more complications
for everybody, including you, so I didn't want to say anything.
And now it's just best that I leave," Desta said.

Colonel Mulugeta reached into his pocket and pulled out a ten
birr note. He apologized that he didn't have more to give Desta, but
he said he'd plan to come to Finote Selam after the New Year—
September 11—and hoped to bring Desta more money then.

Desta thanked him. His Father-of-the-Breast kissed him three times on
the cheeks, and Desta dashed out of the office. Although he had no permanent
place to stay in Finote Selam, he was happy to finally be leaving Fanawork
and her unloving family. He had a smile on his face and a spring in his step.

When he returned to the house, he checked to make sure he had all his
things. Then he prepared to leave. The cook kissed him. Both Menkir and
Enatnesh stood unmoved. Fanawork stepped forward to give him a kiss. Desta
extended a hand instead. She took it and held it briefly in her cold, lifeless palm.
They all followed him as if suddenly regretting his departure. Desta didn't look
back, walking with a confident kind of dignity. He was bloodied but unbowed.

Chapter 34

Just as Desta reached the center of town, he found a loaded truck about to leave for Dejen. "You're a lucky boy," the driver said. "There was supposed to be a man riding with me, but he had to cancel. I'll charge you three birrs instead of the five the man was going to pay, and you can ride in the cabin with me."

Desta hesitated for a few seconds, wanting to make sure he'd have enough for his shuttle bus fare plus future expenses. With the ten birrs the colonel had given him and the leftover money from Asse'ged, he had a total of 30 birrs. He paid the fare the driver asked and got in the truck.

This time the drive to Dejen was heaven. No wind, no fear of falling off—and it seemed they got to their destination in a flash. After spending the night in the town by the Blue Nile gorge, Desta rose early and got on a shuttle bus for Debre Marcos.

He met a young man named Messay on the bus who was going to the capital of the province to take a test for a hospital job. After learning Desta's situation, the man convinced him to take the test, too.

Under the circumstances, Desta thought he might as well. Immediately after they arrived in Debre Marcos, the man and Desta went to the hospital to register. The test would be administered in the afternoon. Although Desta pretty quickly had second thoughts, he took the test, just the same. There were about one hundred other people in attendance. The hospital was looking to hire only fifteen. The results would be released at noon the following day.

Because Desta didn't know anyone in town, the man invited him to spend the night with him and his relatives. A kind and gentle man, Messay smiled with his big eyes, as well as his teeth, as he spoke. Desta couldn't tell whether that was his true self or a cover for the anxiety he was feeling about the test. And he seemed very anxious about getting the job.

At midday Desta and the young man went back to the hospital. They joined the other test takers in a room. The hospital administrator

announced the names of the fifteen people who scored the highest and
the names of five backups. To his absolute surprise Desta was one of the
fifteen. However, his friend from the bus wasn't among the twenty.

Those selected, including the five who were wait-listed, were led to a room
where a Ferenge named Dr. Yakov Petrova greeted them. Once they all sat down,
an Ethiopian man called out their names from a list while Dr. Petrova glanced
at them and checked their names against a copy he had in his hands. This done,
the man congratulated them and explained the nature of the job. At the end he
asked who out of the fifteen wouldn't be interested in taking the job. Desta was
the only one who declined the job. They replaced him with one of the backups.

As the individuals filed out of the room, the man came over to Desta
and told him that Dr. Petrova wanted to speak with him. Nonplused,
Desta followed and was formally introduced to the man. He received a
handshake and a congratulation from the doctor and then an invitation
to his office. After they sat down, Dr. Petrova, who pronounced words
as if they were disagreeable to his palate, said, "You scored the highest
on the test. You are the only one who got a perfect score in English,
science, and math. What can we offer you to change your mind?"

At first Desta thought Dr. Petrova was joking. Desta had taken the exam
halfheartedly. So he assumed he hadn't done that well. "Thank you for the kind
job offer. I've had second thoughts about it because I have bigger goals in life."

"That is fine. You can work part time for us and go to school full time. After
you finish high school, we can send you to medical school in Bulgaria, where I
come from. Your country needs doctors. We think you'd be a good candidate."

Desta, who listened with his eyes on the floor, lifted his head and
looked at Dr. Petrova, intrigued as much by his suggestion as by the
connection between the doctor's accent and his country of origin.

"Again, I thank you for your offer, but I cannot accept. I have
a much larger responsibility than becoming a doctor."

The doctor steadied his face and narrowed his sky-
color eyes. "What would that be?" he asked.

"I'm on a journey to find an important coin."

Dr. Petrova chortled. "You think that is more important than
becoming a doctor and helping your fellow citizens?"

"This is not my choice but my destiny, sir. If I'd had a say in the matter, I'd
have preferred a path less arduous than the one I'm on. Certainly,

your proposition is very attractive."

"Yes, we'll pay for your expenses here as well as for your medical school studies—and that, Desta, is an opportunity you shouldn't pass up."

Desta scratched his head, trying to figure out a way to leave the doctor's office without being disrespectful. It was then that Dr. Petrova asked, "Where do you plan to go to find this coin?"

Desta told him.

"Aha," the doctor said triumphantly. "The Black Sea, one of the largest bodies of water in the world, borders my country. One of the top medical schools there is located in Varna, the coastal capital of Bulgaria. You never know—the person who holds the coin might be living there. This means you could go to our medical school and look for the individual in your spare time."

This piece of information was intriguing to Desta. He remembered the map he saw on the wall of Washaa Umera. It showed Odessa, on the Black Sea, as one of the places where the people who owned the second coin lived. But then he remembered that the same map showed Palestine, back in 1915, as the last place where the shekel had been seen. So the chances of it being in Bulgaria were slim to nil. Then again, if he was to trust the information presented on the walls of the grand cave, no map existed that showed whether the coin was now in Israel or another country.

"I'm sorry," Desta said finally, "as tempting as your offer is, I still have to decline."

Dr. Petrova appeared astounded, as if to say, How can this poor boy who has no definite career say no to such an offer?!

"On the other hand, I'm not beyond proposing a counteroffer, Dr. Petrova," Desta said. "This time I have to break my own rules because my circumstances have been so greatly compromised. If your finances are such that you can afford to offer me all you say, may I be so bold as to ask you a favor? I'm in short supply of cash and I could use some for a bus trip and other things I'll need. Although I cannot promise, I hope to return the favor in some way down the road."

Dr. Petrov's face eased, as if satisfied to have found an alternative outlet for his benevolence.

"How much do you need?"

"Ten birrs or so."

Dr. Petrov tipped his body to the left and reached for his wallet.

His hand returning with it, he opened it and pulled out two crisp red bills. "Here," he said. "I hope this will cover your bus fare and more."

"Twenty birrs is generous and I thank you very much."

With that, Desta rose, shook hands with Dr. Petrova, and left.

That afternoon he took a bus to Finote Selam. The passengers arrived as the night consumed any vestige of light, leaving very little of the day.

Dinknesh's modest house had become a home away from home for Desta, his father, and brother. She was a wonderful human being—all heart. She smiled happily when she saw him. "Your father was here a month ago, wondering how in the world he could find out how you were doing. I am sure he is going to be very happy to learn you're healthy and still smiling," she said, after embracing and kissing him.

The next day, Desta was going to see his family. August was the tail end of the rainy season, but the highlands were still deluged with water, generally in the late afternoon. Desta needed to get going before the river was flooded and the bridge uncrossable. He rose before dawn and left after thanking Dinknesh for her hospitality.

Chapter 35

Melkam's mouth dropped open. "Desta!' she shouted, dashing toward him. She had just stepped out of her in-laws' residence. She hugged and kissed him. After they talked for a few minutes, asking and answering questions about each other's welfare, Desta motioned to enter their parents' home.

"Wait!" Melkam said, grabbing Desta by his arm. "You can't go in."

"Is something wrong?" Desta asked, his face turning grave.

"Nothing very serious, we hope anyway, but Baba is sick with a *beshita*—communicable disease—and we don't want you to catch it."

"Great," Desta said. After all he'd been through, he comes here to rest and have a meaningful time with his family, only to be kept at arm's length. He wanted to say more but it would've made no sense to Melkam. Instead he pressed his knuckles to his nose, narrowed his eyes, and thought hard—but nothing concrete or consequential came to him. Given all that had happened, he should be angry enough to scream holy murder at God, but Desta didn't know how to get angry. He turned to Melkam. "So where can I go?" he asked, as if an afterthought.

"You can come to our house or stay with your mother. She lives in a small makeshift hut down by where the remains of your Kooli are buried."

"I'll go to Mother's," Desta said.

"Do you want me to take you there?"

"If she's staying near Kooli's grave, I'll find her. Thank you."

To Ayénat, Desta might as well have dropped out of the sky. She kissed him and wanted to know how he had spent the rainy season in a place so far away and with people nobody knew about.

Before he finished answering all her questions, she grabbed him by the hand and took him inside her little hut. The space took up no more than seventy-five square feet. A grass roof hung over a split wooden wall, which lacked the usual covering of mud plaster and straw. At places where the gaps were considerable, Ayénat had draped fabric. It had begun raining.

"First it was Melkam who got sick with the disease," Ayénat started saying, describing the sequence of events. She had brought Desta food and drink and was sitting next to him. She continued. "Melkam got better, shortly after your father got sick. It was then all the children said I should move out before I got sick, too. Damtew and a couple of other young men built this shed for me in two days." Ayénat suddenly stopped. Desta followed her eyes. She was watching the rivulet of rainwater that was sliding down the split-wood groove of the interior wall.

"That's new. The roof keeps leaking. Each time we find a leak, Damtew fixes it. The problem and the mending never stops," she said, her eyes still on the runaway rain.

"The spring season is around the corner. That will stop it," Desta said, trying to ease his mother's mind.

"It still rains in September, although not as frequently," she said. She turned to Desta. "Anyway, nobody takes care of your father except Melkam, who brings him the food I prepare."

Desta stopped eating. What he was hearing was upsetting him. He lost his appetite. Five months ago he'd lost a brother who had promised to follow him to Bahir Dar. The family whom he had hoped would be of help to him didn't want him in their home. Now his father, his only hope, was about to die? He still had the eighth grade to finish and then go to Bahir Dar to attend high school and search for the second coin. Why was he being put through this interminable test?

Ayénat tapped him on his shoulder. "Don't worry too much. Just pray. The Lord God will have the answer for all of us."

Ayénat always had a tendency to simplify things like this; she was forever throwing her problems in God's corner.

The rain had begun falling heavily. The rivulet was now a cataract. Ayénat and Desta got up and started moving things away from the water, which was now rising on the floor. Having seen quite a few floods in his young life, he was most concerned about a rush of water from higher ground.

"Has anybody dug a trench around this house?"

"Damtew has built one."

"Oh, good," Desta said, relieved. "We can contain this local breach. What could be a disaster is if an actual flood surge came from the higher slopes."

"I think we are okay," Ayénat said.

Desta sat down. Ayénat stocked the fireplace with logs.

"To come back to your father's situation, the only person who reports to us about his condition is Melkam. We go talk to your father at night, though."

"You go talk to *Baba* at night?" Desta asked, glancing at Ayénat. He wanted to see if her eyes were saying the same.

Ayénat returned the glance. "Yes, outside. We sit near his bedroom wall and talk to him. We sometimes have to talk louder, but he hears very well. And we can hear him sometimes, if he is not too weak. You can talk to him tonight, after midnight."

"Is he that bad?"

"Some days he is bad, and some days he is better."

There was a rustle, something like a snake pulling through dry leaves. Desta turned to see. "Oh, my God!"

Ayénat's eyes followed Desta's. "Good Lord! We're being flooded." They quickly gathered clothes, bedding, and other items and placed them out of the reach of the surging water: on crossbeams, boxes, and atop fire logs. They piled things on top of belongings Ayénat could afford to lose, but they couldn't save the fire.

Desta realized that along with the flood, they were about to be engulfed in darkness. "Ma," he called, "let's at least find some of your heavy gabis and cover ourselves with them. Chances are we are going to spend the night either standing or perched on something."

"You're right," Ayénat said, as she plunged forward. She pulled the heavy cotton fabric from the mountain of clothes and gave one to Desta and kept the other for herself.

They stood side by side and watched as the hot ash from the fire pit turned to steam and the embers sizzled. The brilliant fire was being strangled by the onslaught of water, and they had no power to save it. Every ember and every glowing log was turning to smoke, the warm firelight dying before their eyes. Ayénat and Desta coughed and wiped the ash from their eyes.

The rain had abated but the flood had not ceased. It kept coming and coming, as if being fed by a mighty waterfall high up in the mountains.

Having little choice, they huddled on a stool and became the best of allies. It took rain and a flood for Ayénat and Desta to find friends in each other.

"So much for going to talk to your father tonight," Ayénat said.

"Can't we, if the rain stops?"

"We have no fire to make a torch. How can we find our way there in this pitch blackness?"

Desta contemplated Ayénat's concern.

"I think it's better you talk to him tomorrow night," his mother suggested. "Hopefully, we'll have fire to make a torch with. . . . And as backup, we can also borrow Teferra's flashlight."

Something occurred to Desta. "Why not tomorrow during the day?"

"No," Ayénat said. "We can't because the disease comes out during the day."

"You mean to say it has life and a body, and actually walks?"

Ayénat was quiet for a few seconds. "I don't know about the life and body part but that's what people say: it's not a good idea to talk to a sick person from outside during the day."

"What're we going to do about the night?" Desta asked, wrapping himself tighter with a cotton blanket.

"What do you mean?" Ayénat said.

"How are we going to sleep?"

"Tell you what," Ayénat said. "Let's pull the bench over to the wall, and we can try to get some sleep by leaning against the wall and each other."

So that's what they did. They rose and pulled the long bench to where Ayénat had suggested, and they sat down. They leaned against each other and the wall and tried to fall asleep. No sleep came to either. This was the first intimate moment Desta had shared with his mother. It made Desta wish all the more that Ayénat had shared her feelings and thoughts as he was growing up. He'd never asked her why she was cold and distant toward him all those years.

"Ma?" he said.

"Yes."

"Since we can't fall asleep, we might as well make the most of this strange night. Do you mind if I ask you some questions?"

"Go ahead," Ayénat said, in a cheerful but guarded voice.

"Why have you never shared yourself with me all these years?"

Ayénat went dead silent. Instead of elbowing her to see whether she was awake, instinctively Desta turned toward his mother to get a look at her face. It was no use. Her countenance, like everything else around them, was completely obscured by the night. But then there came a rustling and a clearing of her throat.

"I'm not aware that I have been unfriendly or unloving toward you. Yes, we have had a few incidents, but anything I've done was for your own good, to protect you from the Saytan, to save your reputation and ours."

Not being able to see her face, he tried to read the level of sincerity in her voice.

"You mean that you and I have been like a mother and a son ought to be?"

"Pretty much."

"Have you ever had a warm feeling for me or for any one of your children?"

"What's that?"

"Some people call it love."

Ayénat went silent again.

"Well," she said. "Neither of my parents ever expressed those kinds of feelings while I was growing up. For one, they were divorced before I was five, so I never felt any love, not even from my mother, because she was incapable of showing it. I have those feelings once in a while for all my children, but they never come out. Why—I don't know. It's as though somebody has trapped them inside, particularly with you."

"Somebody?"

"Yes. There is a resistance I feel inside every time I make a conscious effort to hug or kiss you. It's as if there is something or someone holding me back. And then there is this strange woman who comes once in a while and tells me to withhold my feelings toward you because that is the only way you can grow and become a strong man."

"A strange woman? What does she look like?"

"I've never seen her face because she has always covered it, along with the rest of her body. For all I know, she could be a spirit."

"I see. . . . Does she say anything else to you?" Desta suspected she must be talking about the celestial being Eleni.

"She says nothing else, usually. . . . Now I have not seen her for a while, and I no longer have the lack of feeling for you."

Desta was stunned. Not only was he having to deal with the harsh realities of the world but also the spirits and demons who have influence of Ayénat.

"You know, Ma, the years we lost we can never recover," Desta said, "but we can make the best of the time we have left. You have a lot of children. I have only one mother."

Ayénat put her arm around Desta and pulled him closer. "Although I've been barren of feelings toward you, in my mind you're just as important as every other child."

"Thanks for letting me know that it was not your fault. . . . And it's probably the same spirit who influenced the two women I sought as my Mothers-of-the-Breast to reject me, by convincing them that they didn't have it in them to love me or show me their native feelings as my blood mother would have."

Desta detected a lump in his throat.

Ayénat gripped his shoulder. "I hope you have been strengthened by all that has happened to you. We're not meant to be a part of your life. Your father says it's all because of the coin we possess and the mission you're meant to accomplish. . . . It seems to me our purpose as your parents was merely to create you and keep you at home until you were old enough to embark on your journey."

"By nature, I am not a vindictive person, but what saddens me, Ma, is that you reduce to mere fate all that has happened to me," Desta said, staring into the blackness. "No one will take responsibility."

"If it was not for fate, you could have been living here like your brothers and sisters," Ayénat said, turning and staring in Desta's direction. "And no one can punish or bring justice to fate."

Desta swallowed hard. Ayénat's words cut through to his bones. He thought for several seconds. "I'm not seeking justice in the way we know it; ultimately it does no good for me or the people being punished on my behalf—but I know that my greatest reward will be when the two Coins of Magic and Fortune finally unite and become one—that will be the best compensation I can receive for all the hardships I bore."

"I'll pray for you," Ayénat said, almost joyfully. "Let's now go to sleep. We can continue this talk in the remaining days you will be with us, sitting around a roaring fire by then, hopefully." She smiled to herself.

"Thank you," Desta said. "We need to somehow get the sleep you said we would."

With that, Desta's head fell on his mother's shoulder and hers over his head. They closed their eyes and were fast asleep.

Chapter 36

The voice was feeble. Words came in strained and tentative patterns. The patient sounded like he preferred sleep to hearing the same voice and answering the same questions.

After Ayénat turned off the flashlight, the night looked blacker and thicker than normal. The mother leaned over and said, "According to Melkam, he is getting weaker by the day. And he is not eating the food I prepare for him. . . . That's not going to help, of course."

"What would be the solution, then?"

"Time and rest and eating well," Ayénat said confidently.

"But you said he is not eating much."

"I think he is also depressed. Since we lost Asse'ged, he has not been the same. You know how close the two of them were."

"I know," Desta said, "but Baba is a very strong man. Our loss of Asse'ged shouldn't cause him to fall apart like this, to lose his will to live."

"Your being here should help brighten him up."

"Let's hope so."

Ayénat cleared her throat. "We have a visitor!" she shouted.

Abraham was quiet.

Ayénat repeated her announcement.

"Who?" Abraham said, finally.

"Desta is here with me."

"Era! Desta!"

It was as if Abraham was given a shot of medicine. His voice now was louder and projecting into the night air.

"You came all the way from Bichena to see me—who told you I was sick?"

"I didn't know you were sick. I just came to see you all."

Abraham seemed at a loss for words. He went silent.

"I'm sorry you came with me in this condition. . . How are Colonel Mulugeta and his family?"

"They're well."

"When do you plan to go back?"

"In about two weeks."

"Maybe I'll feel better by then and we can have a proper visit."

"Let's hope so," Ayénat interposed.

"This coming school year I'll be in Finote Selam. We'll have a chance to see each other when you come for your court cases."

"You're not going back to Bichena?"

"No."

Abraham went quiet again.

"It's a bit complicated, Baba. I'll be fine. I'll find a way to survive another year of school in Finote Selam."

"That's fine, son. You'll be closer to us, too."

"What disquiets me the most is that I have no place to live when I go to Bahir Dar a year from now. . . . You may have to sell one of your cows," Desta said, chuckling.

"We still have a whole year before Bahir Dar. What worries me is where you're going to live when you go to Finote Selam in two weeks," Abraham replied.

Ayénat said to Desta, "Let's not get him worried over this."

"Don't fret," Ayénat said. "Desta said he will be fine. What would you like for your breakfast?"

"Something hot, like *shorba*—soup—would be welcomed."

"I'll bring you shorva with freshly baked dabo," Ayénat said.

"That sounds even better," Abraham said.

"Get some sleep. We'll talk to you tomorrow night."

Abraham coughed, "Good night."

Ayénat and Desta stumbled home, using Teferra's flashlight as their guide. For the next two weeks, Desta and Ayénat came to visit Abraham. It was during one of these visits that he disclosed his will. In addition to the coin and the coin box, Abraham wanted Desta to have his pistol.

Ayénat explained later that Abraham's pistol was one of his proudest possessions. It had been with him most of his adult life. It was his bodyguard. He used it to protect himself against people who had come to harm him, particularly during the Italo-Ethiopian War.

"Before you became a modern school student, he had willed it to Asse'ged. Then later he thought you should have it because of all your accomplishments;

you had made him especially proud. He also thought you could use it to protect the coin and coin box from those who might try to steal them."

Desta was touched. Abraham had never been overly complimentary in the past. However, just from the way he showed Desta respect and from the closeness they achieved over the years, Desta felt valued and appreciated by his father. For Abraham to express these feelings through the generosity of his will made Desta feel special. His self-esteem and self-image has been badly damaged since his encounter with Dagim. This was just the boost Desta needed.

ON NEW YEAR'S DAY, early in the morning, Ayénat prepared her usual *goozgoozo*—cheese spread over freshly baked double-layer injera, sprinkled with spiced melted butter. She sent one to Abraham and kept one for Desta and herself.

Right after the first cock's crow, Desta joined his brothers for the fireworks, which consisted of torches made from bunched twigs. They took the torches outside, lit them, and raised them in the air, as they danced and women sang, "*abeba ayesh wey?*—Have you seen the flowers?"

After daybreak Damtew brought the meat of a lamb he had killed for Desta and his mother. Ayenat prepared an appetizer dish of *dulet*—a mixture of chopped liver, minced onions, garlic and herbs. Desta and his mother ate half of the appetizer and sent the remaining to Abraham. At noon, Desta and Ayénat went to Saba and Yihoon's home for lunch and to Teferra and Laqechi's home for supper.

Before every meal, the gathered families prayed for Abraham to get better. Desta prayed harder, asking God not to take his father from him.

The celebrations passed, and the spring season bloomed in every aspect—with rain clouds rapidly disappearing—the sun having taken full possession of the valley, tickling the earth to release the forms of life it had kept hidden through the rainy season. Flowers of every kind smiled at one another and at the world, from the hills, backyards, and along growing farm fields. Desta wished he was a kid again and his sister Hibist was with him so they could go running in the fields together, chasing butterflies. But he was a grown boy now, having learned so much in school and about life since his innocent, carefree years.

Maskel—marking the discovery of the True Cross—was the next holiday coming up. It was in September. But Desta was not even thinking about it this year. He needed to prepare and leave for Finote Selam to start the eighth grade. School would open on September 28.

Abraham was getting better but had not yet completely recovered. He still couldn't have visitors, except for Melkam, who delivered his food. During their nightly visits, Desta and Abraham discussed Desta's living arrangements for the coming academic year.

Since it was Desta's final year in the Finote Selam school, Abraham suggested during one of their nightly visits he try to stay with someone they knew, rather than complete strangers. Abraham thought Dinknesh, their longtime host, would be a suitable choice, so long as they supplied her with grains.

"Besides being a wonderful person," Abraham said, "she is also an honest woman. None of what happened to you in Dangila would happen under Dinknesh's roof."

"I agree with you, Baba, but we don't know how she would feel about my living with her," Desta said.

"But I know," Abraham said, "that she is a single woman who has no income other than what she earns from selling drinks and food. She would appreciate the extra supply of grains from us and give you accommodation."

With Desta's living situation in Finote Selam assumed settled, the next challenge was how to transport the sack of grain. Was there someone who could travel on foot with Desta a full day and a half?

Abraham rarely kept donkeys. He usually raised horses and mules. At the time he had only his riding horse, Dama. This meant they had to find a draft animal to carry the grain and someone who would go with Desta and return with the animal afterward.

There were Desta's three able-bodied brothers, but they declined. Each was busy with work—with farming or tailoring. Weeds grew like bushes and they needed to be removed before they took over the grain fields. People needed clothes, especially with holidays coming up.

Desta held back his tears, thinking of Asse'ged, his deceased brother, the one who would do anything for him.

Teferra, the eldest, at least offered his spare mule to transport the teff Desta was to bring to Dinknesh. But there was still the problem of an escort. Ayénat contacted people for hire she knew of, but everyone was already committed.

Then it was decided that Desta could make do without
an escort. He was to bring the loaded animal by himself and
keep the beast until the owner came to collect it.

Not only didn't Desta want the responsibility of keeping the
animal, he was suspicious. What kind of mule was she that Teferra
was willing to risk losing her? He very well knew Dinknesh had no
place to keep the animal and Desta had no time to look after her.

But Desta decided he would not reject his brother's seemingly kind gesture.
He agreed to take the mule and left her safety in the hands of God and fate.

Teferra had his wife, Laqech, bring the mule to Ayénat and Desta.

Desta did nearly an about-face when he saw the animal. She was
a sad, tiny creature—a beast of burden that looked more like a donkey
than a mule. Desta could see open wounds along her bony back.

Noticing Desta's reaction, Ayénat came to the rescue. "Don't
worry," she said, "this animal carries loads like a horse and can
travel long distances without a whimper. That's why Teferra
calls her *Medenek*—the wonder animal." She smiled.

Having no other options, Desta would have to take whatever he was given.

Later when Damtew and Teferra loaded Medenek, she accepted
the sixty-pound teff without so much as a grunt or dip in her back.

"See!" Ayénat said triumphantly. "She is a strong, sure-footed girl."

"After your brothers leave," she said, "I'll escort you two
to the top of the mountain."

"If she is as strong as you all say, I'll be okay, Ma," Desta said,
walking past his mother.

Ayénat went inside her hut and returned with a walking
stick and her netela thrown around her shoulders.

With Desta holding on to the lead and Ayénat following behind
Medenek, they went spiraling up the steep mountain. Ayénat spurred
the mule with her stick when she slowed, and stopped and adjusted the
load when it seemed it might come sliding off Medenek's flank.

They didn't talk much. Desta was taken back to the time when he
climbed the same mountain. He had traveled through the same pathless
terrain with his sister Saba, trying to touch the sky and gather clouds
in a sack. He remembered vividly his excitement when he finally
cleared the mountain, his disappointment when the sky was beyond

reach, and now he pondered the ridiculousness of his attempt.

He had come a long way from those days—when everything was strange and new. If he could now just finish the eighth grade without any interruption or mishap like what happened to him last year. He had more mountains ahead of him, and he'd prefer a rest from the climb.

Once they cleared the top, Desta and the mule would be traveling on more or less level ground along the ridge. At this point, Ayénat kissed Desta and said good-bye.

As he descended the leeward side of the mountain, the load on Medenek's back slid out of the strap and fell to the ground. With nobody in sight to help him remount the sack of grain, Desta waited and hoped for a long while, holding the animal's lead and praying and rubbing the coin image on his chest to bring someone who was traveling the same road.

"What happened to your load, boy?" A man asked, seeming to appear out of thin air.

Desta, startled, collected himself before saying, "It slid out of the strap. Do you think you can give me a hand?"

Desta steadied the mule while the man hoisted the load up onto her back. He arranged the straps neatly over the sack and wound them around Medenek's belly, tying the ends on top.

"Where are you going with this poor donkey?" the man asked, after eyeing Medenek critically.

Desta smiled a little. "She is actually a mule—we're going to Finote Selam."

The man glanced again at Medenek. "Ha, ha, ha, you're right!" he said, as he chuckled some more. "She has all the fundamentals of a mule, but her size and temperament are the spitting image of her donkey father."

"That's why my brother calls her Medenek."

"I'm sorry. I didn't mean to laugh at God's creation. . . . Drive her instead of pulling her on the lead," the man advised. "That way you can tighten the straps if the load threatens to slip out."

The man continued on his journey. Following his suggestion, Desta spurred Medenek from behind with his stick. She jogged along easily on the flatter terrain and scrambled with little effort up the hills.

The next steep climb was up the Yeedib plateau, and the sweet little mule handled it well.

Desta kept company with his thoughts as well as with Medenek.

Assuming Dinknesh would agree to accept his father's proposal, the precious load he was bringing was not just food for him and his host but the bridge to his future—his education and the Coin of Magic and Fortune he would continue to seek. He needed to guard the grain and Teferra's animal with the utmost care until they reached Finote Selam.

The descent down into the plateau on the other side of Yeedib was generally pretty treacherous because the road was often strewn with rocks and cut deep in places by flood waters. Medenek was having a terrible time. She grunted often and her legs trembled as she tottered gingerly and hesitantly down the steep slope. Just a few yards before reaching the bottom, the animal tripped and fell—badly.

With the load still on her back, the mule's body landed in a contorted position, her legs pinned beneath her. Medenek groaned, her glazed eyes fixed on Desta. Desperately, he tried to push or pull her, but she wouldn't budge. Some of the big boulders had hemmed her in. And Desta couldn't reach the ends of the straps because she had fallen on them.

Desta needed a miracle. He prayed for someone to show up from somewhere and help him save Medenek. He began rubbing the coin image on his chest. Nobody came. He tried pulling her legs, then grabbing her ears. Again he attempted to reach the straps to release the load. It was as if someone more powerful than he was holding the animal and load securely in place. Desta stood and looked at the straight road ahead and there was no sign of a human being coming toward them.

He turned and stared at the slope above them to see whether someone responding to the call of the coin on his chest was descending. There was no soul from this direction either.

Medenek incessantly grunted, evidently in pain and perhaps frightened, like Desta, that no one would save them.

Desta continued to rub the coin image on his chest. It was then he remembered Yewegey, the once cross-eyed boy whose eyes Desta corrected with the magical image of the coin on his chest. He lived nearby and wondered whether anyone was at home.

Leaving the mule where she lay, Desta took off in the direction of Yewegey's house. As he ran he kept rubbing the coin image, hoping the boy would be at home and would come help free Medenek.

Desta found Yewegey outside. The boy looked confused and lost.

He locked on Desta, searching his memory, and then lunged forward to hug him. "Great to see you! What brings you to our neighborhood?"

"I'm in need of help," Desta said, trying hard to remain calm. "A draft mule I'm traveling with has had a bad fall and I can't get her up."

"Do you think we need more than one person?"

"Maybe."

Yewegey dashed to his home and returned with his father, Meles. Desta ran, and Yewegey and his father followed.

When Desta returned to Medenek, she was still groaning but now feebly, as if seriously injured.

Together, father and son quickly moved the big boulders. Then while Desta and Meles lifted the mule's haunches, Yewegey untied the leather straps and pulled the sack from off her back.

Afterward, Meles placed both hands on Medenek's body and moved her back and forth. Although groaning no more, she stared through blurred eyes.

"Is she dead?" Desta asked, feeling sorrow rise up inside him.

"No. Her body is still warm," Meles said. "I think she is just exhausted from being trapped for so long."

Meles suggested they pull her away from the road. He held her head and Desta and Yewegey held her front legs, as they raised her upper body from the rocky terrain and gently dragged and placed her down under a tree.

After inspecting her body and legs, Meles noted Medenek's left front shoulder had been dislocated. She wouldn't be able to walk until it was corrected. He pushed and pulled every which way but she didn't budge.

"Where were you going or coming from?"

"I'm going to Finote Selam."

"This animal wouldn't have made it there," Meles said. "The fact that she made no effort to get up"—he noticed the ground was undisturbed around her legs—"shows she was pretty weak already."

Desta sucked his upper lip. He suddenly felt very sad, not so much for his own misfortune but for the animal's.

Meles went to get a donkey, leaving Desta and Yewegey behind. Desta wished Yewegey had gone with his father so that he could cry out. Fear and sorrow were gripping his heart. With this recent string of bad luck, it seemed he might not finish the eighth grade, let alone make it to Bahir Dar to further his education and search for the coin. Tears were generally his soothers, but that afternoon he couldn't shed a drop.

Yewegey turned to Desta and said, "Just moments before you came, I was having a weird feeling—akin to clairvoyance. I was called to go someplace but I didn't know where. I had come out of the house and was trying to orient myself and see which way I was supposed to be heading. And then you showed up. It was the strangest experience."

"I knew you lived nearby and prayed I'd find you at home if I came to ask for your help," Desta said. He smiled benignly.

Meles returned with the donkey and loaded the animal with the help of Desta and Yewegey. They all went back to the house, leaving poor Medenek lying by the tree.

The following morning, Meles and Desta went to check on Medenek. Desta walked with his hand to his chest, hoping she had recovered and was walking about chewing grass.

The delicate mule was not meant to survive. Death had come to her in the most terrible way. Some animals, most likely hyenas, had devoured her during the night. They saw fragments of her bones strewn under the tree.

Shocked and speechless, both Meles and Desta stood without moving a muscle. Meles put his face in his hand and Desta turned away.

Meles dropped a hand to his waist. "I should have fully predicted this," he said, his voice somber. "Hyenas have a great appetite for donkeys. And Medenek was an easy target."

Desta was still standing, speechless, as unmoving as a statue, and terrified of what was to come: What Teferra would do to him, and how he would now get himself and the sack of teff to Finote Selam.

"What do you want to do now?" Meles asked.

"I have no idea, really," Desta replied, holding back his tears. "I still need to go to Finote Selam. School starts tomorrow, which means I need to go today."

Meles thought for a long time. "Let's go home and see what we can do."

Desta wiped tears from the corners of his eyes and followed Meles.

"Be right back," Desta's host said and went inside. He came out several minutes later.

"This is what we'll do," he said, tossing his hand out. "We'll load my donkey with your sack of teff and go to Finote Selam together. What you did for my son a few years ago is worth this trip many times over."

Desta was awestruck. He couldn't speak for a few seconds.
Up to now he was thinking *how he could convince Dinknesh to
host him without being able to offer the teff in return.* With this
generous gesture from Meles, his hope was revived.

All he could say was, "You will?"

"Yes, I'm happy to do it. Let's quickly eat breakfast and get going."

The morning had not yet fully arrived when Desta, Meles, and the
loaded donkey started down the road to Finote Selam. Sorry as Desta
was for the lost mule, he was relieved that he wouldn't have to look after
her in Finote Selam, where there was no place on Dinknesh's property
to keep her overnight. He would deal with his brother's wrath later.

They arrived way before the sun dipped below the western
horizon. Dinknesh was pleased to see Desta. Doubly so for the
sack of teff he had with him—*a true face-saver indeed,* Desta
reminisced, thinking about what his father had said.

Meles took his leave, his donkey in tow, explaining he would be
spending the night with his relatives in town. Desta followed his lifesaver
and donkey to the open plaza, thanked Meles profusely, and they parted.

Chapter 37

Desta had returned to Dinknesh. They engaged in debate. "But I've no room for an additional person in this little *gojo*—hut," she protested, when Desta asked if he might live with her. They stood inside the entrance to her tiny house. On the other side of the living room, a woman and little girl sat on the floor with their eyes on Desta. The woman coughed intermittently.

"I'll be taking care of my sister, who has just come from the country for medical treatment. She has a bad case of asthma, which our traditional medicines have failed to cure."

"I won't need personal attention and I'll not need much space. Just a corner of your *medeb*—raised earthen bunk—will do. My father," he said, pointing to the sack on the floor, "sent this teff for our first month's supply. He plans to bring more in another month or so, after he's recovered from his illness." Desta elaborated on his father's condition.

Dinknesh looked down at the sack of teff. "I'm sorry to hear about your father's sickness. . . . And I appreciate he sent this teff, but there's more than just food you have to think about when managing a household, not to mention individual lives," she said, her voice dropping to a murmur.

"I know," Desta said. "I've lived with enough people to understand what it takes to run a home. . . . I'll make it as easy as possible for you. And I'll only be here for the next nine months, until I finish the eighth grade. *I hope.*"

"Your father sent you, trusting that I'd accept your offer. I suppose that would have been true if my situation were different. . . ." Her eyes drifted toward the entrance to the outdoors. She turned and said, "Could you step outside for a moment? I need to discuss this with my sister. Her comfort here is very important, too. Let me see how she feels about it."

Desta's stomach coiled. He stumbled outside and stood with his arms crossed high on his chest. He pressed the area above his heart while his mind focused on the image of him living with Dinknesh in the months to come.

Moments later his host appeared at the door. "C'mon in," she said, with a lilt in her voice.

"My sister says it's fine with her." Dinknesh gave Desta a lingering, intrigued look. Desta arched his brow, puzzled. Asking what was on her mind would have been intrusive. Instead he cast his eyes toward the floor and contemplated her intent.

Over the years, he had become well-versed in reading people's eyes, faces, voices, and the hidden meaning of their words. This was how he could anticipate potential problems and protect himself from getting hurt.

Dinknesh's look was more of curiosity than malice or suspicion. Not able to know beyond this, Desta simply said, "Thank you. I'll be respectful of your space and privacy."

"Considering that we share the same living quarters, I wouldn't be disappointed if you transgressed," Dinknesh said, smiling a little.

Desta smiled a little, too.

Dinknesh went on, "Per your suggestion, let's have you sleep at that corner then," she said, pointing to the shadowy area near the door. "It's the only spot where the eye and the outdoor light have no direct access. The silhouette of the door offers a measure of privacy."

"Thank you," Desta said. "I'll be happy there."

Almost as an afterthought Dinknesh said, "I have to warn you though. As you have already noticed, my sister—Hiwot is her name—coughs a lot. You may have trouble falling asleep or be woken in the middle of the night. This I cannot help. We just have to deal with it, as her family at home has dealt with it."

"That won't be a problem," Desta said quickly. "I'm not a light sleeper."

Having struck an arrangement, he let go a deep sigh. "Thank you again for the accommodations. You'll make my father happy," he added.

"You're welcome! Your father is a good man." Dinknesh tapped him on the shoulder. "Go have a seat, I'll make us dinner," she said and walked off.

Desta stepped over to Hiwot and her little girl, Beza. He bent a little and said, "Thank you for accepting me as your housemate."

Hiwot stared at him for a few seconds. "Don't thank me, I'm just a sojourner like you, but our being here together may be by design and not by mere coincidence. . . . A pleasure to meet you!" She turned her face away and a succession of productive-sounding hacking coughs ensued, but nothing came up.

"A pleasure to meet you," Desta said, once Hiwot regained her composure.

She nodded in acknowledgement with her hand over her mouth, anticipating another bout of coughing.

"Sorry for your condition," Desta said. "I hope you find a cure for it soon." He walked over and sat on the high curving earthen seat and took inventory of his new home. Dinknesh was not being overly modest about the size of her home. This domicile that Desta would be sharing with two women and a little girl was unpretentious indeed.

The living quarters amounted to a circular dirt floor, edged on the back wall by the long, curving bunk. Above the bunk, the wall broke into a pocket, which fit a bed that slept no more than two people. This was Dinknesh's sleeping den.

Near the entrance a long rickety table claimed a good portion of the floor.

Hiwot and Beza had been apportioned the area directly across from the entrance, near a small pantry. Although out of the way from the indoor foot traffic, their space was just two long strides from the entrance, and close enough that whispered conversations from here could be heard anywhere in the living room.

It was because of this cramped living situation Dinknesh had no fireplace in the house. She cooked in an open-air pit outside when the weather was good and under her eaves or in the neighbor's kitchen when the outdoor conditions didn't permit.

In the ensuing days Dinknesh's warning about her sister's relentless coughing bore fruit. The pills and treatments Hiwot was getting from the clinic had not helped her asthma in the least.

She continued to cough. Sometimes she coughed until her eyes watered. Other times she coughed until she convulsed on the floor and gasped for the very air that kept her alive. Sometimes her coughs were dry and brittle. Other times they were frothy and wet. Sometimes her coughs came in flurries; other times in short, isolated spells, lasting a few minutes at a time. But she also had breaks, a stretch of an hour or two of normal living.

For Desta this state of affairs made sleeping or staying in the house nearly impossible. Most nights he slept just four or five hours. The hours in which he was not sleeping were simply wasted. He couldn't light the kerosene lamp to read or study because they didn't have money to pay for extra fuel. While lying with his eyes closed, he couldn't even hold a thought for any length of time to keep his mind active and engaged. Hiwot's cacophonous coughing was jarring to his senses.

Also Hiwot's constant coughing and occasional production of sputum, which she collected in an open spittoon, lent an unpleasant, and somewhat unclean, atmosphere to the room.

Despite this seemingly insurmountable problem, Desta chose
to approach the issue as a challenge, not a catastrophe. He didn't
complain or whine to anybody. He decided he had to find his own
solution or, as Dinknesh had suggested, get used to the situation.

He stayed behind on campus in the evening, getting his studying and
homework done. In the morning he got up before dawn and studied under the
warka tree, a stone's throw from Dinknesh's house. It's here before anything
else he recited the legends and the selected seven narratives on the new
parchment the mysterious spirit had organized and written out for him.

At home he didn't just get used to Hiwot's coughing, he became
a student, an observer, and an interpreter of the relationship that
developed among his housemates in response to her illness.

Dinknesh stopped her tella and tea business and now devoted all of her time
to the care of her sister. Five-year-old Beza refused to go out and play with the
neighborhood kids because she wanted to be by her mother's side at all times.
When Dinknesh was not around, Beza was the hands and feet of her mother.

She took the spittoon out and cleaned and brought it back afterward.
She washed coffee beans between her two little hands and roasted them in
a pan over glowing charcoal. She took it off the fire when done and set it
aside to cool. She left the task of grinding the roasted beans in the wooden
mortar and pestle to her aunt. Her arms simply weren't strong enough.

She had seen her aunt's comforting hand on her mother's shoulder
when her coughing became severe. Lately, Beza had been offering the same
gesture of support to her mother.

After Desta became personally involved with the affairs of his housemates,
he no longer judged and criticized what he saw and heard. Hiwot's
problem stopped being *his* problem. It was as if he no longer heard or saw
a woman with asthma. The compassion he developed for her superseded
the comfort and peace he needed for himself. He saw Hiwot's struggle for
life as his own struggle to be alive enough to accomplish his dreams.

One afternoon when she had a lull from her coughing, Desta said,
"Considering that things have not improved with your asthma,
what keeps you going, Hiwot?"

"Hope—hope for a miracle; hope I'll one day be cured and lead a normal
life and raise my daughter to womanhood; hope that God will see my struggle

and will one day heal me. Not for me but for this little thing."
She engulfed Beza in her arms.

"Don't give up. Keep praying and seeing yourself as a healthy
woman. God has a way of giving you what you really want."

That night, Desta didn't want to leave Hiwot's wishes up to God.
He decided to invoke the magical powers of the coin. Shortly after he
lay in bed, he rubbed the coin's image on his chest, thinking of Hiwot
and her asthma and imagining her as a vibrant and healthy human being.
He chanted "heal Hiwot" twenty-one times. Then he went to sleep.

The next day early in the morning he went to the warka tree to recite the
legends and chant the "heal Hiwot" mantra. Then he commenced studying.
The birds came down from the tree as if Desta had brought them a basket of
grain. They pecked the dirt around him looking for food. Defaru—he called one
particular bird by this name because it was not afraid of people—stopped in front
of him as if to say something. What happened next was stunning, if not terrifying.

Right in front of Desta's eyes, Defaru slowly grew into a
giant bird, before suddenly turning into a smiling human being.
Desta dropped his notebooks and froze. The smiling face was
comforting, otherwise Desta might've fled toward home.

"You want to help, Hiwot, eh?" the man asked.

"That is my wish, yes!"

"You can help her with your coin but there is something more powerful.
Tomorrow morning be here at the same time and I'll administer the ultimate
treatment for asthma."

Desta stammered, trying to say something, but no words came out. By
this time the man had transformed back into the little bird, which was now
part of the flock busy pecking the ground, looking for morsels of food.

Desta blinked and threw his head back, trying to determine whether
a real man or a phantom had appeared before his eyes. He looked
around but there was no person—smiling or otherwise—to be seen.
The bird was still there busily pecking like the rest of its mates.

Feeling spooked, he hurriedly gathered his books and went home.
Throughout the day, Desta thought about the phantom, wondering whether he
would show up the next morning with the treatment he promised for Hiwot.
That there was the possibility of a cure for her brought a smile to his face.

When he went home in the evening, he noticed that Hiwot was not coughing as much, and when she did her coughs were not as gut-wrenching as usual.

That's a good start, Desta thought. He couldn't wait until
the morning broke and he could go to the warka tree.

HE SAT ON HIS USUAL perch and quickly recited the parchment. Then he
leaned back and waited for the phantom, for the birds to come down. The
creatures of the air finally descended and began their search for food in the
dirt around him. The only one missing was Defaru. Desta started twiddling
his thumbs, wondering whether he was going to come at all. He finally did
come, joining his mates as soon as he descended. Desta kept his eye on the
bird so as not to miss the moment when he transformed himself into a human
being. To his disappointment, the bird remained a bird. Now he was convinced
that he hadn't seen a man at all the day before. He must've imagined it.
Just then the spirit man appeared, literally materialized out of nowhere.

"You're still here! Good!" Defaru said. He reached under his straw-
green jacket, pulled out something that looked like a root, and handed it
to Desta. "This," he said, "is the medicine that will cure Hiwot's asthma.
It should be administered before she goes to sleep at night. Tell her to
chop it into small pieces and drop the bits onto glowing charcoal. She
should then cover herself and the smoking root with a sheet or netela and
try to inhale as much of the smoke as she can. It has a strong odor. By
the following day, she should be cured of her asthma completely."

Desta flipped the object one way and then the other. With its many
hair-like strands, it had more the quality of a strange insect than a root.

He looked up at the man and found himself exclaiming, "Really?!"

"Really!"

Desta had to control his excitement. "Who are you?"

"I'm the voice that has given you messages in the past, but you and I
have never formally met. I'm your family's custodian, a spirit that comes
to help you at critical moments—often invoked by the call of the coin."

"Really?"

"Really!"

"Thank you for showing up. It truly is crucial that Hiwot gets relief from
her suffering; her daughter and sister Dinknesh need relief, too," Desta said.

"Go now and give her that root. Tell her to follow the
instructions I gave you." With that the spirit vanished.

Desta ran home. "Hiwot! Hiwot!" he shouted. "This," he said, waving the strange object before her eyes, "will cure your asthma." He handed her the root.

She flipped it one way and then the other. She looked at Desta and asked, "Really?"

"It's true!"

"Who gave it to you?"

"A man."

"A complete stranger?"

"Not really. We have met before, sort of," Desta said, after hesitating a bit. Then he told her the instructions the man had given him about inhaling the smoke from the root.

Hiwot knitted her brow and narrowed her eyes.

"Don't ask too many questions. Just try it. This is your last real chance, not the pills you have been taking, which have done nothing for you."

"Yes, I will," she said, slowly relenting.

Beza took the root from her mother's hand and started stroking the dangling strands.

"Need to run to school. Am already late," Desta managed to say, as he grabbed his books and dashed to the door.

"Without your breakfast?" Hiwot asked. "Take at least a few slices of the loaf."

"Thank you," he said, retracing his steps. He picked out a couple of slices from the basket on the table and took off running.

THE MORNING AFTER the treatment with the strange root, Hiwot woke to face three pairs of eyes. Her housemates and her daughter had congregated around her.

To everyone's surprise, Hiwot looked like a new person. Gone was the coughing and the wheezing and the tears. Her eyes twinkled like stars and her face bloomed with happiness. "It's truly a miracle," she said, her eyes hopping from Beza to Desta to Dinknesh. "I feel wonderful!"

"You look beautiful," Dinknesh said, wiping her tears.

Desta held back his tears. "I didn't think it would be this dramatic," he said, "I'm thrilled for you."

Dinknesh turned to Desta and hugged him. "I cannot thank you enough for what you have done," she said through her sniffles.

"How can I say this without sounding false. . . . I'll just

say that I'm happy for you," Desta said. Then Hiwot's face
hardened suddenly. "Do you think this is permanent?"

"I think it is. We'll find out in the days and months to come."

"To see her this happy, even for one day, is a blessing," Dinknesh said.

"My lungs feel perfectly clear. . . ." Hiwot was overtaken by her own deep
feelings. She hugged Desta, now crying profusely on his shoulder. Then she let
go, chuckling nervously as she dabbed her tears with the back of her hand.

"You know," Hiwot said, "before I came here I went to see a *deb'tera*—seer.
He said that I'd be living with a person who would find a cure for my disease. I
didn't believe him. I came in part to get the modern medicine treatment my sister
had been insisting I try as a last resort. If the pills hadn't worked, I was facing
death as the ultimate solution to my misery." She succumbed to her tears again.

"I remember you mentioned that, but I was skeptical
because the deb'teras would say anything to get your money,"
Dinknesh said, getting up. "Let me make us some tea."

Desta didn't go to the warka tree that morning. He stayed at home and
celebrated Hiwot's recovery with the rest of his housemates over dabo and tea.

Chapter 38

Beza and her very healthy mother left Dinknesh's house after staying one week more. Desta made Hiwot promise to return in a year and put her daughter in school. Dinknesh recommenced her normal life of making and selling tella and tea and sometimes food. She also resumed having men over, which only continued to disrupt the rhythm of Desta's life. But his host continued to be the even-tempered, kind, and giving person she had always been. Still he couldn't continue to live where boisterous drunken men lingered in the home well past his bedtime. But he was grateful for what Dinknesh had done for him. He successfully completed his first semester of school. However, the unsuitable condition of her home environment caused Desta to seek accommodation elsewhere for his second semester. His wish was fulfilled by an accidental encounter with a man who had the need for what Desta could offer.

While Desta was en route back to school, after spending Christmas break with his family in the country, he ran into the governor of Sekela, *Fit'aawrari*—Commander of the Vanguard—Asrat, and his entourage of a dozen men. A brown-skinned, white-haired man with matching beard, Asrat reminded Desta of his vervet monkey friends, except that they were prettier. He had seen him at a distance before and heard about him from his father. Desta was encouraged to travel with the governor and his footmen, which gave him a chance to get a good look at the man. Asrat sat high on his white horse.

One of the men—Kasey—knew about Desta and his academic accomplishments. He formally introduced Desta to the governor. The first word that came out of Asrat's mouth was, "the *geberay lij*—farmer's son—I heard so much about?" in a voice that was both pejorative and condescending. A pair of small eyes came down from their perch and scrutinized him.

Kasey winced a little. He rested his hand on Desta's shoulder. "Yes, they say he is the best student in the whole school, isn't that right?"

"I don't think so," Desta said with certainty. Kasey's effort was not lost on Desta. He was trying to make up for the insensitive snub hurled by the governor. "There are many who are better than I am."

"What we need is someone like this boy who might motivate and inspire our children," the governor said. He slowed his white steed so that Kasey wouldn't have to trot to keep pace with him.

"I'm sure we can hire a boy like Desta who can work with them," the footman said, looking up to the mountain.

"They are doing fine but are not stellar like some of the kids we hear about. I wouldn't mind trying that. Someone who could come a few times a week or live in even," Asrat said.

"I'll ask around," Kasey said. Then the conversation moved on to politics and disadvantaged youth.

Desta turned a deaf ear. It was true that in all the schools he had been to, the top students always seemed to be the kids from economically disadvantaged families, and from the countryside in particular. They seemed to value education more. Many well-to-do families didn't seem to be getting their children to go to school or encouraging them to open their minds. These kids were rich with stuff but poorly educated. Desta had to admit that he sometimes appreciated Abraham's philosophy of not indulging a child. "Let the child solve problems he faces," he often said. "He will become a well-adjusted and better adult that way."

Later, as they approached the town, Kasey said, "Why should I go casting about for other students when there is one with us here," he said, smiling some. "Would you be interested in living with Governor Asrat's family and working with his children, Desta?"

Kasey caught Desta off guard. He thought if the governor had wanted him, he would have suggested it when the idea was discussed earlier. Also, Asrat's snobbish air had turned Desta off. The governor had given the impression he didn't want his children to be associating with a farmer's son. Now that Kasey was broaching the idea, however, he would have to think about it.

"*Gashe*—honorific—Kasey," Desta said, when they were out of the governor's earshot, "first, you have a leap of faith in people like the governor who just because he sits high on his white horse and is the head of a district feels he has a legitimate right to slight others who he perceives to be less than he is. Second, before you asked me in front of the governor, you should've checked with me. That way both you and I could keep our cards close to the chest. Third, yes, I would be interested if he is serious and would instruct his children to treat and respect me like their equal."

Kasey was quiet. Desta was not sure whether he'd heard what he'd said.

He turned and looked at him. The footman's face and eyes showed thought, but Desta was not sure what Kasey was thinking about. "Did you hear what I said, Gashe Kasey?" he asked, lowering his voice with diffidence.

"Yes, I did. You just caught me by surprise."

"Why—you didn't expect me to think—like you, the adult? Or as the son of a farmer, perhaps I shouldn't be asking or commenting like I have?"

Kasey was quiet again. Then he glanced at Desta. "You're right, I shouldn't have assumed as much as I did . . . on behalf of both you and the governor. I'll ask him first and see what he says, and we'll go from there. Is that okay?"

"I think that's perfectly fine. . . . You brought up a point that I have long thought about but have never shared with anyone. When people know little, they assume too much. When we understand little about people and animals, we take things for granted. Let me explain what I mean by this. When I was a little boy—oh, say, four or five—my dog Kooli and I arrived from the field and happened upon my father and eldest brother. They were outside polishing a metal object. Propped up on two stilts, this thing resembled a sitting dog. I asked them what it was.

"My father, with his eyes and hands busy with what he was doing, said in a very casual and dismissive manner, 'Oh, it's a piece of metal I broke off and brought home from an old abandoned truck.'

"I couldn't believe it. It was not just a piece of metal. It was a *gun*—a 'machine gun,' as I learned later. I knew exactly what it was. I just didn't know what they called it. My father assumed I knew so little that he could've said it was a piece of wood he'd taken from a dead tree, and I would've believed him. I had wanted to tell him I knew better, but what good does it do to challenge people who are so much higher, both in age and height. I was disappointed that he thought so little of me to tell me things that were untrue. But more to the point, I came to realize the wide gap that existed between adults and children sometimes.

"The other observation I had involves my mother. Ayénat would throw spoiled meat to my dog. When I asked her why she gave the animal food she wouldn't eat herself, she would retort, 'He's only a dog.'

"'Ma,' I'd say, 'Kooli has feelings, Kooli knows it's bad because he can smell it, and it's not good food. Kooli knows a lot. He just lacks the language to tell you how he feels and what he thinks of you. The trouble is, Ma, you assume too much. Please don't do it again.' Mother became respectful of Kooli after we had that conversation. . . . In short, this is to say that you'll be on safer ground if you don't take things for granted. Always give others the benefit of the doubt."

"How right you are," Kasey said. "How did you become so wise like this at your age?"

"Because I have seen and felt so much in the sixteen years I have been here on earth. If you pay attention, life can be your best teacher."

Kasey shook his head and went silent again.

Shortly before they reached the point where the road split, one leg going to town, the other leg north to the governor's second home, Kasey trotted ahead, He interrupted Asrat's conversation with one of the other footmen, and shared his thoughts about having Desta tutor the governor's children.

"Sure," the governor said, without hesitating. "Let him come tomorrow and meet my children and the rest of the people."

Kasey gave Desta the directions and some landmarks that would help him identify the governor's compound, on which stood two well-appointed homes.

DINKNESH'S HOUSE was full of people, men sitting around the bunk seat, drinking tella, and talking liberally. Dinknesh kissed Desta endearingly when he arrived and made him as welcome as a mother would have, but inside he felt like a homeless person. With that many people and his small sleeping corner taken, he realized he would have to go elsewhere or stay up until the people left. After having walked all day, he just wanted a place to lie down.

Noticing how exhausted he was, Dinknesh brought Desta a skin mat and a blanket and spread them under the eaves for him. He fell asleep. By the time Dinknesh woke him up, it was near midnight. People had already left. The house was quiet now and welcoming. After eating his dinner, he crawled to his bed in the corner and immediately was lost to the world.

The following day shortly after nine o'clock, Desta left for Governor Asrat's home. He prayed that the governor and his family had room in their home and hearts for him so he could finish out his eighth-grade education.

The children were the first to receive him—one boy and two girls. They ranged in age from nine to fifteen, the boy being the oldest. The children already knew who Desta was, but Desta was curious to know who the children were. With one hand on Desta's shoulder, Kasey introduced Mesfin, Leyla, and Eden. "You know his name, right?"

"Desta!" all said in a chorus.

Desta, surprised that students outside his classroom knew him, felt important and pretty good inside.

"As you all know Desta is a good student. Your father thought it would be good for you to have a student like Desta in your company. He can help and motivate you to be top students like him. Would you like that?"

"Yesss!" the three said in unison.

"Desta, what do you think—would you like to live here and work with these young people?"

Desta thought for a few seconds, assessing his feelings about the children and the general ambience of the place. It was a large rectangular compound surrounded by trees. There was a fence on three sides. It felt like a great place to get lost in any time he wanted privacy and space. "I think I'd welcome it," Desta said finally.

"Great!" Kasey exclaimed. "We'll work out the sleeping arrangements, but what I want to add is that you kids must respect and cooperate with Desta. The primary reason he is here is to help you with your studies. Don't ask him to do things for you that you know you can do for yourselves. Is that clear?"

The three children nodded.

"Now you can go. Desta and I are going to meet Mamita."

Leyla and Eden hopped a little as they headed to the main house. Mesfin walked with his head down behind them.

"Mamita is the cook," Kasey said. "She along with Lema, the groundskeeper, and the children are the only ones who live here. Governor Asrat and his wife live in Yeedib. They come here once or twice a month, and that's when this place can get very busy. Otherwise it's serene and pleasant like this the rest of the time. Mamita is a good disciplinarian— the reason the governor keeps her here. She used to work at their home in Yeedib. Be patient with her. Deep down she is a good-hearted woman."

They found Mamita outside, busy with germinated barley, which she was trying to dry in the sun.

"Mamita, I want you to meet Desta, a student at the school who will be living with you and the children here."

The cook looked disheveled. "Is that so?" she asked, a feigned smile veiling her small face.

"Yes. Desta is one of the top students in the school and the governor thinks, and I agree, that the children need someone like him to help motivate and inspire them."

Mamita's face now became serious and businesslike. "I think it
would be a good idea, particularly for Mesfin. He needs a friend. The
girls have each other," she said, glancing at Kasey. "Yes, sometimes
they can be difficult to manage but I'll keep an eye on them."

Kasey agreed. They took a tour of the two houses so Desta
could decide where he wanted to sleep. The main house was new
and the floors covered with rugs and plush animal skins. Both
houses were painted white inside and out, with dark blue trim.

The kitchen house was dingy but had a large bed and a big window, which
looked out onto a grove of trees. Only the groundskeeper slept here. The choice
was either to share a room with Mesfin in the main house or sleep here on his
own. Desta chose the latter. Lema slept in his own bed in a separate room.

Kasey, the general manager of all the properties the governor
owned, established the rules. After dinner, Desta was to spend one to
two hours every evening studying with the children. He would answer
any questions and make sure they concentrated on their studies. Then
Desta would go to his sleeping quarters in the kitchen house.

"TO HE WHO WEARS a nice set of clothes, tip your head," Desta had heard
his father say, citing the common expression. So as he returned to Dinknesh's
home later that morning, the first thing Desta wanted to do was wash the set of
clothes Asse'ged had made for him before he died. He didn't want to disrespect
his brother by dressing like an orphan. Desta hadn't gotten a chance to wear
Asse'ged's beautifully made clothes until now.

In the afternoon he washed his clothes and then went to a store to
purchase a new pair of tennis shoes with money he had saved.

The following day he went to the governor's compound dressed in
his new clothes and shoes and brought most of his belongings. He had
sent his flying craft home with Abraham shortly after he began living in
Konjit's shack a year and a half ago. The governor, his children, and the
rest of the residents didn't exactly bow to Desta in his new attire, but they
regarded him with respect. Desta, like his father, always looked good
when he dressed up. Like Abraham he walked and comported himself
around people with dignity and self-confidence. He set the tone around the
household; it was a noble quality he hoped to maintain the rest of his stay.

In the main house, two tables with resin-coated floral tablecloths were set up at opposite sides of a room. This was the study hall. During study time, Desta and Mesfin were to sit at one table and the two girls at the other. Each table was to have a kerosene lamp.

It wasn't until Desta saw the study hall that he realized how undefined his role as 'tutor' actually was. Would he simply be sitting at the table and studying and hoping the three children would do the same? Or would he be actively instructing them? The father wanted to see measurable results. This meant Desta would have to make sure the kids committed to their studies in the hours he was with them.

With kids who had been left here without any formal supervision, would he succeed? He couldn't help noticing that Mamita sounded a bit exasperated with the children.

Rules govern people. He had seen them being implemented in every aspect of his life: in school, in church, and at home. So Desta decided to have a list of rules. He would share his list before the start of their first study session.

After they went into their study room, Desta gathered all three children and told them what he called their mutual rules.

"One, we'll have dinner by six o'clock and be here by six-thirty sharp. If any of you want to eat earlier and come here to study afterward that's fine. We'll eventually join you."

Eden rolled her eyes.

"Two, once we sit down to study, nobody should talk or get up and move around the room. We need to keep sitting and studying quietly. We'll be here for two hours with a fifteen-minute break in between."

Eden pursed her lips tight.

"We cannot be eating while studying or getting up and going to get something to drink. You should take care of that beforehand.

"Three, if you have questions, write them down and we can discuss them at the end of the study session. We'll have fifteen or so minutes dedicated just to that."

Eden's mouth twitched as if to say something, but she didn't.

The other two stood stone-faced.

"Any questions?"

"How about if I want to go to the bathroom?" Leyla asked.

"Just get up quietly and go. And don't dawdle. That's fine."

"I sometimes play soccer or do things with my friends after school.

Do I have to be here exactly at six-thirty?" Mesfin grumbled.

"Yes. We all have to be here at the same time and finish with our studies at the same time."

Mesfin rolled his eyes.

Eden piped up. "Is sneezing allowed?"

Desta fixed his eyes on the little girl for a few seconds but didn't answer her. That he was getting this kind of back talk before they even started their study session meant Desta was going to have his hands full with these three.

"Those are the rules. Your father and Gashe Kasey brought me here to encourage you and help you with your studies. If you don't do well, they will blame me. If you don't cooperate with me, I will be forced to write down each incident and report it to them. . . . I hope I won't have to. . . . That will be entirely up to you."

Eyes flashed, lips murmured, but no real sound came out of their mouths.

"Go get your notebooks and let's sit down to study."

Desta sat down at the table dedicated to him and Mesfin. Butterflies took hold of his stomach as he contemplated that the children might never return with their notebooks.

With his eyes on the door, he drummed his fingers on the table.

Mesfin was the first to come back. Then Leyla. The last was Eden. The little girl apologized, saying that she couldn't find all of her notebooks.

Desta looked at her suspiciously.

Leyla corroborated Eden's claim. "She is never organized and she is always losing things."

The two girls sat at their table. Mesfin took the chair across from Desta.

Leading by example, the tutor opened his notebook and began studying with all the concentration he could muster. Mesfin did the same, and so did the girls. Desta sighed silently.

With his ears and eyes he monitored the tables. Leyla was serious and kept her focus on her open notebook. Eden's gaze stole through the room occasionally. She would look up at her sister as if willing Leyla to exchange a nod or a wink.

First came a burp, and then a muffled giggle. Desta didn't see who was responsible. Eden appeared the instigator because she was stifling a smile. Leyla had shielded her face with her hand and was struggling not to laugh.

Mesfin glanced at the girls, then at his mate across the table, and back to his notebook. Desta pretended he didn't hear or see what was going on. Eden finally fell silent. There was another outburst of giggling about ten minutes before their first hour of study ended. This time Leyla had joined in.

Mesfin lifted his face again. He glanced at the girls and back to his studies. Desta continued to ignore them.

When their first hour of study was up, Desta went directly to the girls' table to admonish them. He directed his comments mostly to Eden, indicating that he already had two points against her. To this Leyla said, "She has the attention span of a dog and she forgets things easily. She has probably already forgotten the rules you told us at the beginning."

Desta shook his head in exasperation. "Okay. Eden, from now on we'll leave the door open. The next time you have the giggles when we are studying, go outside and laugh all you want and come back afterward. Can you do that?"

Eden nodded.

"You're dreaming," Leyla said. "She will forget that, too, I'm sure."

"No, she won't. Right, Eden?"

She nodded again.

"Good girl."

"We'll see," the older sister said.

For their break they went to the dining room which was next door to the study hall. Mamita served them tea and dabo which they ate and drank quietly. Desta thought that if he or Mamita were no there watching them, the atmosphere in the room would have been completely different. Soon after they finished their beverage and snack they went back to their room, Desta leading the way.

The next hour passed without any incident. They were concentrated in either their studies or doing their homework.

THAT FIRST NIGHT'S STUDY session was more or less representative of all the sessions they had throughout Desta's stay at Governor Asrat's home. Eden contained herself in the study room and showed more colors outside of it. She was constantly in trouble with the cook and Lema, mostly because she was mischievous—she wasn't a bad kid.

One day while Desta was in the backyard washing his clothes, someone hit him in the back with a fig. He immediately rose to see who threw it. He looked all around, but there was no one in sight. He rubbed his back for a bit and sat on the heels again to continue scrubbing his clothes.

Soon after, he was struck again—much harder this time. He stood and scanned the grounds once more. "Who is doing this to me? Stop it! It really hurts. Whoever you are, just know that you'll be sorry when I find out."

Nervous and wary he crouched again, trying to quickly finish his washing and get back in the house. With a few douses of clean water he removed the remaining soap. He proceeded to wring the water from the clothes and hang them on the line. His nerves eased and he figured the culprit had gotten the message. He was wrong. As he was turning to leave the yard, he felt another hard pelting at his back.

There wasn't a soul to be found. He decided the source of the ammunition, the fig tree, might provide a clue. He walked all over the grounds. There wasn't a fig tree among the foliage. However, he spied a lush and mighty oak along the fence. There he made out the offender. Hidden among the leaves like a monkey was Eden. When their eyes met, she burst into her giggles.

"Come down!" Desta demanded.

"Not if you're going to hit me like you threatened."

Desta contemplated his options. He'd never said he'd actually hit her, and he never would. There was not much he could do. He simply walked home, rubbing all the places where Eden assaulted him.

Another of Eden's stunts, a recurring one, which thankfully didn't involve Desta, would happen in the morning before school. She would go ahead of everybody and hide in the bushes. As her classmates walked past her hiding place on their way to school, she would jump out and scare them, giggling and then guffawing in the process. This worked only the first two or three times, of course. The family was worried that if she happened to startle complete strangers, she could get hurt. Luckily her pranks were limited just to the family and her school friends.

Leyla and Mesfin were more mellow children. Their problem was more with the changes their bodies were going through. They experienced mood swings and unexpected temper tantrums, especially Leyla. There was a particular incident that involved Desta. Leyla and Eden were sitting with their backs to the wall of the main house, crying.

When Desta came upon the distraught girls, he asked them what was wrong. He placed his hand on his mouth and stared at them, concerned.

"Leyla thinks she is going to die."

"What?"

"Yeah, she has been bleeding since this morning," Eden said, wiping her tears.

"Where?"

Eden glanced at her sister and then at Desta but said nothing.

Desta scratched his head. "You don't know where she is bleeding?"

"Yeah, we know," Eden said. "It's in a place *you* cannot see."

When Eden noticed Desta was still at a loss,
she blurted, "You know, *down there*."

Desta had seen that kind of blood before. When he lived in the country, blood as Eden described it sometimes appeared where his sister-in-laws had been sitting.

"I don't think she is going to die from that kind of blood. Go talk to Mamita. She can explain it better, okay?" he said. "I don't know much about it." With this he walked off, relieved.

Later when Desta told the story to Lema the groundskeeper, the man laughed. "That's pretty bad actually," he said.

"Nobody has taught these children what happens to their bodies as they grow older. My father was good about that."

"Yeah, you're right," Lema said, rubbing his chin. "That's pretty funny I must admit." He laughed again. . . .

Living with Governor Asrat's family was very comfortable for Desta. Grain and animals for their food came from the governor's holdings in the country. And chickens were raised in the compound for eggs. The cook prepared their meals in a timely manner, with meat dishes three to four times a week.

Academically, the children did well despite their resistance early on. The wild Eden performed the best of the three children. She was first in her class and earned the highest mark in mathematics.

Mesfin and Leyla finished in the top ten. Mamita, who was the main reporter to the governor and Kasey, said that since Desta has been living with them, the children were better behaved and more diligent in their studies, as reflected in their outstanding academic performance.

Desta himself did extremely well academically, ranking first in his class and earning the highest scores in some of his subjects.

Both the governor and Kasey were thankful and pleased with their decision to have Desta tutor the kids. When the year was out, having met his obligation to the governor and his family, Desta moved on.

Chapter 39

1966

The director of the school had announced there would be a graduation ceremony for the eighth-graders on Saturday, June 25. The students' families and friends were invited. When Desta asked Belachew, his homeroom teacher, what it was for, Belachew had said, "It's the formal acknowledgement of an academic milestone, a valediction ceremony for students who have reached a school's highest scholastic learning, which simply goes by 'graduation.'"

For Desta the term *milestone* meant more than simply 'marker' or 'occasion.' From where he started to where he currently stood, it had been a long journey and he considered his academic achievement to be an incredible feat.

He had come two and half years previously with only the clothes on his back and money barely enough to pay for a week's worth of food. He had neither transfer documents to the new school nor people in town he could live with.

With no accommodations to be found in the towns that had high schools and little financial support from his family, Desta had turned to the greater world—complete strangers who offered him room and board in exchange for his services while he continued with his studies.

He managed to convince the director to accept him into the fourth grade. And he found someone to live with. However, the relationship with this person, as with other individuals later on, was neither enduring nor unconditional. All in all he was forced to move five times, living with five different families for the two and a half years he studied in Finote Selam. The transitions were often difficult and uncomfortable, at times making Desta feel as if he were climbing a steep mountain with nothing for leverage but his hands, nails, and teeth.

During this time he suffered bodily harm. He eventually healed, but the memory of the assault echoed in his head, affecting many aspects of his life, particularly his academic performance. He felt that, through some of his experiences, he had come to know what a dog must feel when he is abandoned—the confusion and sense of loss—and what can happen to a forgotten animal that follows his master's scent.

Although Desta's nomadic life was disruptive to the rhythm of his routines, and he was scarred by some of the awful things that had happened to him, overall he found the past two and a half years to be exceedingly enriching. He knew all that he'd endured was meant to prepare him for the bigger challenges ahead, as he advanced farther into the world and pursued the second Coin of Magic and Fortune.

He had finished his studies one and a half years earlier than expected. He'd gotten good marks in all his classes. These achievements helped him carry on and forget the bad times.

Prior to coming to Finote Selam, Desta had lived with three different families. First, his dear uncle and aunt took him in, but they were soon killed in a bus accident. Then he was permitted to stay with distant relatives on his father's side who starved and physically abused him. The third living arrangement was with complete strangers, whom Desta adopted as his family. He led a good but academically stagnant life while he lived with them. After he finished the fourth grade, he remained where he was because he couldn't find benefactors in the towns that had modern schools.

After all these experiences and factoring in lost time, it took Desta seven years to complete his elementary and middle school education. But based on what he was able to accomplish at the Finote Selam school, if he'd been able to attend school without interruption, he would've completed his early education in just four years—half the time. Desta thought that this would have caused his father's head to grow out like a pumpkin with pride.

No matter, here he was, having finished his education through the eighth grade and ready to be sanctioned a graduate. And ready to move to bigger places, where further adventures and experiences awaited him.

Desta sent his father and mother an invitation to the graduation ceremony. Of course, he went to Dinknesh and personally invited her, and he wrote a note to Alem and Aberra, encouraging them to attend. He also suggested they tell Konjit, in case she wanted to come. Desta asked Governor Asrat's children and Mamita, the cook, who were excited to see him graduate. He wanted to invite Colonel Mulugeta, but there was no way to get the invitation to him. In all he had expected twelve people, possibly thirteen, if Konjit came.

Abraham arrived alone two days early. He said Ayenat couldn't come because they had no one to look after the home in their absence. The father wanted to buy Desta some new clothes, and so they went

shopping. It was common practice to order tailor-made clothing, but
there wasn't time to have a suit sewn for Desta's graduation. Therefore,
they went in search of a ready-made suit. None was to be found.

However, one shop owner named Mikias said he knew of a
customer who had ordered a boy's suit that ended up not fitting. "They
may be willing to sell it to you at reasonable price," Mikias said.

"What's your name?" the shopkeeper asked, bending a little toward Desta.
Desta told him.

"You're the famous Desta!" Mikias exclaimed, his face brightening. "A
pleasure to meet you! My son and his friends talk about you all the time."

He looked up at Abraham. "What medicine have you given this boy
to make him such a good student?"

Abraham smiled, his lips parting past the edge of his chipped
tooth. "Nothing, really. He's just a hardworking student."

"My son studies hard, too, but he doesn't get the kind of marks
your son earns. . . . Look, about Desta's suit, I will arrange to have
it delivered to my store. Check back with me later today."

"Thank you," both Abraham and Desta said and left.

Late in the afternoon Desta and Abraham returned to the store.

"C'mon in," Mikias said with a smile when he saw the pair at the door.

"I went there myself and got it. They were particularly pleased when I told
them who it was for. You see, everybody in town knows about your boy."

Abraham looked down on Desta, beaming. "Let's hope he keeps
up his work at this level or better in the future," he said firmly.

The pair watched apprehensively as Mikias took the
suit off the hanger and spread it out on the counter.

"This looks beautiful but . . .," Abraham began to say.

When Mikias fixed his eyes on Desta's father, anticipating
the completion of his thought, Abraham said, "I don't have
the kind of money for an expensive suit such as this."

"Let's see if it fits him first," Mikias said.

He handed Desta the suit, took him to a fitting room, and returned.
Desta came out smiling.

"What a good-looking suit, befitting a handsome boy!"
Mikias said, as he appraised the fit and looks of the clothes.

"How do you like it?" the shopkeeper asked.

Desta looked at his father first, then down at the suit.

"I like it and it feels good, but I'm sure it's not within our means."

Abraham ran his fingers along the fabric and examined the picture before him with his eyes. "It's very becoming, Desta . . . but I know what you mean."

The father turned to Mikias. "How much?"

"How about half of what it originally cost?" the shop owner said, smiling.

"How much is that?!" Abraham inquired, flustered by Mikias's evasiveness.

"Eighty-four birrs!"

"Take it off, son. I'm sorry, I didn't come with that kind of money."

Desta returned to the changing room to put his clothes back on.

To Abraham's amazement Mikias seemed willing to bargain down to a lower price. "What is the lowest you're willing to go?" Abraham said decisively.

"Forty-two birrs."

"Okay, let's do it, quickly. I want to surprise my son."

When Desta came out carrying the new suit on his arm, like precious merchandise he was about to carefully deliver to someone, the four eyes bore down on him.

Abraham took the suit from Desta and said, "Let's return this to"—he held the clothing high in the air for a brief moment—"Desta," he said finally, grinning.

Desta was confused at first. Then he smiled when it dawned on him. "Thank you so much, Baba!" he exclaimed.

To Abraham's continued surprise, the shopkeeper wanted to give Desta a free pair of leather shoes to go with the suit.

When the father told him that Desta would never take anything for free, Mikias said, "How about twenty birrs, half the price?"

Abraham agreed to pay it.

Father and son left pleased with their windfall. By the time they reached Governor Asrat's home, they were exhausted. Abraham went to take a nap. Desta went on a long walk. He had suddenly been struck with fear and anxiety. The image on his chest was tingling. It seemed a crazy idea at first, but he had a feeling the suit they just bought might have been originally made for his hateful former roommate, Dagim. It was not only the sensation coming from his chest but also the color of the suit itself, which was a very unusual shade of blue, a color he'd only ever seen Dagim wear. He somehow needed to resolve this growing hunch.

That Desta could be wearing something that had been made for

his tormentor was upsetting to say the least. In some ways it felt
as if he was being savagely beaten by Dagim all over again.

Logically, Desta knew this notion seemed farfetched, as Dagim was
supposed to be with his father in Debre Marcos, but he couldn't get the idea
out of his mind. He sat down and placed his right hand over his chest and
prayed, asking God to relieve him of his obsessive thoughts and emotional
upset. A message came to him. It said that Desta must forgive Dagim his
awful behavior. This was the only way he could be free of his anxiety.

Desta picked up a pen and one of his notebooks and went to the
back of the house. He sat down and opened the notebook in the middle,
where there was no writing, and propped it on his knee. With his pen in
hand and poised over the page, he thought for several minutes, forcing
his mind to concentrate on what he must say. Then he began.

> Dear Dagim:
> I hope while you were in jail you had time to think and
> reflect on what you've done. I pray you've been awakened to
> the real problems that plague your world. The only person you
> can count on is *you*. Unless you wish to live on the sweat of
> physical labor, education is one of the surest ways to freedom.
> Wherever you are, I hope you've gotten back to
> school and are continuing your studies. It's the only
> possession no one can take away from you.
> Earn the money you need. Don't take anything for free.
> This will be the beginning of your independence. Only in
> this way will you discover the true meaning of life.
> I hope you find peace and contentment in all that you
> do. I don't hate you. I hold no grudges against you.
> Desta

Afterward, Desta folded the letter into a square so small that
it fit in the middle of his palm. He then dug a hole in the dirt with
a stick and placed the letter there. Finally, he positioned a rock
slab on top, scattered soil over that, and walked away.

Chapter 40

The graduation ceremony was held on the soccer field. They had chairs enough for fifty people but three times that many came. The attendees sat on the grass. Desta's guests were given part of the first row. Abraham sat in the middle of the group.

Tedla, the director, gave a short speech welcoming the guests. Then he congratulated the graduating class. This was followed by the awarding of certificates of completion to all the students, except three. The roll was called in alphabetical order. The top three students were ranked by their average percentile score over four years, or two and a half years, in Desta's case.

After the director passed out the certificates to the unranked students, he turned to the three diplomas he had set aside. He gave a brief talk about the third-ranking student as well as the second, a girl with the highest overall average in math. Then he awarded them their certificates.

Next Tedla talked about Desta: that he had the highest overall average in the graduating class and in the school's history; how he was the first to earn a double promotion in one year, and complete four grades in two and a half years.

He noted that Desta had achieved all these things with no family support or stable home, and in spite of personal traumas that included the loss of his brother. Tedla praised Desta as a model student who had never complained about anyone or anything, and had had nobody complain about him.

The director stepped away from the lectern and handed Desta his certificate after a firm handshake. He slapped him affectionately on the back. "Keep up the good work!"

The crowd stood and applauded. Some of the kids whistled.

Desta glanced at his father.

Abraham just stood and beamed a bright smile, offering a clear view of his chipped tooth, but his head didn't grow like a pumpkin.

After the clapping stopped, some people sat down while others remained standing. Still others wrestled with their seats as they prepared to leave.

The director stepped back to the lectern. He clapped his hands and said, "Attention please. I have an announcement to make. Desta and three other top graduating students will teach the classes this summer." Clearly directing his comments to the parents in the audience, he continued, "We encourage all our students to enroll in summer school. It's a much better use of their time than playing marbles or hopscotch in the street. Classes begin July 10."

The crowd rose and began to mill around. Some started to leave.

Dinknesh was the first to fly over and hug and kiss Desta. She stepped back and said, "How handsome you look in that suit," looking him over. Then came Alem, her husband Aberra, and their children, followed by Fenta, Ato Bizuneh, Senayit and Mamita, Mesfin, Leyla and Eden. They all hugged and kissed him.

Konjit extended a congratulatory hand, followed by an envelope of something.

Desta felt the fruits of his hard work and years of struggle for this moment of glory and fame—to be accepted, respected, and praised. Everybody seemed to want a piece of him, to touch or shake hands with him.

He didn't know how Abraham was feeling inside, but he could tell he was mightily proud. It was the moment that had eluded him with his older boys.

Desta shook hands with and thanked many of his guests as they left.

Konjit tapped Desta on the shoulder as he was about to exit the school's gate with his father and friends. "Can I speak with you for a second?"

Desta broke off from under his father's shadow and lingered with Konjit.

"Could you pardon Dagim," she asked without hesitating. She glanced around.

"I don't carry grudges no matter what people have done to me," Desta said, "This is not because I condone Dagim's behavior but because I seek peace of mind."

"He's been feeling very bad. He would have his own inner peace if you would let him know you forgive him."

"Where is he?"

Konjit looked toward the side of the gate. There he was standing like a statue, leaning against the stone pillar, a hat shading his face.

Konjit waved at her son.

"Say you're sorry," Konjit said to Dagim as he approached.

Dagim repeated the phrase, his eyes cagey and tentative.

Then she turned to Desta, saying, "Can you please say you forgive him."

Saying it like he meant it, Desta offered, "I forgive you."

Desta extended his hand. Dagim took it and held it for a few seconds and then let go. In those moments, Desta looked searchingly into the boy's face to see whether the penitence of his words were also in his eyes.

He saw shame and confusion and not remorse or gratitude. "Good luck," Desta said.

Then he turned to Konjit. "Thanks for coming and for your gift."

"You're welcome! Buy something meaningful with it," she said.

"I will," Desta said.

"The suit looks very good on you!" she said, turning to her son as if for confirmation.

"It does," Dagim mumbled. "Thanks for the letter and your advice."

Desta winced. He glanced at the mother and then at the son for a second. "Letter?" he coughed under his breath. He didn't know what to think or say. He simply dashed to his father, who was now standing outside the gate, waiting for Desta.

As Desta and Abraham headed to the center of town, Desta opened the envelope. He found four red birrs and two single birr notes—totaling forty-two birrs. He felt sick inside.

"Just what I suspected," Desta said, his voice flagging.

Abraham looked at Desta. "What?"

"This suit I am wearing was made for Dagim. I lived and studied with him for one semester."

"How did you know—did they tell you?"

Desta opened the envelope and showed his father the money.

"Era! The same amount we paid to Mikias."

"There is your answer."

"Why are you upset? This means you got a free suit." Abraham smiled.

"I had suspected this from the time I studied the fabric and color in the sun. No kid in town wears clothes like this but Konjit's son."

"I'm mystified by this," Abraham said.

"It's a long story, Baba," Desta said suddenly and dismissively, his eyes far away. He didn't want to upset his father by telling him what Dagim had done—not now, anyway.

"You have to learn to be bigger than any problem, son," Abraham said, resting his big hand over Desta's shoulder. "Don't let it ruin your happy day."

"You're right!" Desta said, forcing a smile. They continued walking toward the center of town. Desta blocked out every thought of Dagim and his clothes.

Dinknesh invited her friends and had a small luncheon celebration for Desta.

Late in the afternoon Deat and Abraham went to Governor Asrat's home. Abraham wanted to take a nap. He went to Desta's room to lie down.

Desta needed to be alone. His head was still abuzz with the day's excitement. He walked out of Asrat's compound and stood. He stared at the new life the recent rains had tickled out of the field, the bushes and trees. Seeing this rebirth of nature usually made Desta happy. That afternoon, however, Desta was anything but happy. He had a sense of emptiness in his heart, a letdown. With his head down, he began walking the open land. He must have gone at least half the length of the vast field when he looked up and saw a familiar figure standing before him like a statue.

"What're you doing here?" Desta asked, surprised to see Eleni.

"I have been here for a while waiting for you," Eleni said, smiling a little. "Congratulations! You made it, finally!"

"Thank you," Desta said, uneasily.

"One of the spirits from your ancestral family sent me here with your graduation present," Eleni said, handing Desta a small wooden box.

"Who?" Desta asked. His mind raced, thinking of the possibilities.

"Open it first and I'll tell you."

Desta flipped the small metal latch from the side of the box and opened it. His eyes grew big. "What's this?"

Eleni stepped closer. "This," she said, reaching and picking up an oblong gold piece attached to a looping leather cord, "is called a cartouche. . . ."

The afternoon sun teased out flake of golden light from its polished surface. Desta jerked his chin. "Cartouche?!"

"Yes," Eleni said. "It's an ancient Egyptian symbol used to write in or engrave the names of the pharaohs. She pointed to the middle of the cartouche. "This hieroglyph means Desta. The line below it says, 'To Whom the Lions Bow, in Amharic." The Wind Woman smiled.

Desta was stunned. "Who made this for me?"

"I don't know who made it but it's sent by the spirit of the person who once had this attribute."

"Would that be Emperor Lebna Dengel?" Desta asked, throwing his fingers over his chin.

"Yes," Eleni said. "Let me tell you about the others."

She continued pointing to a few of the remaining items and said,
"The bee is the ancient Ethiopian symbol of royalty and wisdom.

"The ankh is an ancient Egyptian sign for life and eternity.

"The Maat's feather, also Egyptian, represents truth, justice,
morality, and balance. The rest of the symbols you will find out
about on your own. I need to go," Eleni announced suddenly.

Desta knew about many of the symbols. He had studied them in his
ancient history classes.

"You're always in a hurry," he complained.

"I told you I travel all over. I can't stay for more than a few minutes at
one place," Eleni replied, nonplused. "Before I go," she added, "my friends
and I would like to invite you for an extended visit to Washaa Umera."

"I'd like that but it would have to be after I get
established in Bahir Dar," Desta said.

"When you're on vacation would be best. . . . Wear your
cartouche and let me see how it looks on you," Eleni said.

Desta slid the cord onto his neck, and looked down on the brilliant piece.

"It looks beautiful. . . . Enjoy! . . . Got to go!" With this, the Wind Woman
rose to the air and vanished.

Desta remained standing with his hand on the cartouche, befuddled by
Eleni's sudden disappearance. Then realizing that's how Eleni managed her
time, he walked home, happy with his gift from the spirit of the man who died
defending the territory of Ethiopia and the freedom of his people.

DESTA LIKED FIRES. When he was a shepherd, they radiated
warmth to him when he came home after tending to the animals. He
liked to watch their hypnotic flames as they swayed and nodded when
the breeze came through the open door of his home. Flames always
pointed up and straight when not bothered by wind or breeze.

Fires were festive. There was something light and happy about
them. Fires were powerful. They had the ability to transform things or
consume and blot them out of existence. By this very fact, fires could
bring conclusions to things and prompt breaks with people's pasts.

For all of fire's attributes, Desta yearned to put a fire at the center of
a private celebration. From the eucalyptus grove, he gathered dead twigs

and branches. From the back of the house, he collected logs and kindling. Over a carefully spaced pair of logs, he built a bed from the straight sticks and piled the rest of the dry wood on top. The bottom he reinforced with dry twigs and brittle eucalyptus leaves. Then he went inside. He gathered his old notebooks, his old gabi, and some clothes, placing them in a carton with a box of matches and setting them by the entrance.

At midnight he rose, careful not to wake Abraham, who was sleeping next to him. He quietly opened the door. Then he picked up his carton of things and went to the back of the property, where his mound awaited lighting.

A single match strike produced a vigorous flame, with which Desta lit dry leaves under his piled wood. Flames licked the leaves and then flickered upward onto the twigs, with the help of the ambient breeze, then growing long tendrils, the fire moved on to the sticks and logs above.

With the box of things by his side, Desta watched the flames, mesmerized. He held his hands close to the fire and warmed them. Then one at a time he began tossing his belongings from the box into the conflagration. First his notebooks, then his old gabi, and finally Dagim's suit. He sat down with his legs folded and crossed and watched everything turn to flame, then to smoke, and ultimately into nothing recognizable.

Desta sighed deeply, relieved and happy. When everything was gone, he went home with the carton, content and feeling free. He felt better and slept better that night.

THE NEXT DAY Abraham asked Desta whether he would go home with him and celebrate his graduation with the rest of the family.

"As you heard, I'm one of the four teachers selected to instruct the summer classes. School restarts in ten days. I need to stay and get ready for it," Desta said.

"That's fine, son. All the power to you."

"Let's do it when I come in September," Desta said. "I'd like to see the family before I go to Bahir Dar."

Agreeing on this, Desta and Abraham parted.

Chapter 41

Eighty students registered to take the summer classes. The session ran from July 5 through August 25. Each student was to pay five birrs per month. This meant that each student teacher would earn about two hundred birrs by the end of the summer session.

Out of this money Desta planned to use fifty birrs for his living expenses during the summer months and one hundred fifty birrs to pay for school and cover his other costs in Bahir Dar in the coming academic year. He would have even more to live on if relatives offered support when he went home in September. For now he could only count on what he would receive from the teaching job.

Trying to save as much as he could during the two months he was teaching, Desta ate only one full meal each day, usually at lunch, which consisted of *shiro wat*—ground pea sauce with injera—and a glass of water, from the local restaurant. He paid thirty-five cents for it. He and one of the other student teachers rented a small one-room shack on the side of a house. Desta prepared his dinner at home, usually eating roasted corn with a glass of water. For breakfast, if he decided to have it at all, he ate dabo and drank tea, for which he paid only twenty-five cents.

This austere existence caused Desta to lose a substantial amount of weight, but he didn't mind it. In fact, he found this ascetic way of living during these weeks to have purifying and spiritual effects, which soothed his soul. He taught English and science in grades six and seven, and this teaching experience provided him great emotional satisfaction.

The ultimate fulfillment was yet to come: Going to Bahir Dar, where he would start his high school education and look for the person with the second Coin of Magic and Fortune.

After they let out their students near the end of August, the four teachers divided up their income and went their separate ways. From his eighth-grade graduating class, Desta was the only one who was going to the famed town by Lake Tana. The rest would be furthering their educations in Debre Marcos, the province's capital, or Addis Ababa, Ethiopia's capital.

As soon as school closed, Desta joined his family for the Ethiopian new year, which came on September 11. He hoped to gain a lot of weight in the two weeks he would be spending with his family. Then he would be ready to set off for Bahir Dar.

When he arrived home, Abraham surprised him. To celebrate Desta's academic accomplishments and because Abraham couldn't make his head grow like a pumpkin, he decided to kill one of his mookit goats and have a feast with family and friends. It was the only practical way Abraham knew to show pride in his son.

Although eating large portions of red meat would have been a good way for Desta to regain his weight, he was vehemently opposed to the idea of killing one of the family's goats for food. He'd rather the goat be sold and the money put to good use. He certainly didn't want the goat to lose his life on his behalf. The kind of lavish celebration that Abraham was proposing wasn't meaningful to him. When Abraham suggested a lamb instead, he declined this as well, as he did the few chickens his father finally countered with.

"I appreciate your intentions and I'm glad to see that you're finally proud of me," Desta said. "If you really want to express your sense of pride with some kind of celebration, I prefer that mother make two rye loaves in the shape of the coin, and we can share these among our immediate family members."

Abraham was thoughtful and quiet for a few seconds. "I was hoping to show you off among my friends," he said finally. "Because not only are you the sole modern student in the entire valley, but you've performed ahead of so many others." He choked up with emotion.

"A public display of my achievements is the last thing I want, Baba. Imagine the ensuing gossip afterward, if we held the kind of celebration you suggested!"

Abraham yielded. He and Ayénat got busy preparing the small family affair they planned to hold two days before Desta departed for Bahir Dar. Ayénat decided to make tej along with tella.

On the day of the gathering Abraham went to the river and collected three small bundles of *kettema*—pulpy lime-colored grass—and sprinkled it over the thoroughly cleaned living-room floor, a practice on holidays normally accompanied by the killing of a lamb. This time however the two loaves would replace the lamb, a benign and guiltless alternative for Desta.

Several washed horn and clay cups were arranged on a platter and set aside on the floor. Desta's sister-in-law Melkam had washed and displayed several of the small colorful coffee cups on a wooden tray. She had roasted and ground coffee beans, which were now boiling in a large coffee pot. On a clay burner she had placed several glowing pieces of charcoal and dropped in incense, which immediately plumed into white smoke, adding a new fragrance to the existing coffee aroma.

After the three brothers and sister arrived with their spouses and settled around the nicely decorated living room, Ayénat served them tella in the clay cups.

Then Abraham cleared his throat and said, "We are gathered here this evening to recognize Desta's educational accomplishments, which he did on his own and after living and dealing with so many people—some kind and some not so kind.

"Based on what I know about our church schools, I took the attitude that Desta fend for himself as he pursued his education. As I have found in the past five years, modern schooling is very complicated and the needs of the students are so many. For folks like us it is nearly impossible to put a child through these schools.

"Even then, Desta met and overcame these challenges and graduated at the top of his eighth-grade class. When I heard this news at the graduation ceremony last June, I actually felt my head grow like a pumpkin," Abraham said, chuckling a little. "I'm feeling it grow right now just thinking about that experience." He laughed. The children's eyes were suddenly on Abraham's head, searching hard for any changes.

The storyteller picked up his cup, drew from it, and set it down again.

He scanned the audience and noticed they were all still looking at him. "You took me literally, didn't you?" he said, his chipped tooth catching the light at the center of a now-wide smile. Abraham glanced at the modern student. "Desta, I know I haven't told you directly, but I want you to know that I am very proud of your academic accomplishments."

Desta glanced back at his father and said, "Thank you." Inside he was feeling better than he had in a long time. To be recognized like this in front of all these people, many of whom used to hate him and treat him like an outcast, was something he would cherish for months and years to come.

"Baba, can you forgive me now that you have a son who finally makes you proud?" Tamirat said, recalling Abraham's dissatisfaction with him when he abandoned the priesthood.

"I was disappointed but never harbored ill feelings toward you, Tamirat," Abraham said. "Besides, really, the loss is yours and not mine."

A low murmur went through the crowd.

"Anyway," Abraham continued, "in a couple of days Desta will be leaving for Bahir Dar to continue his studies. I would appreciate your giving him any money you can spare."

Saba, the only sister in attendance, gasped. "That far!"

Just about everybody sang Saba's line in unison, like a chorus.

Abraham countered, "Actually, he has a specific reason for going there. The only cities with high schools anywhere nearby are Bahir Dar and Debre Marcos, and Debre Marcos is very far away."

Another low murmur went through the crowd.

Abraham signaled to Ayénat, who shortly after brought out the two loaves in two separate *mossebs*—round table-like eating baskets, one at a time, and placed them near the father.

Melkam took the coffee pot out and set it aside so that the granules would settle out. She moved the wooden tray with cups closer to the coffee pot.

"I had wanted a more elaborate celebration of Desta's academic achievements—like offering one of my mookit goats, but Desta wisely advised that it was unnecessary. Selling the goat and giving him the money would be more valuable to him than the celebration. So that is what I might do. He neither wanted a lamb nor chickens," Abraham said, looking from one side of the room to the other. "He decided on something that is close and dear to his heart. Two dabos made in the image of our Coin of Magic and Fortune. This is our feast, plus honey wine, I believe," Abraham said, glancing across the room to Ayénat for confirmation.

Ayénat nodded.

"Yes, honey wine, tella, and coffee," he said, with a smile and finality in his voice.

"That is wonderful!" Saba said. "Why waste the life of another animal."

Abraham opened the first mosseb and looked in.

Ayénat quickly brought a kerosene lamp. She wanted

everyone else to look in and admire her creation.

Desta was the first to get up and peer in. "Oh, Ma!" Desta exclaimed. "This bread is a perfect replication of our coin: the man in the center, the channels, and even the letters from the legend. I know you had one of these before, but these are the best!" Desta smiled at his mother.

"I must say so!!" Abraham agreed. He picked up the big knife from the side of the basket, drew the sign of the cross in the air over the loaf, and went to work. He cut seven slices, following the edge of the channels. He passed around the basket with the cut dabo slices and went to work carving the second loaf.

This was followed by the distributing of a cup of honey wine to all who were there. They drank their wine as they munched on the slices of dabo and talked leisurely. Some of the women talked about Desta and his impending travel to the faraway land. The men shared mutual problems with weeds in their farms and all the pests they needed to control for a good harvest in the months to come.

The bread and wine feast was followed with coffee, and everybody acted and talked as if they were having a grand time.

In the end Abraham blessed all the children who had come, praying for a great harvest and peace and happiness in their enclave as well as in the entire valley. The final benediction went to Desta.

"May God protect and guide you," his father said. "May the people you meet and befriend be kind and generous. May the school administrators and teachers be supportive and appreciative as the ones in Finote Selam have been. May you thrive again in you academics! May God steer you to the person who holds the second Coin of Magic and Fortune with the least amount of effort and trouble!"

To this all said amen. Desta and some of the women had stood when Abraham was saying his blessings. They sat down and continued with their coffee and their unfinished morsels of dabo.

Then one by one Desta's siblings thanked their parents and began to leave. Abraham reminded them again not to forget about supporting their brother before he left for Bahir Dar in two days. Just about all of them had said they'd contribute something.

Chapter 42

On the day of his departure Desta rose early, had his breakfast, and awaited his hoped-for contributors. Saba and Yihoon were the first to arrive. They gave him three birrs between the two of them. Next came Damtew and Melkam. They gave him one birr each. Tamirat came by himself and offered one birr.

Abraham and Ayénat had given him eight silver dollars, which was equivalent to thirty-two birrs. Then the father kissed Desta and left for court.

Desta had hoped Teferra, the tailor, who always had a lot of cash, would be his greatest contributor. So he waited for his brother to arrive. The others also waited because they wanted to see Desta off. When Teferra didn't show, he said farewell to all who had come and went to look for his brother.

Teferra's wife, Laqechi, said he was not at the house because he had been meeting with neighbors across the creek. So Desta went there.

"I'll come in shortly. Wait for me at the house," Teferra said curtly, dismissing him with a wave of his hand.

Desta returned and waited outside Teferra's home, pacing the ground and glancing at the street that would bring his brother. The morning was advancing, but there was still no sign of Teferra. Desta's mind was split. Should he leave or just wait a bit longer? Even a little extra money would be worth waiting for, let alone the substantial windfall he might receive from his cash-rich brother.

So he waited. Enough time went by that Desta decided to go to a clearing where he could see the gathered group. He hollered, "Teferra, are you coming or not!?"

The brother hollered back. "I'll be there!"

Desta returned and sat down on a bench and continued keeping vigil. Time had a way of teasing and frustrating one who watched it. This was doubly true when one also attempted to beat time. Desta had to be infinitely patient with respect to both. After all, a great reward was at stake. The morning was now approaching midday.

Neither time nor the narrow path produced Desta's wealthy brother. He swallowed his disappointment and headed to his parents' home, where he gathered his things and got ready to leave. For a snack to have on the road, Ayénat gave him a few dabo slices from the night before. His mother escorted him to the cattle field, they kissed, and Desta got underway.

To save money, he had decided to travel on foot. It was going to take him two full days. The long journey would be well worth the money he'd save on travel expenses. But he hadn't a clue how he was going to get to Bahir Dar. He didn't want to take the mountain route, which was how he and Abraham had traveled. They had gone over the mountain to see Zegay and investigate what turned out to be a dead-end lead in the search for the second coin. It was already late in the day and he knew he couldn't clear the mountains by sundown. So he decided to take the caravan route north and head northeast, once he found a major crossroad that went in the general direction of Bahir Dar. Having no guide he would rely purely on his intuition.

Once he began his two-day trek, he wasn't going to let thoughts of Teferra get him down. The farther along he went on the road, the happier he got.

He was finally on his way to the place of his dreams, on his way to Bahir Dar and to high school there, where he'd also get to look for the second coin— he couldn't be more thrilled. He trundled along whistling sometimes and planning and dreaming at other times. Every so often he would ask passersby to confirm he was headed in the right direction. They told him he was.

When the sun was about to dissemble into the western horizon, Desta went to one of the houses nearby and presented himself as *yegzi-abhare ingida*—a guest of God. The good people received him happily and gave him accommodation. The following morning he got up early and pressed on. After traveling all day, he reached the town of Merawi, the same place where Colonel Asheber's Land Rover had broken down the last time Desta attempted to go to Bahir Dar to look for the alleged possessor of the second coin. The colonel stayed with the car as his family and Desta returned back to Dangila, where Desta was attending school at the time.

On his current journey, Desta spent the night as a guest of God at one of the farmer's houses on the outskirts of the city. When he was about to leave in the morning, his host strongly advised that he take a bus instead of walking to Bahir Dar because the days had been hot and it would be safer in a motor vehicle.

Now he would complete the journey he'd started five years previously and take a bus instead of walking. He reached Bahir Dar early in the morning. In the afternoon he went to register at the high school. Having his certificate of completion from the Finote Selam school, the school officials readily accepted and enrolled Desta for the ninth grade.

The next item of business was to go look for someone in town he might live with in exchange for his services.

It's considered a coincidence when two or more unrelated events occur simultaneously. Desta, like his father, had come to believe that coincidences were predetermined events designed to influence or affect outcomes and people's lives. What happened that afternoon was something no amount of planning or mutually arranged timing could have synchronized.

While walking on the asphalt road with his head down, thinking about the kinds of things he should say to people he planned to meet in town, Desta lifted his face just for a second and saw a remotely familiar man enter a gray stone building. A wooden sign above the door announced, COMMERCIAL BANK OF ETHIOPIA.

Desta stopped, curious to see who this man was. He waited outside the gate, assuming the man would come out relatively soon. The sign above the door had no meaning to him. He was unfamiliar with financial institutions. Desta recognized the man, but he couldn't recall his name. It didn't matter. He would just have to say hello and ask the man if he remembered Desta.

As time went on, Desta grew impatient. Not only did he need to start looking for people to live with, he at least had to find shelter for the night.

The man finally reappeared and walked briskly to the gate. He stooped slightly as if he, too, was weighed down by his thoughts.

Desta might as well have been a statue to this man. He dashed past him without so much as a simple side-glance. This caused Desta to have second thoughts about even saying hello. The air about him and the speed with which the man walked said that he didn't want to be disturbed. Desta watched him cross one side of the street, through the plants in the median, where he stopped momentarily to let the oncoming traffic pass.

This was Desta's moment. He pushed off from the curb. "Dr. Petrova! Dr. Petrova!" he shouted, as he ran toward the man, happy that he had finally remembered his name.

Dr. Petrova turned around, taking a few steps back. He glanced at Desta but then looked down, as if searching his mind for any clue to the identity of the boy standing before him.

"Do you remember me?" Desta asked, looking up at the puzzled face.

"I'm trying," Dr. Petrova said, studying Desta's face.

"My name is Desta. I was one of the people who took the test for the job you had at the Debre Marcos hospital."

"Of course I do—now," the Doctor said, smiling broadly. "What are you doing here?"

Desta told him.

A man with a gardening spade suddenly popped up from among the decorative plants along the median strip. "Could you both step off of the plants?" he said. "You're not supposed to walk through here."

Dr. Petrova apologized. They crossed to the other side of the street and continued to talk.

"I arrived this morning and am staying here at the Ras Hotel," he said, pointing to the tree-shaded building. "I've been transferred to the hospital in town here because there aren't enough doctors."

When Desta told him his situation, the doctor said, "Come see me this evening—at about six o'clock—we'll explore the town together."

"Thank you. I will," Desta said, trying hard to appear calm and casual.

Dr. Petrova gestured toward Desta. "Let me show you my room."

A brief walk along the driveway brought them to the grounds of the hotel. Desta could see Lake Tana through the drooping leaves of a warka tree, which stood tilted over the shore, a short distance from the main building of the Ras Hotel.

To their right, a narrow, low-roofed structure curved under the shade of numerous lush trees. They turned and walked toward this building. "Here is my room," Dr. Petrova said, pointing to the first door. "You should have no problem finding it."

Desta said he wouldn't.

Dr. Petrova glanced at his watch. "Someone is coming from the hospital to pick me up and I need to get ready," he said. "I'll see you later."

Desta left after promptly saying, "See you at six."

As Desta headed down the asphalt road toward the center of town, he heard a loud rumbling sound coming from somewhere on his right and he turned and looked. He noticed an airplane coasting up a grassy field past the end of a short road. Desta had never before seen an airplane on the ground. He was excited. He cut across the two-way boulevard and got onto the street that connected to the airfield. He ran as fast as he could. Getting there, he stood at a distance and watched.

A wire fence circled the airport. A small light green building, which looked like an office, stood at the north end of the field. The plane had come to a halt with its tail nearly dragging and its nose up in the air as if having detected something disagreeable. *What a huge bird*, Desta thought.

A smattering of people waiting to board the plane milled about near the building, glancing up occasionally at the new arrivals, who were dismounting the drop-down stairs near the nose of the plane. A uniformed man with a hat pranced here and there, seemingly arranging and coordinating things. Then he and another uniformed man, who Desta identified later as the pilot, chatted for a few minutes and shook hands. The second man rushed back to the plane once all the waiting passengers had boarded.

The pilot cranked the engine. With this action, the multiple blades at the center of each wing whirred until the blades themselves became invisible. The pilot backed up the bird and then swung it around to face the long stretch of green field ahead.

"Nice to have seen you up close!" Desta said, waving his hand at the bird. It paused for a brief moment, looking downfield like an athlete who calculates the distance he must cover in relation to time and space. Then the aircraft roared louder as it began slowly moving. It had picked up speed and was racing swiftly down the runway. Before Desta knew it, it was taking flight, and vanished into the clouds in mere moments.

Afterward Desta went to town looking for a place to spend the night. Once he secured a room for one birr in a small boarding house, he returned to the Ras Hotel at the appointed time. He found Dr. Petrova sitting on a wicker settee outside his room, reading something.

"We could eat at the restaurant here, but I prefer to go to town," Dr. Petrova said. "It's a nice evening for a walk and I also need to buy a few things."

"Let's go then," Desta said.

Out to the driveway and then left toward the center of town they went. Balmy, the evening was indeed nice, fit for a leisurely promenade along the smooth asphalt road, which now had hardly any traffic.

At the town square, the roads intersected like a three-point star. One went south, the second east, and the third—the one they were on—went west. Dr. Petrova stopped, took a note from his pocket, looked at it, and said,

"We go along this road." He pointed to the road that went south. "If the hotel attendant is right, from here is a highly reputable restaurant," he added. "But I neglected to write down the name."

After walking about fifty yards, they found an eating establishment on the right. It was an old, rather nondescript structure with a pitched roof. The sign on the place said YE ABEBECH MIGIB BET—Abebech's Restaurant.

Dr. Petrova stopped and Desta did, too. The Bulgarian appraised the facade before him. "These kinds of places generally have the best food," he said, as if to allay a reluctant voice in his head. "Let's go in."

The food was indeed very good. Biting into the freshly baked teff injera, their teeth sunk effortlessly into the spongy bread and their tongues danced with delight. The sauces—the chicken, beef, ground peas—along with mixed vegetables and sliced vermillion tomatoes were beautifully prepared, their individual qualities perfectly maintained amid the multiplicity of flavors represented on the sizable crepe, which was served on a large floral platter. They augmented the meal with glasses of water.

Just like an Ethiopian native, the Bulgarian was adept at eating with his fingers—tearing a piece of the injera and dropping it flat on a sauce, then pinching and scooping up morsels of food, and gingerly sliding bread and all into his mouth.

They talked when their mouths were empty and sometimes even when they were full. "I'd love you to stay with me," Dr. Petrova said. "I'll be living out of town and I've no one to run errands for me."

"I told you I'd return your favor of a year ago," Desta said, smiling. "This could work out just fine for both of us then."

Additionally, they agreed that Desta would spend the night in the hotel. The doctor paid the bill and they left.

In town in a sumptuous store owned by a man named Sheik Mohammed, they purchased a number of things. Dr. Petrova got a notepad, pens, canned food, toiletries, and some fruit. Desta bought his school supplies—notebooks, pens and pencils, an eraser, and a ruler.

Each lugged his acquisitions in a bag and they headed back to the Ras. Dr. Petrova stopped in the middle of the road and said, "This is our dessert!" He took a long, deep breath and then exhaled slowly, savoring the moment and experience.

The man seemed in a trance. Desta looked at him, expecting a follow-up to the sudden exaltation and throaty gesticulation. Dr. Petrova said, "The air!

It's so much like the atmosphere in Varna, my hometown on the Black Sea."

"How wonderful! You must feel at home then," Desta said cheerfully.

"I love it!" Dr. Petrova said, now resuming his walk. His bag of merchandise brushed against his leg.

Indeed! The evening had gotten cooler, yet there was something elemental and salubrious in the breeze that was now coming off the lake. It felt nourishing and invigorating both to the body and spirit. Desta loved it, too.

The hotel room was large, with two beds that could be cordoned off by means of a partition wall. They visited for a while. Then Dr. Petrova said, "I need to go to bed. Someone will come get me early in the morning." He pulled the divider across the room, undressed, and went to sleep.

Desta took off his shoes and sat at the edge of the bed. The cool tile floor felt good under his feet. His eyes were on the floor, too, but he was gazing inward, not at anything within his frame of reference. He was thinking, amazed by the coincidence, grateful for the day's outcome.

"Of course not," he whispered suddenly, having caught himself in the common fallacy people make about the convergence of two or more unlikely events. It was not a coincidence that he was in this room, next door to his future benefactor.

He could see it all like a picture now. It seemed to Desta that everything that happened to him in Finote Selam had to lead to this meeting with Dr. Yacob Petrova—first in Debre Marcos a year ago and now here in Bahir Dar.

While their first meeting happened after a series of random events, their second encounter that day ensued through the convergence of events, measured in split seconds: Desta looking up and seeing Dr. Petrova at the very moment he was crossing the threshold of the bank. If Desta had been a few seconds later arriving at the spot or had not lifted his face at that precise moment, he knew his evening would have been completely different, and his future might've been as uncertain.

His meeting with the doctor could not be dismissed as a random event or mere coincidence. It must have been either encoded in the coin or planned and orchestrated by something or someone greater than any human being. He rocked his head up and down, agreeing to his own interpretation.

While in Finote Selam staying with Fenta to living with Alem to Konjit's shack to Colonel Mulugeta's home, which led to his following them after they transferred to Bichena and finally his returning to Finote

Selam when his living situation with them didn't work out. All the people he lived with and the things that had happened to him appeared like steps on a ladder he was climbing to reach Dr. Yacob Petrova.

He scooted to the center of the bed, drew up his legs, and folded and crossed them before him. Absentmindedly, Desta slid his index finger over the pad of his thumb—moving it up and down—but his mind wandered, focusing on all the homes he had lived in and all the things that had happened to him. *But did I have to be physically hurt and mentally scarred for my meeting with Dr. Petrova to be fulfilled?* He was thinking of what Dagim had done to him.

Did I have to be mocked and teased? He was thinking about his beloved brother Asse'ged, who had abandoned his farming work and became a tailor so he could support Desta when he came to Bahir Dar. After Desta thought he was set with his accommodations for his four years of high school, his brother was suddenly taken from him.

Desta bit his lip and stared into space, grimly thinking about the suffering Asse'ged had endured. He shook his head, as if to chase away the spiraling eddies of emotion.

Ironically, it was shortly after his brother had died that he'd found out, upon returning from his vacation, the family he had adopted had abandoned him. He followed them to the new town, but when living with them had become unbearable, he returned to Finote Selam. During this trip back he stopped at the Debre Marcos hospital to take a test for a job he ended up not taking.

The side effect of this exercise was that he met Dr. Petrova, who not only had wanted him to work for the hospital but also proposed to send him to Bulgaria for medical school once he was done with his high school education. Who in their right mind would call this series of events mere coincidence or random happenings?

"To answer your earlier questions," said the familiar voice that rose up out of nowhere, "given the quest you're on, sometimes you are bound to get knocked down or hurt. . . . You're right! Your meetings with the doctor were not mere coincidence. In fact, everything that happens to you is never a coincidence or a product of good or bad luck. Just about everything is predetermined. That your life path came to a full circle with this man is prearranged. He will be a source of critical information regarding the second Coin of Magic and Fortune."

"Really?" Desta said, astonished. "How is Dr. Petrova going to help me find the holder of the second coin, if he is new to the town like me?"

No reply came.

Desta sighed deeply and closed his eyes, disappointed he couldn't hear from the ethereal being any longer. He crossed his arms over his chest, kept quiet for a few seconds, and thought. Now having realized all that had happened to him in the past two and half years was for the benefit of his missions, Desta felt he needed to acknowledge all those who played a part in it.

He said, "You all who have served as a rung on the ladder of my mission and enabled me to finally be here in this town, I thank you. That means: Fenta, Alem, Konjit, Colonel Mulugeta and family, and Dinknesh and Governor Asrat and David Hartman. Those household members who challenged my resolve and fortitude, I forgive you but also thank you for your contributions to my purposes in your own ways.

"The difficulties you subjected me to caused me to move. Each move, it turned out, was for my own gain. If it were not for your actions, I wouldn't have met people like Dr. Petrova, who now has offered to have me stay with him in this strange town where I knew no one. By your behavior and deeds, I was strengthened. I needed you just as much as I needed those who were kind and benevolent to me. You both were two sides of the same coin. Thank you and good-bye!"

Desta tossed his hand over each shoulder in turn, symbolic of his throwing his past behind him. He needed to start with a clear mind. He needed to be unencumbered and free.

Desta was now looking forward to being a high school student, to meeting the teachers and students in his classes. He was excited by the prospect of living with the Bulgarian, with whom he would practice speaking English every day. And he was anxious to find out the critical information he supposedly held about the second shekel.

He wanted to record his thoughts and feelings of the moment for his own future reference. He reached into the shopping bag by his bedside and brought out a notebook. He retrieved a pen from his pocket. He opened the notebook at the beginning. Pen in hand, he searched for the precise words that would capture his moment of joy. His mind went blank. His feelings had subsided. In the end all he could come up with was:

DESTA
To Whom the Lions Bow

He put the notebook and pen in the bag. He undressed and got under the covers. He turned off the lamp. The shadow of the night filled the room, making Desta disappear but not his thoughts. He lay on his back thinking about the person called Sweet and Sour, the holder of the second Coin of Magic and Fortune—the person Desta believed lived in this town and the main reason he'd come here instead of going to Debre Marcos for his high school education, as his eighth-grade classmates had done. Believing he could find the woman here and finally unite the two identical coins that had been separated from each other by three thousand years thrilled Desta once again.

He took a deep breath, rested his hand over his chest above his heart, and closed his eyes. Shortly after, he no longer thought or heard anything.

———————————

Acknowldegements

My wife, Rosario, has been the ardent supporter of my work. Her undying faith in the Desta stories and the value she feels they would have to the readers have kept me going even when at times my own faith seemed to waver. They say writing is a lonely experience, and Rosario allowed me the quiet and secluded space I needed to write these books. I am thankful for this and her limitless grace and patience.

I'm eternally grateful to my father at whose knee I learned all the fundamentals of life and from whom I borrowed the many great personal traits that appear in the character of Abraham in the book; and to my mother who taught me I can do anything I want if I apply myself, including becoming a writer.

I extend my many thanks to Merrill Gillaspy who edited the manuscript, to Vincent Cusenza who proofed it and to Philip Howe for his artistic wizardry with all of the Desta covers and for his patience and understanding of my need to make the illustrations as authentic as possible, even in a situation where the images he reproduced were flights of my fancy. I thank David Klein for his web work and his poetic genius.

I am also thankful to Dr. Alula Wasse, Dr. Worku Negash, and Getachew Admassu for their enthusiasm, support, and encouragement for the Desta series. They and my nephew Tadesse Alemayehu in Ethiopia have been my reliable sources for some of the cultural details that appear in the book.

I thank Dr. Helen Bonner for taking a special interest in Desta and for her cheering me on in my efforts. I extend my thanks to my friends from Writers Unlimited—Monika Rose, Dave Self, Antoinette May, Glenn Wasson, Ted Laskin, Joy Roberts, and Linda Field.

Last but not least, I am grateful to the Creator, who gave me healthy faculties so I could record what I saw, read, heard, and experienced to use as material for this and the first two novels.

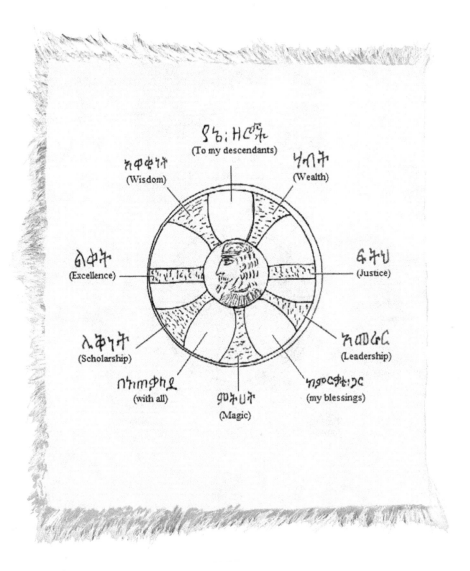

*Legends connected with the Coin of Magic and Fortune,
illustrated and inscribed on a goatskin by Desta's
grandfather's spirit and given to him to recite daily and
adapt the messages in his own life.*

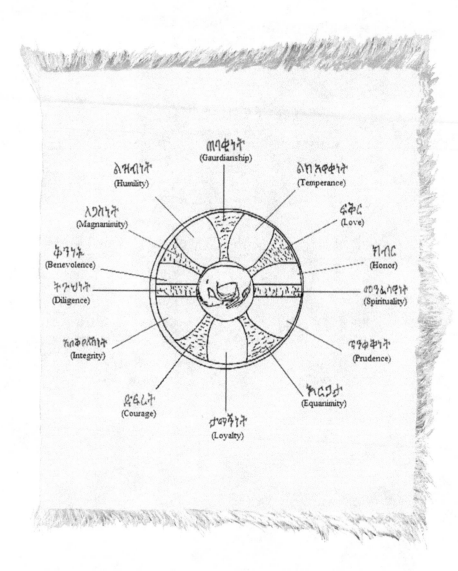

Legends connected with the Coin of Magic and Fortune, illustrated and inscribed on a goatskin by Desta's grandfather's spirit and given to him to recite daily and adapt the messages in his own life.

DESTA'S CHARACTERS

Abebech – a restaurant owner in Bahir Dar

Aberra – one of Alem's boyfriends who later became her husband

Abinet, Colonel – Bichena's former head of police

Ahmed Gran – the Muslim leader from Eastern Ethiopia who, from early to mid 1500s, had attempted to usurp the Christian country in the west and convert it into an Islamic state.

Amare – a grain merchant

Aklilu – a clothing merchant, the man who introduced Desta to Alem

Alula – Yeedib's governor

Asrat, Fit'awrari – past governor of Yeedib

Bekalu – tailor who made the clothes Asse'ged bought for Desta

Belachew – the eighth grade homeroom teacher in Finote Selam

Belay, Girazmachi – Abraham and Desta's distant relative who unraveled their ancestral heritage and the previous owners of their Coin of Magic and Fortune

Beza – Hiwot's daughter

Bizuneh – Fenta's uncle

Cristóvão da Gama – the son of Vasco da Gama, commander of the 400 soldiers who came to help fight against Ahmad Gragn of 1541

Defaru – a bird Desta met under the Finote Selam warka tree which later transformed into a human being. It was this man who brought the root that cured Hiwot's asthma.

Dinknesh – A friend of Abraham and Teferra who later became Desta's host and supporter

Eden – Governor Asrat's youngest child, a girl

Emnet – the girl sired by Alem's father from their servant who later became a victim of jealousy.

Enatnesh – a girl who worked in Col. Mulugeta's household

Fanawork – Colonel Mulugeta's wife

Fenta – Desta's best friend

Ferenge – a term applied to all white people

Fikade – the Finote Selam elementary school English teacher

Fikray – Asse'ged's son

Girum – Alem's second boyfriend

Glawdewos –Emperor of Ethiopia, son of Emperor Lebna Dengel

Goosa, Aba – nickname for Yisehak, the director of the Yeedib school

Girma – Desta's sixth grade seatmate, a boy

Hailu – horse renter in Tilili

Hiwot – Dinknesh's sister, sick with Asthma

Kasey – Governor Asrat's property manager

Kibret – Alem and Konjit's aunt

Kidest – Alem's aunt

Konjit – Alem's sister

Laquech – Teferra's wife

Lebna Dengle – the former emperor of Ethiopia, Abraham and Desta's ancestor

Lema – ground maintainer at Governor Asrat's second home

Leyla – Governor Asrat's second oldest child, a girl

Lulit – Asse'ged's second wife

Mamita – Cook and guardian to Governor Asrat's children

Medenek – a name Teferra, Desta's oldest brother, had given to his mule beast of burden

Meles – the man who helped Desta transport the sack of teff after Medenek, had an accident and was eaten by hyenas overnight. (See Yewegey)

Melke – Alem and Konjit's mother

Menkir – Colonel Mulugeta's step-son

Merid – the top student in Desta's seventh-grade class in Bichena

Mersha – Alem, Emnet and Konjit's father

Mulat – a shop attendant at Aklilu's store

Mulugeta, Colonel – the head of police in Finote Selam, Desta's Father-of-the-Breast

Muneet – Colonel Mulugeta and Fanawork's servant

Senayit – Ato Bizuneh's wife

Sitotaw – a guard/custodian at the Finote Selam school

Tekle – Abraham's friend in Zegay who introduced him to Girazmach Belay

Tessema – One of Alem's boyfriends

Tiwab, Emma— hotel owner in Finote Selam

Yisehak—the director at the Yeedib school

Yacob – Emperor Lebna Dengel's youngest son

Suseyenos – Emperor Lebna Dengel's grandson who was also Emperor of Ethiopia

Trufat – Emnet's mother, Alem and Konjit's parents' former servant

Matias – the young man Desta met on a bus trip from Dejen to Debre Marcos, who talked him into taking a test at the hospital for a job

Petrova, Yakov—the Bulgarian doctor Desta first met in the Debre Marcos hospital, who offers to be his future benefactor when reconnected in Bahir Dar

Tamrat – Desta's third oldest brother who had once aspired to become priest

Tedla – the director of the Finote Selam school

Yewegey – the boy Desta helped correct his crossed eyes a few years earlier, who along with his father, Meles, helped dig out Medenek from pile of rocks which had hemmed her in after she fell.

Yimer – One of Alem's boyfriends

Yodit – Desta's sixth grade seatmate, a girl

Zelalem – Col. Mulugeta and Fanawork's second oldest son

The Winds of Washaa Umera are represented by the seven rainbow colors: red, orange, yellow, green, blue, indigo and violet.

The seven Winds Desta met while visiting Washaa Umera were:

Almos -- red

Wesret – orange

Senbi –yellow

Setsobeck –green

Seth-blue

Kamoon –indigo

Rasums – violet

The reds are the youngest, having left their organic bodies within the first one hundred years. Violets are the oldest, three thousand to tens of thousands years since existing as free spirits. . . . When they sit, they always take the pattern of the rainbow.

Cultural terms and their definitions

Aba – father, a generic term of respect applied to most elderly men.

Areqey – a double or single distilled home-made whiskey.

Asmat—spell

Ato – the Amharic equivalent of Mister.

Awwe – yes, less formal than (see ishee)

Ayzoh – be strong, a cheering term

Birz – honey diluted in water

Beshita – communicable disease

Bete seboch – family

Betru – with good

Budas – In Ethiopian folklore, Budas are a class of people considered
to have evil eyes. Budas haunt gravesites looking for newly buried
bodies to dig out and bring home to eat. Budas supposedly use
the hyenas as their draft animals to carry the corpse home.

Chinet – load

Dabo Kollo – In the countryside, this is apricot-size dried bread
travelers bring with them as a snack. In cities, dab kilo
comes in different sizes and is served as snack anytime.

Dabo – loaf

Deb'tera – seer

Dehna neh – you're well

Dulet – Liver

Era – An expression of surprise, not really a word.

Ferenge – a term for all white people, similar to
the Mexican's Gabacho or Gringo.

Firfir – minced injera or loaf

Fit'aawrari – commander of the vanguard

Gabi – a double ply heavy cotton cloth, roughly 7 feet by 6 feet, worn for warmth over the shoulders like a blanket.

Gashé – honorific—a term of respect, used to address an older male, usually as prefix to the first name. Example: Gashé John, Gashé George, Gahé Tom, etc.

Gedam – monastery

Gibtse – Egypt

Gojo – hut

Goosa – an old monk who lives in a forest who often is invisible to ordinarily folks.

Goozgoozo – two layers of injeras, topped with cheese and red pepper paste and garnished with spiced, liquefied butter.

Injera – a spongy, flat bread made from fermented dough of teff, barely or wheat

Ishee – yes or okay—formal, for the servile form (see awwe)

Kettema – a tall pulpy grass, often sprinkled on the living room floor during a holiday.

Konjo – beautiful

Madd-bet -- kitchen

Makfalt – The bread (injera) the church goers break their fast with

Maskel – the finding of the True Cross, celebrated in Ethiopia on the 27th of September.

Masinko – a bunched horsehair string instrument played with a bow also made of bunched horsehair

Medeb – a raised, earthen bunk seat

Medehaneet – Medicine

Mehan – childless

Mekina – vehicle

Meto – one hundred

Meto amsa – one hundred fifty

Minim aydel – don't mention it

Negaday – merchant

Mookit – applies generally to a male goat or bull whose testicles have been pounded to a pulp of tissue so that it won't waste its energy chasing she-goats or cows. This goat or bull becomes fat and big, fetching top price when taken to the market.

Mosseb – an often colorful basket with skirt-shaped bottom and a circular top used to serve food. Its top is cone-shaped and often has similar color and pattern as the bottom basket.

Netela – a single-ply fabric, worn mostly by women as a shawl or to drape the shoulders with.

Paleo – old (paleo Hebrew)

Ras – a title equivalent to Duke

Set'adaree –an euphemistic term for a prostitute, literally means a single woman who lives on the sweat of her labor

Shash – a white fabric that is worn around the head

Sewasew – grammar

Sholla – related to the warka tree but less rugged. It produces a great number of green figs which turn into fire red upon ripening, becoming fleshy and edible afterward.

Teff – the smallest grain in the world which comes as either brown or white variety, and is the staple food of Ethiopians.

Tej—honey wine

Tella – a black or brown home-made beer made from hops and barley

Tenquay – wizard

Tsion – zion

Waga – price

Warka – a spreading, large-trunked tree with broad, thick, leathery leaves and long, hefty branches, perhaps related to the sycamore tree.

Weizero – Mistress (Mrs.)

Zebegna – custodian, guard

About the Author

Although Getty Ambau was educated both in the natural and social sciences and has run his own businesses over the years, writing has always been his inner calling. He has written books on health and nutrition which have sold internationally. *Desta: to Whom the Lions Bow* is his third in a series of novels. He lives in the San Francisco Bay Area with his wife, Rosario and a devoted terrier called Scruffy—perhaps not as devoted or self-sacrificing as Desta's pet and friend, Kooli.

CPSIA information can be obtained
at www.ICGtesting.com
Printed in the USA
BVHW071113280821
615433BV00003B/315